The Mad

David Maidment

The third book of the Madonna Trilogy: sequel to 'The Child Madonna' and 'The Missing Madonna'

ISBN: 978-1-326-11916-4

PublishNation, London
www.publishnation.co.uk

This book is dedicated to two men who have inspired me to persevere with writing and publishing 'The Madonna Trilogy' – Rev Dr Andrew Pratt, the Methodist Minister at Nantwich in the early 1990s, to whom I gave my manuscript of 'The Child Madonna' for comment and who was sufficiently enthused to pester me to get it published for years before I acted on his advice, and secondly the author, John Houghton, who critiqued the first two novels and gave me the idea for 'The Madonna and her Sons'.

All royalties from this book will be donated to the Railway Children charity,
Charity Commission registered no. 1058991
www.railwaychildren.org.uk.

Previous titles by David Maidment:

Religious Novels
The Child Madonna, Melrose Books, 2009
The Missing Madonna, PublishNation, 2012

Railway Fiction
Lives on the Line, Max Books, 2013

Street Children Non-Fiction
The Other Railway Children, PublishNation, 2012
Nobody ever listened to me, PublishNation, 2012

Railway Non-Fiction
The Toss of a Coin: an autobiography of a railway career, PublishNation, 2014
A Privileged Journey, Pen and Sword, 2015

Author's Note:

The name 'Jesus' is a Greek translation of 'Yahoshua' (shortened version 'Yeshua') commonly rendered in English Bible versions as 'Joshua'. I have therefore used this name throughout.
His full Aramaic name was 'Yahoshua ben Yosef', ie 'Joshua, son of Joseph'.

'Mari' or 'Mary' is a shortened version of 'Mariam' or 'Mariamne'. I have deliberately used the variation 'Mari' throughout as a reminder that this is a work of fiction.

CONTENTS

Family Tree of Mari and her Siblings
Family Tree of Eli and his Sons

			Page
Chapter 1	Mari	AD 5	1
Chapter 2	Mari		9
Chapter 3	Mari		15
Chapter 4	Mari	AD 8	28
Chapter 5	Mari	AD 9	37
Chapter 6	Mari	AD 12	45
Chapter 7	Mari		60
Chapter 8	Elizabeth	AD 13	71
Chapter 9	James	AD 16	86
Chapter 10	Mari	AD 21	98
Chapter 11	James	AD 23	105
Chapter 12	Mari		124
Chapter 13	Mari		133
Chapter 14	Mari		151
Chapter 15	Mari	AD 24	160
Chapter 16	Mari		177
Chapter 17	Mari		190
Chapter 18	Mari	AD 25	209
Chapter 19	Mari		225
Chapter 20	Mari	AD 26	237
Chapter 21	Mari		255
Chapter 22	Mari		270
Chapter 23	James		277
Chapter 24	Mari		286
Chapter 25	Mari		302
Chapter 26	Mari		322
Chapter 27	Joseph of Arimathea		331
Chapter 28	Mari		337
Chapter 29	The Watcher		346
Postscript			352

Family Tree of Mari and her Siblings

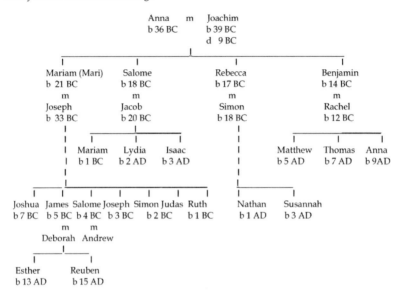

Family Tree of Eli and his Children

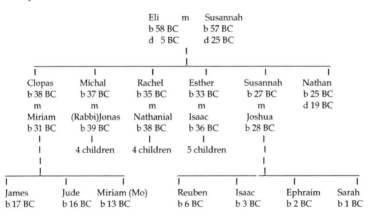

Chapter 1
Mari, AD 5

'Where's Joshua?'

'Don't worry about him, he'll be alright. It's good for him to be with the older boys instead of with younger children all the time.'

So we don't worry and assume he's somewhere with the group.

The festival is over and we've already arrived back by the river. It was lovely to see Elizabeth again, looking so well and so energetic still despite her age. John must be quite a handful. He's big and strong. He's as different from Joshua as he could be, yet they seemed to have such a rapport. We all went up to the Temple together after our Passover meal and we parted from Elizabeth and John in the city, when they went back with some of their neighbours because Ein-Karem was out of our way. Joshua went around with his eyes on sticks, he lapped everything up and asked us so many questions. When we were in the Temple he asked about each detail, why this, why that. I think some of the men got fed up with his questions. I know Joseph told him a couple of times to be quiet and listen.

Anyway, it's time to set up camp for the night. I meet up with Joseph and ask him again where Joshua is. We have a quick look, but can't find him. He'll be with the other lads. They're up front somewhere. We're a big caravan from several villages around Lake Galilee, there must be nearly a hundred of us including at least a couple of dozen children who are now of age.

Next day we set off and at lunchtime we sit down by the river where there is a wide expanse of meadow beside the turgid water. I get our loaves out – I must find Joshua, it's not fair that he's eating someone else's lunch. I find Clopas's boys and ask where Joshua is. They look blankly at me.

'He's not with us,' says Jude. 'I haven't seen him since Jerusalem.'

I begin to panic. I rush round asking everyone if they've seen Joshua, but no-one has. I tell Joseph and he searches too. It's fruitless. We can't think of anywhere else to look. Has he been kidnapped? Has some bandit caught him at the back of our caravan and spirited him away? I know they say it's dangerous on this road, but I thought we'd be safe in such a crowd and there were plenty of soldiers about. Surely someone would have noticed if something was wrong. But no-one seems to have seen him on the return journey at all. The last time I remember seeing him was when we said farewell to Elizabeth and John, but we were still in the city then. Surely he can't have missed us then and got lost? I realise of course that this is his first time in the city and it's very easy to lose your way, even for someone who knows the city reasonably well, especially when it is so crowded. What should we do?

There is nothing for it but to go back. It must be a two day walk which means we'll be on our own through the desert area above Jericho, but it can't be helped. Clopas volunteers to come with us and then his two boys offer as well. I don't want to put them out like this, but I feel safer with them, especially if Joseph takes ill. He's been a bit breathless again today and being so worried about Joshua won't help. It takes us nearly two nail-biting days to get back to the city, luckily without any undue alarms, but where do we start looking for him? We spread out, Clopas and his boys search the east of the city, Joseph and I go to the other side which we know best as it's nearest Bethlehem. We arrange to meet at sundown in the outer courtyard of the Temple.

We arrive hot and frustrated after the long afternoon and evening's search. I'm distraught now. After all the promise, all the sudden expectations aroused by our conversations on the way here, is it all suddenly in vain? 'What have you done, Lord?' I cry in my heart. I pray fervently. He must be here somewhere, mustn't he?

We find somewhere to stay – at least the city's emptying of pilgrims now, so there are rooms to be had. The next day is just as bad. We've been everywhere and Joseph is looking grey. Although it is still two hours before we're due to meet up with Clopas and his sons, I persuade Joseph to return early to the Temple. It's still hot outside and Joseph is exhausted.

'Why don't you go inside the Temple itself, into the shade and rest. Go and pray to God, go and ask the priests to help us.'

Joseph doesn't want to leave me but he knows women can't go into the main part of the Temple, so reluctantly he goes. I just sit down on the steps in the outer courtyard and start weeping. It's awful. I'm tired out and scared. What can have happened to the boy? What is he feeling now? Is he scared and tired like us? What will he do when he realises he's lost? Surely he won't try to come home alone. I suddenly realise that if I were in his place, I'd probably think of going back to Ein-Karem and finding John and Elizabeth again. Yes, that's what we must do. Tomorrow morning we must go to Elizabeth. He must be there.

I've just concluded this and allowed myself to feel some relief, when Joseph comes running over. I panic because he looks so agitated. Has something dreadful happened? Has he found our boy injured or even dead?

'Mari, Mari, come quickly. I've found him. He's here. He's in the Temple.'

'Oh, thank heavens! Is he alright?'

'Yes, the stupid fool's sitting there as bold as brass arguing with three of the Temple's chief rabbis. The cheek of it! I could wring his neck, I could. Just wait till we get home. He's not heard the last of this.'

'Don't be so angry, Joseph. Just be thankful that we've found him. I was beginning to think we'd never see him again.'

'Well, look how upset he's made you. I'd never have believed he'd be so thoughtless. James, yes, but Joshua! Just shows how you can misjudge someone. I never dreamt that he would do this to us.'

'Perhaps he was lost and thought that this would be the most likely place to find him.'

'I'm going back in for him. Don't be too soft with the boy. There's no excuse for his behaviour.'

Joseph turns back and disappears into the Temple building. I whisper a prayer of thanks to God and try to wipe the tears from my face. I don't want Joshua to see I've been crying. I'm sure he didn't realise how much we'd worry about him. It's a long time before they emerge. I was beginning to wonder what on earth had happened. Did he not want to be found by us? Has he run away? I can't believe that, but the minutes drag on and my mind is whirring with silly fears.

At last I see them coming. Joseph has got hold of Joshua by the shoulder and is propelling him in my direction, but two of the rabbis are coming with him. What has he been up to? Has he misbehaved and shamed us? My stomach lurches again. Then I notice that the rabbis are smiling. Only Joseph is looking angry.

'These rabbis have asked to see us. I dread to think what they want to say. Joshua, you can begin by apologising to your mother. You can't begin to understand the distress you've caused let alone the inconvenience. Five whole days you've been here. What did you think you were doing?'

Before Joshua could open his mouth, one of the rabbis holds up his hand and interrupts.

'You are this boy's mother?'

I nod.

'Let me explain. Don't be too hard on the boy. It is true that he got carried away listening and talking to some of the rabbis who were teaching in the Temple. When he realised that your party had gone without him, he spoke to one of the rabbis and inquired what he should do. We asked him where he thought his parents would look for him when he was missed and he was adamant that you'd look here first. We never thought you would be so long. Didn't you miss him earlier?'

'I assumed he was with some of the other boys in our party. We are part of a large caravan come down from Galilee, from Nazareth, Capernaum, Kana and Nain. I didn't get concerned until well into the second day, then we came straight back. We've been searching the city ever since. My cousin and his boys are still looking for him. Where on earth has he been, what has he had to eat?'

'Don't worry on that score. We told him to stay with us. He slept in the Temple with the priests on duty. We fed him, don't concern yourself about that. He's a remarkable lad though. He's been listening to the rabbis every day with rapt attention and asking all sorts of questions. Some of them really had the teachers hard pushed to give an answer that satisfied him. You have a very bright boy there. Are you from a priestly family? Is he destined to be a priest or rabbi?'

I stammer a 'no' to that.

'A pity. We could do with someone with his wit and understanding here. He's a lot brighter than most of the boys we are training. He must have a very good teacher back in Nazareth.'

The rabbis bow to us and give Joshua a friendly pat on the shoulder. Joseph looks a little abashed and bites his tongue.

'Couldn't you guess where I'd be, Mother? I thought it would be obvious.'

I feel ashamed to own that it was nearly two days before we missed him. 'Did you feel scared when we didn't come for you? Weren't you bored, having to stay in the Temple for so long with all those old men?'

'No. Why should I be? It was really interesting. I could have listened for hours to them. And they let me ask questions and they didn't mind when I argued with them. One of the younger ones seemed to think it was funny.'

We wait on the steps of the Temple for Clopas, James and Jude to find us before we can resume our journey back home. We'll have to find lodgings again, it'll be dark before we can take the road down to Jericho and everyone has warned us not to risk it after nightfall. While we wait, I ask Joshua what he talked about for so long. What sort of questions had he asked?

Joshua gives me a long hard look.

'I asked them about the Messiah. I asked them what sort of Messiah they were expecting. When one of them said that they were expecting a leader who would restore Israel to the Jews and throw out the Romans – the priest was very careful to say this very softly so no-one else could hear – I asked him how he squared this with the prophecies of Isaiah who forecasts a peacemaker, someone who will suffer, not a great conqueror. He found it difficult to answer me and said Isaiah must have been thinking about a teacher or priest, not the Messiah. And I asked them why they thought God was only concerned with the Jews. Didn't the people we used to live with in Egypt count? And they said there were many Jews in Egypt, God would care for them. So I asked if God would protect a bad Jew and not a good Egyptian. The priest changed the subject.'

'Goodness me! Didn't they get upset? Didn't they think you presumptuous to answer them back like that?'

'I don't think so. More and more rabbis came to join in and I listened to them arguing with each other. They don't all think the same, you know. Joel and the other rabbis in Nazareth always say the same thing. I never heard them arguing – well not about God and our scriptures anyway. Only about taxes and which Roman laws we had to obey and which were against our laws. Anyway, I asked lots more questions. I can't remember them all now. I asked why some people seem to suffer through no fault of their own. I was thinking of Rachel and my friend Benjamin you told me about and our friends in Pelusium and Alexandria who were so generous and yet so poor. They quoted Job to me. Will Rachel and Naomi and Annie and all the other children become rich in the end like Job was? They couldn't answer that. I know I asked why some of the laws were so strict, did they all matter equally to God or were some more important than the others. That got the rabbis arguing for a whole afternoon. That was great fun.'

'Were there any other pilgrims talking with you to the rabbis?'

'One or two hung around listening, but I don't think anyone else asked any questions.'

'What was the most important question you asked?' I am really curious. I wonder if he's really thought about this. He doesn't hesitate.

'Oh, I asked them why we are here. What is our purpose? Does our existence have meaning? If God has a plan for us, how will we know?'

'And did they have answers?'

'Not really. They tried. They waffled a bit. They quoted lots of scripture but when I asked what it meant they just repeated the phrases as though that made sense and when I still pushed them, they said I must recognise the authority of the scriptures and anyway God was mysterious and we couldn't know the answers to that now.'

I'm in deep thought.

'And you,' I ask, 'do you know the answers?'

He hesitates a moment. He looks at me for a moment and smiles. 'You know the answer to that one don't you? When we talked beside the Jordan on the way here, I thought you knew everything. I thought you were telling me what I needed to know, what I had to do. That's why I thought you'd soon find me in the Temple.'

I repeat my question. Joseph is listening with increasing confusion. He doesn't know what either of us is talking about now. Neither of us has mentioned the frank and deep discourse we had beside the Jordan River.

'Joshua,' I say once more with great emphasis. 'Do you know the answers?'

He stares at me. He looks a little sheepish and embarrassed at his reply.

'I think I do.'

Chapter 2
Mari

'Are you sure, Joshua,' I say, 'do you know what you are saying?'

'I think I do,' he replies, once again, looking me straight in the eyes.

I am too astonished to say anything more. It seems so precocious, so arrogant and yet it does not come over like that. He'd said it so shyly, so reluctantly. I'd asked him a direct question and he'd just answered as honestly as he could. I am awestruck. The more I think about it, the more shaken I am. I know now. I know that everything I've been told, everything I've experienced is part of the plan. It is all coming true. All the doubts I've had, all the heartbreak and troubles, all the pain, all of it was worthwhile because of what my twelve year old son has just said. I should have asked him more. I should seek his answers to the questions he'd asked those rabbis. But I am too taken aback at his reply to think of any further response and now he's walked ahead by himself leaving me to ponder the implications of the words he's just uttered. It is almost as if I fear to ask any more.

*   *   *   *   *

I've had twelve hours to reflect on the events of the last few days. I've not seen the boy since he uttered those words; he walked ahead to spend some time with his father. His father? That's an irony. Joseph must have been hurt when he talked of being in his father's house. That's what he called the Temple. 'My father's house'. I'm not sure if Joseph noticed it at the time, because he was so angry at finding Joshua unconcerned at our distress. The boy just seemed to assume that we'd know where to find him. 'In my father's house', he'd said, 'I thought you'd know'. Just like that. I'm sure the pain of the phrase will have hit Joseph now. Perhaps that's why Joshua has gone to spend time with him. Joseph has been so good with him. He's always looked on him as his son, he's treated him exactly the same as the other sons he's fathered. Sometimes I thought that he favoured James, but that was, I'm sure, because their interests and temperament were so similar. Then as the other boys and Salome and Ruth came along, he treated them all the same. But Joshua was always the eldest boy and given that due respect.

It could have been so different. My husband's never really sought my explanation. I've never had to explain every detail of the boy's conception - not that I could give him an adequate account even if I wanted to. Sometimes I thought he held back because he was fearful of the truth and wanted to believe what I'd told him. He and my mother had worked together to save me from the consequences at the hands of the Nazareth rabbis. He'd had a dream, had a revelation that he was to trust me, but I always wondered; did he manage to suspend his disbelief or were there occasions when he must have allowed a doubt to creep into his mind?

'My father's house'. Joshua's words come back to me again. I remember with a shudder my time before the rabbis when I first uttered those words, 'Please God, help me and have pity on me and on your son!' Their fury was nothing compared with the shock I gave myself as those words were torn from my lips. I'd not planned them. They just came out in the stress of the moment. They were the last things I should have said at that crux of my judgment, yet I could not help myself. But I said it and despite the blasphemy, I survived.

There have been long periods in my life since then when nothing extraordinary has happened. Well, plenty has happened, but I could not always see what was so special. My story is not unique. Other women have babies in less than

10

ideal situations, many others are forced to flee from oppression, too many are forced to live in abject poverty, others are then blessed after such travail with the love and responsibility of a large family. But every so often, something does happen that renews that promise that my son is special. That he survived at all despite the threats of the rabbis and then escaped the second threat when Herod sought to kill him. The odd things that apparent strangers say, those outcast shepherds that forced their way into our cave only minutes after I'd given birth, the old couple at the Temple when we took him to be dedicated, those Babylonian astrologers, Malthus, the rabbi in Alexandria. I'm sure he knew Joshua was special although he never said anything outright. But the way he looked at the boy, the hints he dropped. I'm sure he'd guessed something.

Some of the other women had joined me and had tried to chat, but I'd been silent and they'd soon realised that I'd wanted to be alone. I didn't know them and they didn't know me and after an initial attempt to involve me in their chatter, they'd ceased to be curious, or if they were, they'd refrained from further questions. After we'd found Joshua, we'd waited until we'd been told of another caravan going north. It was too dangerous to go on our own now that we'd left our village party. Clopas and his sons were with us still – they'd been so good in coming back with us to look for Joshua. Now I think of it, we'd all taken a big risk – just the five of us going back up from the Jordan valley on the infamous Jericho – Jerusalem road through the hills infested by bandits. Luckily there were Roman foot patrols still keeping an eye on the stragglers leaving the city after the extended Passover festival. This group of villagers from the north of Galilee are travelling via the Samaritan route. They don't seem bothered about going through potentially hostile territory as they have sufficient tents and provisions with them to not need any foreign hospitality. We've got a tent too, although I'll need to get some bread and water at one of the villages we pass through tomorrow.

I catch up with Joseph and Joshua as the sun is nearing the horizon to our left behind the rolling hills. They are walking in silence, but I notice Joshua has his hand in that of his father. That's good. I was worried that Joseph might still have been angry with the boy and might have shunned him. I wonder what Joshua has said to Joseph. Has he tried to explain his behaviour? Has Joseph thought about what the Temple rabbis said? As I join them, Joshua gives me a quick smile, loosens his hand from Joseph's grip and trots off to catch up his cousins, James and Jude. We are at the back of the party now. Everyone has slowed their pace, I'm sure the men ahead are now looking for a suitable place to set up the tents and settle for the night. We walk for a while in silence. I'm wondering if I should say anything. I must really.

'Are you still angry with the boy?'

Joseph doesn't answer immediately. He is thinking. I can almost hear his brain thumping like the rhythmic sounds that emanate from our workshop.

'Of course I am, though I've tried to say nothing further to the boy. Not yet, anyhow. Let's get home first, then I'll be having a long and serious chat with him. He can't get away with treating us like that. Whatever his excuse, he had no right to let you get so worried. It was thoughtless at best. If he knew what he was doing, it was selfish and wrong of him.'

'I'm sure it was not deliberate. He just got caught up in his exchanges with the rabbis. You know when he concentrates on something, it's as if the rest of the world is no longer there. And it's as much our fault as his. We should have checked before we left Jerusalem. With all those crowds it was only too easy to get cut off. We should have checked, Joseph. Don't put all the blame on the boy.'

'You're too soft with him, Mari. You always find excuses for him. You judge him differently from our other children. They'll notice it, you know. They'll get jealous.'

'Well, he is different. You know that perfectly well. I try my utmost to treat him no differently to the others. But of course he is special. You know that. And finding him holding his own with those teachers of the law, well that just proves it. More than holding his own, actually. You heard what those rabbis said when they brought him to us. They were astonished at his learning and answers. I've always wondered when he would show unmistakable signs of being the Messiah we've been promised. I think that was the first real sign we've had from Joshua himself. We mustn't blame him for that.'

'I've still a good mind to have a long talk with him about thinking of us a little more – well, of you anyway. He needs to know how much we love him and that such thoughtless behaviour hurts.'

'Are you thinking of me, Joseph, or your own hurt?'

'What do you mean? I was no more upset by his absence than you were.'

'Are you sure about that? Yes, of course I was worried sick when I'd thought we'd lost him, perhaps for good. But when he talked of being in 'his father's house', didn't that upset you more? After all you've done for him these last twelve years fulfilling every duty of a good father, and yet he seems to imply a different allegiance. Didn't that hurt you more?'

'Nonsense, Mari. I've always known he was only my son in name.'

'But to hear him say it, in the Temple of all places, in front of some of the most revered and influential rabbis in the land – didn't that seem too pointed, too public a humiliation for you?'

'I didn't take it that way. I'm sure the rabbis didn't understand what he meant. If they'd really taken it in, they'd have been angry themselves, they'd have accused him of

13

blasphemy and challenged us instead of marvelling at his wisdom. Forget it Mari. That doesn't bother me. I just want him to grow up still respecting us as a family and not growing apart from us. I don't want him to use us before going his own way, leaving us behind, not needing us any more.'

I wonder though. The boy is growing up. That really was the first sign of his independence. He'll always be my son, but I can't help wondering whether his future ties to Joseph will be so strong. And the bond between a boy, especially the firstborn, and his father ought to be strong. But then, who is his father?

Chapter 3
Mari

We camped outside a Samaritan village last night and continued along the narrow path between the poor shacks this morning. This means we are strung out over quite a distance as we can only go two abreast at some points along the way. To my surprise Joshua drops back to walk with me. For a long time he is silent. Then suddenly, when we are far enough away from anyone so that we cannot be overheard, he suddenly speaks.

'Mother, can I ask you something?'

'Of course, son.'

'It's personal. You won't mind, will you?'

'Go ahead. I'll do my best to be truthful.'

I wonder what on earth is coming. Have I been rash to promise to be honest with him? He makes me quite uncomfortable sometimes as though he knows what I'm thinking.

'Mother, I hear rumours about my birth. I heard someone say that you were not married when you had me and that the rabbis nearly had you stoned to death. And yet you were saved. Is it true?'

I pause for a long time. I have always dreaded this question. I knew it would come one day. I'll have to do my best and pray that God will cause my words to come out right.

'Yes, son, it is true. But it's a long story.'

'Can you tell me? I want to know.'

For the next hour I tell him everything, how I kept meeting the stranger, what he told me, how he was conceived, Eli's wrath and my ordeals before the rabbis. I didn't elaborate on this but skipped to my meeting with Elizabeth and Zechariah and then my return and Zechariah's letter and Joseph's dream and how I was saved.

Joshua thought for a long time.

'Did they hurt you, mother?'

I'd said that I would be honest.

'Yes.'

'What did they do?'

'It doesn't matter, Joshua, you don't need to know that. God protected me and kept me safe.'

'Please mother, tell me, I need to know.'

'Why, Joshua, why?'

'I don't know. But I just need to know.'

'They flogged me, Joshua and told me to get rid of you.'

'But you didn't.'

'No.'

'So what did they do then?'

'They brought me before the rabbi's court in the synagogue and threatened to stone me to death.'

'And you didn't do what they wanted.'

'No, Joshua.'

'And God saved you.'

'Yes. And he saved you too.'

'I thought so.'

'You thought so? How Joshua? How do you know that? Who has spoken to you about this?'

'I think I've always known. I know you nearly sacrificed yourself for me. One day I'll have to do the same.'

'What do you mean, Joshua? What are you saying?'

'I don't know yet. I just feel it. I want you to tell me everything you did, what they did to you, how you felt. I need to know.'

'Why Joshua, why do you need to know?' And I start to cry. As I try to tell him, it all comes back. I don't want to say, I want to protect him, but he puts his arms around my

16

shoulders and for a few minutes it is as though I am the child and he is the adult.

When I have stumbled through my confession of my humiliation and punishments, he just looks at me.

'Thank you for telling me, mother. I understand. It makes sense.'

'It makes sense? How can you say that?'

'I understand some of the things the prophet Isaiah said now. You think I'm special in some way don't you?'

'Of course, Joshua. Every mother thinks that of her sons.'

'I've got to think about what you've said.'

And with that he strides ahead and rejoins his cousins. I walk on in silence on my own. What have I done? What have I started? Is this the sign? Does he know he is the Messiah after all?

I don't even see him for the next two days. I think he's somewhere ahead with some of the men. I walk with Joseph again until we are nearly at the border of Samaria. For a long time I wonder if I should tell him what Joshua's just been saying. We see Shechem in the distance where we will camp the night. Just before we break up, I hold Joseph by the arm.

'He knows.'

He asks no questions. He understands exactly what I mean.

*   *   *   *   *

I've been watching him so closely now since we returned to Nazareth. He's different, very different to his brother James, but I ask myself, isn't that quite normal? Most siblings are different from each other – just look at my two sisters. He's clever, there's no doubt about that. Joel and the new rabbi, Jonas - the husband of Clopas's sister Michal - soon picked that up and were pleased to give him extra lessons. He has a phenomenal memory and can quote great chunks of the scriptures without any apparent effort. What's more, it's not

17

just rote learning. He genuinely seems to understand what he's reading. And he likes to play games just like the others, though he's not quite as athletic as James. I find his company very rewarding, he likes to chat with me and asks me all sorts of things. James is a typical lad – never tells his mother anything! I wonder which of them the other boys will take after. James, I shouldn't wonder.

But he's a good lad is our Joshua. I know Joseph thinks him amiss in causing us so much heartache in Jerusalem, but I still think it was mainly our fault. Look at him now. There aren't many twelve year old boys who help so much around the house. He's wonderful with the younger children, just like I used to be, so my mother keeps telling me, but I was a girl and it was expected of me. He can get our twins to do nearly anything he likes and both his sisters adore him. Only James seems sometimes to cross him and likes to tease or annoy him. James is much more like other boys of his age, boisterous and mischievous. I think he believes Joshua is too much of a kill-joy. It's rot of course, Joshua likes his fun and has a good sense of humour, but James can be quite cutting and I've had to reprimand him on occasions for bullying the younger children. Joseph – I normally call him Joe to differentiate him from his father - looks up to James and is closer to him than he is to Joshua. I don't think Joe is as bright as either Joshua or James – even the twins seem to me every bit as advanced as he is. Joshua tries to explain the things the rabbis teach, but Joe is not very good at listening and he is easily distracted by James who seems to find it funny to lead him astray.

Most children of his age are thoughtless, they don't mean to be, but they get engrossed in what they're doing and forget others. Joshua never seems like that. He is extraordinarily sensitive to others, he knows what they're thinking, when to speak and when to be silent. It's a lovely gift, but not one I associate with a great military leader which I assume is the role of the future Messiah. It was only the other day that Rabbi

Joel talked to me at length about the boy, for he was party to the decision to accept my claim. He asked me if I still believed. He said the boy was bright and confident but he'd seen no signs of anything abnormal. There again, he said, wasn't Moses middle-aged before he was called to lead the Israelites out of Egypt. 'Who are we to understand God's ways?' he argued. 'We just need to be patient. God will show us, I'm sure, in his good time.'

I do still believe, of course. But whether he's to be a great soldier who'll drive the Romans out, that's another story. Plenty of our neighbours resent the foreign presence, but Joshua doesn't seem interested. Perhaps that's my fault. I've never found the Romans that bad. I know Eli didn't like that and accused me of consorting with them. That was a lie, I never did, but I didn't hate them like he did either. And Joshua doesn't get worked up about their presence like some of the other boys do. I used to think that he might get picked on by the other boys because he's gentler than they are, but he seems to hold his own. He's respected. They seem to know he cares about them and I notice if any of the children are upset about something, it's Joshua they go to first.

*   *   *   *   *

Joseph has taken the boys into his workshop to show them some of the things he's made which are waiting collection while Salome helps me prepare the evening meal. She's a great help to me already, even though she's only nine. Ruth wanted to help too, but she's not old enough to be of real use yet – she's so willing, but just gets in our way when we're in a hurry with such a houseful. My husband seems to have recovered a little – I was quite worried earlier, he looked so tired. We're just ready when my mother hobbles in – her arthritis seems to be getting much worse these days.

'Mari, let me help you. What can I do?' She fusses immediately round me, picking things up and putting them down again.

'Mother, for goodness sake, sit down and rest. There's little more to do. Just wait a few minutes, Salome and I've got everything under control.' Well, all except Mother. Despite her affliction that causes her so much pain, she hates doing nothing.

'Ruth, go and sing to your grandmother!' At least that keeps them both out of my way until the meal is ready.

Afterwards, as I'm cleaning the pans and dishes, and getting the younger children to be quiet and roll out their mattresses, I hear Joseph telling Joshua to walk out with him for a few minutes. I guess he's going to reprimand the boy now. I hope he won't be too severe with him. I catch Joseph's eye and cast him a meaningful wink. I think he gets my gist.

When they come back a few minutes later, I look to see if Joshua is upset. I don't think so. At least he says nothing and doesn't try to avoid my eye. He takes Joe under his wing – the twins and Ruth are already on their bedrolls and look to be asleep – probably pretending. He's telling Joe about the sights he's seen in Jerusalem and Salome joins them, eager to miss nothing. James doesn't seem that bothered.

'I'll be going up to the Passover next year, won't I, Mother? Then I'll see it all for myself. There's no need for Joshua to tell me.'

'That's alright, James. He's not forcing you to listen. I just thought you'd be interested.'

James goes outside and I hear him calling to one of his other friends. If he wants, he can stay out a short while until Joe and Salome are settled, then I'll get the two older boys to go up onto the roof if they want as it's now warm enough and will give us a bit more room inside.

Joseph comes back from his workshop. He looks grey in this light and I'm anxious. He was getting breathless in

20

Jerusalem, but I thought it was the tension then, fearing Joshua was lost. When everyone is settled, I whisper to him, hoping no-one else can hear – least of all my mother, because she'll only worry and there's nothing she can do about it.

'Joseph, are you alright? You look all in.'

'Stop fussing Mari. I'm just tired. It's been a long day.'

'You've not had any more of the pains you had in Jerusalem?'

'It's nothing Mari, it really isn't. I've just been carrying a fair amount of baggage so it's no surprise that I'm getting twinges from one or two muscles I don't normally use.'

I'm not convinced by this. He does plenty of lifting and carrying in his work, so he should not be troubled by a tent and a few extra changes of clothes. But he's not going to admit anything further. Perhaps he's trying to stop me worrying. All his reluctance to admit any problem just has me worrying the more. Well, I might as well accept it. That's Joseph and I'm unlikely to change him now. I lie there still listening to him. I think I hear a slight groan at one point and I'm wide awake, tense, straining to hear his breathing. I slowly relax and at last I hear him snore, softly at first and then louder, uneven, with an occasional sudden disturbance, then it begins rhythmically again. I begin to relax myself and in the end fall asleep.

*　　*　　*　　*　　*

It's morning, the children are out of the house and I'm alone with Anna, my mother. She's been waiting for this moment. Salome and Ruth are scarcely out of the door when she turns to me.

'Tell me, Mari, what happened. How did Joshua get lost? Where did you find him? We were worried sick when Susannah and the others arrived home without some of the menfolk and said that you'd had to go back to look for Joshua.'

'He was in the Temple, Mother. He'd been discussing our religion and history with the chief rabbis there after he'd found we left without him.'

'You left him alone there?'

'We didn't mean to. I thought he was with the rest of the party. He'd spent a lot of the journey to Jerusalem with the other boys and young men. I assumed that's where he was when we set off home.'

'But didn't you check? Surely you could have seen he was missing?'

'We were a big party, Mother, nearly a hundred of us from several villages. Of course we should have checked - I know that now. But we didn't. I thought Joseph had seen him, and he thought I had.'

'You were lucky to find him. It was sensible of him to stay in the Temple where you'd been. Didn't you look there first?'

'Hindsight is a great thing, Mother. We split - Clopas and his sons searched one quarter of the city, Joseph and I went back to where we'd lodged near the Bethlehem Gate. I did look in the Temple Courtyard. I didn't think of looking inside. I'm not allowed further in as you know, and it was three days after the end of the Festival so we didn't think anything would still be going on there.'

'He was right inside then? What was he doing?'

I tell her everything I can remember. How he was fascinating the elderly rabbis with his knowledge and wisdom and how some of the younger students studying in the rabbinical school there came to listen and dispute with him. They say he held his own with some of the brightest scholars. My mother does not seem to be astonished.

'I know he's a bright lad. Why don't you talk to Rabbi Joel? He could train to be a rabbi just like Clopas's brother-in-law, Jonas. Joel has reached the status of judge now, replacing Eli, alongside Jethro. But Jethro's getting old, he's not very active

22

there these days. They'll be seeking another rabbi in a few years' time.'

'Yes, Mother, I know. I'll talk to Joel sometime - he took a lot of care with me and his daughter Hannah even though we were girls. Perhaps he'll give Joshua special tuition. I'm not sure if rabbinical ordination is a must for preparation for the Messiah though.'

'Why not? Many of our great leaders have been learned men too. Think of King David and Solomon. And the Judges of old that our Scriptures tell of - they were men of letters and spiritual power as well as military leaders. Why don't you talk to Joel today? Why don't you go to see him now while the children are out of the house? I can look after Salome and Ruth if they come back early. Salome can go for the water if she returns before you do.'

So I pick up my mother's suggestion. If I don't she'll keep on at me and I shan't get a moment's peace until I've done it. In all probability Joel will be free as Jonas usually teaches the boys of the village together. Joel sometimes takes the older boys for some special teaching. But it's not far, so I might as well go and see if he's available for a quick word. I'd rather talk to Joel than Jethro - the old man is very deaf now and I'm not sure that he ever really believed in me, but just went along with Eli when that man changed his mind and accepted my claim that I was carrying the future Messiah.

So I pull on my shawl and set out before the day gets too hot. Most of the women will be down at the well at this hour where I would normally have been too. Joseph is busy in his workshop. The early morning hammering has given way to silence as he has a farmer from over Sepphoris way negotiating some new order. I think that perhaps I ought to share my mother's suggestion with him before I go to the synagogue, but when I poke my head around the door of his workplace, I see the two men are deep in conversation and Joseph doesn't even notice me. I'll tell him later what Joel says

- it will only be advice at this stage - nothing definite, I'm sure. We've never talked of the possibility of Joshua training as a rabbi. Clopas would have been the obvious one, I know Eli was disappointed when he showed so little interest, so he championed his daughter Michal's husband's cause instead and celebrated his ordination just before he collapsed and died.

I've never really liked Jonas that much. I remember Eli seeking his opinion when they'd proposed to have me publicly whipped after they said my carelessness had betrayed my father and his companions to Herod's soldiers and it was only Clopas who'd stopped them. But Jonas and Eli's other son-in-law Nathaniel had both pressed for a punishment, so they'd compromised and had me beaten in the privacy of my own courtyard. At least I was spared the humiliation of disgrace before the whole village, though Jonas and Nathaniel as well as Eli seemed happy to be witnesses to my shame. Only Clopas seemed embarrassed. It's odd. Even now when I see Jonas, I remember that day and blush. I don't know why - I'm a grown woman now of twenty six with seven children and then I was only just of age, not yet thirteen. It's another world and yet when I look at Jonas I feel like that young girl again as though I'm naked before him and he sees into my very mind.

Anyway, I don't need to see Jonas now. He'll certainly be busy teaching the boys. When I get to the synagogue I can hear the children chanting from the Torah. I spot Joel but he's got someone with him. I turn to retrace my steps, but he catches sight of me and beckons me to stay, indicating he won't be long. I listen to the boys. Joshua, James, Joe, Simon and Judas will all be there. I listen to see if I can distinguish any of their voices. I think my family must make up a goodly proportion of the class. My family is one of the largest in the village and no other mother has five sons. I'm lucky to have retained my health and not had any problems in childbirth. So many others

24

have had stillbirths or given birth to crippled or blind children. Even the twins arrived without complications. After so many children I have to admit I've lost my slimness that I'd retained until after Joe was born. My husband does not seem to mind and he doesn't look at other younger women like some men I know. I trust him absolutely. He's devoted to me and our children.

Eventually the man Joel's been talking to takes his leave, nodding to me as he passes by. I know the man by sight but can't remember his name. I know many in the village now - certainly most of the women. I follow into the alcove where Joel is standing.

'Peace to you, Mari. It's good to see you this morning. I've heard all about your alarm in Jerusalem. I celebrated Passover here this year with my family, Hannah sends you her greetings. You two used to be such friends, but she doesn't see you now since she married and moved to Sepphoris. Her husband is a rabbi in the main synagogue there and they have four bonny children.'

'Please send her my greetings when you next see her. I've fond memories of our times together when you used to give her and me special lessons after the boys had gone home.' I pause.

'Have you come for any special reason?'

'Of course. I want to ask your advice about Joshua's further education.'

'He's a bright boy. I pick him out with a couple of others to give them extra work. But he's the best scholar. It's not so much his memory, though that's good. It's the understanding he seems to bring to the texts. He seems mature well beyond his age. Have you ever thought of having him trained for rabbinical ordination? He could do it, you know.'

'That's what I wanted to talk to you about. When we lost him in Jerusalem, he'd been back in the Temple disputing with the chief rabbis there.'

25

'So I heard.'

'And a couple of them came out to meet us when we eventually found him and told us how much he'd impressed the teachers there with his knowledge and intelligent questions. They said he must have good teachers here,' I add smiling at Joel.

'Thank you for that compliment, Mari. I do my best, but I think one of these days soon Joshua will outstrip me. He needs to obtain higher learning, perhaps in the synagogue in Sepphoris or even Tiberias. Or you could think of trying to enrol him in Jerusalem itself although the competition to get a place there is stiff.'

'I think he's too young for that. And we need him here in Nazareth to help in his father's workshop. My husband isn't old but he does seem to tire easily these days and I look forward to the time when Joshua can take on some of the heavier work from him.'

'Well, another couple of years here is the most I think he'll still get benefit from. After that you should think of getting him to study for rabbinical ordination - it takes several years, so he shouldn't leave it too long. He could still train at a town synagogue in Sepphoris, Magdala or Capernaum or even in the rabbinical school in Tiberias on the lakeside and get home frequently enough to give your husband a hand with the carpentry. Think about it. You've probably got another couple of years before you need to decide. What does Joseph think?'

'I haven't discussed it with Joseph yet. He got angry that Joshua stayed behind to talk to the chief rabbis. I don't know what he'll think of the boy training to be a rabbi. I'm sure he intends Joshua to learn his trade and take over the business as a family concern in due course.'

'Do talk to your husband about it. Suggest he comes to see me and I'll discuss the options with him. And I'll start giving Joshua more extra tuition to make the learning easier later. I'll be able to assess his interest and commitment to a life of teaching. I suspect he may find that more to his taste than a lifetime of carpentry, noble though that trade is.'

'Thank you, Joel. You've given me much to think about. I will talk to Joseph soon.'

I will. I'm not sure how he'll take it though.

Chapter 4
Mari, AD 8

The family are growing up. James had his 'bar-mitzvah' last month and we celebrated Salome coming of age earlier in the year. We'd long outgrown our accommodation in the compound that our Pharisee ancestor Eli had made available for us, and his son, Clopas, helped us purchase a house with a small workshop attached nearer the centre of the village by the market place where most of the traders are clustered. And now our house seems too small with such a boisterous group of youngsters round me all the time. For much of the year several of the children sleep on the roof. Joshua and James have their bedrolls in Joseph's workshop. James is there at the moment assisting Joseph. Joshua is going shortly to the rabbinical school in Sepphoris. We had quite a tussle to get him to enrol there.

Rabbi Joel, at my suggestion, came to see us a few days ago. I'd already sounded Joseph out on my conviction that Joshua should go to further his learning, but Joseph had been reluctant and Joel had offered sometime ago to give further advice on this. Joseph knew why Joel was coming and after initial courtesies and the drinking of a cup of wine together, I offered to leave the two men together to discuss the issue.

'Mariam, stay with us. I'm sure your husband will not mind and your insight is valuable too.'

Joseph nodded. I'm not sure whether he really wanted me there, but he was not going to argue with Joel.

'Joseph, I'm sure you have had your own plans for Joshua, but that young man is quite exceptional. I've been teaching him now since he was a young lad. You know how bright he is. For the last couple of years I've been giving him additional tuition apart from the other boys of his age as he far outstrips them in both knowledge and understanding. Having him in with the others is not good for him or them. He has the ability to learn much more, but I cannot help him further. He needs teachers more learned and experienced than me.'

'Rabbi, I appreciate what you are telling me. I know he is a talented boy, but I have a large family now and I need his help to maintain my business. Seven youngsters is a big family to feed and clothe and working the hours that I do, I get tired. There is more work available if I had the extra hands to help me and I was looking forward to Joshua, then James, both learning the trade. They are already helping me but I wanted to really involve them so that they'll be capable of undertaking some orders on their own without me constantly looking over their shoulders.'

'But Joseph, you know that your son is marked out for a special mission in life. You've not forgotten that, have you?'

'Of course not, Rabbi. But he's plenty of time for that. In five years' time his brothers will be able to train as well and he'll have gained strength through the heavier work he'll undertake. Surely that will be more valuable for his future role than more book learning?'

'But he needs to build on his learning now. In five years he'll have forgotten much and will need to start again. And he'll find it harder to gain admission to a good school in Tiberias or even Jerusalem. The authorities there will not see carpentry skills as a proper introduction to the training necessary to become a rabbi.'

'Jerusalem? Why there? That'll take him right away from his home and our influence. I won't even think of that. And in any case, why does he have to be a rabbi to prepare for his role as the promised Messiah? Will he not need some military training and will not the extra maturity of another few years hard work not fit him better for that?'

'Our famous leaders of the past have been skilled in books as well as war. A Messiah, if he is to challenge the authorities and gain support of the nation, will need to understand our history and our religion if he is to be a great leader. He will need to know enough not just to save us, but to rule in righteousness and justice when the nation has been restored.'

'And what do the other rabbis think? Do Jethro and Jonas agree whither your thinking?'

'We've discussed it a lot. Jethro is fully behind recommending Joshua for rabbinical training at one of the best schools. Jonas has been more doubtful, but he has to admit that the boy is at the limit of what can be offered to him here. We can't just continue with him attending the synagogue here for a few mornings. He'll become bored. He's already straining to learn more and is asking deep questions that none of us feel totally competent to answer. If he leaves us and works for you full time, how will his enthusiasm and curiosity be satisfied? Will he be content with such a life or will he rebel?'

'My boy is a good and loyal lad. He'll not disobey me.'

'But you'll be putting him under a lot of tension. I think he knows his destiny. If he believes God is leading him in a direction that conflicts with your plans for him, won't that put him under great stress? It's not fair to put a boy of fifteen in the position where he believes he has to disobey either his father or his Lord God.'

'Are you telling me that you know that God is already calling him to be a rabbi? Has he told you this? Or is it something you've discerned yourself?'

'He's said nothing explicitly, no. But I sense that he is turning such thoughts over in his mind. He asks us so many questions about the promised Messiah. He wants us to interpret the prophecies and when we explain to the best of our ability, he comes back with further questions that go deeper and raise issues we cannot answer for fear of leading him astray. He needs the guidance of some of the best scholars and priests if he is to avoid error. His mind is questioning, sometimes perhaps too far. He needs steering into a proper understanding and only priests and rabbis of the rabbinical schools can provide such authoritative scholarship that he will respect.'

'Are you saying that he's in danger of blasphemy?'

I couldn't help stop myself interrupting here. The talk had too many throw backs to my own experience. I could almost hear my Pharisee Uncle Eli warning me about my questioning of the scriptures and being told not to be so presumptuous. I was beginning to get alarmed.

'No, Mari, don't get excited about that. He asks questions because he isn't certain, he can see other possibilities and he needs experienced thinkers who've had the time and scholarship opportunities to have thought such thoughts before. It is good that he questions. But he needs those with the wisdom to give him answers that will satisfy him. He won't accept an argument that just quotes a phrase from scripture. He wants to know why it's right. He sometimes quotes apparent contradictions, words which even I've not seen the meaning he discerns. He needs to sort his ideas out now, not let such thoughts and questions fester on unanswered over the next few years.'

'I'm not sure, Rabbi, I'd set my heart on developing the lad to take over my work for a few years yet. Are you really telling me that I should think again?'

'What do you think, Mari?'

The Rabbi had put me on the spot. I did not want to take issue with my husband, but he surely already knew my views.

'My husband knows that I think Joshua should take advantage of the training that you recommend. But I'm mindful of what Joseph says. It is hard for him and he does need help in the workshop.'

'Joseph, I don't ask you to rush to a decision now, but think about what I've said. If you do conclude that Joshua should seek entry to a rabbinical school, I will do all I can to press his claim for enrolment in the school that will stretch him most. If you feel Jerusalem is too far, then I recommend that he attend the school in Tiberias, as many of the most gifted scholars are attracted there by the development of that seat of learning in our district's administrative centre.'

'I'll think about it, Rabbi, I promise you that. I'll talk further with Mari and with Joshua himself. Has he expressed any desire to take the road you are suggesting? Has he asked you to speak to me?'

'No, Joseph. The boy has said nothing. He believes I can answer all his questions. It's very flattering, but I know I can hide the truth from him only a little longer. He will soon find me out and become impatient for more than I can give.'

When the rabbi had left us, Joseph turned to me and I feared he was going to rebuke me for encouraging Joel to come to back up my own views. But I had misjudged him. He just sighed and smiled at me.

'It's what you've always wanted for the boy, isn't it. I promise, Mari, that I'll think about it properly. I'll take the rabbi's words seriously. Although I had been so hoping that I'd be able to make Joshua a genuine partner in the work I do. I suppose that's the ambition of any father for his son. Let's leave it a few days while I get used to the idea. Then we'll both talk to Joshua, to see his views. We might get a surprise. I can never quite guess what that lad will come up with. He might have quite different ideas.'

I relaxed. At least Joseph had promised me to think about it and he'd not been angry or distressed.

*   *   *   *   *

A few days later my sister Salome is visiting and the children are talking to her. Joseph is still in the workshop with Joshua and James. It's a good opportunity, I think, and go in to them and suggest James joins the others. As he leaves the room, Joseph looks at me and realises what I'm doing.

'Joshua,' he says, 'leave what you are doing for the moment.'

'Shall I join Aunt Salome also? Do you want a quiet word with Mother without me?'

'No, son, we both need to speak to you. It's time we had a good talk with you about your future.'

The boy looks up at us with interest, but says nothing.

'The rabbis think it's time you considered your further education. They think you should enrol in one of the rabbinical schools. Is that what you want?'

'Oh!' The boy is silent for a moment while he takes in what Joseph has just said.

'Don't rush. But tell us what you really think.'

'Father, do you think that would be right for me? I know Rabbi Joel thinks that, he's hinted several times that I should learn from scholars in Tiberias or Magdala. But I always thought you wanted me to train fully as a carpenter so I can take over from you when the time is right. Isn't that your plan for me?'

'That was what I've always hoped, yes, Joshua, I won't pretend otherwise. But I want to do what's best for you. I have to think of your future. What do you want to do? What direction should your life be taking?'

'Think, Joshua,' I say, 'what is God wanting you to do? Are you aware of his prompting?'

The boy fiddles with a piece of wood for the moment. His fingers feel the smooth surface, and hesitate over a rough patch. We are waiting.

'I feel strongly that I need to explore God's laws further and obviously studying to become a rabbi would help me do that. But what about you here? How, Father, will you cope? Do you not need me here until James is strong enough to assist you more?'

'Son, if God needs you to learn more of him through becoming a rabbi, then I must not stand in the way of God's will for you. I admit that I'd have liked you to stay with me a while longer, but I must not stand in your way if you feel strongly that God is calling you to a special mission.'

'You know that I am being marked out in some way for a special mission then?'

'We've always known it, Joshua, both your mother and I. And you feel it too?'

'Yes, Father. But I don't quite understand everything yet. Perhaps it can wait a while until James is old enough to help you fully and Joe too and even the twins.'

'But Rabbi Joel says they can't teach you any more here. He thinks you should go to Tiberias or even Jerusalem to learn.'

'Mother, is that what he said? Jerusalem? You weren't very pleased when I stayed there before to talk to the teachers there.'

'That was three years ago, son. And it wasn't that we didn't want you to talk to the rabbis then, it was just that we didn't know where you were. Do you want to go to study in Jerusalem?'

'I don't know. One day perhaps. But not now. I want to stay with you. Isn't there a way I could do both, begin to study further and still help here in the workshop?'

'I don't know, son. Even Tiberias is three hours' fast walk away. If you studied there during the day, you'd scarce have time, let alone any energy, to help me when you returned home in the evening. And I wouldn't like to think of you walking alone that distance through the mountains at the edge of the lake. It's not safe, there are bandits in those hills.'

'Isn't there anywhere closer I could study? There's a school at the synagogue in Sepphoris. If I went there, I could come home each day and do some work for you.'

'I don't know about that, Joshua. I'll have to talk to Joel further to see what he says. I don't know if the rabbis there can teach you any more than Joel or Jethro.'

'Joshua,' I say, 'you do want to go to a rabbinical school, don't you? You think it's right. If that's so, we must find a way. I'm sure we can manage here. We must do what's right for you.'

*   *   *   *   *

We left it at that for the moment. I thought Joseph was very good. I know he's disappointed that Joshua will not be available to work with him, but he's seen that it is not the best way of preparing Joshua to be the Messiah. Joshua came back to us several times and said that he was prepared to go to Sepphoris, so he could continue to help his father and I know that Joseph had a couple of conversations with Joel to check whether the school in Sepphoris was adequate. I think Joel was doubtful, but agreed that it might be a suitable compromise for a limited time, perhaps a couple of years, so we gradually came to accept this as the way forward. Joshua was adamant that he would not go anywhere that would leave his father short of the help he needed.

'Mother,' he said to me one day, 'Father's not really well is he? He gets tired and breathless sometimes and James or I have to lift things for him.'

I tried to dismiss his worries, but he's right. Despite my yearning for Joshua to start his mission and even go to Jerusalem, perhaps the timing isn't right. I'll be glad of his presence here for a while longer.

Joshua was finally persuaded to go to the Sepphoris synagogue school so that he would be able to travel home each day and give Joseph further assistance in the evenings. He was so keen to help that I think he'd even have done extra work for Joseph on the Sabbath, but Joseph wouldn't hear of it and it would have caused great offence in the community. Joshua is funny sometimes - in many ways he is very religious, yet he seems to treat some of our laws with scant regard. He once said to me that surely it was more important to help Joseph meet a deadline for a customer than to obey all the petty rules meticulously and let someone down.

It's time we thought about Joshua getting married too. Joseph and I had a long talk about that last week. He's sixteen now and even if we found a suitable girl for him in the next few months, by the time we observe the usual betrothal ceremonies and waiting period, he'll be over eighteen before he's married and ready to start a family of his own. None of the girls in our immediate family is old enough for him, my sister Salome's Mariam is only ten. Clopas's sisters' children are already married, apart from Esther's youngest, Leah, who is fourteen. I don't know that family very well, they live in a village the other side of Sepphoris, but from gossip I hear when the family get together, I gather the girl is not very bright and we must find someone that Joshua would respect. I think my friend, Hannah, Joel's daughter, might help us here. She has four fine children, one of whom is a girl. I see her quite often when Hannah is visiting her father. She must be about the right age. Joseph and I decided that it would be worth speaking to Joel about her to see if she is already in negotiations for a marriage elsewhere.

Chapter 5
Mari, AD 9

Salome and Ruth have gone for water, the younger boys are at school and my mother and I are about to tackle some of the sewing work we need to do as soon as I've finished sweeping out. There is a sudden crash. I assume at first that some wood has fallen over in the workshop, then I hear a cry. It's James shouting. I don't pick up his words at first, then he appears in the doorway, looking flustered.

'Mum, come quickly, it's Dad. He's collapsed. I don't know what's wrong, but he's breathing heavily and he seems to be unconscious.'

I rush into the workshop and find Joseph lying on the floor amid some planks of wood which have been disturbed by his fall. Dust is still rising. I peer at my husband and see that what James said is true. He is unconscious. He is breathing but his lips look blue. I'm scared. James is looking up at me. He is frightened too. I suddenly realise my mother is standing behind me in the doorway.

'Get him through here onto a mattress. James, give your mother a hand to lift him. Then you can run and fetch Matthaeus.'

Matthaeus is the nearest we have to a physician in the village. They say there are properly trained physicians in Sepphoris, but it'll take several hours to get there and persuade one to come here and treat Joseph and cost a lot that we can ill afford.

'James, you lift his feet when I take his weight.' I grasp his arms, slipping my hands under his shoulders. He is heavy but somehow my panic gives me extra strength and we carry him through to the living area where Mother has unrolled his mattress and we lay him down as gently as we can.

'Go quickly, James, run!'

My words are superfluous. James is already out of the door. I damp a cloth and wipe Joseph's face and loosen the clothes around his head and neck. He twitches a couple of times, his face grimaces as if in pain, then he seems to relax. His breathing is noisy but gradually seems to calm down. I don't know what more I can do. I just hold his hand and whisper to him. I feel my mother's hand resting on my shoulder. She doesn't say anything, but it is comforting to know that she is here and her knowledge and experience is available.

The wait seems interminable. I'm not sure if Joseph is still unconscious or whether he's just sleeping now. He's so still. I look at Mother and find my eyes beginning to water. It must be the shock. I'm cold and shivery and mother brings me a draught of water which I gulp and then splutter, setting off a coughing fit. At last we hear footsteps outside and James bursts in followed by Matthaeus.

'Is he alright?' asks James trembling. I take the boy in my arms and give him a hug.

'I don't know yet, dear. Let Matthaeus have a good look at him and see what's best to do.'

I explain to the physician what has happened and he examines Joseph and listens to his breathing. As he does so, Joseph stirs and begins to mumble something although I cannot make out any words.

'He's recovering, Mari. It's probably some malady of the heart. He should rest. He must lie here and not seek to get up until he feels stronger.'

'Do you have any treatment or herb you can prescribe?'

'Don't give him wine or beer at present. Just water and a little bread. Get him to eat fruit - figs and dates are better than meat. But above all, make him rest. His work is heavy. He must not try to undertake such labour until he is completely rested and fit.'

I'm not confident that the man knows exactly what he is prescribing. I know he can suggest remedies for common ailments, for a fever or a chill. He has some knowledge of plants and herbs that can help, but people in the village who can afford it send for a physician from Sepphoris if they have a relative who is more seriously afflicted. We have been fortunate in our family's health so far. Our children are all robust and have shrugged off minor childhood diseases without too much alarm, but many families have had the death of a child to cope with, or a mother's loss in childbirth. There are few with seven children for whom tragedy has not struck. I thank God constantly for our good fortune in this aspect of our lives and now my prayers must be for my husband. I have been worried about Joseph before. There were times when he seemed too tired and breathless for a man of his age, but he always seemed to recover and he dismissed any suggestion that he should take things more easily. 'How can we?' he would say. 'We've a large family to support. One day James and Joe will be fit to take over from me. Then I'll deserve my rest.'

Joshua comes home at last and I meet him and take him outside to explain what has happened beyond Joseph's hearing.

'He's recovering now. He's sitting up and taking notice though it's best for him to rest and sleep.'

'Should we not obtain a physician from the city? I'll look for one tomorrow?'

'I think you'd be better here. Don't let your father worry about the work that's still outstanding. The best treatment for him will be to stop him worrying. You and James know enough, don't you, to finish the orders your father was working on? You both help him. He's told me often you have the skill and James is shaping up well. Can't you both stay here and work for the moment? You can surely let your studies delay for a while until your father's quite recovered?'

39

'Of course, Mother, if you think that's the best thing. Frankly James is as expert as I am although perhaps he needs a little more strength. But he'll soon acquire that. I'm sure between the two of us we can keep things going. Don't worry about it, Mother, and don't let Father worry either.

'Well, tell him yourself. He'll not be so restless if you and James can assure him of all you're doing.'

* * * * *

And so we settle into a new routine. Joshua and James work together every day from morn till evening. They are keeping abreast of the orders, so they say, and I don't hear too many arguments between them. I chat to the customers when they come to collect their implements or order new carpentry and they seem to be satisfied with the quality of what the boys are making. Joshua has a good head on him and can cope with the financial side of the business. He knows what to charge and has a fine way with the customers. I wondered if someone would try to cheat them, but everyone knows Joseph is here and able to give advice and he has sufficient respect from the villagers for them not to want to take advantage of his illness.

In all our worries, the need to find a wife for Joshua has become a low priority. I haven't wanted to bother Joseph or get him stressed about this. Joshua himself seems unperturbed and is not pushing in any way, he seems remarkably unconcerned and when I raised it once, just said that there were many other priorities at the moment. I'm having a job stopping Joseph taking on physical labour again. He's been up and about for a few weeks now, and I've persuaded him to do no more than watch the boys and give advice when appropriate. I've got my sons to promise that they will not let their father undertake any physical work and if he tries, to call me immediately. Joseph knows this and is aware how cross I'll be if he tries! Anyway, he seems content with the quality of

40

the work the boys are doing. I know he's frustrated though and I don't like the fact that he still gets pains in his chest and arm. He often has to stop and rest.

The other children have been good, though I can tell the younger boys are anxious. Little Joe in particular - well it's silly to call him little, he'll be of age soon and we need to plan his 'bar-mitzvah' - he fusses over his father and wants to fetch and carry things for him, and he keeps asking me if Joseph will really be alright. I wish I could reassure him. Salome is very sensible and is a great comfort to me and she and Ruth spend a lot of time together.

We're just settling down into this routine, with Joseph gradually regaining his strength and seeming determined to get back into the role of the main breadwinner of the family, when my worst fears are realised. One evening, when Joseph has been active most of the day in the workshop, and we are walking to the synagogue to see Joel, he complains of a sharp pain in his chest. We return quickly and he takes a rest while I prepare the evening meal. My concern is heightened because it is rare for Joseph to admit to any pain and it is clearly bothering him badly. I'm just wondering if I should send for Matthaeus, although I'm not sure what good he'd be, when Joseph suddenly shouts out and I turn and see him grimacing in pain clutching his chest and gasping for breath. James takes one look at me and rushes out of the door. I've no need to tell him what to do. Joshua has gone to Joseph. He looks at me. There are tears in his eyes. He knows. I know this time. I take Joseph in my arms and hold him tight. He is gasping for breath, groaning, jerking in my hold as the pain grips him anew. Then suddenly he goes limp. His rasping breath is stilled. I feel Joshua's hand on my shoulder. The other children are staring at us open-mouthed. Joe suddenly bursts into tears. My mother puts her arm around the twins and Ruth and draws them from the room.

'Come, my children, let us give them room. Come with me and help me get some water. They'll be needing some.'

Mother hasn't been to the well for weeks. Each step is painful for her now. But she knows what has happened and she wants to get the younger children out of the way.

I have one arm round Joseph and the other clasps Joe who is weeping uncontrollably in my lap. Joshua still has one hand on my shoulder, with the other he strokes the head of Joe, trying to soothe him. My tears have not yet come. I'm still shocked. It was so sudden, so quick. I know this worry has been gnawing at the back of my mind for the last couple of years and especially since his first collapse a few months ago, but I'd really thought he was recovering - well, I supposed I wanted to think so and had persuaded myself that he was regaining his strength. I feel Joshua's hand softly replacing mine behind Joseph's back and he lays him gently on the mattress. He kisses his father on the forehead and closes Joseph's eyes. The tension in Joseph's face seems to fade away, the muscles round the cheeks and jaw slacken.

'I'm not ready yet, Mother. I don't think I can do anything more now.'

I hear what Joshua says but I can make no sense of it. I don't know what he is talking about. I'm not really listening, perhaps I misheard. Joshua has prised Joseph from my grasp. He is not being callous - he is seeking to ease my pain. I hear him, somewhere in the distance of my mind speaking to the others.

'Joe, Salome, let's leave Mother alone with our father for a few minutes. Come with me. We'll go to the synagogue and tell the rabbis.'

I was going to tell them to stay, it didn't matter but they were gone. I'm alone with Joseph now and the tears can fall. At first I let myself go and clutch at his body, but then I pull back and sit beside him and look and think. Joseph, my husband, the only man who has known me so completely, every inch of me, and me of him. Seventeen years I've known him, sixteen of those we've lived as man and wife. Father of six of my children and father, yes, father to Joshua too, father in all but the moment of conception. Generous Joseph, who could have rejected me, could have refrained from intervening, not shared with my mother the endeavour of saving me from the widespread condemnation. Joseph who shared the privilege of caring for our God-sent son, why oh why could you not wait to see the fulfilment? My thoughts go back to my own father who spent his life fighting the Roman occupation and praying for the Messiah who would vanquish the invaders, when I knew that we were at the very threshold of all his fervent wishes. And now my Joseph, even he will not see the culmination of all that's been promised to us. And I cry for Joseph, for his unfulfilled dreams.

I'm still weeping silently, staring at my husband's lifeless body, when James bursts in, followed by Matthaeus.

'I'm sorry we were so long, Mother, but I couldn't find him. Here he is now. Is it too late?'

He looks at me, then at the still figure of his father and his face crumples. Matthaeus looks at me too and goes to check the pulse of my dead husband. He nods.

'Yes, son,' he says, 'we are too late. I don't think even if we'd got here quicker that we'd have saved him. You must comfort your mother now. She'll need you to be strong for her.' He glances round. 'Where are the others?'

'Thank you for coming,' I say to Matthaeus, 'but there is nothing you can do now. Leave us to grieve together.' Matthaeus nods once more and backs quietly out of the door. James looks at me. He is flushed from running, it makes him look angry.

'Why?' he shouts. 'Why us, why my Father? We prayed for him. Why didn't God listen to us?' And he bursts into tears.

I wait until he has calmed a little.

'I don't know, James, I don't know. But I've felt myself in God's protective arms all my life. I'm sure he'll not let us down now. Your father has not been a fit man these last few years. God saved him long enough for you and Joshua to be older and strong, able to support us all. We're going to rely on you and your brother now, James. Be strong for me. Weep for your father, yes. But be strong, help your brothers and sisters to cope as well as me. We're still a loving family. Let us be united in our grief and in the way we pull together to overcome our sadness.'

Joshua returns at this moment with Joel who reaches out to me immediately.

'Mariam, I'm so sorry. Joseph was a good man. Please accept my condolences. You have a fine family here...' - he indicates Joshua, Salome and Joe who've accompanied him – 'and I know they'll be a great comfort to you. And your friends will support you too. My wife and family... anything you want, you have only to ask. I had great respect for Joseph, the whole town did.'

Then he is silent. He puts his hands on the shoulder of Joshua and prays with us. Only his voice and the muffled sobs of the children break the silence of the night.

Chapter 6
Mari, AD 12

It's been a difficult three years since Joseph's death. At first everyone pulled together and supported me in the weeks after the funeral. Joshua stayed at home and worked with James in the workshop. I thought he'd given up his intention of becoming a rabbi and had settled to domestic life with us in the village. I was in two minds about this. Obviously I was pleased to have his company and he quickly gained the confidence of Joseph's customers and our income held up despite early fears. But I couldn't dismiss the prophecies about his future and acting as a village carpenter did not match the expectations of a future Messiah. After Joe's bar-mitzvah, he too joined his brothers in the carpentry workshop and Joshua soon told me that the boy had a special gift for the work. James was quick and businesslike, but Joe seemed to have an extra love for the work, exhibiting patience with detail and concern for the quality of finish that matched his father's skill.

After a few months, I spoke to Joshua about my concerns and he agreed to continue his studying at Sepphoris once he was sure that James and Joseph could maintain the business. Joshua would still come home in the evenings and cast his eye over the products finished during the day and maintain the records of the sales and income to ensure we had sufficient to meet our living costs. He also took charge of purchasing the raw materials needed for our work, making use of his time in Sepphoris to contact reputable suppliers of good timber. Occasionally he would take on a small contract in Sepphoris itself, undertaking a home repair or meet some request for an influential customer there and then he would often stay overnight as a guest in the house of the person employing him.

This meant that my worries about our ability to maintain our home and feed the children and my mother largely disappeared and I began to think about some of my other responsibilities, in particular finding wives and husbands for my children. Joshua was already nineteen and I felt strongly that he needed a suitable girl who would not be out of place as the wife of a rabbi, a girl perhaps who would know enough of our history and religion to understand should Joshua reveal the destiny I believed was before him. I had spoken to him several times about choosing a partner for him, and sought his views about any likely girl, but he showed little interest, and seemed fully committed to his studies and oversight of the family business.

I had a long talk with my brother Benjamin a couple of years ago. He had been allocated a couple of fields from Eli's property by Clopas and worked closely with him and his sons in sharing in the grape harvest and producing wine that was the source of most of the family's income. Ben's young family - Matthew, Thomas and new baby Anna - were healthy and he was well supported by his wife, Rachel, the daughter of a scribe from Nain. Although most of his time was taken up with his own affairs, he'd kept an eye on me since Joseph's death and asked me one day about the responsibility for negotiating successful marriages now Joseph was not around to undertake the father's role. He agreed to assist me in that duty and turned his attention first to finding an appropriate young girl for Joshua. I mentioned my friend Hannah who moved to Sepphoris when she married a young man studying to be a rabbi there and Ben agreed to contact her and her husband to see if their fifteen year old daughter was spoken for.

I was very disappointed when Ben reported back that the girl was already betrothed, but my brother promised me that he would stand in for my husband and take the responsibility for helping me to find partners for all my children when the time was right. He was as good as his word and both James and Salome are now betrothed, James to Deborah, daughter of one of Susannah's friends in Nain and Salome to Andrew, son of our village baker. But Joshua is still without a partner. I've spoken to him many times and asked him to help us find someone suitable but he tells me to stop nagging him - he says it with a smile on his face, but it doesn't get us any nearer settling him down.

*   *   *   *   *

And now, today, they're all here. We've been celebrating the marriage of Salome this week and we're all a little exhausted and fraught after all the eating and drinking. My sisters and Ben and all their children have just gone home and we're looking at the debris from the meals and the general muddle after the presence of so many small children. I think Joshua especially must be shattered. He's been the centre of attention of so many of the youngsters. He tells them stories and they love it, and clamber round - and over - him all day and he doesn't seem to tire of it. Certainly James doesn't seem to have his patience and gets cross with them if they pester him too much, so most steer clear of him and go to Joshua or Salome. And Salome has had her own priorities to attend to this week!

Salome and Andrew are about to leave us. I shall miss her presence here although she won't be far away. They'll be staying at Andrew's parents' home until they can find somewhere of their own. At least we are sure of a good supply of fresh bread - Salome has promised me that! She's talking to my mother at the moment and Andrew is with Joshua, James and Joe in the workshop looking at some of the things they've made. Judas and Simon are outside somewhere talking to some of the other lads from the village.

'Well, Ruth, it's just you and me now. And I guess it won't be long before you have your own young man to take you away from me.'

'Oh Mother, I'm not ready for that yet. It'll be a long time yet.'

'I was married at your age, you know. Well, betrothed, anyhow. I'll have to get your Uncle Ben to start searching for the right man for you.'

'What about my brothers? They're older than I am. Are you going to look for twin sisters for Simon and Judas so they can all stay together?' she says laughing. 'And what are you going to do about Joshua? He's getting left behind.'

I give the girl a hug. She's so like me in many ways. She's really blossomed in the last couple of years, become her own person. She used to trail round after Salome all the time and I worried that she'd be lonely when Salome got married and moved away, but she's good company for me and she spends a lot of time talking to Joshua now. I've taught her to read and she's begun to ask questions about some of our scriptural prophecies of the Messiah. I haven't said anything to her about Joshua's destiny but I'm beginning to wonder if he's said anything to her that's aroused her curiosity. In fact, I've not shared anything with my children about Joshua's special role. Perhaps I ought to. Or should I? I'm in two minds. I don't want to push Joshua before he's ready and I don't want to create problems and jealousies between the children. On the other hand it seems such a momentous thing and it seems odd to say nothing - will the other children feel let down that they've not been able to share this knowledge that is so important to me and that I'm sure Joshua himself is exploring in his own way?

Salome comes back.

'Grandma's tired and has got a headache. I told her to lie down and get some rest, but she wouldn't before she gave me her blessing. She seemed to think I was going away. I told her,

I'm only five minutes' walk away, less than that. I'll still see you a lot. I shan't spend all my time in the bakery.'

'I know you won't, Salome. But your first priority is to your new husband and his parents. Don't forget that. But I know we'll still see you around. I think it's time you and Andrew went back to your new home. His people will be waiting for you.'

We embrace.

'Mother, where's the coin in your wedding necklace? There's a gap.'

I look down and squint at where it should be. I hold the necklace up and then to look properly, I take it off over my head and stare. As Salome said, it's missing. The small silver coin that was given to me by Joseph while we were in Alexandria after everything had been stolen from us during our escape from Bethlehem. He'd had it made into a new wedding necklace for me, even though we were still only betrothed, to avoid awkward questions from our Jewish neighbours there. My heart misses a beat. I can't have lost that surely.

'It must be here somewhere. It must have fallen out today.' Someone would have noticed, just as Salome has now. 'Ruth, can you help me search for it? Salome, don't you worry, you get going with Andrew. I'll get the boys to help me look for it in a minute.'

I try to concentrate on saying farewell to Salome and Andrew for the moment, but I'm panicking inside about the loss of my wedding coin. It means so much to me, especially now that Joseph's physical presence is no longer with me. As soon as they're gone, I start the search. Ruth and I look in the obvious places first. I pick up a torch from the wall. The flame's reflection should pick out the shiny surface of the coin. We can't see it. I go to where my mother is lying.

'Mother, have you seen my missing coin? Did you see when I must have lost it?'

'What coin, Mari? What are you talking about?'

'The coin from my wedding necklace. It's gone.'

'Oh. I hadn't noticed, dear. Yes, I can see now. When did you lose it?'

'That's what I'm asking you, Mother. Did you notice it was missing? When did you last notice it?'

'I'm sorry, Mari. I hadn't realised you'd lost it until you said just then.'

I've already swept the room with my eyes and can't see it.

'Mother, can you get up a minute? I want to see if it's fallen near your mattress and you're covering it at the moment. I'm sorry, I just want to make sure.'

My mother pushes herself up laboriously and Ruth helps her to her feet. There is nothing on the bedroll and I lift it and shake it. Nothing. The ground beneath is empty too.

'Can I help you look for it?'

'No, Mother, lie down again. I'm sorry to have disturbed you. It must be around here somewhere. I'll get the boys to help me.'

Ruth interrupts.

'I'll get them.' She goes to the workshop door. 'Joshua, James, Joe, come and look for Mum's necklace. She's lost the silver coin from it.'

As Joshua and the others enter, Ruth makes as if to go outside to fetch Simon and Judas.

'Ruth, there's no need to call the twins. Let them be. There's enough of us here to do a thorough search. Any more and we'll just get in each others' way.'

Joshua gets the broom and begins methodically to sweep the room. We all try for ten minutes or more, going back over the ground we've already covered. We pick up piles of clothes and shake them. We look among the discarded and soiled pots, pans and dishes. We pick up the water jars and look underneath.

'Have you been into the workshop or yard, Mother?'

I try to think. I can't remember going into the workshop but we search there just in case. In vain. I've probably been into the yard. That's harder in the darkness. We can see nothing from a superficial search.

'It's hopeless, Mother, can't we leave it until daylight in the morning? We'll help you then,' shouts James in exasperation.

I can understand his feelings. What he says is true. Of course it'll be easier in the morning. James and Joe stop looking and come back inside. Joshua stays outside still searching for a while. Ruth goes to help him. Then Judas and Simon come back indoors and wonder what all the fuss is about. I try not to let them see that I'm crying. It's silly, it's only a piece of jewellery and I shouldn't get so worked up about it, but it's one of the few keepsakes I have of Joseph and it's important to me.

We give up. We eat a few of the remaining figs and then one by one to children lie down to rest for the night. I'm fidgeting around, still looking although I know we've already searched everywhere two, even three times, but I can't tear my eyes away. Joshua notices and comes over to me.

He speaks very softly. 'Don't worry, Mother. I know how precious it is to you. We'll find it in the morning. We'll persevere until we find it. Try to rest now. Trust us. Don't fret yourself any more.' He gives me a gentle hug.

*   *   *   *   *

I've been awake half the night. I really shouldn't get so het up about something as insignificant as a small coin. 'You can soon find another one,' said James quite rationally but he doesn't realise that it would not be the same. Joshua understands. It would be one more loss, one more diminishing of Joseph's presence. It would be so easy to forget him amid the turmoil of our daily life, so many mouths to feed, so much activity around me. But I do not want to forget. And that

51

necklace, that coin, was a constant reminder as I fingered it from time to time.

As soon as it's light I want to be up and looking, but everyone else is still fast asleep and I do not want to disturb them. Then I hear movement. Joshua's head appears around the workshop door. He comes to me and whispers.

'I've searched the courtyard already. I don't think it's there. Where else have you been?'

Before I can answer, I see Ruth is stirring.

'You went with Ruth to the well several times yesterday, didn't you? Perhaps you caught your necklace while you were hauling the water up.'

I think. I suppose that's true, although I can't remember doing so. We were so busy with everyone around and making sure all was well with the celebrations, I suppose I could have done something to loosen or catch the necklace without noticing as my mind would have been elsewhere.

'Come and have a look with me.'

He knows I can't wait any longer. Ruth is getting up as well. She wants to come too. We tiptoe out of the house trying not to disturb the others and go slowly down the street towards the rough path leading to the well. It's really too early to see our neighbours, for the sun is barely up. We go carefully looking at the earth beneath our feet, searching for anything that glints in the sun's rays. We eventually arrive at the well. No-one is there. At first we see nothing. I'm disappointed. I'd hoped against the odds that we might find it. We'd had a couple of false alarms. An exclamation when Ruth or Joshua saw something shiny, then the realisation that it was just a fragment of broken pottery or a smooth pebble polished by the wind and rain.

Then, suddenly, 'Look, over there at the foot of the well parapet. There's something there.' Joshua has called out and Ruth rushes over to where he is pointing.

'It is, I'm sure it is,' shouts Ruth in excitement, and picks it up and comes dashing over to me, holding a small coin in the palm of her hand. I look. It is, I recognise it. A huge wave of relief overwhelms me. I suddenly burst into tears. Ruth looks up at me in alarm, but Joshua just meets my eyes and smiles.

'You see, Mother, you needn't have worried so much. I told you we'd find it in the morning.'

We go back. The earth suddenly seems a fresher place, the sunshine now bathes the barren hills and the shadows are lifting. Only a few houses in the depths of the valley are still shaded from the morning shafts of light. When we get home, I find all the children are up and rolling up their mattresses.

'Look!' I shout as we reach the doorway. 'We've found it. It was by the well. Joshua was right, he said that's where it would be.'

'Give me your necklace and the coin, Mother. I'll reset it in the workshop while you and Ruth prepare our breakfast.'

A few minutes later, as we're sitting round, eating, Joshua comes back with the necklace, the coin restored to its rightful place in the centre. He comes up to me and places it over my head and kisses me on the forehead.

'There you are, Mother. Everything back to normal. You can relax now and finish the celebrations in good heart. We've a double reason now. Salome's first day of marriage and your lost wedding coin is restored. Our father is still in our hearts. We still remember him with love and respect, Mother. And we're all still here for you. We don't say it very often, but we say it now. We all love you and are here for you now. It's up to us to look after you, Father gave us this sacred trust.'

The children are all looking at me. I'm lucky to have such a close family. But the first of my children has just left us. James is still here with Deborah, but Salome's move to her parents-in-law's home is our first change since my husband died. It seems a moment of importance, to be conscious of the change that is taking place. And another thought comes to my mind.

Joshua will be twenty soon. He's a young man, soon he will be revealing his calling, I'm sure he will. I ought to say something to the other children. I've never said anything until now, because I didn't want them to treat him any differently. But I'm sure he knows that his life will soon be changed dramatically and I wonder how the others will respond. Will it be too much of a shock? Will they blame me for not telling them what is going to happen? Will they believe it or think I'm mad, or that Joshua is as well? Should I tell them now? Should I ask Joshua's permission? Perhaps he will not want to be revealed. I'm torn in two minds, but should I leave it to him to break the news in his time, or should I say something now to get them prepared for the fact that their brother is the Messiah they hear foretold each Sabbath in the synagogue? I ponder this all day and at nightfall I'm no nearer coming to a decision on what I should do. Perhaps I'll just warn Joshua that I must say something.

The opportunity comes the next day. James and Joe are busy in the workshop. Ruth and Deborah have gone to fetch water. Simon and Judas are with Clopas's sons working in the fields. And Joshua has just come home from Sepphoris, earlier than I expected. I intercept him before he walks through to the workshop.

'Joshua, I need to talk to you.'

'Yes, Mother, what is it?'

'It's about your special mission, son, you know what I'm talking about?'

Joshua is silent for a while. I'm waiting, wondering again if I should have brought the subject up. Should I have waited until he takes the initiative?

'Yes. What do you want to know about it?'

'I'm not going to press you any more, but I need some guidance from you. When are you going to reveal yourself? Do I need to do any more to help you? Do we need to find you a wife first? How much longer do you need to study in

Sepphoris? Do you need to go to Tiberias or Jerusalem to study? Do you...'

'Steady on, Mother! That's a lot of questions.'

'I'm sorry, Joshua, I didn't mean...'

'It's alright, Mother. But let me try to answer as best I can. You know what I've been called to do. You've always known it, haven't you?'

'Yes, of course, Joshua, you know that.'

'But you must realise what a momentous thing it is. Do you think I'm ready yet?'

'I don't know, son. Only you can judge that. What more do you think you have to do? You've been studying our scriptures for many years now. Joel says your knowledge already outstrips his. I know your studies in Sepphoris have been interrupted, but do you need to learn any more? The rabbis in Jerusalem were pretty impressed with you many years ago.'

'It's not just about knowledge and learning. I have to think about many other things. I have to be sure of what God is expecting of me. Some of the things I may be required to do and say may cause controversy. I have to think things through. Be aware of the implications. Be sure I can cope with the consequences. Do you understand that?'

'I'm sure you're right on that. But it's not necessarily a matter of age or maturity, Joshua. God will lead you to do what's right and protect you if you trust him. I know that, I was much younger than you when I was called to break all our traditions and rules and face opposition from so many people.'

'Mother, you've often hinted at the problems you had. Tell me again. What did they do to you? What was the worst you had to face?'

I hesitate. It's true. I've never been explicit. Should I tell him everything?

'They had me whipped, son. Whipped in the synagogue, the full thirty nine lashes. They wanted me to have you aborted. When I refused they threatened to have me stoned. No, wait,' I say, holding up my hand to stop him interrupting, 'the worst thing was the grief I was causing my mother and my sisters. I don't think your Uncle Ben was old enough to understand. But your aunts knew. You ought to talk to Grandmother. Has she never said anything to you about this?'

'No.'

'Then ask her sometime. She knows you're special. She knows my secret and yours. She is wise and can advise you. I know she doesn't have the knowledge, she was never taught to read or write like I was, but she has much experience of life. She has much to offer you, Joshua. But she won't say anything unless you ask her. She's been watching you closely. She often talks to me about you, wondering when you will be revealed and what it will mean for all of us.'

'How old were you when these things happened to you?'

'I was just thirteen, Joshua. Perhaps I was too young to have thought through all the consequences of what I did… or rather, what I allowed to happen. If I'd been older, perhaps I would have been more careful, more cautious, perhaps I'd have thought more about the likely threats and punishments. I was naïve, foolhardy.'

'No, Mother. You were very trusting. You heard God calling you and you just trusted him. I need to be able to follow that example. But I am older, I know the probable consequences of what I might have to do. Therefore I now need to be sure of how I'll manage. You suffered and you were strong enough to hold fast. I always knew you'd had to be strong, but I didn't know that it was that bad. How did you cope? Surely the pain was too much for you to bear?'

'I bore it, son, because I had to. I had no option other than to deny God's call to me and renounce you, let them tear you from me. And I couldn't do that. I had the support of my mother and my sisters, then later I had your father too. But what I did was considered scandalous. When you are seen to be the Messiah, then people will flock to you. You may find opposition from the authorities, but the people will protect you, they'll not hurt you like they tried to hurt me.'

'I'm not sure, Mother. I'm not so sure that what I have to do or say will be so easily accepted. I may have to face what you endured.'

'Surely not!'

'That's why I need more time. I'm not ready yet. I need to prepare more thoroughly. I need thinking time. I need to spend time with my cousin John, because he's been called by God too. I need to understand his role and mine.'

'Then why not go to stay for a time with John and Cousin Elizabeth - I'm sure they'd be delighted to have you. James and Joe are quite capable of running the carpentry business. The twins are already helping in the fields and Clopas has promised them some land of their own to cultivate. Go while Ruth is still with me to help around the house and assist me in looking after my mother. But do have a good talk with your grandmother. I'm sure she will give you much wise counsel.'

'I think that's good advice. And I think spending some time in Ein-Karem and Jerusalem with John is an excellent idea and one I should pursue. I'm ready to move on in my studies. I need to ask more questions of the teachers and philosophers in Jerusalem. The rabbis in Sepphoris are learned but they get bogged down with the minutiae in the texts and are unwilling to speculate or challenge orthodox interpretations. John and I can go together and listen to some of the most experienced teachers in the Temple. We will hear them disputing and arguing. They are more likely to be open to challenge and encourage new insights.'

'If that's the way forward, I need to ask you another question. If you're going to be a rabbi, you'll need a wife.

Should we not find you one before you take that next step? Or should we wait until you return from John?'

'I'm not sure I need a wife, Mother. The way ahead may be hard. It may call for me to be on the move, never staying in one place. It may not be fair to commit a young woman to such a life. I'll need to be sure of God's priorities and not have to be restrained by my commitment to another human being. Let's wait and see. Perhaps when I've spent time with John and his mother and spent time in Jerusalem, I'll be sure. Leave it until I return.'

'So you will go to John and Elizabeth then?'

'I'll join the group going up to the next Passover, and seek to stay on afterwards with my cousins. I can check out then whether that is acceptable to them. It's only another couple of months away. In that time I'll make sure that James is introduced to our suppliers in Sepphoris and is competent to keep the accounts and knows how to bargain to avoid being overcharged.'

'Then there's one other thing I need to raise. We must tell your brothers and sisters.'

'Of course.'

'I don't mean just about you going to Jerusalem. I mean about your calling. The fact that you will be our Messiah.'

'I'm not sure about that yet, Mother. It may be many years before my full calling can be revealed.'

'But we need to share the good news with them, Joshua. They need to know you are special, that you and I have together had a special role to fulfil from God. Imagine how they will feel when you declare yourself and they will say we lived with him for nearly twenty years and never knew.'

'Is it not better that they treat me like an ordinary brother? If we make out that I have a special task, set by God, will that not cause friction, make them jealous?'

'Nonsense, son. They should be delighted, privileged that our family should be so chosen.'

'I'm not so sure about that. I can't stop you saying anything after I've gone. But is it wise now?'

'I think they should know. You need to share with them your thoughts, your plans. Perhaps they will help you, support you. You can test your ideas with them, as well as with me and my mother. We're a family, Joshua. We should have no secrets from each other.'

'Well, this has been a secret that we've kept from them for many years. Did my father know everything?'

'Yes, Joshua, he did. You've always known he wasn't your natural father. He only accepted that because he knew of your exceptional source and calling. He was proud to have been chosen to care for you in your formative years.'

At that moment Ruth and Deborah burst in with two large water jars and our spell is broken.

'We'll talk some more,' I say, and Joshua greets his sister and sister-in-law and goes to find James and Joe in the workshop.

'What was all that about?' Ruth is curious. We'll have to tell them, I'm sure of it.

Chapter 7
Mari

Salome came to see me this afternoon. She brought me some fresh loaves and we had a quiet chat. I'm reassured. She tells me everything is well, Andrew is content and she's been made welcome by his parents. That's a great relief. I didn't expect any problems, but you never know. I'd be devastated if we'd made the wrong choice for her. Then I had an idea. I invited her to bring Andrew to our evening meal, with this extra bread we have more than enough food. Now is the time to tell them about Joshua's call. If I put it off, I'll find excuses not to tell them and it'll become harder. I think I persuaded Joshua that it was the right thing to do.

So we're all assembled in the flickering light of the torches round the room. We've had our fill and everyone is reclining, chatting. Ruth has been quizzing Salome about married life and the boys are swapping banter with Andrew and Salome causing the poor girl to blush, which is obvious to all even in this dim light. I think it's time to spare the girl any more embarrassment, so I call for silence and tell them I have something important to say. The hubbub gradually subsides and they all look at me expectantly. I find I'm nervous. I look at Joshua and he is looking at me with some concern. But I've said it now. I must go on.

'I've a big secret I want to share with all of you. Only Grandma and Joshua know it and I think it's time I told you. I think it might shock some of you, but listen all the way through before you make any judgments.'

I pause. They are all attention now. The only sounds are the distant bleating of sheep in the hills and the scuffling noise of our hens in the yard. Even our donkey is quiet. I take a deep breath.

'Many years ago when I was a young girl, about as old as Ruth here, I had a very strange experience. I met a stranger, he said he was a messenger from God, and he would appear from time to time and converse with me when I was in the fields caring for our livestock. Then one day, he told me I should bear a very special son, a child sent by God, not by any human father. I just had to accept God's will and it would happen. I worried how this would come about and what my family and the rabbis in the synagogue would say, but in the end I gave my consent.'

James interrupts me. 'Was this before you met our father? Or was he the stranger?'

'No, James, I did not know your father then. This was a very strange young man. He had the habit of appearing and disappearing. I was confused by him. I think now he was an angel. He said he was a messenger from God.'

'You didn't believe that, surely?'

'I was young, James, and he said such beautiful words. And he told me things that no stranger should have known about us. You know your Aunt Elizabeth in Jerusalem had your cousin John after many years of being barren. This man told me that she would have a child despite her age and later I found out that what he'd said was true and no-one at that time knew about it. How could he have known unless he had some special power? Anyway, I believed him. And then one day he told me that I would have this child and he would be the long promised Messiah, the saviour of our country.'

I look around. They are struck dumb. They are looking at me as though I'm mad.

'And it happened as he'd said. I became pregnant even though I'd had no husband. Although I'd met your father Joseph by then, we'd never been alone together. There was a terrible scandal, you didn't know your Uncle Eli, Uncle Clopas's father, who was a rabbi here at the time. He and the other rabbis were furious and accused me of adultery and blasphemy and had me whipped and sent away with instructions to have the child aborted and I was sent to stay with Aunt Elizabeth. You know all this is true, don't you Mother?'

My mother nods. All the children look to her for confirmation.

'What Mari, your mother, says is true. It was an awful time for all of us. But your mother was strong and steadfast and wouldn't bow to any of their demands even though they threatened to kill her.'

'How? What did they want to do to you?' It's Joe that interrupts this time.

'The punishment for adultery and blasphemy is stoning. In fact, either offence could draw that death sentence. I was judged guilty of both.'

'How did you escape then?'

'Your grandmother pleaded for me. Your father sought my release. Elizabeth's husband, Zechariah, who was a rabbi in the Jerusalem Temple believed in me and wrote to the rabbis here. Eventually the rabbis here were persuaded of the truth of my claim and convinced a meeting of the men of the village who'd been called together to judge and condemn me.'

'What happened to the baby? Was a boy born as the stranger promised?'

'Yes.'

'Where is he? Who is he?'

'Don't you know? Can't you guess? It's your brother, Joshua!'

All eyes turn to him and stare. Joshua is silent. He is not smiling, his eyes even seem to be watering.

'I don't believe it. You can't believe it, any of you. It's a story you made up to hide your shame. Whoever heard of seeing an angel? I ask you! These things don't happen.' James looks furiously at me and then looks round at his siblings.

My mother speaks quietly. 'James, don't shout at your mother like that. What she says is true. I can attest it.'

'But you only have her word for it. I don't doubt that she caused a scandal and all the things she said happened then are true. But surely you don't believe her story of the angel and her innocence.'

And he turned and looked at Joshua.

'You're a bastard, that's what you are. You've no right to be in our family and get all the privileges of the eldest son. That's my right. All this special attention and going off to be a rabbi. It's all wrong.'

'James, please, don't be like that. Blame me if you like, but not your brother. It's not his fault. And you can ask Rabbi Joel at the synagogue and Rabbi Jonas knew as well although he was not a rabbi then. And the old man Jethro, he was convinced in the end, although he was very sceptical at first.'

'I believe you, Mother.' Ruth says this quietly and looks at the others. They say nothing. They don't know what to say. Some of them are looking very uncomfortable. They don't want to join in James's outburst but they don't look very convinced. Perhaps it was a mistake to tell them.

'Joshua, what do you think of all this nonsense? You don't believe her, do you? Or has she filled your mind with these fairy tales and perverted your common sense?'

Joshua looks hard at his brother and is silent for a long time. All are waiting to see how he will react.

'You heard what our mother said. You know her love and care for us. Do you think she is mad?'

'You don't deny it then? You're mad as well! You'll come to no good. If this rumour spreads around people'll crucify you. They'll watch every step you take, criticise every word you utter. Life will be impossible for you. What are you going to do? Are you just going down to the synagogue tomorrow morning and shout, 'I'm the Messiah, let's throw the Romans out! You won't last five minutes, they'll tear you apart.'

'No, James, it won't be like that. I need to go and talk to my cousin John in Ein-Karem. I know he feels he has a special calling too. I need to share my thoughts with him, we need to test our call to see that it is true, that we are not deluding ourselves.'

'So you think you might be wrong, then? That your mother was hallucinating?'

'No, James. I believe her. But the nature of my call, how and when I make any move, these things are still a mystery to me.'

'So you're going to leave us and go to John. Leaving all the work here to Joe and me. You have all the privileges of the eldest and then you intend to abandon us. Hard work with your hands is too demeaning for you, is it?'

'James, stop it! You're being totally unfair. You can shout at me if you like, it was my decision to tell you now. I thought you all deserved to know and not suddenly find out when Joshua's role is revealed and you all feel foolish because you hadn't been told before. I don't think Joshua really wanted me to tell you.'

'You know now what Mother has said. I've told you that there's still much preparation and thinking to be done. I promise to share my thoughts with you, your support and ideas will assist me. But for now, I think I should withdraw. I see this has been a shock for most of you. I think you should talk about it among yourselves freely without the embarrassment of me being here and you all having to check every word you are saying.'

He turns to me. 'Come, Mother, and you, Grandma. I think we should leave them to talk amongst themselves. They'll be more honest with each other if we're not listening.'

He's right, of course. He usually is. We go to move towards my mother's room, but Joshua guides us towards the door to the street.

'Let's get right away. Let's look at the stars.'

I feel his hand on my shoulder and he slips his other arm around my mother to help her up. We leave the silent room, as we move outside we hear a sudden burst of conversation. They are suddenly all talking at once. We move out of earshot.

'Was that wise, Joshua?' I ask. 'James will persuade all the others now that it's all nonsense, even a fraud. Should we not have stayed and argued?'

'If we'd stayed, the others would have said little. They've got minds of their own. You heard what Ruth said. She's already committed herself and said that she believed you.'

'I think Joshua's right.' My mother makes her first contribution. 'The others will have a chance to make their views known now. And it's only a beginning. It was a shock for them, James overreacted, he'll think it over and come to a more sensible and considered standpoint.'

'Do you think I was wrong to broach it with them now, Mother?'

'No, not necessarily, Mari. They had to know sooner or later. It was always going to be a shock. The longer left, the harder it would be. I've often wondered if you were wise to leave it so long.'

'Why didn't you say anything before then?'

'I have to trust you, dear. Too many times I've wanted to guide you and subsequently found that your intuition was right. Or rather, you discerned God's will and shamed my thoughts, so I've learned to be quiet and let you decide. If I'd had my way twenty years ago, Joshua would never have been born, for I was party to the decision to send you to Elizabeth in the hope that they'd help you rid yourself of the child. If I'd known all along that you were being approached by the stranger, I'd have forbidden you to leave the house without being chaperoned.'

'But you did support me. It was your intervention and your persuasion of Joseph to stay loyal to me that saved my life. Mother, I've always meant to ask you. That dream that Joseph

65

reported that changed the rabbi's mind. Did he really dream those texts, or did you prompt him about the texts that Eli'd given me when I came of age?'

'That's my secret, Mari. That's one I'll take to my grave. God inspired all of us to act as we did and it had the perfect outcome, of that I'm sure. I can't remember the exact details now, it was a long time ago.'

'Of course you can remember, Mother. You don't forget things like that.'

'Well, I have forgotten, so it's no use you trying to get me to say otherwise. I can't remember. You were saved. Let's just leave it at that.'

'Oh, Mother!'

Now I don't know what to believe. Did she really make up the story of the dream and the miracle texts that persuaded the rabbis that my claim was from God himself? Perhaps the miracle was that Joseph went along with it despite the offence my pregnancy must have caused him. Then there was Zechariah's letter. It wasn't just Joseph's dream. It doesn't matter now. Joshua is here and so am I. That's the miracle.

* * * * *

We stay out in the cool of the night for a long time. We wander to the edge of the village and stand, just gazing at the blackness of the sky and the contrasting array of stars. After all the argument we find it restful just to stay silent. At first I feel the tension, the need to ask Joshua more questions, to discuss the probable outcome of the conversations now taking place among my children. But gradually this pressure seeps away. Both Mother and Joshua seem content. Then Joshua takes my hand and looks at the heavens spread out before our eyes.

'Leave it to God, Mother. You've said what needs to be said. My brothers and sisters will react in their own ways. Some will believe. Others will remain sceptical. Accept it. Love

66

them equally. Do not ask them to conform. I'll go away for a time. They'll get used to the idea.'

He squeezes my hand.

'I think it's time to go back now. You go back together. I want to spend some time on my own to think and pray.'

*   *   *   *   *

The men left yesterday with others from the village to make pilgrimage to Jerusalem for the Passover festival. All my sons went, together with Clopas, Miriam and their two sons. Ruth has stayed with me and Salome says she'll visit me each day as her Andrew has joined the party also. Joshua is intending to stay there after the Passover and spend time with John and Elizabeth as we'd previously agreed.

The last couple of months have been very difficult. The children are in disagreement about Joshua. James has remained hostile to the idea and his wife Deborah has clearly been influenced by him and regards me with great suspicion now, although she says little. I can tell it though from her attitude and silences. Ruth is a great support. She chats to me and has asked me many questions and is more enthusiastic than ever at searching the scriptures, listening avidly to the rabbis when we attend the synagogue on the Sabbath. I think Salome believes too although she is circumspect in what she says as I don't think she wants to commit herself in front of Andrew who is clearly dismissive of the whole story. Apparently he told his parents and now the gossip has gone round the whole village and everyone is looking at me as though I've lost my wits. Well, not quite everyone, there are still those who were present at my trial before the rabbis in the synagogue nearly twenty years ago and who were among those who heard Eli, Joel and Jethro proclaim that I was bearing the future Messiah. But then I went away, and many forgot or put it to the back of their minds. Now this tale is opening up the controversy for I'm discovering that many who heard Eli's speech were not necessarily convinced by his argument, but were reluctant to condemn to death a young girl they'd all known and liked.

As for the boys - well, the twins are not hostile like James, but they seem to joke about it, not take it seriously. I suspect they are reluctant to argue with me but I guess when they are with other village boys they laugh it off in order to avoid being teased about it. Joseph - I haven't a clue what he's thinking. He gets on quietly with his work with James, but never says anything to me. I've heard James trying to speak to him about the issue too, but Joseph ignores him and only opens his mouth when James changes the subject. I notice that James has stopped talking about it to Joseph as a waste of breath. I honestly don't know whether that means he believes but hasn't the intellect or strength to counter James or whether he's blotting out the whole episode as something he doesn't want to think about.

Deborah was feeling a little unwell this morning, so Ruth has gone alone to fetch water. We don't need as much now all the men are away. I thought at first that Deborah was just missing James - she went with him last year to the Passover - and this is the first time they've been apart since their marriage. We're alone at present as Mother is visiting a friend a couple of streets away. I expected her usual silence that has descended over her since I told them about Joshua's birth and destiny, but she suddenly starts talking to me - perhaps she feels less inhibited when James is not there.

'Mari, there's something I need to tell you.'

My ears prick up. Is she going to say something I don't want to hear?

'I think I'm pregnant. That's why I haven't gone with James this time.'

'That's wonderful, Deborah. I'm so pleased for you.'

68

'I'm a bit nervous about it. I hear so many stories from the other women about the pain and dangers of childbirth and my own mother is not here.'

'Deborah, you can talk to me any time. I've had seven children now. I think I've sufficient experience to be able to pass on some advice to you - words of wisdom shall I say, from living through it, not from old wives' tales.'

'I'm feeling queasy a lot of the time, even at this very moment.'

'That's quite natural, Deborah. It'll ease during the day and cease altogether as the pregnancy becomes more advanced. That was my experience anyway. Look, sit down, there's no need to do any more sweeping. Ruth will finish it off when she returns. And don't think you've got to help me with the cooking if the smell of certain foods makes you feel worse.'

Deborah looks very pale and is breathing heavily. I leave her for a while and when I return colour has come back into her face. She's an attractive girl, and very level-headed. I've always felt she was older than her averred sixteen years. Sitting there on one of the old stools that Joseph made for us, she looks younger now and more vulnerable. I sit beside her.

'Feeling better?'

'Yes, a bit.'

'Just relax, don't worry. It'll pass off in a few minutes I expect.'

She is silent while I attend to a few household chores.

'Mari, I'm sorry that my husband says such awful things to you. It made me very embarrassed when he argued with you and shouted at Joshua. I don't know what to believe, but he shouldn't have treated you like that. I feel guilty that I didn't stop him.'

'It's not your fault, Deborah. You can't be held responsible for what he thinks.'

'But I should have stopped him. I should have apologised to you then.'

'You're apologising to me now, aren't you?'

'Yes. But I should have done so at the time.'

'Don't let it be a matter for you to argue about with James. I don't want it to cause quarrels between you. Salome has a similar concern with her husband, Andrew. I know it all sounds far-fetched. When it happened to me, I found it incredible too, but it happened as I was promised. The proof will come, Deborah. But be patient. Just have an open mind for the moment. Don't worry about James. He'll find out the truth in his own good time.'

Chapter 8
Elizabeth, AD 13

Let me introduce myself - you'll have seen reference to me earlier, but I've been asked to look after my cousin Mari's son, Joshua, for a few weeks. My name is Elizabeth. I live in Ein-Karem, a small town about ten miles north of Jerusalem. My husband, Zechariah, was a senior rabbi in the Jerusalem Temple but unfortunately he died over eighteen years ago. But I've not been alone. I conceived a child after I'd almost given up hope, and John, my son, has been a great comfort to me ever since. He's a strong young man now in the prime of life, twenty years old. I know he has a special mission in life. When we prayed for a son after years of frustration, he was promised to me to alert the nation to the coming of the Messiah. I keep wondering when his time will come, but he's said he'll not leave me while I have need of him. And now his cousin, Joshua, has come to stay with us. And he is the one who is to be that chosen person. I'm sure this time will be of great importance.

John joined the group from Nazareth for the Passover. Clopas and his sons and Mari's boys had the Passover meal here with us and then they all went into the city each day to celebrate the festival - all apart from me for I'm too old for walking far now. I've reached my allotted 'three score years and ten'. I've been so blessed to have such a son and I'd just like to live long enough to see him fulfil his call, and Joshua too, but perhaps that's too much to ask. I have a feeling that John is waiting until I'm no more. He's never said as much, but he knows I'm frail and I'd struggle if he left me on my own for too long.

When they all arrived here the first night Joshua asked me if he might stay a while. I was delighted and asked him to remain with us as long as he was able. He and John really need to get to know one another properly, as they've only met briefly during previous Passover gatherings when there has been so much to do and see. Everyone's gone back to Nazareth now apart from Joshua. They told me all the news as soon as they got here, I knew James was married and I was hoping to meet his bride but she's not come this time. The big news was Salome's wedding. We'd been invited, but I couldn't possibly go that far now and John wouldn't leave me. I said that my neighbour would keep an eye on me, but John said it would have been too long - nearly three weeks with the week long celebrations and the journey either way. And it's not safe, they tell me, either route to Galilee if you're not in a large guarded party. They say there are terrorist groups in the mountains between the Samaria road and the Jordan as well as the local brigands and thieves. We don't see much of the Roman soldiers on these roads unless it's at festival time.

Joshua's a fine young man. He's more thoughtful than John. My son can be very blunt and sometimes speaks first and thinks later. He's been under the influence of a group called the Nazarites. They've persuaded him to go on special diet and not to cut his hair. Goodness knows why, it makes him look very dishevelled and I often tell him to tidy himself up. He just laughs at me. He's promised to take Joshua to meet some of those he knows. I hope he isn't persuaded to do the same. Underneath John is a gentle giant but he looks awesome and I think he frightens some of my neighbours a bit. He teases the children and they run screaming from him, but I think it's a joke and they like the excitement of the chase. They ruffle his hair up and he pretends to be a wild animal, a lion or a wolf. I thought Joshua was a bit serious at first but he joins in the games with the local children as well and makes them laugh too. But he does it more by telling them stories. He's really good at it, I don't know where he gets all his tales from. I know some are the stories from our scriptures, the escapades of Isaac and Moses and King David, but often he tells them stories he's made up about life in his village and on the neighbouring farms.

They're both in the city today. John helps in the Temple assisting the scribes and those administering the rituals there. He receives a small income from the priests and brings me money regularly as the Temple authorities maintain all the widows of those who've been employed there as scribes or rabbis. My husband was revered in his day as a very wise counsellor and when he died they suffered a great loss that the other priests told me was hard to fill. I'm not sure quite what they make of John. He's hardworking so I'm sure they have no qualms on that score, but he can be argumentative and outspoken and I've heard it said that some of him consider him intemperate and undisciplined. Apparently he's too inclined to criticise if he sees anything he thinks wrong. He doesn't wait for any explanations or excuses but comes straight out with it. I don't think that endears him to many and I've often advised him to hold his tongue. He might take more notice of Joshua if he gives him similar advice!

When he comes home, he'll often be all indignant at something he's seen, some priest being pious one minute and then speaking ill of some poor soul behind her back; or when he sees some trader in the Temple Outer Court overcharging one of the pilgrims, especially if it's someone who can ill afford to purchase the obligatory sacrifice. I used to think that he would be a priest like his father. We are both from priestly tribes and what better way to prepare everyone for the coming of the Messiah than to proclaim it from the Temple itself, I thought, but I don't think John wants to take that route. He's lost respect for many of those who officiate there. There are just one or two teachers of whom he's fond and those are the ones he assists and learns from.

I must get back to preparing our evening meal. The sun is sinking and the men will want to be home before nightfall. It's difficult to decide sometimes what to get for John since he's taken up with the Nazarites, as they won't eat meat or drink wine. I milked the goat earlier and there is sufficient for John, but I think Joshua will have a cup of wine with me. I have bread and some figs and grapes, but for some reason John won't eat grapes either. I'm not sure why that prohibition exists, it's not that he doesn't like them. He used to eat plenty. He's associated himself with the men who've taken a vow to separate themselves and purify themselves from sin. They come to the Temple to make offerings as part of their vows, I think. John's attracted to their austerity and their repudiation of the corruption he sees around him. I don't really understand all he tells me. He talks about Samson and Samuel a lot, but I'm not sure what they have to do with the coming of the Messiah. The rabbis used to talk about the prophet Elijah being the forerunner of the Messiah, but I haven't heard John mention him.

Ah, that's the pair of them arriving now. They'll be hungry and dirty from the road, I've no doubt. I'd better pour out some water – they'll need to wash their feet.

'Cousin Elizabeth, we'll do that. We can bend better than you!'

Joshua fetches the jar over and pours some into a basin. He slips his sandals off and looks round for a cloth. John goes into the adjacent room and brings back a clean piece of rag he's found.

'Sit down, Joshua, and let me do it.'

'Alright, but I'll freshen your feet afterwards.'

The deeds done, Joshua looks at me.

'Come on and rest, Aunt. I would imagine you've been on your feet most of the day. Let your feet soak a while.'

I try to protest, but the two young men laugh and both take an arm and give me little option but to accede to their suggestion. Joshua gently washes my feet – I must admit it feels good after a hot and tiring day. Then John grabs the towel from Joshua and dries them. They're both still laughing.

Eventually they let me go and I serve the food I've prepared for them. I've guessed right. Joshua is not averse to a cup of wine or a handful of grapes.

'Sinner!' cries John, trying playfully to grab the goblet from Joshua's clasp.

'Careful, boys, you'll spill it and that'd be a waste of good wine.'

They settle down and eat the bread and figs. I've not got any meat because of John. I know Joshua is used to fresh fish which traders bring to the markets in Tiberias and Sepphoris but we can only get dried fish here as we're too far from a source. An occasional catch is brought into Jerusalem from the coast, but it won't keep in the warm seasons and John is happy to let me buy local produce from the farmers here. It's getting dark now and I light the torches and place them in the brackets on the wall. Our shadows flicker on the rough stonework and the men begin to discuss what they've been doing during the day. I leave the discarded platters lying and listen, for Joshua is able to challenge and question John in a way I could never do, and I find it refreshing.

'What did you make of Malachi?' John lies back and looks quizzically at Joshua.

'An interesting man. I'm not sure I agreed with everything he said, but he raised some good points, issues I need to think about.' Joshua looks at me. 'This man, I thought he was a priest at first, came to the Temple and we heard him disputing with some of the teachers and rabbis there. We overheard some of the conversation – they were quite heated at one point – so we attached ourselves to the group and listened. We followed the man – his name was Malachi – and talked to him at length. He was one of the Essenes, they are in many cities, but this man came from a big settlement out at Ein-Gedi in the desert hills between Jericho and the Salt Sea.'

'I've heard John talk about the Essenes sometimes. Are they the same as the Nazarites you often talk about? They seem to be very critical of some of the ways the priests run the Temple.'

'With good reason, Mother. Both groups criticise the priests, but they're not the same. Some of the things the priests do are disgraceful. Some are corrupt. They line their own pockets at the expense of some of the poorest and most vulnerable people. They pick on the most ignorant and bamboozle them in the name of religion.'

'Don't the Chief Priest and the senior rabbis stop these excesses?'

'Joshua, I've told you before. They're some of the worst offenders. They've got no interest in stopping the corruption. They get a good income from the fees and profits of those who exploit their permission to trade around the precincts. These Essenes repudiate such things and hold themselves apart from such a travesty of our religion.'

'But what do they do to stop it?'

'Well, you heard the argument today. They show by example how life should be lived. They believe that only by being pure in deed and spirit are they entitled to criticise and advocate a better way.'

'That's all very well, but is shutting themselves away in isolation in the desert the best way to do the Lord God's will?'

'I'm sure they have to start by protecting themselves against the evils of this world. They learn to discipline themselves, to purify their lives, to practice healing for themselves and for others. We need to hear their voice. This nation badly needs to hear their message of repentance and purity. We've become too contaminated by this world. The Temple priests have sought accommodation with the Romans and thereby compromised themselves and the purity of our faith.

'That's fine if their isolation is a temporary measure, a time of preparation before taking action to change things. But you can't have much influence if you isolate yourself in the wilderness.'

'The Temple priests should go to see them for themselves instead of criticising them as being impractical idealists. When do they ever go out of their cocooned luxurious abode and see how the people live, or see this alternative lifestyle?'

'Well, you could turn that argument on its head. When do these Essenes mingle with ordinary folk and advocate their message? How do they know the pressures that most people experience, the struggle to maintain their families, feed their children? They even hold themselves free of family ties, so they do not experience life as lived by everyone else.'

'Well, what about us? Neither of us is married. Are you saying we cannot know what is right without being married and having a family? What about you? Do you intend to take a wife? Isn't your family putting any pressure on you? Your brother and sister are married. They're both younger than you. Is your celibacy a deliberate decision?'

'I'm not sure yet. I've plenty of experience of family life, after all I have six brothers and sisters and I've lived the last few years amid my cousins and their children. But I'm reluctant to commit a young woman to a partnership that might call her to hardships and seeming abandonment. I might be forced to decide between my commitment to God and to a wife. That would be very unfair. But I'm still open on the subject. What about you?'

'I'm sure I must not take a wife. I've argued with you many times, haven't I, Mother?'

Indeed, he has. I've given up on this. I'd hoped by now to have a daughter-in-law and grandchildren. But I can see it's not to be. Mari is lucky. Even if Joshua remains unmarried, she's got her other children around her and it's only a matter of time before the first grandchild arrives.

'I've taken a vow, Joshua. I'm tempted to do the same as Malachi and visit his community. They do not marry there. I intend to keep myself apart from the temptations of the flesh.'

'It's not a point of principle with me, but one of practicality. One part of me envies my brother and would like nothing more than to settle down and raise a family of children. I love them, I've always enjoyed the company of children and believe I'd be a good father. But I'm uncertain of my true destiny at the moment. I'm sure I have to wait until I'm clearer.'

I interrupt. 'You would be a good father, Joshua, I know you're right about that. I've watched you with the village children here. Why are you so reluctant? The priests and rabbis all marry. Why is your call so different?' I'm on Mari's side here. I think he'd make a marvellous family man. A woman who married him would indeed be a fortunate girl.

'I might, Elizabeth. I haven't finally decided yet. But I don't want to rule out all the options before I'm clear about my mission.'

'Joshua, would you be interested in coming with me to explore the Essene community and their style of life?'

John sees my glance, I can't help displaying my anxiety which he picks up at once.

'Don't worry, Mother. I'm only suggesting a short visit – I'm not intending to abandon you.'

He turns to Joshua again.

'What about it, cousin? Malachi said he'd be in Jerusalem for a few days. Why don't we make contact and go back with him, just for a week or so. I'm sure we'll see him again in the Temple. He'll be back, he won't resist further disputation with the rabbis. I think he was enjoying himself more than they were.'

'Maybe. If your mother can spare us for a short while. It would be interesting, to be sure. I'd like to make my own mind up by direct observation. I want to see if their lifestyle is as honest and pure as they say it is. I'd like to find out what influence, if any, they really have. How spiritual they really are.'

I'm a bit nervous about this. I do hope Joshua is as good as his word and does not fall under their spell as my John seems to have done with the Nazarites and now the Essenes. But he seems genuine in wanting to see for himself and test their ideas. There can be nothing wrong with that.

They both go into the city again the next day to search for Malachi, but assure me they'll be home tonight and will ensure I've sufficient provisions to see me through the following week. In any case I can still get as far as the baker's to buy bread if I take my time and I've got wine and water – John refilled my jars last night. I'm not at all convinced by this venture of theirs. I was promised that John would prepare the way for the Messiah, not hide himself in the desert. I'll have to be patient though. There's little I can do these days to change my son's mind. He's determined to foreswear the company of women and to seek this purity he yearns for. And I've heard that these Essenes are unpopular in Jerusalem. How will John get his message over when his time comes if he's ostracised by the authorities as I've heard? Surely he'll need all the support he can get? The influence of the two priests he assists seems to be weakening. If I were younger, I'd go to the Temple and ask their advice, but it's too far now. I'd like to ask Joshua's advice, but he spends all his time with John and they go into the city together. Perhaps I can find an excuse for him to stay with me one day.

They came back in good time. They found Malachi easily enough. He's planning to spend the Sabbath in the Temple – John said that there's no way that he'd consider travelling on the Sabbath for apparently one of his quarrels with the Temple authorities is their lax observation of that day. So they've agreed to set forth on the first day of the week, stay with our distant relatives in Bethany and complete the journey to the desert community the following day. They'll only stay a couple of days – they promised me that. So we'll see. I have no real confidence in that statement, because if it really attracts their interest, they'll get caught up in it and be reluctant to tear themselves away. But Joshua gave me his promise. We'll see.

*   *   *   *   *

They did come back as they promised. They arrived late last night, weary after the climb up from the Salt Sea – they'd made it in one very long day, having set off before dawn. They were too exhausted to say much but just grabbed a crust of bread and some milk and were asleep before I could satisfy my curiosity. They both refilled my water jars first thing this morning – they won't let me go now despite the odd looks they get. Well, to tell the truth, most women are used to John's presence as he's been fetching water for me most days for the last couple of years. You don't see any women of my age at the well, their daughters or daughters-in-law and even granddaughters perform that ritual.

As we settle around the breakfast meal, I can contain myself no longer.

'Well, what did you find? Was it what you expected?'

'It was very impressive, Mother. It was a huge encampment with common living areas, dormitories and you should see their gardens! Right out there in the desert, they seem to have mastered the irrigation of their land. They've made ditches from the Jordan and storage basins for rain water. It doesn't just supply the ground they use for crop cultivation, they have long communal baths used for both cleansing and their ritual purification ceremonies.'

'And what did you think of it, Joshua?'

'As John said, it was impressive. There's no gainsaying that. They are totally self-sufficient. They need for nothing. And they are spiritual people. They certainly are different to the priests and rabbis at the Temple.'

'I can hear the 'but' in your voice, Joshua!'

'Come off it, Joshua,' says John. 'You know you were amazed at what you found. Don't be so negative.'

'I haven't said anything against it yet.'

'But you were going to, weren't you? See, you said 'yet'.'

'Well, there were some very impressive things about the community. They are serious about sin and its consequences. They are an ascetic people; they live simply. And surprisingly, they are humble. They don't boast about their spiritual and moral superiority, though they must be tempted sometimes.'

'But?'

'Well, I think they're half right. They've preserved themselves from sin. They lead good lives, they don't hurt or injure anyone else. They seem cheerful in their way. But they don't exert much of a positive influence, do they? They abstain from doing wrong rather than doing what's right.'

'There's lot worse you can say of people.'

'Of course, I'm just saying I think they lack something. They're too passive.'

'How can you say that when you hear them arguing with the Pharisees or Temple priests? Passive is the last thing they are. They're revolutionary. They'd sweep all the Temple authorities away and install a simpler purer form of ritual and worship.'

'But it's about ceremony and ritual, not about relationships and care for society.'

'On the contrary, they are extremely caring. They have no property – they share everything. No-one is poor among them.'

'I grant you, that is an admirable trait. But they just care for each other. They're an inward looking community. They've isolated themselves from reality.'

'With all the wickedness in Jerusalem, don't you think that's a good thing?'

'As far as it goes, John. But what is their purpose? Are they just about maintaining their own purity and keeping themselves from the contamination of the world?'

'They do have gifts they share outside. They're well acquainted with the mysteries of herbs and healing. They do not hold that back from others who seek their help.'

'I grant you that. But you have to go to them. And it's a long and dangerous route to reach their settlement and if you're ill or crippled, how would you make the journey?'

'You were very interested in their healing methods.'

'Yes, I was. As well as the herbs and ointments they use, I was impressed with their understanding of the mind, the power of suggestion and of prayer. Very often it seemed to me that the healing takes place without the need for medicine or physical treatment. I'm sure one can learn their methods. If I were to spend any time there, I think I'd make that my priority. But when I'd learned, I wouldn't stay there. I'd want to take my understanding into the cities and villages where such skills are most needed.'

'But would you be able to exercise such skills in the hurly burly of the cities among people who wouldn't have seen such healing and therefore be sceptical about its effectiveness?'

'Why not? Are you saying you can't be close to God in the towns? That you can only develop spiritual powers in the desert places?'

'I don't know, Joshua. I only think it would be much harder. I think I'd need constantly to return to the desert to build up my spiritual strength.'

'Elizabeth, it's certainly peaceful and quiet out there. The water rituals are symbolic and calming. But it's strange. There are no women or children. You do not hear footsteps in the sand. For a short time, yes, I liked it. But I wouldn't want to commit myself to dedicating my life to a community in such an environment.'

We stir ourselves and attend to a few necessities before it gets too hot. Then later under the shade of our home sitting in the yard watching the hens and goats scavenging, we sit and Joshua and I share a draught of wine, while John partakes of goat's milk.

'They believe in the coming of the Messiah,' says John, giving Joshua a meaningful look. 'You could do worse than spend more time with them. I know some are scholars who are copying out the scriptures, but they believe they are preparing for the Messiah's coming by purifying themselves in readiness.'

'They are certainly very disciplined. I'm not sure though how worthy it is to be such a slave to rules. Do they know why many of their rules exist? What their purpose is?'

The virtue is in the discipline. They learn self-control, to be masters of themselves. They wish to be ready for the end time when evil will be confronted and a new kingdom will be installed. The role of the Messiah is to bring this new kingdom about.'

'But what sort of kingdom is it, John? What sort of Messiah do they look forward to? I got confused for they seemed to be looking to different characters. Sometimes they spoke of a military leader who will drive out the Romans and establish peace in Jerusalem to be ruled by the righteous, with the existing priestly hierarchy being thrown out with their Roman masters. The next moment they are talking of a Messiah priest whose kingdom is spiritual. Then again they talk of a Teacher of Righteousness – some as though he was their founder, others as though he's still to come. Is this all one person or three different people? Are they all Messiahs? And will this paradise to come just be for themselves and those that believe like them or is it for everyone, or at least open to all who are just and on the side of good?'

'They study the prophets, Joshua. They revere Isaiah and his prophecy of the new creation, the reborn Jerusalem. The time when the evil priests will be overthrown, and they, the righteous remnant will rule justly. Then trees and plants will flourish in the holy city, just as they are cultivating a foretaste in the desert.'

'But do they mean this literally - or is it a figurative image that they have? Is it an earthly kingdom, or a symbol for a celestial spiritual end time?'

'You need to spend more time with them to understand these things, Joshua. We both do. We were only with them three nights.'

'I was certainly interested in their concept of a new kingdom. But do they believe it's possible now or only after earthly death? I want to explore more about that. God's kingdom. What would that be like, John? A segregated holy group, pure and sinless, apart from a doomed and defeated evil world? Or a present world transformed in which ordinary people are able to be Godlike, inhabit God's mind and love peace and care for those less able than themselves? Do they take the prophet Amos's words seriously and value justice and make this an integral and essential element of the kingdom?'

'It'll have no Temple priests, that's for sure. Didn't you hear them say that the Temple would be destroyed and rebuilt in purer form. I presume they meant the systems of organisation and administration, not the edifice itself.'

'The world won't be put to rights by just condemning the priests.'

'No, the whole structure of the establishment must be swept away – the priests, the rabbis, the scribes, the Sanhedrin and the Roman governor, the occupying powers, Tetrarch Antipas and all his ghastly court.'

'You really are a revolutionary, John. You'll have to be careful what you say or someone will take you seriously. And then you won't last long enough to see any of your dreams come about.'

'You have to dream, Joshua. I have to believe that there will be many who will turn from sin and be ready for the new kingdom. And you're going to be with me one day, aren't you? You are, you know. It's my job to prepare the way for you and you know it, don't you?'

I listen to all this and I'm both excited and scared for them. And such talk goes on for days. They argue and they develop their ideas. They walk out together and roam around the hills. All they seem to want to talk about is the nature of this kingdom. I can't help them now. My brain reels at the thoughts they express. To me life was simpler. I heard a call from God and I obeyed. I trust now that others will take forward the vision. My part is over.

Chapter 9
James, AD 16

It's time my voice was heard. After all, I seem to do all the work round here. My so-called Messianic brother has deserted us again and gone off with his equally misguided cousin, John, to the Essenes' hideout in the Judean Wilderness to contemplate their navels once more. This is the third time. The first time was only for a few days, though Joshua stayed in Ein-Karem for several weeks. Then he was away for nearly six months. This time he's been away for nearly a whole year.

'You've got your brother to help you,' he said. Huh! Joe. I suppose he does his best, but he's so slow. Every single thing he makes he thinks is a work of art. I can't get him to hurry up. It doesn't matter how many deadlines we're about to miss, how many impatient customers are queuing up, it's all the same to him. He just plods on, for ever planing another bit off here, smoothing a bit there, or rejecting a half finished piece he's already spent days on because he discovers some tiny split or knot. It's left to me as usual to sort things out, make sure we get new business, get over to Sepphoris each month to fetch new supplies and order stock and then cost everything out and make sure we get paid. Joshua used to do some of these things, but ever since our crazy mother spouted about his 'miraculous' birth and destiny, he's lost interest in us and goes gallivanting off to explore her flights of fancy. I used to think he was sensible and practical, but her words seem to have turned his head.

As I said, he's been gone over a year now. I thought he'd be back with the returning Passover crowd. He went with them last year, but apparently he was still out at Ein-Gedi when it was time for them to return. I didn't go this year as our youngest, Reuben, is only a few months old and Deborah is finding Esther a handful. She's just mastered the art of running everywhere and my wife can't handle both her and the baby at the same time. I know my mother and grandmother are here, but one is too arthritic to help much and I want to keep an eye on what tales my mother is feeding to Deborah. If Ruth had still been at home, it would have been fine as Esther adored her and would do anything that Ruth told her to do, but she got married last year and has moved to Tiberias with her husband Simon, who's boat repairer for the fishermen there. Frankly I thought we could have done better for her, but apparently the man has a good enough business with his brothers and the girl seems content. She's a big loss here though. And it was a disgrace that Joshua failed to come home for the wedding. He must have known it would have been celebrated during the year, yet he still chose to isolate himself to prepare himself for his calling. That was his excuse. An odd set of priorities if you ask me.

'James, James, can you hear me?' That's my grandmother calling me. As well as being arthritic, her eyesight is failing. I guess she's mislaid something again. I don't know why she still struggles with the sewing work. We don't need the income now from that, not that it ever yielded much. But she's obstinate and will not give it up. Mother's down at the synagogue again talking to Joel. He encourages her in her illusions, unlike Jonas who, like me, thinks the whole thing a nonsense. I get this constant interruption now that Deborah has the two children to keep an eye on and Simon and Judas are both working with Clopas's sons in the fields. It's no use asking Joseph to go. He'll take hours picking up again where he left off. Better to leave him at it and do whatever old Anna wants myself.

'Yes, Grandmother, what is it?'

'I want to go to see Benjamin.'

'Alright.'

I wait. She's going to ask me to take her. If Mother was here she'd do it, but it's me again that has to drop everything. There's a stack of orders awaiting completion and I'll have to work half the night to keep on top of them. But it's no good letting her go on her own. She'll only fall or be helped by one of our neighbours who'll spread the rumour that I'm heartless, letting my crippled grandmother struggle without assistance.

'You'll come with me, won't you, James?'

'Yes, Grandmother, you know I will.'

'I know, I'm a burden to you, aren't I?'

'No, don't you worry about it. It's not your fault. It's just that I'm hard pressed to finish our orders these days. I thought Joshua'd be back to help after Passover, but I don't know when he'll be back now.'

'I'm worried about you, James. I want to ask Benjamin if he can help out in some way.'

'I'm alright, really I am. There's no need to bother Ben, he's got his own family to support.'

'He spoke to me the other day and asked if I thought you needed assistance. He said he could help out if you thought it useful. I know you're hard pressed. You get very frustrated and stressed sometime and you get bad tempered with Deborah... No, James, don't protest. I know it's only your tiredness and overwork talking.'

'It's Joshua's fault. Our father trained him in the business and expected him to shoulder the burden as first born.'

'Don't blame your brother all the time. Your income is good, you could afford to hire someone in to help you. Why didn't you train Simon and Judas instead of encouraging them to work with Clopas? I know Joshua was all for that.'

'Well, I didn't know Joshua was going to abandon us then, did I? If he knew that the twins ought to be brought into the business because he was setting his sights elsewhere, he should have said. I didn't want any more in the business then because I didn't know that the income would be enough to sustain more than three families.'

'Can't you stop criticising your brother all the time? It upsets your mother.'

'Well, she shouldn't have been so naïve and credulous. It's her fault that he's developed these preposterous grandiose ideas of his.'

'You don't know the half of it, James. I saw what your mother went through, the opposition and scandal she faced, her guts and tenacity. At one time it was her as a thirteen year old girl against the rest of the world.'

'Well, that should have made her realise the stupidity of her argument.'

'You don't understand her at all, James. She convinced me, your father, Rabbi Joel, even old Eli who was the hardest of all and resisted until the end. Why won't you believe her?'

'Grandmother, look at us. We're an ordinary family. We're tradespeople. I know Clopas has property, but he's nothing compared with the merchants in Sepphoris let alone the priests and scribes and government officials in Jerusalem. Who on earth ever heard of a Messiah coming from such stock? The Messiah will come from a royal bloodline, so it's no use looking here. I know father was from the tribe of David, but if what Mother says is true and she was really a virgin, it destroys her whole argument, for then Joshua can't possibly be of royal lineage. I have a better claim to that!'

'You'll learn. One day you'll regret you've said these things.'

'No I won't. I'm going to keep my sanity whatever other people think and do.'

'It's no good arguing with you, James. But I tell you, you'll change your mind one day.'

It's useless trying to convince her. In the meantime we've been walking slowly towards Uncle Benjamin's home on the edge of the village, a home he built with my father's help when he got married. Old Anna, as the other village woman call her – she's younger than some of them frankly, but she's stooped so she looks older – is gripping my arm hard as she nearly stumbles over the ruts in the cart track. If her intention is to have a serious talk with Ben, she'll have her task cut out, as I'm sure his children will be demanding her attention. They insist on hearing stories about the past whenever she calls on them – another family led astray by whimsy. I'm surprised Ben doesn't intervene and constrain her.

When we arrive, we discover their house surprisingly quiet. The lads, Matthew and Thomas, long out of school for the day, are apparently playing down by the stream beyond the well. Little Anna, a bright seven year old, is learning to do simple stitch-work with her mother. Old Anna goes over to her and kisses the child and they have a quick hug, then the girl goes back to her task. My uncle – well I don't think of him as that as he's only a few years older than me – pours us a glass of wine and we settle in the shade and after the usual pleasantries, my grandmother raises the issue that has prompted her visit.

'Ben,' she says, 'it doesn't look as though Joshua will be home for a while yet. James is finding it hard to cope with just Joe to assist him. Are you really in a position to help as you hinted to me the other day?'

'It's certainly easier in the fields now we have Simon and Judas as well as Clopas's two. I help Clopas keep tally of the produce, sales and tax, but I'm not required to spend so much time in the fields on the physical labour as used to be essential. I could spend some time with you, James, if you would like me to help. I know you go to Sepphoris a lot for ordering and getting your supplies. I travel there often on behalf of Clopas, I could easily combine his interests with yours. And I'd be happy to do your accounts and tax calculations if you want to concentrate on the carpentry which is your skill and which I cannot help you with.'

I hesitate for a moment. His offer would be helpful, but I haven't discussed the idea with Joe and I suppose I ought to. However, I'm sure he'll just be satisfied if we leave him to carry on producing his masterworks in his own good time. If Ben were able to take on everything except the actual carpentry, it would mean that I could undertake all the regular functional orders on which we depend for our livelihood and let Joe do the decorative stuff, which has a laxer timescale. But I have to get one thing clear. I have my pride.

'That could be of value, Ben. I need to talk to Joe, but I'm sure he'll do what I say. It's on one condition, though. We'll pay you a fair rate for the job.'

'That's not necessary, James. I have enough and there will be no reduction in the work I do for Clopas.'

'We can afford it. The work is coming in thick and fast and Joshua takes no income from us now. He doesn't do any work, so why should he?'

'He'll need something when he returns home.'

'If he returns home. He can earn some money from the business if and when he contributes to it. If we get a couple of young lads from the village to train, Joshua could take that on board. We'll need more hands if we want to expand our work. There's no shortage of demand. We could get contracts in Sepphoris, Tiberias and Magdala if we wanted. There's just one carpenter in Nain and another one in Kana and I'm told they're in no position to take on more.'

'That's not a bad idea. I could have a word with my sisters. Salome's Isaac and Rebecca's Nathan could be interested. It might give them a more secure income than farming. Or in a couple of years my Matthew could start learning. But it does depend on Joshua coming home of course. Have you any news? I thought he'd intended to return with the Passover pilgrims. I gather he's stayed on with John and his mother.'

It's a thought but can I trust my brother to come home? And even if he does, will he stay? I can't have him back and get everything lined up for him to teach the lads and then find he leaves us again before they've learned enough to be useful.

'What about it then, James? Do you want to think more about it or discuss it with Joe? I'll help you with all the supplies and accounts work and if you insist, I'll take a modest wage as long as the business can afford it.'

I've just agreed when we hear footsteps and my mother appears at the door.

'How did you know we were here?'

'My mother said she hoped to have a word with Benjamin this afternoon. We've been worried about you, James. You've taken too much on your shoulders.'

'That's your fault as much as anybody's. If you hadn't encouraged Joshua to waste his talents in studying to become a rabbi instead of sticking to a trade that makes money for us, I'd not have been stressed, as you put it...'

Ben interrupts. 'James, don't speak so unkindly to your mother. You should be honoured that your brother is accepted in so many schools of learning. I'm sure your mother has done what she feels is best for all of us. We all owe a large debt to her for what we are.'

'Why, what reason is there for you to be indebted to her?'

'When I was a child, your mother, my older sister, was often mother, father and teacher to me. With all respect to you, Mother,' he turns and indicates Anna, 'I know how difficult things were and how much you relied on Mari to care for us all and keep us amused and out of trouble.'

I say nothing. There's no point on upsetting my mother and grandmother here in front of Ben's wife and the child, Anna. If I speak my mind, I'll only be further rebuked by Ben. I need his help with the business so there's no point in annoying him unnecessarily. So, it's agreed. Benjamin will join us. And I'll endeavour to find out when Joshua intends to return.

* * * * *

I went up to Jerusalem for the Feast of Tabernacles. Mother and Grandmother agreed to see that Deborah was coping and I was fortunate in finding that Joshua had returned to Ein-Karem to look after the widow Elizabeth who had taken to her sick bed and was ailing. John apparently was still with the Essenes – Joshua said that he was intending to join the sect there – but when Joshua saw how near the end Elizabeth was, he agreed to fetch John back, while I looked after the old lady.

They just got back in time. Elizabeth died only a few hours after their arrival. I think she was sufficiently conscious to recognise them both and give them her blessing. She's as mad as my mother, convinced that her son has a call from God, though how he expects to make any impact in that god-forsaken desert, I've no idea. As soon as his mother was buried I heard him tell Joshua that nothing could stop him now from joining the Essenes and being fully inducted through their rituals into acceptance into the community. He tried to persuade Joshua to join him – I heard them arguing one night – but luckily I'd already got to Joshua and convinced him that his place was back home where he was badly needed. I laid it on a bit thick intending to shame him into returning with me and although I'd expected a series of excuses and was geared up to giving him a hard time, he was surprisingly open to my arguments. Indeed, he went one stage further and I got the impression that he'd already intended to come home anyway.

Frankly, I don't think he was as enthusiastic about the Essenes and their teaching as John was. He had a certain grudging admiration for them and I gather had picked up a number of useful tips about their medicine and healing techniques and had also valued the space and time to meditate – who wouldn't? I don't think he realises what a luxury that is for people like me having to pick up all the responsibilities of the family back in Nazareth. As soon as I told him of Ben's suggestion of training Salome's and Rebecca's boys, he saw the logic of this at once and told me he'd return with me without any hesitation. There was just one moment when I thought all my plans were unravelling. When John went to take his leave after he'd secured the house and made safe everything that could be stolen – giving most of his mother's belongings away to neighbours – he embraced Joshua and said quietly – but I heard him:

'You'll be following me here, I know you will. It's your destiny, Joshua. You'll not resist it for long.'

Joshua, however, would not be drawn. He just wished his cousin peace and embraced him, but said nothing, nothing that I could catch in any case.

I expected to have to argue with him all the way home and to be subjected to a barrage of words about his Messianic quest and all he'd learned at Ein-Gedi. But he was very quiet. He seemed genuinely concerned about our workload and Grandmother's health and I forbore therefore to press him further about his neglect of us. I thought at one stage that he actually regretted his decision to stay in the Wilderness. I asked him outright if he thought it had been a mistake.

'No, James,' he'd replied after a moment's thought. 'It was very useful, but it's taught me what's wrong as well as what's right.' I thought at first he was talking about Moses's commandments or the detailed rituals and rules and thought after all his years of schooling, that surely he'd know all that. They drummed it into us at the synagogue. I didn't see how he could have missed that. Then I realised he was talking about their decision to cut themselves away and condemn the rest of humanity to sin and destruction. Perhaps he's seen some sense at last and will return to our fold in all senses of the phrase.

When we arrived back in Nazareth, I found we'd hit another emergency. No sooner had Benjamin taken it upon himself to act as our agent in Sepphoris, than he'd been badly beaten up and robbed on his way to order a new supply of timber for us. He'd not been carrying too much money – just enough for the next month's purchases – but he'd suffered a bad injury to a leg that made it impossible for him to continue that journey and had lost the sight of one eye where he'd been clubbed with a heavy stump of wood.

Joshua immediately went to spend time with him and Rachel and the children and apparently gave Ben much needed pain relief with ointments that he'd learned to use whilst with the Essenes, so I suppose some good had come of it. In fact, he went to stay with Ben's family for several weeks until he was at least able to move around, albeit in a restricted fashion, and could do some straightforward accounting, although the strain on his good eye was bad and he was subject to frequent headaches. Joshua not only took over our money transactions and the trips to Sepphoris and Magdala, but started helping Ben with the similar work for Clopas. Mother was nervous now about letting Joshua make frequent trips alone over the route where Ben had been attacked, but he seemed quite relaxed about it and told Mother to stop worrying and trust God. I know she'd been robbed when she was in Egypt, so I can understand her fear.

I really thought we'd settled down and that Joshua had turned his back on his pretensions. He never talked to us about his future and if he ever discussed it with our mother, it was never in my presence. He was as good as his word in taking Isaac and Nathan into our workshop for training. I must say that he had a great skill in teaching the boys, developing their interest and balancing the hard work with fun and lighter moments so that their motivation remained high and I could see within a year or so that we'd have two very useful additions to our team.

He never did get married though. In due course, when Ben's Matthew celebrated his 'bar-mitzvah', he took his training on as well, so we now have three lively keen young lads helping me and Joe. Joe still pursues his leisurely pace –

I've given up trying to make him work faster and he's happy turning out more intricate woodwork. But Isaac and Nathan are now capable of making the simpler equipment and can start off other items which I then finish to the required standard. And he spends a lot of time with my children who adore him. I can't think why he hasn't married since he's so good with kids.

I thought he'd forgotten or put aside all thoughts of practising as a rabbi despite nearly completing the studying in the synagogues of Sepphoris and Jerusalem, and was satisfied with the turnover of family life here. There was more than enough to maintain his interest. Our business grew – nothing too ambitious and the Roman tax collectors made sure we never had excessive profits! The number of children in the family multiplied and he acted as favourite uncle to all of them. Mother seemed to be more like her old self, watching over us all, managing the household, almost forming a partnership with Joshua to keep the family together. They dealt with the usual family crises, the sudden fevers, the children's squabbles, the occasional minor injury. Simon, Judas and Ruth all got married in the same year and Joe, who'd married before Joshua went to Jerusalem for the second time, now had two young children for my mother and grandmother to spoil and Joshua to entertain. For four or five years life went on with no great alarms or disturbances. Susannah's husband, Joshua died. That was a shame, he was always popular in the family. Much more so than his other brothers-in-law, Michal's husband, the rabbi Jonas and Rachel's and Esther's husbands although we see little of them except at weddings, funerals and festivals.

Then one day, Joshua suddenly announced, 'It's time for me to leave you. I have to go back to Jerusalem and meet my cousin John.' It caused turmoil. The boys in the workshop were upset. The smaller children were distraught. Only my mother and my grandmother seemed unsurprised. And perhaps Ben, though I'm not sure. He didn't say much, but he did not join in the general protests. I thought Joshua had grown out of it. How wrong I was!

Chapter 10
Mari, AD 21

Joshua told me yesterday before he told the rest of the family. I was not surprised. Several times recently Joshua has mentioned to me that he thought that the others had forgotten. I hadn't. I was wondering when he would make a move. He's grown in so many ways. Sometimes I feel as though I'm his daughter instead of being the other way round.

'I have to go back to Jerusalem. You know that, Mother, don't you. I need to complete my studying with the rabbis in the Temple. I need to talk to John. I'll return. I'm not quite ready yet, but it'll be soon.'

'You'll stay for my niece Susannah's wedding, won't you? She's been betrothed now for over a year and Rebecca will be devastated if you're not able to be present. And Susannah will be very disappointed.'

'Yes, I'll stay and come with you. Does your mother feel up to it?'

'She'll make an effort. It'll be a great strain for her, but she won't want to be left out, of that I'm sure.'

'She can ride the donkey cart. We'll need that if we are all to stay for the whole of the celebrations rather than travel daily. The young ones can travel to and fro, that is if they don't dance the night away and sleep in the open.'

Having satisfied myself that Joshua will not disappoint everyone by departing from us before the family wedding, I was neither surprised nor unduly unhappy at Joshua's declaration. Whilst I like having him here with us, I'm impatient to see everything that has been promised come to pass. I have lived with this knowledge for so many years and sometimes have been impatient, at other times even doubting, because Joshua was showing no signs of fulfilling the destiny that I thought had been announced to me by that stranger so many years ago. But the news, when Joshua told the others of his intention, met a much more mixed response. All the boys – well I still think of them as my boys even though they're all young men with wives and children now – they all expressed their shock and dissatisfaction, that after so many years of returning to us and being of such great help to me and the business, he should think of throwing everything away again.

'Why are you taking it so calmly, Mother?' asks James in righteous anger. He, I should have realised, would be the one to take it badly, considering his opposition to everything Joshua had done and said years ago. 'He's abandoning you just when you need him most.'

'In what way do you think I need him specially now?'

James is a bit reluctant to spell it out. He thinks I'm getting old! I know I'm over forty, but I don't feel my age, even despite bearing seven children, and I'm blessed with good health. I have my other children around me, the girls are not far away and the grandchildren are a delight.

'Well ...' James hesitates. 'Your mother needs a lot of assistance and you won't always be fit enough to do everything for her.'

'James, I've got you and Deborah living here with me. Joseph and Leah, Simon and Rhoda, Judas and Martha all live in the village. So do Salome and Andrew. Ruth and her husband are not too far away. My sisters live nearby. And Benjamin and his family are here also. We are not dependent on Joshua. It is time for him to fulfil the destiny that's been foretold for him. You should be proud of that, not critical.'

'Mother, you know what I think of that. I've not changed my mind. I used to think you'd gone crazy, then you'd accepted the truth as Joshua returned to us. You've not believed that stuff about him being the Messiah all these years, have you?'

'Of course I have. You don't forget such momentous prophecies. Not when you've had the experiences I've lived through. I've had to learn patience. God honours his promises although his times are not necessarily ours. I'm pleased that we shall now see great and miraculous things happen. You'll soon see the truth of what I've been saying.'

'I await events with some trepidation. If he really is foolish enough to announce publicly that he is the Messiah, he won't last a minute. The Roman authorities will have him locked up and executed before he can cause any insurrection. Either that or they'll see our Jewish leaders scorn and ridicule him and then perhaps the Romans will ignore him as long as he vegetates in some village in Galilee and stays out of the cities.'

'You're a cynic, my son. You have little faith in what God has been doing throughout our history. Don't you ever listen to the rabbis each Sabbath? Does it all wash over you? Are you a complete unbeliever in our God?'

'Of course I'm not. But they are speaking of eons of history. Not now. Why now? Why here?'

'Why not?'

There's no point in either of us continuing to argue. We let go and talk about the practicalities.

'James, you know all there is to know about the business. Your reputation as a skilled carpenter is known in Sepphoris and the surrounding villages as well as here. You've got Joe whose work is renowned. You've got Isaac, Nathan and Matthew who are all experienced in the trade and could keep the business flourishing even if anything happened to you. Why do you think Joshua will be indispensable here? Come on, tell me!'

'Well, you'll miss him.'

'Of course I will. We all will. But we mustn't stand in the way of him. Our destinies are tied up with his. Whether he is here or not, we will be reflected in the renown that he will earn.'

'Or in the ridicule and disgrace. That will reflect badly on us too. People will say, 'Why didn't you stop him? What sort of control did you exert as his family? They will, you know.'

The others didn't say much – they were not as outspoken as James, but I knew they were sceptical and were disturbed that our routine would be broken, responsibilities would change. But they're all preoccupied with their own families now – Joe has his two, the oldest nearly four now, Simon had his first last year and Judas's Martha is expecting at the moment. My mother is the only one in the house who is as supportive to Joshua as I am. She doesn't say a lot, but she gives me the reassuring look, the squeeze of the wrist when she thinks James or the others are being articulate about their scepticism. I think Ruth will be pleased too, although she won't yet know of Joshua's decision. The news will spread when we assemble for Susannah's wedding.

I get a chance to speak to Joshua alone the next day when the men are busy in the workshop. I'm in for a few more surprises, for Joshua is more hesitant than I expected.

'When you get to Jerusalem, will you be revealing yourself to the priests and rabbis in the Temple? Will you be seeking their support straight away?'

'No, Mother. I'm not ready yet. I'm still learning. I need to spend more time listening to the teachers there. I need to go once more out into the Wilderness. I need to test some of my plans with John, with the community in which he lives.'

'But you have power, Joshua. I've watched you these last few years. You know exactly what people are thinking, you know intuitively what to say and what to do. The children are drawn to you, those who are ill or anxious, they come to you for sympathy or advice. You are patient with them, you listen. And people go away different, changed. You have a power, Joshua, even if you won't admit it.'

'I'm not sure about it yet. It frightens me sometimes. I'm frightened of what I can do. I'm frightened of how I could use

101

the gifts I have. They are not mine to use. They are God's gifts. I need to know his will. I do not need the distractions around me.'

'Can you not do something that will demonstrate your vocation to your brothers? They don't believe in you. I do. Show them, Joshua. Help them to change their minds. Help them to support you, work with you rather than against you.'

'All in good time, Mother. But don't push me, don't crowd me. They'll see and have to make their own mind up. They won't all believe. I can't force them, just as I can't force everyone else. They'll see and hear me and will have to decide how to react.'

'It would be easier for yourself if you could convince them now.'

'Mother, I know you mean well. But let me find my own way. You've done so much, given so much love and support. But you have to let go. Trust me and trust God. It's not going to be easy for either of us. You know that. You've had your suffering on my behalf. Let me be and concentrate your care now on the rest of the family. Deborah needs you. James frightens her sometimes. She needs your reassurance and support.'

'What? He's not violent with her surely? I've never seen him hurt her.'

'No, not physically. But he can be harsh, intense. And she doesn't understand his words when he's frustrated with life. She thinks it's her fault, that she's being blamed. He doesn't mean everything he says but she takes it too much to heart. Find out what's eating him. I think he's a bit jealous of me. And he misses his father so much. Even now.'

We leave it at that. I watch James and Deborah extra intently after that warning. I notice nothing at first, but I thought I caught Deborah weeping the other day. I asked her what the matter was, but she wouldn't tell me; said it was nothing. Then Esther comes to me and curls up on my lap. It is so unexpected of her. She is not usually so demonstrative of affection. She's normally a tomboy, playing with her brother and father. I cuddle her for a while. She yawns and I can see a tear drop in her eye.

'What's wrong, love?' I give her an extra squeeze.

'Daddy hit me. It isn't fair. I didn't do anything. Reuben just fell over when we were playing. I wasn't anywhere near him.'

I don't say anything. I mustn't undermine her father, but I'll have a quiet word with him. I hold her for a while, give her another hug and in the end she brightens up, gives me a kiss and scrambles to her feet, and disappears out into the yard to continue her play.

Later Deborah has taken the children with her when she goes to fill our waterpots and Mother is resting. I poke my head around the workshop door and see a hive of activity. Matthew and Isaac are working together, one holding a plank of wood, whilst the other is sawing. Nathan is carrying left over scraps of wood into the yard. Joe is hunched in the corner over a lamp holder he is carving. James is writing something at the table. I beckon him.

'Could I have a word, James?' He looks up but stays seated. I indicate with a movement of my head that I wish to speak to him privately and he gets up and follows me.

'James, why are you being so cross with everyone?'

'I'm not. What on earth makes you think that?'

'The people around you are not happy. Something's wrong.'

'You've got things wrong, not me. I don't know what you're talking about.'

'I thought there might be something you could share with me. I don't like to see you and your family unhappy.'

'Oh, Deborah's been complaining about me, has she?'

'No, James, but I've just been watching you all. I can sense something's not right.'

'Nothing's wrong at all. And you can mind your own business. If Deborah wants to say anything she can say it to me. And she's not said anything to me at all. So nothing's wrong, now are you satisfied?'

He is vehement. His very body language confirms my worries. But he's not going to confess anything to me. The more I say, the less likely is he to listen to me. I'll have to wait until he's ready and be there for Deborah and the children. It's coming at me from all directions. Patience. I'm not very good at waiting, but now I have it from both my elder sons. Oh well, I'll have to learn and wait for the right moment, the right opportunity. It'll come, I know it will.

Chapter 11
James, AD 23

It's another annual pilgrimage to Jerusalem for the Passover. My brothers Simon and Judas are with me. Joe has stayed at home to look after Mother and Grandmother, widow Anna as she's known. I intend to find my brother Joshua to discover what he's up to. My mother made me promise I'd find him and bring news back. It's two years since he left us and when we came up for the Passover last year there was no sign of him. Cousin Elizabeth was dead and the home sold to strangers. John was gone too, presumably back to that Wilderness community of his. My guess was that Joshua was with him, but no-one knew. We tried our distant relatives out in Bethany but they couldn't tell us anything.

We went straight to the Temple today along with the rest of the party from Nazareth and bought doves for sacrifice and made our offerings. Then the group split up and we made our way down the winding road through the desolate escarpments to Bethany, along with many pilgrims unable to get lodgings in the city. We were made welcome last year by our distant cousin, Lazarus and his sisters, Martha and Mariam and Martha's husband and they told us we'd be welcome again if we came this year. It's a bit of a trek out of the city but during this festival period it's safe enough as long as we travel during daylight hours.

The three of us are greeted effusively by this hospitable family and we are soon gossiping around the stove as Martha prepares an evening meal for us after we've washed the dust from our feet and hands. We explain that Clopas and Miriam are staying at home this year and that their sons have found other lodgings in the city. They are keen to reassure themselves about the health of Mother – they'd heard much about her in the past from Elizabeth and John. Their parents had both died the previous year and we express our condolences. It isn't long, however, before the conversation soon veers round to the subject of Joshua and John.

Lazarus tells me all about it.

'Yes, we see Joshua now quite frequently,' he answers to my enquiry about the whereabouts of my brother. 'He seems to divide his time between studying with the rabbis at the Temple and visiting the Essene community in Ein-Gedi well out into the desert towards the Salt Sea. He calls on us each time he passes and breaks his journey. We're always pleased to see him. He's been a good friend to us and comforted my sisters after the sudden death of both our parents.'

'Where is he now?' Simon has joined me while Judas is still stowing our tents and ass in their yard.

'I last saw him about a month ago. He was joining John the other side of the Jordan. I presume you've heard all about John and his preaching?'

'No, what's that about? I thought he had been inducted into the Essene community.'

'We thought so too. But apparently he left them a few months ago and started preaching in the open air down by the river. He's become quite famous. It's a wonder you didn't hear about him earlier when you were in Jerusalem.'

We pause for a moment as Judas rejoins us. Despite they're being twins, my brothers are so unlike in appearance. Simon takes after our mother, dark and thin-boned and quite animated. Judas is more like Joe and our father, thickset and stolid – well not quite as pedestrian as Joe I grant you. And me? They say I take after my mother too, dark and sharp-witted, but unlike in many other ways. Some say that we quarrel because we're too alike, impetuous and intuitive. The trouble is our intuition is polarised. And nothing divides us more than what we feel about Joshua. I'll have to be careful in what I say here for Joshua has obviously ingratiated himself with our hosts. I don't want to make things awkward and appear ungrateful as they seem so pleased to see us.

'So tell us more. Have you seen John? Or has Joshua just told you about him?'

'All Jerusalem is buzzing. People are flocking out to see him every day. We see groups of people from the city from all walks of life making their way through our village to see him.'

'So what does he do? Does he think he's a prophet or something? Is he political? Does he cause trouble?'

'He preaches and everyone hangs on his words. Apparently he's a very powerful speaker. He tells the crowds that they're full of sin and evil and they lap it up. He tells them to confess and repent and he immerses all those that do in the Jordan. They say it's like a mass madness; grown men weep like babies when they hear him. Even the authorities from Jerusalem go out to listen to him, though I think they are wanting to keep an eye on what he's up to, in case he threatens trouble with the Romans.'

'And is Joshua mesmerised by him too?'

'I don't think so. He's interested in what John has to say, but I don't think he agrees with everything he does. John's brought many of the rituals from the Essene community to his actions and words. All the ritual washing he's got from them. And Joshua says he uses many words in his preaching from our prophet Isaiah, words he learned from the Essene teaching. He seems to be demanding that people repent and prepare themselves for a new beginning.'

'I'd like to hear him for myself.' Simon looks at me and adds, 'Why don't we all stay on after the Passover and go out to see what it's all about?'

'Mother has asked me to find Joshua, so if he's with John, that's what we'll have to do. I will, anyway. I promised Mother.'

'It'll just be for an extra couple of days. We can afford that surely.'

'That's assuming Joshua doesn't come back here for the Passover. Aren't you expecting him back for the festival, Lazarus?'

'I wouldn't be surprised. It's not like him to miss such an occasion and he knows he'd be welcome here.'

And Lazarus is right. Joshua turns up the very next day.

* * *

And he's only been here less than an hour before we quarrel. I suppose it's my fault. It always is, so Mother says. As long as we're indoors in the company of Lazarus and his sisters, I manage to keep my temper. However, he goes out into the yard and I follow him.

'Why haven't you come home? Your mother's worried sick. It's over two years since we've heard from you. Have you totally abandoned us? Don't you care about us any more?'

'James, Mother knew I had to come here. I told you all. I didn't keep it a secret. I have to spend time with the rabbis at the Temple. She agrees with that, in fact she's always been anxious that I live out the life that's been anticipated for me.'

'But why so long? Anyway, you haven't been at the Temple all the time. You've been wasting your time out in the wretched desert with fanatics and escapists.'

'I've been much of the time with Cousin John. We are bound together by our mission.'

'Mission? What sort of word is that? You're not still on about the Messiah thing, are you? Be a rabbi if you must. I think you're opting out of your family responsibilities, but I suppose it's a respected calling. Most rabbis get married, settle down and father children. Why can't you do that rather than disappear into the Judean Wilderness and get hooked up with a rabble rouser?'

'I respect John. He's taken on some of the most powerful people in the country and is telling them things they do not want to hear. He's courageous.'

'It sounds more like foolhardiness to me. You're stupid to get involved with him. I always said that you would finish up in trouble. Just don't involve us in it is all I ask now.'

'If you don't want to be involved, I won't involve you. It's as simple as that. I can invite you, but I'll never force anyone.'

'Anyway, are you coming home now?'

'Not yet. I need to go back and spend some more time with John.'

'In the name of Baal and Beelzebub,' I explode, 'haven't you wasted enough time with that fake prophet? He thinks he is, the fool, and you're just as bad. You're arrogant, you're selfish, you're a disgrace to your family!'

Simon and Judas hear my raised voice and come out to see what's going on. I turn to them.

'This traitorous brother of ours intends to abandon us once more and go back to squander his life in the desert. He doesn't care about you or me, his mother or his grandmother. All he thinks about is the fame and glory of deceiving people into thinking he's the Messiah.'

'James, can't you keep your voice down. Lazarus and Mariam can hear every word you're saying. We shouldn't be revealing family conflict at Passover time.' Simon tries to pacify me.

'Well, don't you think your brother deserves our scorn? Or don't you think family values and traditions come first any more?'

'What do you say to that, Joshua?'

'Simon, you and your brothers have families to care for. You live in Nazareth and are close to our mother and grandmother. You are conscientious. I know they are well cared for. I have no dependents. I am being called by God to something very different. Would you that I turn my back on

God's voice and finish up like Jonah? Do you really need me? If my presence is essential, then I will come. But you'll have to have good reason.'

'It would be good to have you at home. The children miss you. Mother misses you.'

'I miss you all too. But I have to obey God. That has to come first.'

I can contain myself no longer.

'So, how do you know what God's telling you to do? Couldn't it be your pride, your own wishes for aggrandisement?'

'That's why I need to stay here. I have to test my calling. I have to be sure that it's not just my inclination, my will, my pride as you put it. I can only do that by debating with the Temple rabbis, reading the scriptures and listening to their interpretations, seeing John at work, trying to understand the ascetics at Ein-Gedi.'

'You don't sound very sure.' Judas has made his first intervention.

'I'm not. I nearly am, but I have to be completely sure, otherwise when things get difficult, as they will, I'll not have the conviction to persevere.'

I don't know how long our arguments would have persisted, but at that moment Martha calls us to say that the meal is ready. We call a truce and manage to be civil to each other over the next couple of days during the festival itself. We have the Passover meal with Lazarus and his family and we all go to the Temple during the subsequent days, make further offerings and watch the pilgrim crowds. The Temple is a bustling place, full of life and energy, but Joshua seems unhappy with it all. I thought he would have been extra devout within its walls, but he seems uneasy there and wants to get away as soon as he's spent time in the inner parts of the sanctum. He hasn't bought any sacrifices either. When I question him about that, he says it's unnecessary – God just wants the sacrifice of our lives. Just! Hark at him. If he doesn't finish up arrested by the Romans, he'll get accused of blasphemy by the priests. Does he think he knows better than them?

We're due to go back home tomorrow and I make a last effort to persuade him to join us. It's obvious, however, that he's made his mind up.

'Why don't you come and see for yourself? I understand that if I'd not come back for the Passover, you were planning to look for me in the Essene community. In that case, why not come out and judge for yourself. Come and listen to John. See if you think it makes sense. Don't judge him without hearing what he has to say. Don't judge me without seeing this bigger picture and trying to understand it.'

'It makes sense, James,' says Simon and I see Judas is ready to go along with Joshua's suggestion.

'You're just as curious as all the rest of the city population,' I say, waving my hand at another throng of people tramping past our house towards the desert.

That evening I discover Lazarus is keen to join us also. So next day we set off, travelling as light as we can. It's nearly a day's journey to reach the river and as we get near I'm astounded at the size of the crowd streaming towards where John is said to be. I can see a man standing high on a rock overlooking the river and know at once this must be him. The man looks wild. He's wearing a crude tunic of rough cloth and his hair is tangled and matted. His voice carries and the crowd seems spellbound. We join at the edge of the milling throng and try to hear what he is saying. I catch snatches of his sentences. He seems to be castigating the rich, telling them to repent and share their clothes, their food with the poor. That message will not go down well with some of the well dressed men I see around me. Then he starts to criticise the Tetrarch and his wife and I hear cheers from men near him. Some of the people near us look a bit smug about this and I see some knowing glances exchanged. He'd better watch his words or he'll find himself in prison and that'll be the end of him.

Then he climbs down from the rock and disappears from our view.

'What's he doing? Where's he gone?' I ask Joshua.

'He's baptising those who've repented from their wrongdoing.'

'He's doing what?'

'Those that wish go down into the water and John baptises them – he immerses them in the river. It's symbolic. It represents the washing away of all their past sins and starting a new life.'

'Do many want to do this?'

'Hundreds. He'll be doing this from now until sunset.'

'Is everyone so credulous?'

'There is a real renewal of the nation going on. It's most impressive. Even Pharisees and Sadducees have buried their differences and gone forward together.'

I shake my head in amazement at the gullibility of so many. The crowd is gradually edging forward. Some of the men near us are breaking away and leaving the scene.

'Come with me.' Joshua beckons us to follow him and he leads us downstream along the edge of the crowd to where it is thinning out by the river, which looks quite deep at this point as it narrows between the gaunt sandy cliffs. We find a scree slope beside the water's edge and can just see figures going down into the river. There's a long queue of them all waiting to speak to the figure of John and one by one he takes them and lowers them into the turgid water. People between us and the procession of those awaiting baptism by John gradually slip away into the queue or leave quietly after watching for some time and we are able to move nearer although we can't hear what is being said.

It must have taken us a full hour or more before the crowd has dwindled to a handful of men still waiting their turn. John looks up and catches sight of us. I must admit I'm repelled by the look of him. He's unkempt, unshaven and badly clothed. I can see now that his garment is just rough camel's hair, badly cut and ill fitting and he's wet through as he's up to his waist in the water. He's a giant of a man, though. I wouldn't like to meet him alone on a dark night out here. Goodness knows where he got his physique from. Elizabeth was quite small and I don't think his father was abnormal – he was just a Temple priest of simple tastes, so I'm told. I'm wondering why we bothered to come out to see such a man – he's clearly demented as many of those seeking his baptism must be. I never knew so many must have had such guilty consciences. Perhaps his attraction is his raving against the rich. That's a popular message for the masses though it won't last if the authorities feel he's gone too far.

Joshua looks at me. He must see my jaundiced look.

'Don't prejudge him from his looks,' he says. 'Wait until you've had a proper conversation with him. We've got all evening.'

We wait until John has finished baptising the last man in the crowd. The sun has lost its heat and the man, quite elderly by the look of him, shivers as he steps into the water. I can't help wondering what sins he's confessed to John – he's obviously had plenty of time to commit many, unlike some of the spry youths I noticed in the water earlier. I try to catch his words as he whispers to John but I see John just nods before grasping his shoulders and pulling him downwards, his other hand supporting his lower back. I feel sorry for the guy as he shuffles, water dripping from his sodden tunic, but the man suddenly pulls it over his head and retrieves his overgarment where he's laid it on the bank and draws it over his naked wrinkled body.

John doesn't seem worried by the fact that he's just as wet. He looks at us again.

'So you must be this man's brothers?' He grunts, pointing to Joshua. 'Come to drag him back home or to see what we are doing?'

Joshua must have told him about us and our reservations at his presence here. John doesn't seem annoyed though. He just grins at us.

'Come back to my home if I can honour it with such a name. It's just a cave in the sandstone cliff a bit upstream. It's only a few minutes' walk away – I try to keep it hidden from the crowds who come out to see me. If they find it I'll probably have no peace. However, few are happy to stay here after sunset – they want to get back to Jericho or Bethany before the roads around here are too dangerous to use.'

We follow John along the water's edge and, as the banks crowd us in, we are forced to remove our sandals and wade through the eddying water as it rushes through the narrows.

'Watch where you are putting your feet. There are a few deep hollows and if you're not careful you'll find yourself up to your neck in the muddy water.'

Joshua obviously knows his way well and he turns from time to time to indicate a treacherous spot and help us through. John is striding ahead as the surging water makes no hindrance to his muscular thighs.

We stop after what must be getting on for a full mile and find the entrance to the cave and obvious signs of a fire having been lit there. John immediately sets about making it up with dry wood he's collected and stored inside the cave and squats beside it rubbing two flints together, patiently waiting until one of the twigs catches fire. Gradually the glow from the fire illuminates the cave, for darkness has fallen rapidly during our tramp from the baptism spot. We've brought some loaves and wine with us and I offer John a hunk of bread but he refuses politely. Apparently he's refrained from any food other than what he can gather from the natural world around him. I scour the landscape with my eyes. From what I can see, he'll have a pretty sparse diet. I knew he didn't touch alcohol, so I've not offered him any wine. While we eat, he uncovers some scraps which look cooked and shrivelled and shovels a couple of handfuls into his mouth.

'What on earth were those?' I ask.

'Insects. I catch a few that hover round the fire. They're enough. I don't need more.'

I shudder. They look revolting. 'How can you survive on that?'

'From time to time I come across some honeycombs down by the grasses and papyrus that grow beside the river. There's a stream that feeds into the main flow a few hundred yards further upstream and I find honey regularly there. And I get milk from wild goats that I come across, to supplement water from the stream. Look at me! It hasn't done me any harm, has it?'

I have to admit the man looks fit. Despite his unkempt appearance, his body is taut and strong, as I can see now since he's stripped off his hair garment, which is laid by the fire to dry. We all eat. We hold back our curiosity until our hunger has been satisfied. I take a long swig of the sweet sticky wine and wipe my lips.

'Well,' says the fake prophet, 'what do you want to ask me? I presume that's why you've come.'

My twin brothers are dumb. I know their curiosity is unbounded but they are strangely silent when they have the opportunity to speak. I'd better hold back lest my obvious scepticism spoils the atmosphere too quickly. It's Lazarus who ventures the first question.

'How many men did you baptise today? We saw you receiving a queue of people for over an hour.'

'That was the third group today. I don't count them. I don't know. Probably between two and three hundred in all.'

'And how long have you been doing it?'

'Lazarus, I really don't know. I don't measure the days or seasons.'

Joshua indicates. 'I think he's been out here at least six months, since around the time of the Feast of Tabernacles.'

'That means you must have baptised at least fifty thousand souls,' says Lazarus doing a quick calculation in his head. That's incredible, that's as much as the whole population of Jerusalem.'

'Probably not that many. The numbers built up slowly in the beginning until people got to hear of me. Now they come from all over Judea, from Samaria and Galilee, from Perea on the other side of the Jordan. I've even had a couple of Roman citizens come to talk to me although getting baptised was beneath their dignity.'

'Why do they come?' My brother Simon has found his voice.

'Out of curiosity mostly. But they stop to hear what I've got to say. And my message hits them. They know in their heart of hearts that the state of our nation is rotten. They see the presence of the Romans as a punishment from Jehovah. So they're ready to admit their guilt when I challenge them.'

'What sins do they confess?'

'Corruption, desecration of the Temple. That building which should be the centre of our worship resembles a market place at times, with fraud and cheating wherever you look. The priests are time servers, inheriting the job from their fathers without conviction. They are complacent. They don't have to work, they are sustained by the donations of the poor. It's grossly unjust.'

'Do people actually admit that they are part of the corrupt system?'

'Well, I suppose I'm exaggerating a bit. I see that evil and want to expose and publicise it, so I rejoice when I get one of the Temple crowd or traders to own up to such greed. Most people confess personal things. Family quarrels, cheating,

116

arguments over land. A few men even confess unfaithfulness to their wives or neglect of their children. I found at first that no-one felt guilty about their neglect of the poor, so I've been drumming that message home and now most men confess their lack of care for the vulnerable in their villages. Hopefully they go home and do something about it.'

'Aren't you nervous of arousing opposition? The Temple authorities must have marked you out as a danger to their lifestyle.' I feel it's time for me to have my say at last.

'So what? I'm not scared of them. What can they do? Come out by night and kill me? If they do they'll get lynched by the mob back in Jerusalem, who'll start a riot. The Romans won't like that, so they'll be careful. And even if they kill me, the message will go on. This man here will carry it on, won't you, Joshua?'

'You know I will, John, although not necessarily in the same way as you.'

'I'm only the start. This man is the real prophet. I've come to announce his coming, he'll preach the arrival of the 'Kingdom of God'. You must know he's the Messiah we've been promised for centuries.'

'John, don't say these things. I'm not ready yet. They don't believe, they will shut their ears if you say such things and not listen to the other things you're saying.'

'If you say so. They'll have to make up their minds soon. I won't be out here for ever and your time will come. As James said, the authorities will get me in the end. I'm in no mood for stifling what I think. I've got God's message to proclaim and I can't keep quiet. I'll have to get personal soon and there are some people in high places who won't like that. They'll probably fake some wild animal has got me like Joseph's brothers intended before they sold him into slavery.'

'John, don't you think this Messiah claim is wrong? I'm not accusing you of lying deliberately, but isn't it just your imagination? Aren't you and Joshua just victims of what you want to believe?'

'If you don't believe my words, you'll soon have to believe your brother's. He's got power, I know he has. He could do things now that would amaze you. If he wanted he could do something now to prove it to you. He could render you speechless, dumb. He could make you lose your sight or the use of your legs and then restore them to you. Why don't you, Joshua? He'd believe you if you did that. He wouldn't be such a thorn in your side then.'

'No, John. I'll not persuade him that way. Any powers I have must be for the good of those who are suffering or in trouble, not for demonstration purposes even if my brother is tempting me!'

'See, he won't accept your challenge. He knows he has no special powers. You're just making it up.'

Lazarus wants to change the subject. He doesn't want Joshua and me to clash openly.

'Is this what the Essenes do, John? Do they baptise?'

'Yes, it's part of their induction process. Before acceptance into their community you are immersed totally in one of their ritual baths. You are then pure enough to start a new spiritual life in their community, set aside from the temptations of the world.'

'But you've left that community. Did you fall out with them?'

'No, but your brother persuaded me that I'd change little by remaining cut off in the desert. So I compromised. I go out and preach and challenge men to change their ways, but they have to come to me. I stay in the desert, my home territory. I'll not profane myself by entering their contaminated cities.'

'Did they accept your decision?'

'Not easily. They reminded me of my vows and said that I'd be tempted to revoke the good they'd instilled in me and become tempted by the devil. They take a dim view of the

118

resilience of the human spirit. They send messengers to me occasionally to see if I've fallen into the trap they forecast and seek my return to their community by retaking my vows and being ritually purged, but I think now that I'm so well known, they've given up on me.'

'Do you still believe their message even if you've moved on from their practices?'

It's Lazarus again who now challenges John. But it's Joshua who answers before John can reply.

'We don't agree on everything. There are some Essene practices that John is faithful to, which I would question.'

'Such as?' This could be interesting, I muse. Can I open up a rift between them, can I yet reclaim Joshua for our family?

'The Essene community is male. They do not marry or they renounce their wives when they join. They will not baptise women. John doesn't either. I'm puzzled. Don't women need repentance? Do they never sin? Does not God want their allegiance? In my family it seems to be the women who understand things – my mother, Eli's daughter Susannah, my sisters Salome and Ruth.'

'That just proves my point. They're too credulous. They'll believe anything. We men are more down to earth, we understand more of the world.'

'So why are all those who come for baptism by John male? Are they all as naïve as women, as you allege? You can't have it both ways.'

'What do you think, John? You haven't said anything.' I'm keen that John should say something that challenges Joshua's view.

'I do what I've learned at Ein-Gedi. We've withdrawn from female company to avoid temptation and concentrate on our service to God and honouring his commandments. If the men repent and act justly, their women will follow. The men will ensure the morality of the whole family.'

119

'John and I beg to differ on this point. God created all equal. Women are just as capable of greatness or evil as any man. Look at some of our ancestors. Queen Esther, Judith – or on the other side of the coin, those icons of wickedness, Jezebel or Delilah. And we underestimate the capacity of children as well. My mother says that her main support during her controversial pregnancy were her siblings, our aunts, Salome and Rebecca and her younger brother Benjamin. When all around were condemning her, failing to listen or understand, those children knew intuitively that she was right. They knew when to trust. They are good judges of character, they can discern the genuine and the fake.'

'We've argued over this lots of times. I've spent too long with the Essenes to change my mind. I respect Joshua's view. He'll bring many new insights to us I'm sure. He thinks I should recruit some female followers. But it's hardly practicable out here, is it?'

'You have followers, disciples of your way of life?'

Lazarus is curious as we've not seen any obvious men who could fit this description.

'Yes, I've colleagues, but they're in the city at the moment. They're letting people know where to find me. They're encouraging the people to seek a better way of life by coming out and turning their back on their former sinful ways. They sometimes help me by controlling the crowds seeking baptism. Without them, especially at festival times, the crowd would surge and push us all into the water. That's no job for a woman.'

'To which my answer is, come out of the desert and mingle with the people. Go where the ordinary people are. Let them see you are sensitive to the needs and desires of women and children as well as men.'

'I think that's something you may do, Joshua. It's a big enough challenge to get so many to repent of their deeds and pledge to a new and moral life. I'm clearing the way, removing the things that hinder the minds of these people. You will come with the positive messages, new insights, new teaching, the fundamentals of the Kingdom of God. All I can say is that it is coming. Be ready for it. You'll bring it.'

This conversation is getting out of hand. I can see Lazarus is getting quite interested in the way the exchange of views is flowing. Even Simon and Judas look attentive and don't seem to want to question them.

The fire is burning low. John announces his intention to rest shortly as he arises before dawn to collect honey and to look for wild goats to milk. He says the first visitors from the city will arrive shortly after sunrise and he has to be ready to engage them in conversation, and there will be a big enough crowd within a further hour to require him to get up on the rock and preach to the first would-be baptismal applicants. Joshua too leaves us.

'I need to be alone and think over the day's events,' he explains. 'This is a good time to pray, because it is so quiet. It is possible to hear God's voice in the stillness.'

So he's hearing voices now, is he? I knew he was mad. The pair of them are, but I keep it to myself. The remaining four of us sit for a while as the embers blacken and die. I thought we should maintain the fire to keep animals away but John said he has to gather the scarce firewood in the morning. Sometimes the river brings down branches after a storm or flood further up river.

'Don't worry,' he'd says, 'animals don't bother us. God's entrusted us with a message for Israel. He won't throw it to the winds by allowing us to be killed by his beasts.'

'That's no guarantee of safety for us,' I mutter. 'We've no magic message and therefore no automatic divine protection.'

'You'll be alright,' he'd replies. 'I know you will.'

I just wish I had his confidence.

*   *   *   *   *

I didn't sleep very well. I could hear John snoring loudly in the cave almost as soon as he'd left us. Joshua came back a long time afterwards and I was still awake. I watched his silhouette against the stars, but he did not stop. I think my twin brothers were restless too, though I'm sure Lazarus, like John, was soon dead to the world.

Perhaps I was dozing when I heard movement and became aware that John was leaving the cave. He'd pulled on his rough hair garment. I guess it was still damp, though the heat of the sun will soon dry it before he's back in the water. It's a wonder he doesn't succumb to a fever as he never seems to be dry.

I'd intended to spend a full day and a further night watching John and putting pressure on Joshua to come home. I quickly realised that we'd not learn an awful lot more than we'd gleaned already and I was certainly not looking forward to another night in such primitive conditions. We'd listen to his first morning sermon, I thought, then as the baptisms started we'd take our leave and get back to Lazarus's sisters in time to pack ready for going home the next day and catch up on our sleep. I couldn't see any point in staying all day on the off chance that Joshua would change his mind.

Joshua stirs shortly after John has left the cave and he too makes to leave and walk out into the empty dawn. Going to pray again is my guess – I prefer to get my praying done by the priests. At least they should get the words right. Despite prayers being learned by rote and repeated ad nauseam in the synagogue in my youth, I can never remember the words from even the best known psalms. Joshua notices that I'm awake and beckons to me to join him.

'I don't want to pray. I'm not a fanatic like you.'

'Don't worry. We can just talk.'

So I accompany him along the river a little way and then turn alongside the tiny stream as it flashes sparks of light reflecting the sun's orb behind us in the east over the low hills above the far river bank. We don't speak at first as the water gurgles through the rocks, then reduces to a trickle as its source disappears under an overhanging clod of earth. Joshua sits on the barren ground. I pull my cloak around me to ward off the chill I feel.

'You know I'm staying, don't you. My time is coming now. I have to think through what is in store for me. I need to get away from everyone, even John. I know you don't believe it, but I have power, James. It frightens me sometimes. I've been tempted so often to intervene, to use the power I have for my own ends. But I must use it wisely. I could persuade the people by the use of power they'd think were magic, but that would be to abuse that power I sense within me. I have to use it for others, to be drained and used up for the poor, the oppressed, the vulnerable.'

'That's a pretty speech. I still think you're being selfish. Or, the best I can think is that you're delusioned. Do you actually think you're the Messiah that Israel's been promised for centuries? Do you really, in all honesty, think so?'

'Do you believe I'm the Messiah, James? Do you believe it?'

'No.'

'Then I'm sorry, James. Our ways will part. You've been honest with me. Take my love to my mother and sisters and all who care for me back in Nazareth.'

I think to say more, to argue, to remonstrate. But it would be useless. The man will regret his decision. He'll learn he's wrong one day. The mission he thinks he's got will fizzle out in failure before it's even begun. What's the point of saying any more? I can tell Mother I've seen him and he is well, though out of his mind. I've done what she asked me to do. Time to go home.

Chapter 12
Mari

'Your son's crazy! There's no other word for it.'

He's hardly even greeted me on his return from Jerusalem before he's criticising his brother. Judas and Simon haven't said a word apart from the greeting when I saw them all come in together. James hasn't even asked after Deborah and his own children yet.

'We spent a day with him and John out in the Wilderness, a day's journey from the city. John's notorious now, he's really stirring up the people. He'll not last long, he's upsetting too many people – and the wrong ones at that. And Joshua will go down with him.'

'James, for goodness sake, go and see Esther and Reuben. They've been looking out for you every afternoon for the last week. Reuben's learnt some new songs at the synagogue school and he's dying to sing them to you. I'm sure they saw you all coming, but Deborah's held them back. She can't hang on to them much longer. You can tell me all about Joshua and John and our Bethany friends later.'

Then I look at the other boys – well men, actually, but I still think of them as my boys – and they are hovering there. Judas goes to fetch Joe who has carried on planing wood without a pause, even though he must know his brothers are home. He comes out as if in a trance. I can't believe he was so wrapped up in his work that he didn't hear them. The twins greet him and James gives a brief acknowledgement, then he's back on the attack again.

'I pleaded with him to come home, Mother. I told him how much you missed and needed him, that you'd sent us specially to find him, but he's selfish and obstinate. He doesn't care about us. He's obsessed with this so-called 'mission' of his and that ruffian cousin of ours does nothing but encourage him. I should just forget he's your son. He's not worth it.'

'James, I'm not going to argue with you now. Just calm down and go and greet your wife and children. They're your priority at the moment. You can talk to me about Joshua another time. And you two,' I add turning to Judas and Simon, 'aren't you missing your families? Get off back home, all of you. There's plenty of time to talk about your experiences in Jerusalem and Bethany in the morning. Just tell me, though. Is Joshua healthy? And Lazarus and Martha and Mariam?'

'I told you, Mother, he's mad. He can't be in his right mind.'

'He's fit enough, Mother,' says Simon. 'And all Lazarus's family.'

'Thank you, Simon. That's all I wanted to know at the moment. And now, go! All of you! No, not you, Joe, not if you want to finish the work you were doing. I meant these others who've not seen their families for a couple of weeks.'

Simon raises his eyebrows at me. Judas gives me a sheepish smile, but they both file out to remove their baggage from the ass. James hesitates. Perhaps I need to hang on to him a moment until he's cooled down. I don't want him to go storming into Deborah in this mood and he'll be short with the children too.

'James, just rest a moment and refresh yourself with a cup of wine. You must be tired after such a long journey.'

'I thought you wanted me to go immediately to Deborah.'

'Well, yes, but not in this mood.'

'What mood? I'm not in a mood.'

'Forget Joshua. Think about your own responsibilities. I don't want to argue with you about Joshua now. You can tell me all about it tomorrow.' I pour out the wine as I'm talking to him and hand him the cup. He sits down, thank heavens.

'James, I'm just pleased to see you all home safely and to know Joshua, John and Lazarus and the women are well.' I see

125

him about to open his mouth again, but I interrupt him. 'No, James, I'm not going to discuss mental health. I'm satisfied for the moment that none of them are sick. Just relax and drink your wine. Get ready to greet Deborah and your children. You've been away a long time. They miss you.'

'Well, Joshua's been away even longer and you miss him. That's far worse!'

'James, I don't want any more of this right now. I told you that I'm not going to argue, although that doesn't mean I agree with you.'

He grunts. And at that very moment two heads appear around the door. Seven year old Esther and her younger brother burst in and hurl themselves at their father, almost knocking the cup from his hands. He nearly shouts at them, and then, mercifully, he restrains himself, puts the cup down and takes each of them into his arms. I watch as he physically relaxes, letting the boisterous children gain his attention, as his natural care and love for them takes over.

'Let me finish this,' he laughs, and lets himself be dragged up, one child pulling on each arm. I watch them go with some relief. At least the children have transformed his mood. I hope it carries over into his greeting of his wife. I worry sometimes about that relationship. I don't think he realises sometimes how nervous Deborah is of upsetting him. I do my best to reassure her, but I often hear shouting and he can speak very abruptly to her on occasions.

When they've all gone, I sit down and pour myself a little wine. I've little to do now. Deborah got all the water we needed earlier, and I can prepare the evening meal for my mother and myself after Joe has gone home to his family. I looked in on Mother just before the men returned home and she was sleeping peacefully. I thought she'd wake up when she heard voices, but she didn't stir. I look in again to make sure. She turns over awkwardly even as I look, but stays asleep. I think she has very restless nights because of the pain from her arthritis, and therefore needs to catch up on her sleep during most afternoons. I look at her and feel sad that she finds movement so difficult these days. She'd love to spend more time playing with her great grandchildren, but she does not want to frighten them by trying to play, then shouting out in agony if a child bumps into her or sits awkwardly.

I sit down again and take another sip of sweet wine. I blame myself for the hostility that has arisen between James and Joshua. I should have handled things better when I told the children of Joshua's special mission. But if I had my time again, I'm not sure how I'd have done it differently. Should I have told them all when they were tiny children, so they grew up with the knowledge? Then everyone would be watching him all the time. I'm not sure that would have eliminated any jealousy. And if I'd left it longer, then what story would I have made up about Joshua's absences? Wouldn't James and the others have resented his absences even more if they were unexplained or contrived. I just feel vaguely guilty about it all.

*　　*　　*　　*　　*

James has been in the workshop all morning. I don't know why he worries himself so much there now. He's never trusted Joe with the finances. He believes that Joe, if not supervised, would bankrupt the family and reduce us to paupers, he's so unworldly. But we've my three nephews, Isaac, Nathan and Matthew and they're all skilled now and are more than competent to run the business. However, James has been going over the transactions enacted while he's been in Jerusalem in case they've made an error or overlooked to follow up a bill that should have been paid. Doesn't he trust Ben either? He finally emerges just as the sun is at its zenith. Mother and I are having a bite to eat and he joins us. Noise from the workshop has ceased also, although I can hear the occasional sound as Joe is continuing to craft his latest creation

127

while the others have stopped to eat. Deborah joins us also with Esther and then Reuben bursts in, back from his studies at the synagogue.

'Well, James? Is all in order?'

'Yes, I can't find anything wrong.'

'What did I tell you? You're lucky to have such good workers. You've no need to get so worked up. You're not indispensable, you know. The business will carry on without you.'

James doesn't say any more.

After we've eaten, Mother goes to rest, Deborah takes Esther to wash clothes down at the well and Reuben goes to play with a number of his friends. James gets up, as if to return to the workshop.

'Where are you going now, James?'

'Back to the carpentry shop.'

'Why?'

James hesitates.

'Do they need you? Are they behind on orders?'

'No.'

'Then stay and talk to me. Last night you were only too eager to go on about your brother when you should have been with your family. Don't you want to talk now?'

'I thought you didn't like what I was saying. I thought it was best to shut up. You seem determined to think the best of him, so what's the point of me telling you that I think he's being selfish?'

'Talk to me about Deborah. I don't like the way you treat her sometimes. You upset her often and the children are beginning to notice this. Esther especially, I think sometimes she's frightened of you.'

'I thought you wanted to talk about Joshua. Why this sudden mention of my wife? It's my concern, not yours.'

'James, they're family. You are my son. They are my grandchildren. I love you all. It pains me to see strife and unhappiness. Are you unhappy?'

'What nonsense, Mother! Of course not.'

'Then why do you go around with such a long face so much of the time? Why do you shout at Deborah and the children? Why…'

He interrupts me. 'I don't. You're exaggerating.'

'I don't think you realise just what you're saying sometimes.'

'Well, it always seems to fall to me to take care of the family. I should have some help. Joe's useless, bound up with his work and oblivious to everything and everyone else. Simon and Judas have their own homes and occupations. Uncle Ben gets tired these days with that bad leg and headaches – I don't want to bother him. And all the time Joshua who should be here and head of the family, well, he's off gallivanting around the countryside with that good-for-nothing cousin of ours.'

'I knew it was really about your brother. You know, I don't think you realise how fortunate we are. Clopas has been so good to us since Eli's death. We have all got homes. We don't starve. We've all got wives and children who are healthy. You've three able young men in the workshop in addition to Joe who are expanding the business and Joe's work is held in high regard even if you are so quick to disparage him. Why are you so resentful of Joshua's calling? You don't need him here. Let him pursue his vocation. I'm more than happy – I knew this was always going to be his destiny. Why does it upset you so?'

'He's irresponsible. It's his duty as the eldest to care for us all, well, I mean, at least see we are cared for. He should be married and be giving you grandsons. He should be caring for you. People are talking. His neglect is damaging our family's reputation. And now his dalliance in the Wilderness with John

– that's dangerous. You'll see, John will get himself arrested soon, and Joshua'll be next. And then who knows? All of us will come under suspicion. It's damned reckless of him. He's not even thinking of the consequences for us.'

'James, he can't reject his call. From his very birth, he's been destined for this. If he were to come home and settle here and forget his mission, everything I've done, everything I've been through, will have been in vain.'

'Then more fool you, Mother. No-one asked you to be careless with your virginity and then ignore the opportunities the rabbis gave you to get away with it without condemnation. All I say is that I sense catastrophe coming. And don't complain when it happens. You've brought it on yourself and possibly on all of us. Remember that I told you and don't expect me to put my neck and those of my children on the line when Herod Antipas's soldiers or the Romans come for him and all who follow his deluded presumption. Who'll help you then?'

'God.'

'You think you and you alone know God's will? What about the priests? What do they think? You should hear John going on about the priests in the Temple. It's sacrilege, it's blasphemy. I could understand it if he criticised the Romans or their collaborators. Understand, mark you, not condone. But he condemns the priests, even the High Priest and Joshua doesn't stop him. What sort of religion is that? The priests guard our Jewish faith from all the pagan influences the Greeks and Romans would import and John makes out that they're worse than them. And just to make sure he upsets everyone, he attacks the best and most influential Jewish families. If the Romans or Antipas decide they've had enough, no-one will come to his support. He's offended everyone.'

'I'm sure Joshua knows what he's doing.'

'Yes and that's why I condemn him. He's no right to compromise us all, put us in danger. Someone's got to stop him.'

'How, James? You've obviously tried and had no success.'

'He'll listen to you.'

'And you're expecting me to journey at my age through the barren hills all the way to Bethany or Jerusalem to stop him doing the one thing that God has prepared us both for? Don't be ridiculous, James.'

'I'm not saying you should go to Jerusalem. He'll have to come back here sometime. Tell him then. Tell him how worried you are, that he's neglecting his filial duties. It's the only chance...'

'No, James, you've got it all wrong. God has promised that he'll be our Messiah. He's been faithful so far, everything that has happened has been within God's protection. Why should he abandon us now?'

'I give up, Mother. It's useless arguing with you. If he carries on this way I'll disown him. He'll not be my brother and he has no right to be called your son.'

'James, all you've done is criticise Joshua. You've not told me anything that John actually says. You said he was famous, well notorious actually, but what is he actually saying and what does Joshua say?'

'What's the point of telling you? I've already told you that they'll make trouble. That's all you need to know. You don't need to know any more.'

'Why not, James? Don't you think, as his mother, I have a right to know? Are you one of those who think women should have no opinions? If so, you've got the wrong mother.'

James is silent at last.

'Go on, James, tell me. You're so forthright, let me have it straight.'

'Well, if you insist on pushing this, you're all too credulous – you, your sisters, Salome, Ruth, Aunt Susannah. And Cousin

Elizabeth was worse than the lot of you when she was alive. I even think you've warped Deborah's mind. You want to avoid spoiling the relationship between me and my wife? Well, stop bringing her round to your point of view over Joshua. She's my wife, she'll think and do what I say.'

'James,' I say softly, 'your father believed. You idolised him when you were small, you grieved when he died – I think you felt it more than the others. Can't you respect his memory?'

'That's unfair, Mother. I don't know why he believed. Perhaps he didn't want to upset you. Perhaps he pretended to believe.'

'Oh my son, do you really think your father risked defending me when I was first accused, married me despite the child not being his, went through all the privations during our escape to Egypt, just to keep up his pretence?'

James says nothing for a long time.

Eventually, 'You'll see, Mother. One day you'll see. You'll see I'm right.'

Chapter 13
Mari

Joshua is on his way home. James went to Sepphoris yesterday with Reuben, Susannah's oldest son, who has also joined us to learn the accounts and supply side from Ben and James, to get fresh timber supplies and discuss a new contract for the supply of doors and other household requirements for a new batch of houses being built on land that was cleared during the Roman sacking of the city several years ago. There they met a couple of merchants who'd been in Jerusalem and had travelled back via the Samaritan highway and they were full of rumours and even what they'd seen at first hand. They told Ben and my brother came back with James and Reuben to share the news.

'Mari, good news,' exclaimed Benjamin as he greeted me. 'James and Reuben met men who've seen Joshua and told us that he was making his way back to Galilee. Apparently he's drawing crowds as he's stopping in the villages and towns on the way and is being invited into synagogues to preach from the scriptures. He's even talking to crowds in the open air in Samaria.'

'When will he be home?' That was my first reaction. I'm so looking forward to seeing my son again and hearing at first hand what he's been doing. I want to hear it from his own lips – not the garbled negative version I hear from James.

Reuben broke in, anxious to tell what he'd seen.

'The men we met saw him in Shechem. They were on the edge of a crowd listening to him. They didn't catch everything he said, although they reckoned that his message was not unlike that of John. We talked to them for some time. They said that all Jerusalem knew about John and the way he was baptising men in the Jordan about twenty miles from the city, but they hadn't been out to hear him themselves as they had too much business to attend to. If Joshua comes straight to us from Shechem he could be with us tomorrow or the day after. But if he stops at every village, every synagogue on the way, it could be a week or more.'

'See, Mother, he's not even hurrying now he's coming home. You'd think he would come straight to us and not delay. And why on earth he's bothering to preach in Samaria beats me. That heathen crowd will never take any notice. He's wasting his breath. He'll be lucky not to get stoned and chased out of their villages.'

'If he's started to announce that he's the promised Messiah, that news is for the whole country – it makes sense for him to stop and tell everyone on his way home. He won't have to go back and retrace his footsteps.'

Reuben stops me there. 'I don't think he's preaching about being the Messiah. If he was doing that, I'm sure the merchants they met would have mentioned it.'

James added quickly, 'If he'd been shouting that he was the Messiah, he'd never reach here. He'd have got himself arrested before he's cleared Jericho, if not before.'

They hadn't really any more information to impart. We'll just have to be patient. It's been two days since that conversation, and we've heard nothing more.

*   *   *   *   *

It's now over a week since Reuben and James told me that Joshua was on his way to us. Two Sabbaths have gone by and there's been no sign of him. I've questioned others who've been in Sepphoris but none of them had heard anything more. Then this morning someone mentioned in the market that there was a new preacher causing quite a stir in Magdala. That can't be Joshua surely, I thought. Magdala's north of here. He could have gone directly through Sepphoris though our village is so close, surely he'd have stopped by to see us and

134

stayed for a few days. But it seems a big coincidence that there's another preacher in the area. Every day now I go into the market even if I have no need to buy anything. I ask everyone I meet if they've heard anything. I ask Salome and her husband for everyone frequents their bakery, I ask Judas and Simon to listen to the gossip in the fields, but no further news arrives, not even any rumour.

This evening I can't stand it any longer. Judas and Simon drop in after their toil in the fields and James and Joseph join us for a quick chat before returning to their families.

'Boys,' I say, 'are any of you able to go to Magdala and find out if this preacher is Joshua? James, surely you're on top of things in the workshop? And you two,' I say, turning to the twins, 'how busy are you in the fields? It's not harvest yet. Surely you're not too busy to take a day or two away from your labours?'

Judas and Simon look at each other. Both start to speak at once, then Judas holds back and Simon replies.

'I'll go if you like. As you say, harvest is still a few weeks off. It's mainly weeding and watering now and one of us can manage that. What do you say, brother? Do you want to go or are you happy to stay here while I do what Mother's asking?'

'You go if you like. I'll look after things here.'

'I'll come too.' James is emphatic. I thought he might be reluctant, not want to leave the workshop, but I think he is curious and wants to put his own slant on things if they find the preacher to be Joshua. 'It'll only take us a couple of days. And if it is him, I'll drag him back here and find out why he's not had the courtesy of coming via us and telling us what he's up to.'

`*   *   *   *   *

And so they went. 'Two days', they said. It's been over a week and they're still not back. They must have found Joshua.

135

If the preacher in Magdala had been someone different, they'd have been home straight away. There's no problem here. Joseph seems happier than usual, I hear him singing as he works. I suppose he's not got James breathing down his neck all the time and the other young men with him are managing perfectly well without James bossing them around. I'm about to take a short rest before preparing the evening meal, when I hear Mother stir. I'll go to her in a minute, but she calls out before I'm ready.

'Mari, Mari, can you come and help me?'

I hurry through to where she is lying. She is straining to get up, but her face is red, she is gritting her teeth.

'What's the matter? Can I get you anything?'

'I can't get up. You'll have to help me. It's silly, I know, but I'm locked in this position.'

I hasten to her and reach out. She grasps my hand and I pull, but she is too weak and I have to put my arm around her whole body and draw her up. Her face contorts in pain. I think back to the Mother I knew when I was a girl and I feel my eyes watering. She's not sixty yet, but it's an old woman whose thin body is now reliant on mine to raise her to her feet.

'Careful, Mother. Give me your arm. Come and sit over here.' I think of calling Esther to come and give a hand and talk to her great grandmother, but the courtyard seems silent, and I guess she must have gone out with her mother to the market or the well. Anyway, I can keep my mother company as I boil water and peel onions ready to add to the stew I've half prepared already.

'I'm sorry, Mari, to trouble you like this. You've enough to do without having to see to me all the time. I've outlived my usefulness. I've prayed to Jehovah to let me go.'

'Don't say things like that, Mother. My children are grown up, they don't need me. You're my first priority now.'

'But you haven't stopped worrying about them. Even the oldest. I know you're on tenterhooks waiting for James and

Simon to come back with news. You think he's finally revealing himself, don't you, and you don't know whether to be pleased or frightened for him.'

'Of course I'm pleased. At last all the promises we had, all the signs, finally he's acting.'

'Have you no doubts, Mari? Haven't you sometimes wondered if you'd got it wrong?'

'Of course not. Well, I've not doubted that he would fulfil his foretold destiny in the end. Admittedly sometimes I've wondered how what has happened has fitted into God's plan for him. I know I should have not worried so, and relaxed and trusted more. And now at last they say he's revealing himself. Why shouldn't I be pleased? You've supported me all these years, surely you believe in him, don't you?'

'I suppose so, Mari. I know you believe. I can't comprehend – I never could – exactly what happened to you and I had to do what I thought was best for you at the time. But I don't like the way you and James argue all the time. You don't think I hear, you think I'm asleep, but I know. It's not good for a mother and son to be so at odds. Can't you get Joshua to seek a reconciliation with his brother? Can't you take James's side sometimes and at least see his point of view?'

'Do you really think that would help? Can't you get James to be less critical and accept what Joshua is trying to do. He might listen to you. He knows I defend Joshua always so he doesn't take any notice of what I say.'

'I'm too tired, Mari. Why would he listen to an old woman like me? You're more likely to persuade him. At least you're certain of where you stand, or you say you are. I don't know anyway. When I listen to Joshua, I believe him. Then I hear James's arguments and they seem reasonable. I don't know what to think any more. It's too much to think about and makes my head ache.'

I'm disappointed. I always thought my mother a staunch supporter of both me and Joshua and everything that

137

happened. Has she just ceased thinking properly as she's wracked with so much pain or has she always doubted and convinced herself never to inquire too deeply in case she learned what she did not want to hear? Then I catch voices in the courtyard. I'm sure that's James calling out to Deborah. I peer out of the door. I see James's back disappearing into his home, but Simon is there and he turns as he hears our door hinges creak. He waves and comes over.

'Did you find him, Simon? Is Joshua well?'

'Yes, Mother. But we had to go all the way up to Capernaum right to the far end of Lake Genneseret before we found him. He had been in Magdala, but he'd left there several days before we arrived so we asked around and everyone said he'd gone further north, so we followed. He's established himself there. He seems to have found some followers among the fisherfolk and is staying for a while. But he said he'd be back to visit us soon.'

'Did he say when?'

'No, but soon, I think. He told us he has further things to do there, but he'd be back. It's extraordinary, really. Everywhere he goes crowds follow. We heard him speak and watched him. People are saying that he's a healer and some men and women assured us that they'd been ill or crippled and he'd cured them, but we didn't see anything ourselves. We were able to talk to some of the friends he seems to have made in the town there and they were very impressed with him. He's certainly very popular there. Although he said he'd come home, I don't think the locals want him to leave.'

'Are you going home now or do you want to eat with us and tell us more?'

'It's too long a story. I want to get home to my family. I'll come and see you tomorrow. James said we'd both see you in the morning and tell you everything we've found out.'

So I have to be patient and wait. At least Simon says he's well and is coming home. But why didn't he call on us before going all that way?

*   *   *   *   *

'Yes, we found him. Hidden away in a fisherman's cottage near the shore, cringing from the crowds.'

'That's not true, James. He was resting. They said he'd spent the whole of the previous day talking first to a crowd in the Capernaum synagogue, then later in the open air, because there were just too many people who wanted to meet him to get into the synagogue. No wonder he was exhausted.'

We're all sitting round in a circle in my house. My mother is reclining in the corner. As well as Simon and James who've come to tell us where and how they found Joshua, Joe, Nathan, Isaac, Matthew and Reuben have left their labours and are sitting cross-legged with me in a circle, sipping beer and chewing on some dates.

'The man mystifies me. Instead of coming home to us, he's deliberately ignored us and preferred the company of some uneducated fishermen. What's the point of all the education he's supposed to have been picking up while he's been in Sepphoris and Jerusalem, leaving all the hard work to us?'

'Did he say whether he was coming home to see us?'

'Yes, he said he'd be with us soon.'

'But he didn't say when. Typical! We'll be lucky to see him for a few weeks yet. We're very low on his priorities.'

'But he said he went there because he was sent for. Someone from Capernaum met him down in Sychar or Shechem and invited him there. Said they implored him to go there first.'

'Well, couldn't he have dropped off here and told us where he was going? What was the hurry?'

139

I must admit I feel a little hurt. I try to defend Joshua against the cynicism and bitterness of his brother, but Joshua doesn't make it easy for me. I don't understand why he could not have come here first. I sometimes think he sees the need of everyone else except that of his own family.

'Is he alright? Is he being looked after if he is so exhausted?'

'Yes,' says James, 'they're making a fuss of him. One of the fishermen has invited him into his own home, primitive though it is, and the women in the house are swarming around him, ministering to his every need. No wonder he doesn't want to come home.'

'You say he's been preaching there.' Judas has put his jug down and looks at his twin brother. 'What's he saying? If he's drawing large crowds, he must be saying something of interest. Did you listen to him?'

'He gets the crowd very excited. He says God's kingdom is on the point of being founded. I think some of those who hear him interpret it as a rebel movement to oust the Romans.'

'Yes, Simon, that's just the problem. I haven't a clue what he means by this so-called kingdom, but it's dangerous talk. I've told you before, it'll cause nothing but trouble for him and all of us.'

'How does he hold the attention of the crowds for so long?' I ask. 'If he spends all the afternoon in the open air as you said, he must have a lot to say that creates this interest.'

'Oh, he stops from time to time and individuals come and talk to him. And people bring their kids, I don't know why he bothers with them. Sometimes there are great long queues of children who aren't even in the synagogue schools yet, girls even, and he wastes his time talking to them when he could be resting or doing something more important. He seems to attract some of the poorest and least educated people. He promises them freedom and riches – I think he's speaking figuratively, but I'm sure some of them take him literally. He's raising expectations and he won't be able to fulfil them. It's dangerous twaddle.'

'But has he said that he's the Messiah?'

'Not in so many words. But he keeps quoting words from Isaiah's prophecies and the crowds assume he's talking about himself. If they ask him directly, he doesn't answer them properly, but just tells them to watch what he does and judge for themselves.'

'And he's recruited a group of friends round himself, just like some of the best known rabbis in Jerusalem do, he calls them disciples...'

'And that's another thing,' butts in James. 'You'd think he'd choose educated men like the rabbis. People who know our scriptures. Damn it all, he's been mixing with such men in Jerusalem and Sepphoris. He could have found learned students in Magdala or Tiberias. And he has to go and pick a bunch of fishermen – he didn't even pick the owner of the boats. They're a rabble. I doubt if he can have a sensible conversation with any of them. They won't know what the hell he's talking about.'

'That's where you're wrong, James. Didn't you listen properly to him? He's very simple, direct. He tells stories. He doesn't use the language the rabbis and scribes use. When he quotes scripture he always repeats it in the common language. That's why I think he draws the crowds. They're used to being bored stiff on the Sabbath. He even encourages questions and gives people a straight answer, even if it wasn't the one they wanted or expected. And he heals people from their afflictions – they say he's better than any doctor.'

'You've said it. "They say." Did you see any healings? I didn't. I just saw a huddle round him and then the word went round that they'd been cured of all sorts of diseases, lameness, blindness – I ask you! I bet he gets them to say that to drum up interest. How do we know they were really afflicted beforehand? We've only got his word for it.'

141

'James, are you accusing your brother of being a monstrous fake, a charlatan? That's too much. Joshua's a good man, he's always been kind and truthful. Take back what you said, please.'

'Alright Mother,' he says grudgingly, 'I don't say he's deliberately deceiving the crowds. But he's exaggerating and letting those round him, in their excitement, get carried away and claim all sorts of preposterous things to get the limelight and the crowd's attention. Some of these people have been ignored or neglected for years. Who blames them for seeking a bit of glory by appearing to be blest by this new miracle man?'

'What do you think, Uncle Simon?' says Matthew quietly. 'Do you think he's a fake or are the healings real?'

'I don't know, young man. I know we've not always agreed with your Uncle Joshua but I've never found him untruthful.'

'I didn't say he was lying, did I? I said he's getting it into his head that he's the Messiah. Ever since Mother told him so. It's turned his head. He's deluding himself. I've stopped caring what it does to his own reputation and safety, but I resent it when the things he says and does puts us in danger. And they will, I'm telling you, they will!'

'Well,' says Simon, 'he says he'll be home soon. Then you can judge for yourselves. I'm not prejudging anything.'

'Well said,' whispers a soft voice from her bedroll. 'When he comes here, watch him carefully and listen to what he says. Then see what you think. If he is capable of healing diseases, let's see him do it here in Nazareth.'

'Fine, Grandmother. But I'll be watching him very carefully. He'll have no chance to pull the wool over my eyes. It'll be a good test. That is,' James adds, 'assuming he does come home and the reason for him not coming so far is that he's afraid we'll find him out.'

* * * * *

He came home last night. The first I knew of it was when I heard raised voices in the courtyard. James and Joshua were having a blazing row. I nearly went out to stop them, I could hear James's voice full of anger. I'm afraid I was a coward and kept out of it. There's no reasoning with James when he's lost his temper. I felt sorry for Deborah and the children, because they'll have got the backlash when Joshua eventually made his escape and came to me and Mother. He came in very subdued, shaking his head.

'What was all that about?' I asked anxiously, but he was silent, clearly upset. I poured him a cup of wine and he sat down and I waited for him to say something.

Eventually he pulled himself together.

'I'm sorry, Mother. I'd hoped for a better reception than that. I'm tired. I didn't get much sleep last night and I've been with crowds all day. I only managed to get away when some of my friends in Capernaum drew them off as we neared Magdala.'

'Are you hungry?'

'A crust of bread will be sufficient.'

He drained the cup and lay back as I went to fetch the freshly baked bread that Salome had brought that morning and blow me, when I returned with a hunk of the loaf, he was already fast asleep. My mother called out and I went into her.

'Did I hear Joshua?'

'Yes, you did, Mother, but he's tired and already asleep.'

'And what was the row I heard earlier?'

'James was having an argument with Joshua.'

'What, already?'

'Yes, I'm upset about that too.'

'What was it about?'

'I don't know, but I expect James was having a go at him for not visiting us earlier. If he makes him feel that unwelcome, he'll soon be on his way again.'

Now, this morning, I've got up and Joshua is nowhere to be seen. Surely he's not deserted us so soon? Is he so sensitive that he can't take James's criticism? Well, I suppose the word 'criticism' is rather understated. There was real anger last night. Anyway, I get up and after checking that Mother is still asleep, I go to the well to fetch water. My daughter Salome is there and I greet her. I'm about to tell her Joshua's home, then I refrain in case he's really gone. She usually asks if we've heard from him anyway, but on this morning, strangely, she doesn't. And then, when I get home, I find him there. He's already cooked breakfast for both of us.

'Some fish,' he says, 'a present from my friends in Capernaum.'

'Where have you been?' I ask. 'I thought you'd left us already.'

'I go into the hills to pray every morning. I can't get through the day without the strength and support of God, my Father. I went to the big fig tree down towards the stream, you know, the one you showed me once where you said you used to go and pray.'

We eat in silence. Still my mother hasn't stirred. Soon the men will be arriving in the workshop. James will be here again. I begin to feel tense. Is there going to be another big row?

'How is Grandmother?'

'She sleeps a lot these days. Her arthritis is very painful. Sometimes I think she'd be better if she made a bit more effort. I think she's given up. I know she's had a very difficult life and that the pain must be draining, but I do wish she'd try to get about and occupy her mind. She dwells on her problems too much.'

He is thinking. Perhaps he can help her. They say he's healed many from all sorts of ailments although James says it's just rumour, not fact. Perhaps I should ask him. But before I can say anything, he starts talking.

144

'James accused me last night of neglecting the family. No, he put it a lot stronger than that. He said I'd been deliberately shunning you all and that I'd disgraced you, him, the children, everyone, that my name was reviled in the village. Is that how you feel, Mother?'

'No, of course not, Joshua. He's expressing his own views. I don't know why he feels so strongly about you. I often wonder if it was my fault. I think he resents you being the eldest – he somehow feels that you've usurped his position and then not followed the traditions of the eldest son.'

I pause. Then I add, 'But we were a bit hurt, Joshua. We heard you were coming this way several weeks ago and were sure you'd come home and spend a few days with us before resuming whatever it is you feel you have to do. Why didn't you come to us before you went to Capernaum? Was it so urgent for you to go there first?'

'It seemed to be out of my hands. I didn't miss you all deliberately to hurt or offend you. But I leave my comings and goings to God's spirit to move me, to show me where to go, what to do. I leave my life in his hands. I can't say what I do, or act in the way I do, without his strength, his lead. And I felt at a crossroads. I was coming back to Galilee. Should I use my own village as base or should I go somewhere I wasn't known, where I would be judged for what I said and did now and not as the boy everyone knew as the carpenter's son?'

He waits to see I'm still with him. I am. I will him to go on.

'And I got this overwhelming urge to travel farther north and was wrestling with this thought in my mind when I met two men from Capernaum in Shechem where I was staying overnight and they implored me to visit their town. And so I went there single-mindedly, and I knew immediately it was right. I have no home, Mother, now. I'm everybody's. But I need a base, somewhere I can reflect and be quiet. I don't think I can do that here. Not easily anyhow. And I needed to be sure of that before I came here. It may sound strange, Mother, it's not meant to hurt you or cause offence. Do you understand?'

I nod. I think I do. I'm disappointed, but I think I understand. We'd not give him the space he needs here. We'd put pressure on him, try to influence what he did and where he went.

'Have you people in Capernaum who'll support you? Feed you? Find somewhere for you to rest? Have you met up with Ruth?'

'Yes, Mother. I saw her several times in Tiberias and she fed me and her husband introduced me to men working with him repairing their boat. They were fishermen from Capernaum, humble folk, but very sincere. When their boat was ready, I went back with them. Capernaum is a large fishing village and the men are close to nature. They understand and are in sympathy with the natural world. They accept my message and want to be part of it, they don't argue and dispute, looking for flaws and loopholes like some of the scribes, rabbis and Pharisees in the towns do.'

'Are you going back there?'

'Yes, some of the men and women there want to travel with me and learn from me and help as best they can. I thought I might bring some here with me, but I wasn't sure of my reception and I didn't want to expose them to strong opposition before they've got more confidence.'

'Joshua, is it true that you can heal people? Simon visited you and said he saw you healing many in the crowd who flocked to see you, but James said it wasn't true, people weren't really better. They were just excited and buoyed up by the attention.'

'Yes, I learned many ways of healing when I was with the Essenes. I learned how much is in the mind, how much belief can affect the physical as well as the mental state. If people really believe me and want to be restored, I can bring about positive changes in their lives. But they must believe, they

146

must be half way there and I can, with God's help, do the rest. I have been given this gift by God and I will use it when I can. But it's draining, it exhausts me and I do need co-operation, not scepticism, for the gift to be effective.'

That is giving me food for thought. Perhaps he can heal my mother's arthritis. But will she believe enough? Can I convince her?

I'm still wondering about this, teasing the thoughts in my mind when I'm interrupted by the arrival of Joe, followed quickly by Isaac and Matthew. They swarm around Joshua and embrace their brother and uncle and, thank goodness, do not start asking him why he hasn't come before. They at least seem genuinely pleased to see him. They're still chatting and lead Joshua into the workshop to show him the latest things they've made, when James arrives. I stop him going straight into the workshop because I want to talk to him first.

'James, please, no rows with Joshua this morning. I've talked to him, he didn't mean to cause us any offence. He had a reason and I'm satisfied with that. Please don't argue any more. It just upsets me too much. I love you both and it pains me to see such anger and bitterness. Please promise that you'll not start up more arguments again.'

'Has he apologised?'

'He's explained. It was not a deliberate snub. He needs a base where he's not so well known.'

'So he can deceive people more easily?'

'James, please no more of that. Watch him here. He's explained to me how he heals those who come to him. He uses their belief. Why can't you trust him and see for yourself? Be open-minded. Why, I believe he could cure my mother from her affliction, wouldn't that be proof enough for you?'

'That I want to see. Alright! I'll say nothing more until he's tried to heal Grandmother. But if he won't or doesn't, then that proves he's a fake.'

'Steady on, James, you've got to believe him. If you treat it as a test and you don't really believe in his power to heal, then perhaps he won't be able to do it.'

'It's not up to me, is it? Surely, if what he says is true, it's up to your mother to believe.'

What have I done? I didn't mean to turn the possibility of Joshua helping my mother into a test of faith for James and all those whom I'm sure he'll soon tell if Joshua cannot help her. I'd better tell Mother what I've done and at least see that she is willing for Joshua to attempt a cure.

I wake her up gently. I bring her a bit of the fish that Joshua brought, a great treat. I watch while she eats and I help her wash and put on a fresh garment. James is in the workshop and I hear a murmur of voices, which sounds hopeful. No raised voices anyway.

'Mother, Joshua has the power to heal. Won't you let him see what he can do to help you?'

'It's too late, Mari. I've lived with it too long. I've had enough. I just want to rest. I've had an eventful life, I've crammed in more than others experience in twice my years. Let nature take its course. Don't interfere.'

'But Mother, if Joshua can ease your pain you'll feel energetic and youthful again. You'll want to carry on then, you'll have a new lease of life.'

'What for, Mari, what for? I'm a useless old woman. I've done my bit. I supported you through your crises, you've got your Messiah. It's up to you and him now. There's nothing more I can do.'

'Please, Mother, I can't bear to see you in such pain. Give him a try. Whatever happens, you'll be no worse off than now. Let there be a possibility of change.'

'Just for you then, Mari, if you really want it. I don't care.'

'I don't understand your attitude. I'd have thought you'd have been eager to seize such a chance of a pain-free new life.'

'I don't want to build up hopes, that's all. I'm not ready for another disappointment, so I'll assume the worst and be surprised if I'm cured.'

'But Joshua says that for a person to be cured, they have to believe. He won't be able to help you unless you're more positive than that.'

A few minutes later all the men troop in from the workshop. James is almost pulling Joshua who looks very reluctant.

'I've told Joshua that if he has the power, then he should cure Grandmother of her arthritis. It's his chance to demonstrate to us that he has this power, this calling that he talks about. We can settle it once and for all. If he can cure Grandmother, I'll believe him and stop my criticism. I'll even become his disciple.'

'James, my power doesn't work like that. Your grandmother has to want to be cured, she has to believe that I can help her. If she doesn't I'm powerless.'

'That's an excuse. You're setting out your excuses for failure before you even try.'

Joshua turns to my mother.

'Grandmother, do you want to be cured? Do you believe I have the power to heal you?'

'If you say so, Joshua. I'm too old really, it's too much trouble, but if you think you can, do it to please Mari. She believes you can.'

'Do you, Mother? Do you really believe I can?'

I say 'yes'. I can say no other. But in my heart of hearts, how can he if Mother is so half-hearted about it? And James there doesn't believe, I know he doesn't. Is my belief strong enough to carry us through despite all this or is my knowledge of the unbelief of my family undermining any trust I have myself. I want to believe so badly. Joshua is looking at me. I can't look him in the face. He knows my doubt. I want to ask him to take away my lack of faith. But I say nothing further and will him to go on.

He goes over to my mother and puts his hands on her shoulders and closes his eyes and concentrates. His brows furrow, he is screwing up his eyes, he is mouthing words. He waits. We all wait. I look at James. The man is grinning. He believes he's won as if it were some sort of competition, not something that could relieve my mother of so much pain. I'm angry with him.

Joshua looks at me and shakes his head.

'I'm sorry, Grandmother. There's no power there. Your daughter has tried for you but she cannot bear you up all on her own. There's a lacking of faith here in this house. I'll find it hard to help you all here in this village. I ought to go back to other villages in Galilee where I can use the power I've been given.'

'Please, Joshua,' I say, 'please give our village a chance. Go and talk to Rabbi Joel. He'll remember all you learned from him. He'll give you an opportunity to show this village what you can do.'

Joshua comes to me and puts his hand on my arm.

'I'm sorry Mother. I know you believe in me, but I cannot operate in this atmosphere. Your mother doesn't even want to be cured. James doesn't believe. The others are just curious. I doubt if it will be any different anywhere in Nazareth, but to please you, I'm prepared to give it a try. I'll go and see Rabbi Joel as you suggest.'

He gives my arm another squeeze and departs without looking back.

James looks me in the eye, finding it difficult to hide the satisfaction he's now feeling.

'I told you, Mother. I told you he couldn't do it. Now will you listen to me? Stop trying to come to his defence. Let him go to Capernaum and forget he was your son. He'll bring you nothing but trouble.'

Chapter 14
Mari

It's the Sabbath and I'm sitting in the Women's Court of our synagogue with Deborah, Esther, Miriam, Salome and her two daughters, and Benjamin's wife, Rachel, and daughter, Anna. There are at least another hundred women and girls waiting patiently and the same number of men and boys inside the main part of the synagogue. We're waiting expectantly because Joshua told me that Joel has asked him to expound the scriptures to us today. He knows Joshua has studied with the best scholars in Sepphoris and Jerusalem and he has persuaded the other rabbis to let Joshua take a leading role. Old Jethro doesn't take an active part these days, his voice is feeble and few can hear what he has to say. Certainly out here in the Women's Court, we can hear nothing on the few occasions they let him participate. I suspect Jonas was less pleased at Joel's decision, but he has to defer to Joel as he is by far the most senior of the rabbis here who still have all their senses.

We chant through two of the psalms composed by our illustrious King David and listen while Jonas reads from the Law, then Joel picks up one of the scrolls from the altar and beckons Joshua to come forward and take the seat reserved for the rabbi or scribe chosen to interpret the scripture reading.

He stands and reads from the prophet Isaiah. His voice is firm and clear. We can hear every word. He reads slowly and with authority. He does not rush or mumble as some of those invited to speak do.

'The Spirit of the Lord is upon me,
because he has chosen me to bring good news to the poor.
He has sent me to proclaim liberty to the captives

and recovery of sight to the blind;
To set free the oppressed
and announce that the time has come
when the Lord will save his people.'

We all hold our breath. This is one of the most prophetic sayings about the coming of our longed-for Messiah. Did Joshua choose this or did Joel select the reading and ask Joshua to interpret it? Joshua has handed back the scroll to Rabbi Joel and sits down again on the chair in front of the altar. Everyone is staring at him. I will him to speak, to say things that will bring him favour from those around me. I'm so nervous, it is worse than if I was asked to speak, not that that is ever a possibility. Perhaps it feels like when I had to defend myself before Eli and Jethro so many years ago, accused of blasphemy and adultery.

Then he speaks.

'This scripture is coming true at this very moment, even as you hear me reading it. The Lord's spirit is here in this synagogue, in this village, in Galilee, in Judea. His spirit is in me as I speak to you inspiring all I shall say. It is in you too as you hear my words and they are working on your heart. This passage of scripture has been read so many times that the listeners hear it no more, yet I tell you, this scripture lives and its truth is being revealed to you now. I say again, now. At this very moment!

It is good news for the poor. It is therefore good news for most of you. The Lord of all cares for you. The rich, the learned, they do not think you are important. But you are the most important in God's kingdom. He will put you first. He knows your needs, your travail. He sees when you are ignored, when you are cheated, when you are patronised by those who hold themselves to be of influence. God will use uneducated men – yes, and women too whom you think as of little account. They will understand his kingdom. Children will be of consequence. The Lord God values the trust offered by girls and boys, just as you value and love your own children. So you may not have much of this world's goods, but if you have the friendship and respect of your neighbours, the love and care of your mother, brother, cousin, the peace of a clear conscience, then you are not poor for these things are the riches of God's kingdom.

Isaiah proclaims liberty for the captives. I tell you this. In the kingdom of God there are no captives. You are free to come and be a citizen, no-one forces you, you are free to love your king and to love your fellow citizens and be loved yourself. You will be free from the consequences of evil, free from the shackles of your own guilty thoughts and consciences, for in God's kingdom brother forgives his brother, fathers forgive their children, children forgive their parents and God forgives all who are sorry for their wrong-doing and determine on a new direction of right living and respect and care for others. You can enter this kingdom now. If you have a quarrel with your brother or your neighbour, go from this building and make it right with him. Then your are already entering God's kingdom.'

I couldn't help but think that this remark is directed at his own brother and I wonder what James is thinking. Is he applying it to himself or is he offended by Joshua's words, seeing them as a rebuke? But I cannot ponder further because Joshua, after taking a draught of water from the vessel beside him, continues to speak to the people of Nazareth who are spellbound by his words.

'The blind are being given their sight back. Yes, this is literally true. In Capernaum last week two blind beggars could see again. Their wonder and joy was a marvel to behold. They ran around waving their arms thinking people were trees and trees were people. Their joy was infectious, children screamed with laughter and God rejoiced. But you are blind when you fail to understand the scriptures, when you do not see how

God's Law applies to you. And now we are seeing life in God's word, we see that it applies to us, we see that it gives us guidance which if we follow it, opens our eyes to truth and brings fulfilment to our lives. I've seen my cousin John opening the eyes of many beside the river Jordan as they see their lives for what they are and turn again, vowing to renounce their evil ways and start afresh. I can help you open your eyes. Love the Lord God. Love his word. Love your family. Love your neighbour. Love your enemy. Open your eyes and see that you are loved too. That is the kingdom of God. It is in your heart, in your very being.

So you feel oppressed, the weight of your cares bears down on you, life is a drudgery, you are afflicted by illness or those who would exploit you, unfair masters, uncaring pedagogues, those with spiteful tongues? But you can be released. The Lord God will save you from such oppression if you will but listen to his word to you. He loves you. He cares for you like a father. If he cares for you so much, what matter the petty conduct and meanness of those who would demean you. Feel loved by God, know he values you and that oppression will slip from your shoulders. You will be free in your heart. His message will save you from your despair.

And, my fellow citizens of Nazareth, I repeat, this opportunity is with you now. I am offering you a new way of thinking. The kingdom of God can be in your hearts here in this village and if it is, your relationships with each other will be transformed. Care for each other. Be there for the poor. Open the eyes of the blind. Let the oppressed be free. The spirit of God can be within you. Let this spirit take over your lives and the kingdom of God will be yours. Now! At this very moment! Isaiah has spoken to you through my words. Engrave them on your own hearts.'

He has stopped speaking and looks expectantly at the congregation. It is the time when the men can ask questions.

There is a buzz of conversation, out here among the women as well as from the men.

Then questions are hurled at him, many before he can attempt any answer.

'Who are you?'

'Aren't you Joshua, son of Joseph the carpenter?'

'Haven't you lived here in this village nearly all your life?'

'How do you know so much?'

'Aren't your brothers in this room? And your sisters outside? What do they think of all this?'

Around me, many of the women are expressing their astonishment at Joshua's words.

'Where did he learn such things?'

'Well, I must say, that was much more interesting than we usually hear.'

'I'm not surprised that crowds go to listen to him if he always speaks like that.'

'Do you think he could make blind men see here? Really, I mean?'

Above the hubbub of remarks around me, nearly all expressing astonishment at his knowledge and eloquence, which makes me feel proud, I try to listen to the questions still being shouted out by the men. At last they give him a chance to answer. The last question I heard was 'People say you can work miracles of healing. Can you do that here in Nazareth? Can you show us what you do so we can believe your words?'

And that's when it begins to go wrong. Joshua holds up one arm to silence the hubbub and pauses until they are all looking at him.

'You all know the proverb, "Doctor, heal yourself". I find I can heal many adults and children of their diseases everywhere except here. It is very difficult to be a prophet in your own village. Why? Because you all know me. You've known me since I was a boy and you find it difficult to believe that I can help you in this way. You just want to test me. But

155

my power comes from God and you can't put God to the test like that.'

I hear a few sharp drawings-in of breath at this, as a few of the congregation think he's claiming to be God, blasphemy to them.

'In order to be healed, you need to believe. And if I'm so familiar to you, you find it hard to believe.'

Someone shouts out, 'Have you tried?'

'Yes, he has and he's failed. He tried to cure my grandmother, Anna, from her arthritis and he couldn't do it.'

I recognise James's voice and I'm embarrassed. Why won't he keep quiet? There's no need to publicise our failings – and I'm sure it's our own lack of faith. Joshua said so himself.

'My brother is correct. He does not believe that I have the power to heal. It is hard for him, for he's lived nearly thirty years alongside me and when you're that close you can be blind to certain things. It is difficult though. Our history is full of examples where God could not act through prophets in their own country. Elijah went to a widow living in Zarapheth in Sidon even though there were many widows in Israel at the time of the great drought, because only she, a stranger, had sufficient trust to feed him and thus benefited from the miracle he wrought to sustain her until the rains came. And Elisha could have healed many of their diseases, but who asked for help? Why, it was the foreign general, Naaman, who had leprosy. There must have been many in Israel who had the same dreaded skin disease, yet must we believe that only he had sufficient faith to ask? And even then, it came about only through the faith of a small girl child. Look at you – all you men of irreproachable morals, so you think – sitting there in the forefront of this synagogue, Pharisees, Scribes, Israelites all, praying weekly for a deliverer, the Messiah, yet full of scepticism, wanting to test the spirit of the Lord before you'll trust. And outside in the courtyard are women and children, foreigners. Some of them believe. You need to be trusting like

156

children... Only then will I be able to do the work with you that I have performed elsewhere.'

He doesn't get any further. There is a roar of disapproval. Rabbi Joel grabs back the scrolls from Joshua's hands before they are damaged for already men from the front row have plunged forward and are trying to grab Joshua. Now everyone is standing up and shouting. Then there is total chaos, Joshua disappears under a struggling group of men that is surging towards our courtyard. Some of the women have stood up in alarm, others are joining their menfolk in protest at what Joshua's been saying. Before I have got my wits together, I see Joshua being manhandled in the midst of an angry mob. The noise of protest and anger is joined by the screams of frightened children and I find myself knocked out of the way as I try to get up and move towards my son.

I see James on the edge of the crowd and shout, 'James, can you reach him? Help him, please!'

But all James does is shout back, 'I told you he'd get himself in trouble. I'm washing my hands of him. Just get off home and lock the door before the crowd turn on us.'

Esther and the other girls are crying. 'Miriam,' I shout above the pandemonium, 'can you get the children home before they're trampled in the mob. I'm going to see if I can help Joshua.'

'Don't be stupid, Mari,' she shouts. There's nothing you can do. You'll get hurt yourself. But I'll get the girls out of here anyway. But stay away from the mob.'

Deborah has put a restraining arm on me, but Salome gathers us up and we follow the crowd of men who are now rushing towards the edge of the town. Joshua is nowhere to be seen – he must be buried somewhere in the middle of the angry men. One or two boys and older men have dropped out of the mass of men which is still driving its way up the roadway to the edge of the village and I realise with horror what this angry mob is going to do. For the road leads out of the village along the ledge of the quarry before dropping into the valley. They're so incensed, they're going to push him right over the cliff, they're lynching him. I panic and try to redouble my steps, but Deborah and Salome hold me tight.

'Stay back, mother,' pleads Salome, 'there's nothing you can do.'

'Pray hard, girl,' is all I can think of saying. The men are chasing ahead as fast as ever and we can't keep up with them. The main core of the mob is almost out of sight ahead of us now, only the stragglers are with us. They are not turning back, though. They are continuing because they are curious, they want to see what is happening. We eventually catch up with the men. I'm breathless and distraught and fear what I may find, for the group has stopped at the edge of the quarry where it drops sheer, some fifty feet or so, onto the rubble and debris of the stones that have fallen from the area most recently quarried. I can't get to the edge to look over because too many men are milling around. Then I realise that they are not peering into the quarry depths as I'd feared but seem to be wandering around aimlessly, their anger turning to frustration as in all the headlong rush they seem to have mislaid the object of their retribution.

'Where is he?' I hear the shout go up. 'Who's got him?' Then everyone is repeating that refrain. They can't believe it – and nor can I.

'What have you done with him?' Someone rounds on me. Someone else sees me and spits in my face. 'Whore that spawned this monster!' Salome pulls me away and puts herself between the accusers and me. We go and stand under a tree beside the roadway and wait as the crowd of men gradually breaks up and begins to disperse. When, eventually, they've all gone, we go nervously and peer over the quarry edge. Nothing. It's deserted. The grey stones shimmer in the heat of the day, shining, almost blinding me as I stare. I breathe a sigh of relief. Where has my son gone? How did he escape?

We make our way back home and find a group of men outside the courtyard of our home. When they see me, Salome and Deborah, someone shouts, 'Open up and bring the blasphemer out. Don't hide him.' Someone throws a stone which thumps against the wall of my house. James emerges, and shouts back, 'Go away – he's not here. I have no idea where he is.'

'Let us see for ourselves, he must be here somewhere.'

James gesticulates to a couple of the men. 'Andrew, Ishmael, come and look for yourselves and then tell everyone else. He's not here, I assure you.'

The two men stumble into our home and brush past James and into the area where Anna is asleep. Then they peer into the workshop. They shrug their shoulders and go back outside.

'He's not there. I don't know where the bastard's gone. Is he hiding in Clopas's house?' And the group make their way there.

'Is he?' I ask James nervously.

'Not that I know of,' answers James. 'I haven't a clue how he got away. One moment he was in the thick of the mob, and the next, he'd disappeared. I don't know how he did it, but he was very lucky. They'd have killed him. I told you he'd be a danger to us all and I was right. Wherever he is, I just hope he stays away from us now.'

I kept expecting Joshua to turn up over the next few days. I assumed he'd hidden in the fields or in one of the olive groves and would reappear when it was dark to get some food before making his farewell. But he never came. Weeks went past and we heard nothing of him. Then someone travelling through the village said he was preaching, and healing crowds of thousands around Capernaum again.

I look at James hopefully.

'No,' says James. 'Not this time. I'm not going.'

Chapter 15
Mari, AD 24

We didn't hear any news about Joshua for several months – other than that he'd managed somehow to escape unscathed from our Nazareth riot and had returned to preach and act where his presence was more acceptable. We experienced a few days of hostility, which was mollified to some extent by James telling anyone who would listen that we all thought Joshua was mad and had no further dealings with him. I told James that his views were his own and were not shared by many of the family, but James told his brothers and sisters to say nothing more, so that everything would blow over sooner. I know Simon and Salome do not agree with James, nor do Susannah and my sisters, but they've been told by their husbands to say nothing to prevent hostility in the village arising again. Rabbi Joel came to see me and apologised for asking Joshua to speak and being inadvertently the cause of the upset.

'Joel, don't blame yourself. You gave my son the chance to proclaim his message and he took it. The fact that some of the congregation were offended by what he said was not your fault.'

'I feel bad about it though. I thought the reaction against him was extreme. The mood changed very suddenly. His actual interpretation of the passage from the prophet Isaiah was both thought provoking and eloquent and, on the whole, was well received. It was only during the asking of questions afterwards that the mood became ugly. The words of your son, James, were a bit inflammatory. If he hadn't said what he did, and require an answer from Joshua that was too direct for the hearers, I think we'd have had no trouble. It was a pity. He said a number of things I'd have liked to take up with him.'

'So you do not excuse the actions of the men that Sabbath?'

'No, Mari, I do not. I agreed with a lot of what he said and I'd have liked to have said more in his defence, but the mob didn't give me a chance. I'm afraid my colleague, Jonas, was behind much of the opposition. He was strongly against giving Joshua the scroll to read from and interpret, but Joshua is a learned man, expert in the interpretation of our scriptures and he is gaining a remarkable reputation in northern Galilee. It seemed natural to ask him to speak. Many people are saying that he's the Messiah, you know. I'm sure you'll be vindicated one day. I'd love to see all that you were sure you'd been promised come true. I just hope I live long enough.'

Life went on without many further excitements. The carpentry business flourished and we had no worries on that score. The boys were able to repay Clopas much of what he'd invested to help them when they needed support most. We celebrated a couple more births in the family. Festivals came and went. Benjamin's daughter, Anna, another of my many grandchildren, was betrothed although she'll wait until she's fourteen before we have the wedding ceremony. I don't see as much of her as I'd like, but she comes occasionally to the house when Benjamin calls to discuss the accounts in the workshop. Benjamin doesn't go to Sepphoris now, but he advises James and Reuben who have taken on the regular supply of materials and keep their ear to the ground about potential work or likely contracts they could bid for.

Anna is with me today. I think she's come for a bit of advice. She sits down at my feet and twiddles some of the cloth I've been sewing in her fingers. She looks up at me, and goes to speak, then thinks better of it. She's embarrassed to ask me, I can tell.

'Well, young Anna, out with it! Don't be shy with me. You know you can ask me anything, don't you?'

She still hesitates. She's a pretty young thing, slim and quite delicate. I wonder if it isn't too soon to be arranging a marriage for her. Eventually she plucks up courage.

'Grandma, you've had lots of babies. I've heard people say that it's my duty to give my husband a son as soon as possible after we've wed. Is that right?'

'Who's telling you that, my love? They've no right to put pressure on you. And how can you choose whether your first born will be a boy or girl?'

'Oh, just people. I heard Nathaniel's mother talking to her sister the other day.' Nathaniel is Anna's husband to be, the son of a merchant in Sepphoris that Benjamin has had many dealings with.

'Don't worry, Anna. I'm sure when the time comes and you have a baby of your own, everyone will love the child, whether it's a boy or girl.'

'Will it hurt, Mari?'

'Is that what's bothering you, child? Hasn't your mother told you all about that?'

'Well, yes, I s'ppose so.'

'But you don't know whether to believe her so you've come to your old grandma?'

So we have a quiet chat. I'm really surprised how little she knows. Her mother's obviously told her the basic facts, but not the feelings, the things that girls – and boys – really ought to know. When I've said all I have to say – for the moment anyway, she suddenly changes the subject.

'Where's Uncle Joshua, Grandma? Why doesn't he come home?'

'Why, do you miss him, Anna? I know he used to play with you all, but didn't know he spent much time with you.'

'Oh yes he did. He's my favourite uncle. He used to teach us lots of new games and tell us stories, all the children like him best.'

'Well I never did! I knew he was popular.'

'He used to meet us in the fields when we were weeding or harvesting and he'd help us sometimes. And then afterwards we'd sit down and he'd make up stories for us. We used to shout out a word and he'd invent a story round that word. Why do people criticise him now?'

'Who criticises him, Anna? Do your mum or dad?' Perhaps I shouldn't put her on the spot like this, but I want to know what Benjamin really thinks. I see him as one of the most objective and open-minded of the men and he always defended Joshua's decision to go for training in the rabbinical school. But perhaps Anna hears different things in her own house. Benjamin might watch his words in front of me because he doesn't want to admit he doesn't believe my story.

'Oh, no, Grandma. It's my uncles and the other girls. When we're at the well or in the fields, I hear the gossip. They often talk of when Uncle Joshua caused a riot in the village and they say he said some really bad things about the people who live here. Did he?'

'Well, it depends whether you thought what he said applied to you. They wanted him to do all the things he was rumoured of doing in Capernaum here in Nazareth. And he said he couldn't because people here didn't believe he could do it. You see, everyone thought they knew him because he'd grown up among them and they found it hard suddenly to think of him as a miracle worker and even as the promised Messiah. Now let me ask you a question. What would you think if your father suddenly told you that your big brother, Matthew, was a prophet and would be the Messiah foretold in our scriptures?'

She laughs. 'Matthew? Of course I wouldn't believe it. It's ridiculous, I know him too well, I know his secrets. I know he's my brother and I shouldn't tell tales about him, but, well, you have to behave yourself and be pious, don't you, to become a prophet?'

'There you are, then. You see how hard it was for people who knew Joshua well, especially his brothers, to think of him as the coming Messiah. Not that I ever found Joshua's behaviour such that would rule him out for that reason. But pious? I don't think the Messiah's got to be pious. Belief and trust in the Lord God, yes. My Joshua has a very sincere faith, but he has no particular concern for the rules and rituals of our traditional ways of religious observance. That's one of the reasons why some people, especially the most outwardly religious, criticise him. They think he's making up his own rules as he goes along.'

'Do you really think he is the Messiah, Grandma? You must know him better than anyone. Don't you find it hard to believe?'

'Yes, Anna, I do believe he is. Sometimes I've doubted, that's only natural, but there are reasons for my belief I've told only a few people. I think you need to know. Things happened to me when I was your age. Your father and Aunt Salome and Aunt Rebecca know and supported me when my life became very difficult. Curl up here, my love, and let me tell you.'

And I tell her everything. She listens open-mouthed to me and even cries when I tell her about the threats to me and the unborn Joshua. When I tell her about Rabbi Eli and the whipping in the synagogue she gets all indignant and angry and I stroke her hair and tell her to calm down, because it all ended happily. But has it? It hasn't ended yet.

*   *   *   *   *

Benjamin and Reuben came to see me earlier today when they got back from a visit to Sepphoris to obtain payment for a contract that had just been completed. They'd picked up all sorts of gossip about Joshua and what he was said to be doing all over Galilee.

'Mari,' said my brother, 'he really is a phenomenon. There's too much being said for it to be idle gossip. Apparently stories are coming back and circulating widely that he's leading a new movement, a real swell of support throughout towns and villages not just in Galilee, but over in Perea and in the Decapolitan cities as well. They say he's performing extraordinary miracles of healing – no-one has a clue how he does it. He is even able to heal lepers, they say, and wretched beings whose mental faculties have long since abandoned them. And his preaching – they say he's extraordinary. People flock to hear him because they can understand him, his stories and examples are very earthy and come from real life. He's practical, not like the priests and rabbis.'

Reuben nods. 'Yes, it's just as Cousin Ben says. Joshua's famous. Loads of people are apparently following him round listening to his every word and he has a large band of followers. Many of them are saying that he'll be gathering a rebel force to drive the Romans out.'

I'm worried when I hear that. I think it over for several days and go to see my brother again.

'Ben, what you were saying about Joshua the other day. Do you think he's in danger? If his words and deeds are so well known, won't the authorities move against him? Won't they fear he'll lead a rebel army?'

'I think the Roman spies are pretty sophisticated. I don't think they'll worry about a motley crew of Galilean peasants chasing after a miracle worker. Spies will have seen what he really does. Curing people of diseases won't come high on the fears of the Roman occupying forces. And, from what I can tell, the things he says are more likely to upset the traditionalists, the Pharisees and scribes, rather than the military authorities. That's what I've heard, anyway.'

'I'm still worried for him. These things can be so easily misinterpreted and the authorities don't exactly check too carefully before they act. Remember what that brute Herod did when he heard the rumour that a possible claimant to his throne had been born in Bethlehem. He didn't stop to check, but acted ruthlessly to cut out any possibility. Why are the authorities now likely to be any different? Do you trust them? I don't.'

'Well, there's not a lot here we can do about it. He's far away and he has a lot of support. He's unlikely to back off now, even if his horde of followers and hangers-on would allow him to.'

'I'd like to see for myself and talk to him. Can't we find out where he is and go to see him?'

'Is that really what you want, sister? Would that put your mind at rest? If so, I'll have a further word with others in the family. Perhaps we should all go to see him.'

'Please, Ben, please would you talk to James and the others. I'd like him especially to come as he's been so unbelieving. He must see what's really happening.'

'Alright, Mari. I'll do as you ask. I'm inclined to agree with you. We must make another attempt to get together with him again, see if we can reconcile him to our village and get him working here as he's obviously done so successfully elsewhere. Leave it with me for a few days and I'll see what the others think.'

*   *   *   *   *

We set off earlier today. We found out yesterday that Joshua was last heard of in Bethsaida at the north east end of Lake Genneseret. It'll be best to journey via the western coast rather than take a boat across the lake, as we'll be going through Capernaum and we believe people there will have the best news of where Joshua is exactly. There's a good crowd of us who are determined to meet up with Joshua and persuade him to return back to us if possible, or at least give our village another chance. Most of us are agreed on this. James and Judas and Clopas's sons are still adamantly opposed, citing the danger to Joshua himself and us, his family, if we have a repeat of the synagogue incident. But I've argued, and Benjamin and Simon have supported me, that if Joshua can work here as he's obviously done elsewhere, and if he brings many of his supporters with him, the danger is minimal.

So, as I've said, we're a crowd. There's my sister, Salome, her boy, Isaac and my brother Benjamin. His daughter, Anna, has come too – after our earlier heart to heart, she pleaded with her father to be allowed to come. Cousin Susannah was visiting us and heard of our intentions and asked to come also. Then James, Simon and Judas have all come, leaving Joe, and my nephews and cousins in charge of our business. Andrew, my daughter Salome's husband, is with us and Clopas's two sons, James and Jude. James has recruited them as he didn't want to be outnumbered by those of us whom he thinks will be too easily persuaded by Joshua's eloquent words. James wanted Rabbi Jonas, Clopas's brother-in-law, to come too, but he refused. He's always opposed any link with Joshua and has disputed with Joel over him in the past. Jonas's opposition goes right back to the time when I was accused of betraying my rebel father's presence to Herod's soldiers and subsequent pregnancy which he always maintained was both adulterous and blasphemous. So that makes twelve of us in total. I think five of us are either believers in Joshua or at least hoping that he is all that many say he is. Four are definitely non-believers. I've no real idea of the views of the other three. I just hope they are open-minded enough to give him a good hearing.

We're staying in Kana tonight. My sister Rebecca will welcome us and I want to persuade her to join us. She, like sister Salome and cousin Susannah, has been my friend and confidante for years and would, if she feels able to come, be a great support for me, should anything go wrong. Perhaps her son, Nathan, can be persuaded to join us too – her daughter

Susannah now has a young child so I doubt if she'll be able to leave home.

I leave the men, on arrival, to unload our two donkeys and set up the tents while I take Salome, Susannah and Anna to greet Rebecca.

'Greetings, my dear sister.' She kisses me on both cheeks. She is, as always, overjoyed to see me.

'And to what do we owe this pleasure? You've a veritable army with you. What expedition is this? You're going the wrong way for Jerusalem!'

So I tell her. Salome and Susannah crowd round her and confirm everything I say. She looks at Anna who's said nothing so far.

'Well, my lovely little bride-to-be, so you're venturing on this exciting trip as well rather than staying at home to get everything ready for your wedding. Have you finished all the preparations already?'

'No, not yet.' Anna blushes and looks down.

'But she pleaded to come. She's always loved her uncle and hopes we can persuade him to come back home and reveal himself as Messiah and prophet and stop all the silly opposition. I'm sure she still has plenty of time to complete her wedding preparations.'

'Of course. I didn't mean to criticise her. I think it admirable that she wants to see him for herself. And that brings me to my own view. I'd like to join you – may I?'

'Of course, Rebecca. You can share my tent. I'd love to have your company. What about Nathan – do you think he'd join us too?'

'I'll ask him, but I fear it may be a bit short notice. He's got family responsibilities now and I suspect he'll be reluctant to leave his farming activities to others, even for a short absence. But I'm longing to see your son in action. Ever since you confided in us children in the fields, I've always been curious about Joshua and the claims you made for him and now it all seems to be happening, I hear…'

'What have you heard?'

'That he's a great prophet, that he's attracting hundreds of followers, of course. Why, haven't you heard?'

'How do you know all this?'

'I thought everyone knew. It's common knowledge in Magdala and other villages round the lake.'

'And do your children believe all they've heard?' I turn to Susannah. 'And what about your boys? I've never heard Reuben express a clear opinion, although he's aware of the rumours about Joshua as he hears them from his visits in Sepphoris.'

'Well, we've discussed it, of course,' answers Susannah. 'I wouldn't say they're believers as they've not been to hear him. They think it interesting, though, and tell me everything they learn about him from those who've seen him in action. They find his healing work most praiseworthy but I've heard them express doubts about some of the things he says. They say he sometimes appears to forgive people who confess their misdeeds. I'm not sure about that – I thought that was something only the Lord God can do. But perhaps he's been misreported. It's easy to get details like that wrong.' Rebecca is listening with great interest.

'That's similar to the rumours I hear around here.'

'Well, Rebecca, why don't you come with us? We'll find out at first hand exactly what he does say and do. We'll hear it from his own lips.'

And so, next day we set out, now thirteen of us – with nearly half of us now believers in my son's mission and deeds. We travel downhill on the highway leading into Magdala and buy provisions for the next leg of our journey, including fish fresh from the market by the harbour. I love it here. While the men barter for our provisions, Anna, Susannah and I sit on the harbour wall and watch the fishing boats going in and out.

The lake shimmers in the heat, I have to shade my eyes from the glare. It's over thirty years since I've seen this lake on that fateful trip to see my father in the caves high up in the cliffs. Here it seems friendlier, the water is calm, lapping placidly against the wooden stumps to which several fishing boats are moored. I tell Anna and Susannah about the harbour in Alexandria and the huge ocean-going boats I saw there coming in under the lighthouse from Rome and Athens and other exotic places. I'm afraid I'm making Anna envious, so I have to remind her it's not always quite so simple – not when you're a refugee as I was, anyway.

The men with Salome and Rebecca come back with ample provisions from the market and we make our way out of the town and by nightfall we've nearly reached Capernaum. We stay in sight of the lake all the way. There is action to see all the time – sails catching the glow from the western sun, setting behind us as we veer eastwards along the northern shore. We eat a satisfying meal by the waterside. The tents are grouped in a circle and the cool of the evening is pleasant despite a plague of gnats that pester us for a while until darkness falls. I'm happy now. We seem at last to be a real family group. James has not voiced his views nor have Clopas's sons, so there's no arguing or bickering. It's been a long time since I've felt so relaxed.

I get up early in the morning and wash myself in the lake. I watch the sunrise over the low hills on the far side. They're so clear in this early morning light. The pink reflections glisten in the water hurting my eyes if I stare at them for too long. Then my sisters join me and give me a hug. We sit and chat about the time when we were children playing at the well or in the fields.

'Come on, Mari,' they say. 'Tell us one of your stories you were so good at making up!'

'Oh, I can't remember any now. That was so long ago. I don't need to invent stories when my life has been so extraordinary. If you really want some good stories, you'd better ask Joshua when we see him. They say he tells wonderful stories now. He always did entertain children in the village with his tales, but they say he gives much of his message in riddles and down to earth examples from our everyday life.'

Anna and Susannah join us for a while, before we decide that we'd better prepare something for our breakfast otherwise the men will soon be complaining. We've bought plenty of bread and have the fish we purchased in Magdala. There's no harm in eating it all now, as I'm sure we can get a new supply in Capernaum as fishing is said to be its main occupation.

As we begin to move off towards the town, which we can see nestling on the shoreline about a couple of miles away, we spot half a dozen small fishing boats making their way towards Capernaum's small harbour. They've obviously been out all night. I wonder how much they've caught. We should just about be in time to buy fish from the night's catch.

When we approach the town, I notice a number of people looking at us – they seem to be a little alarmed. I realise that we must seem quite a crowd of strangers and cause some curiosity although I'm sure we can't look threatening. Anyway, one of the men we pass as we reach the first houses of the village calls out to us and asks us our business. Benjamin answers that we're Joshua's family from Nazareth and have come to look for him. The man then grins broadly and comes over and clasps Ben firmly on the shoulder.

'Welcome, friend. You'll find many here who will tell you everything you need to know and help you search for the prophet. He can't be far away. Many of our men and even some of the women have followed him. But talk to the ordinary people. Don't bother to ask the priests and the clever ones. They pretend they're not interested in what Yeshua has to say.'

'Yeshua?' I wasn't sure if I'd heard right. The man's voice was rough, a stronger Galilean accent than in our village.

'Yes, you mean Yeshua, don't you? The prophet from Nazareth.'

So he's even changed his name from that which we used at home. I know his real name was that, but we've all called him Joshua all his life. Has he wanted to signify a complete break from us? I don't know why, but I feel a little disappointed at this. It's such a small thing, but perhaps it signifies something I'd rather not accept.

We confirm that it must be the man we're seeking.

'You must look for Simon's house. It's one of the fisher cottages down by the shore in the centre of the town, you can't miss it. Everyone knows Simon. You won't find him there at the moment, he's a friend of your Yeshua, but his family will know where he is, I'm sure of it.'

'Simon's house? Is he a fisherman?'

'Oh yes. Everyone knows Simon. Big man, loud, speaks first, thinks afterwards, but a great heart. If you ever needed it, Simon'd give you the last shirt on his back. His family are the same. You'll find Rachel, his wife, at home with the kids. Ask anyone, they'll direct you to the house. And Rachel will welcome you, although you're a bit too many to expect her to feed you. She'll be most put out that she can't look after you all. She's used to feeding a crowd because Simon brings Yeshua home with all their friends. A right houseful that is, I can tell you.'

So we enter the town around mid-morning. There is a bustling everywhere, the market is at its height with animals mingling with the people going about their business. You can tell it's a fishing village for there are many stalls selling fresh fish and the smell pervades the market. Ben enquires the whereabouts of Simon's house from one of the fish stallholders and we are directed down the gentle slope towards the lake shore, from the open square and the synagogue into the narrow streets that wind between small cottages that apparently belong mostly to the town's fishermen. We stop outside one of the bigger cottages.

'I think this is the one,' says my brother. We look at it but it appears to be shut up. 'We can't all appear at the door, it'll make whoever is there nervous. Why don't you and Salome knock and tell whoever answers who we are and what we're seeking?'

So I knock on the wooden door and at first there is no response. But I think I can hear movement in the yard behind the house, so I knock louder. I hear footsteps and the door is drawn half back and a woman's face appears and gapes at me. Then she opens the door wider and I see a dark haired woman of around thirty years of age, holding a toddler. Behind her in the darkness I can see the silhouette of a couple of young girls who come forward shyly to peer at me. She looks at me quizzically.

'Are you Simon's wife? It's been suggested that we make contact with you.'

'Who are you?' she asks quickly before I can introduce myself. She hands the small child to one of the girls, presumably his sister.

'My name is Mariam and this is my sister, Salome. We're here with our family from Nazareth. We're looking for my son, Joshua. I'm told you know him and might be able to tell us where we can find him.'

'Joshua? Oh, you mean Yeshua, the rabbi, do you? The miracle-worker from Nazareth?'

'Yes, that'll be him. I understand he lives here in this town although he travels around this area teaching and preaching. Do you know where he is now?'

'My husband Simon will be with'im at the moment but I don't know exactly where'e is. You better come in. Rhoda', she says turning to the girl nearest her, 'go 'n fetch cups and the water jar. These people'll be thirsty. Oh, by the way, I'm Rachel. My husband's a friend and follower of your son.'

'Don't put yourself to any trouble, Rachel. We're a crowd. My other sister, brother and my children are all with me. Just tell me where you think I might find Yeshua and your husband and we'll all be on our way.'

'Nonsense, you're all welcome if you're Yeshua's family. You can all come in, it'll be a bit'a squash, but as long as you don't mind...' She flings the door wide open and beckons the rest in who have been waiting in the street a few cottages back.

The cottage reeks of fish and I see James wrinkle his nose as he enters the dimly lit room, for there's only one small window through which the sun's rays slant. Rachel disappears for a moment and we squat on the floor as best we can in the confined space. Rhoda has lugged a large water pot in and has gone back to get some cups, then Rachel reappears with a loaf of bread.

'This is all I got, I'm afraid, but if you wait for a minute, I'll slip out to the market and get some fresh fish for you.'

'Rachel, please, there's no need. We'll be stocking up in the market before we leave Capernaum if Yeshua is any distance away. A drink of water will be welcome, but that's quite sufficient.'

The woman makes to protest further, but gives way when the men back me up and then concentrates on making sure her two daughters hand out the water without spilling any. When we've made ourselves comfortable and drained our cups, I repeat my request about Yeshua's whereabouts.

'Why, is anything wrong?' We've aroused her curiosity.

'No, but we want to find him. We hear so many rumours of all he is doing and saying that we want to see for ourselves.'

'Oh, 'e's doing everything that's rumoured and more. My Simon and his brother are so impressed that they're following 'im everywhere. And some of the other fishermen, they've gone too. It was a problem at first as two boats lost their main crews and we 'ad to rely on hired help. But ole man Zebedee, 'e sorted that out for us, so we can manage though I'd like it if my husband was around more than 'e is. The children miss their dad. Does Yeshua 'ave 'is own family? 'E's never mentioned one.'

'Do you know him well? It's just Yeshua, he's never married. But he has four brothers and two sisters, all with wives and husbands and many children. We've left most of the younger generation at home, but we're curious to see him.'

'Well, Yeshua stayed 'ere with us last month. 'E was in the synagogue every day speaking to crowds – not just from 'ere. Many came from other villages around to hear 'im, and some brought sick people for healing. I think most came 'cos they was curious and wanted to see 'im healing people. In the end 'e got very tired and went into the hills behind the town to rest and be alone. Simon went back to fishing for a few days, then when 'e returned, Yeshua was all fired up and wanted to be on the move. That was a good month ago, as I said. I 'aven't seen them since then, but they went off to the east towards Bethsaida and I wouldn't be surprised if you'd find them there. That's the best advice I can give you. One of the disciples of the rabbi came home briefly last week and said they were still in the smaller villages around Bethsaida. So I'd start looking there if I was you.'

It is clear that Rachel has said as much as she can to help us. She offers us another drink and again presses us to have a meal with her, but we want to get on our way and find Joshua, today if possible, although I think we'll probably need a further night's camping before we can find him.

We eventually make our farewells to this hospitable woman and continue eastwards along the shoreline, watching the fishermen who are checking their nets after the night's catch.

James is busy grumbling to his cousins, James and Jude, and I catch some of his grouse. Trust James to be critical. I hear what seems like some disparaging remarks about the woman who has just been so helpful to us. He didn't like her accent and thinks the fishermen's cottages dirty and smelly. I thought her home was spotless although I grant that the fishy aroma was strong. I guess if you're married to a fisherman you soon get used to it. But I know what he is thinking. He is again judging Joshua by the company he keeps. He thinks he ought to be mixing with rabbis and teachers in Jerusalem, rather than with what he calls the common folk here. I don't think that he looks down on such people but he doesn't believe in a Messiah who disregards the most learned and religious. And that they clearly aren't. It's odd the way James seems to split his mind. On the one hand he doesn't believe Joshua is the Messiah. And on the other, he expects him to behave as though he thinks the Messiah would. When I tackle him on this, he says that if Joshua were to spend his time with the authorities and religious high-ups in Jerusalem, then perhaps he'd believe Joshua's calling, but when Joshua did just that in the Temple and with John out in the Wilderness, he rejected him and his arguments completely. I just don't understand my son. How can he be so different? When he was small, he and Joshua used to play so happily together – James always wanted to do everything that Joshua did. Now look at them!

Chapter 16
Mari

We arrived in Bethsaida on the far bank of the Jordan River in the late afternoon and after the men erected the tents on the outskirts of the town, Salome and Rebecca prepared the evening meal using the fish and bread we'd bought in Capernaum. The tents were ready long before the meal, so my twins, Simon and Judas, offered to go into the town and see if they could discover Joshua's whereabouts. I thought they must have found him for they were gone much longer than I expected, but when they eventually returned, they said that he'd left Bethsaida a couple of days earlier to tour the villages on the far side. They'd been directed at first down to the little harbour as apparently Joshua and his friends had arrived on a fishing vessel belonging to Simon and his brother. They'd found the boat moored there, but it was deserted. A fisherman on another boat shouted that they'd been sleeping overnight on the vessel until a couple of nights previously and he'd heard one of the men say they'd be away for a few days as they were planning to go to some of the outlying tiny villages. Apparently he'd added that we'd soon find them as half the population of the town seemed to have abandoned their normal activities in order to see this new celebrity.

So we settled for the night and set out the following morning. Several people confirmed as we wound our way through the town that the rabbi and his disciples had turned towards the inland villages north east of their town and we were pointed to the track where everyone said they'd gone. We could see a lot of confirming evidence for the track was very dusty and crops at the edge of the fields flattened as though trampled by a herd of bullocks. We came across our first village and it was nearly deserted. There were a few old people and a couple of young women with babes in arms, but everyone else had disappeared. 'They've all gone to see the miracle man' was the response we got from everyone we spoke to.

We saw them in the early afternoon. We'd stopped for an hour to rest in the shade of an olive grove when the sun was at its highest and as we breasted the brow of a low hill, we saw them. We were astounded. The hill on the other side of the valley was black with people, hundreds, if not thousands. There must have been half the population of Bethsaida there as well as folk from all the surrounding villages. I could see it stopped James in his tracks. At least that's proof that many are taking him seriously. We continued down to the valley floor with renewed vigour, our goal now in sight. We could hear his voice above the hum of the crowd although for sometime we could not distinguish all the words he spoke, only catching an occasional one. Anna was skipping on ahead – she forgets that I'm not as young as I used to be. Susannah and I were content to bring up the rear along with Benjamin whose leg gives him quite a lot of pain these days.

Anyway, we eventually reach the edge of the crowd. There's no obvious way we can move through the throng to get to Joshua and I suggest we wait until he's finished speaking and the crowd disperses, but James and others are impatient.

'That could be a long time,' says Judas. 'Come, brother, we'll find a way through and tell him we're here. He'll finish then and send the crowd away – they'll need to get back home to prepare their evening meals soon.'

So I watch Judas and his twin, Simon, weaving their way between the men and women sprawled out on the grassy hillside listening to Joshua. I'm getting a bit deaf and still can't hear everything he's saying, but I think I get the gist. People are calling out questions – I can't hear what they're asking but I do hear most of his answers. Someone must have just asked him about a family quarrel, for he's talking about the need to forgive each other.

'How often?' I hear someone yell out very loudly. He's obviously getting fed up with one of his relatives or acquaintances. Then I miss the rest of the sentence when the man drops his voice.

'Seventy times seven,' says Joshua loudly and I see some startled faces round me. If he means that much then he must mean we must always forgive for no-one will keep a tally that long. Then he goes on to talk about the need to live at peace with our families and neighbours and starts telling a story about a man who owes a lot of money, but is let off and promptly demands the repayment of a much smaller loan from someone else who pleads to be forgiven. He seems to have started quite a lot of discussion because everyone round me starts arguing about whether the second man was within his rights or whether he now had a moral obligation to be equally generous. It's fascinating to watch how Joshua engages the crowd in what is now a real dialogue. He's getting them to answer their own questions, although he's gently nudging them in the direction he has planned. He's very different from our rabbis, even Joel, who even when they encourage questions, expect to be the absolute authority to give the answer. And the answer is usually a quotation from the scriptures, rarely their own words.

I can see Simon and Judas have reached the group of men standing next to Joshua – I guess they must be some of the so-called disciples or friends from Capernaum. Joshua breaks off from his discourse when one of them comes forward and whispers something to him. He suddenly raises his voice.

'Friends,' he declaims in an echoing voice, 'I'm told members of my family are here and wish to see me. But why should they have priority? You are all members of my family if you listen to what I'm saying and obey my words. You are my brothers, sisters, mothers, children if you do the will of my Father above.'

And then he carried on with the story he was in the middle of telling when he was interrupted.

'Hell and damnation,' exclaims James. He is furious. 'The man's publicly snubbing us. How dare he! We're his own family and he's rejecting us. That's it. I've heard and seen enough. The man's no respect for us whatsoever. There's no point in waiting any longer. I'm off home.'

Cousins James and Jude look equally angry though they're not saying anything at present. The others are looking bemused. I feel hurt too. That was a very humiliating thing for him to say in front of these thousands of people. Everyone is looking round to see if they can spot us. People near us are looking at us because they heard James's outburst. Others are watching where Simon and Judas are going for most have picked up that they were members of the family who'd approached the friends standing round Joshua. All in my family are looking at me, waiting for my reaction. I try to think of something to stop James's anger, to soften what he is saying.

'I don't know what to say,' I stammer. 'I'm sure he didn't mean it as a snub. We'll have to ask him why he said it later.' I can feel tears coming to my eyes and I turn away for I don't want the others to see how upset I am.

'What makes you think he'll see us later?' says James. 'You heard what he said. He thinks everyone's his family. We're no more important to him than anyone else. So much for gratitude. I don't know why you try to defend him seeing all you've been through on his behalf. He's an ungrateful bastard and he doesn't deserve you.'

Rebecca and Salome both come and give me a hug.

'Don't listen to him, Mari,' says Rebecca. He doesn't know what he's talking about. I'm sure Joshua didn't mean to hurt us. He didn't say we were not important. He just said everyone else is equally important.'

'Rubbish!' interjects Jude. What he said was quite clear. He doesn't want us. So much for coming all this way. It's been a complete waste of time.'

Then there is further embarrassment. The people around us are looking at us and some are shaking their heads. Then someone shouts out,

'Will you lot over there be quiet? We're trying to hear what the rabbi's saying and I can't hear a word with all your noise.'

Then it gets more embarrassing still when others turn round and 'shush' us and a couple call out 'hear, hear!'

We get up and retreat to the edge of the crowd. Then I notice Anna is crying. I go over to her, no-one else seems to have noticed. I was about to ask her what the matter was, then I realise that's a foolish question, so I just squeeze her wrist.

'Don't cry, love. Let's wait for Simon and Judas to come back. Perhaps he said something different to them.'

She doesn't say anything but rubs her eyes and tries to look as though she's not been weeping. We all gather at the edge of the crowd and wait for my two sons to rejoin us. No-one is listening to what Joshua is still saying, we're too preoccupied with our own thoughts. As far as I'm concerned, we're out of earshot. All I know is that Joshua is still in full flow and is holding the attention of most of the audience – well all of them in fact, other than the small group around us who've been distracted by our presence and raised voices.

Simon and Judas eventually stumble out of the seated bodies listening to Joshua and we crowd round them.

'What did he say to you?' About three voices simultaneously ask the same question including mine.

'He didn't say anything to us,' answers Judas. 'We never got to him. We were stopped by a couple of his burly friends. From their accent and smell, I guess they were his fishermen friends.'

'We asked one of them to take a message and say that we were here and would like to speak with him. The big one, I think it's Simon, said he would and then you heard what Joshua said.'

'They wouldn't let us any nearer. I asked if we could speak to Joshua himself, after all we are his closest relatives. But the man came back and said, 'No way, not at the moment. Not now anyway'. So we had to turn back.'

'Might he see us later?' I say hopefully.

'Perhaps,' says Simon. 'Joshua's friends said we were interrupting. He was talking to a huge crowd who'd come many miles to see him, and that we were rude to expect him to break off and send everyone home. We were told to wait.'

'Did Joshua say that himself?' says Ben.

'No, one of his disciples passed the message on. I don't know if Joshua said that or whether it was the man's own idea.'

'So let's wait and see,' I say with some relief. 'Perhaps Joshua will come and find us when everyone's gone home.'

'Well, prepare to stay all night,' says James angrily. 'Heaven knows when this lot will have had enough and be willing to go home. They won't unless they get too hungry. Then they'll go, but that could be hours.'

So we congregate at the edge of the grassland adjacent to a field of wheat. Despite James and Clopas's sons being fed up and wanting to go, the rest of us persuade them to wait. After all, we've got to camp somewhere and it might as well be here as anywhere else. So we wait. We've brought food with us and the men find some skins of wine and gradually their bad temper is assuaged. Benjamin and Andrew, Salome's husband, have said little, but seem happy enough to wait for Joshua and see what he has to say. I do hope he comes and doesn't let us down. If he goes away with his new friends without looking for us I'll know he really has washed his hands of us and that'll break my heart. And Anna's too, I

182

think, as I watch her. She's said nothing more and just looks a bit solemn.

I begin to think the crowd will never go home. I think Joshua has stopped talking to them, but although some are drifting off, most are clustering around him. I don't know what he's doing. Then I hear someone say that there's a queue of people asking him for help – people who've been carried here by friends, others who have walked but have a sickness or injury they think Joshua can cure. The sun is going down and we've finished our meal before the crowd eventually disperses and I see Joshua coming our way flanked by about four of his disciples.

But it was Anna who saw him coming first. She'd obviously been watching and she suddenly shoots off. When Joshua sees her he opens his arms and envelopes her as she flings herself at him, gives her a hug and puts his arm protectively round her as she leads him to where we are camped. He walks into the centre of our camp, noticing the embers of our fire.

'Anyone got anything to eat? I'm famished.'

To be honest, we've eaten nearly all our provisions. All the fish is gone. I find a few hunks of bread and luckily we still have some wine. I should have thought of making sure something was left for him, but I'd begun to think like my sons that he wasn't coming. And then he gives some of the bread to his friends. Presumably they've been here all day without any food either. Surely they know what to expect by now? I find another couple of cups, swill them out with the remaining water and drain our supply of wine. I know what James is thinking but I refuse to look at him. He's had his fill and he doesn't need any more. We can buy more food and wine tomorrow back in Bethsaida.

'Where are you staying tonight?'

'I thought you wanted me to stay with you, so here I am. I'm used to sleeping in the open air. I don't need a tent.'

'What about your companions?'

183

'They'll make do, the same as me. They're used to my ways. Anyway, they're fishermen. They're accustomed to staying out all night on the lake, so sleeping rough is no hardship for them.'

I don't know whether I should challenge Joshua about what he said earlier. He seems to be at ease now as though totally ignorant of any slight he may have caused. He can't have meant anything by it. I don't want to risk spoiling the atmosphere by raising the hurt he's caused, he must have just been thoughtless. Then of course, James jumps in, both feet first.

'So why did you humiliate us in front of the crowd? Why did you make us wait? Why did you reject us as your family?'

'I didn't reject you, James. I'm here now. And I've brought my friends with me to meet you. This is Peter – we've renamed him. There are too many 'Simons' round here, it gets very confusing and so we chose a name that suits his character. And his brother Andrew and these are John and James – another James – they're the sons of Zebedee who owns many of the fishing vessels in Capernaum.'

'But you snubbed us when we said we were here and wanted to see you.'

'I got your message. Andrew told me. But couldn't you see I was in the middle of talking to hundreds of men and women? What did you expect me to do? Did you think I'd leave everyone there and come over to see you? Surely you knew I wouldn't do that? They've come from their villages especially to see and hear me. Surely you could wait until they'd gone home. I told Andrew I'd see you later.'

'But we'd come specially to see you too – we've come all the way from Nazareth, farther than any of those here, I'm sure.'

'But I knew you'd be staying near here, whereas the men and women in the crowd would have to go back to their villages to cook their meals and put their children to bed. And, what's more, many had brought their sick. I couldn't leave them suffering, could I, while I came to eat with you?'

'I understand what you're saying – although I didn't hear Andrew say you'd see us later.' My son, Simon, has spoken up. 'But why did you have to tell the crowd that they were your family, that they were more important than us. That's what really hurt.'

'I didn't say they were more important. They're equal. God values all of us. He values you, he values every single one of the crowd sitting on the hillside. He values the women, he values the children just as much. Therefore, if they are ready to reject the sins of their past lives and try to follow the principles I'm sharing with them, they're God's children, just as you and I are. That makes us all brothers and sisters together, doesn't it?'

'But we're your family, your real family. You should put us first!' James won't let it go.

Joshua looks at him. He shakes his head slowly and just says 'James!'

James looks sheepish and mutters under his breath, but he refrains from arguing further. I feel like pointing out to James that it's not long ago that he was declaring that Joshua no longer belonged to our family, but I keep quiet as there's no point in reminding James of his inconsistency. He doesn't see it. He's not thinking straight but is allowing his emotions to gain the upper hand. I think underneath that he's actually jealous of Joshua but he won't admit it.

We stay talking for a while. Anna is asking him questions which he is answering patiently and Susannah is hanging on his every word. The men are indignant that he's wasting his time talking to the women when he should be giving them more attention. Well, I sense some of them are. Benjamin doesn't seem bothered and seems proud that his daughter has restored her spirits and is getting Joshua to take her questions seriously. John, I see, has joined our menfolk and is busy describing all that Joshua has been doing since arriving in Bethsaida. I think he has a task on his hands if he is seeking to convince them though to be fair, they are listening. Eventually people gradually drift away. The disciples go back to join their other friends – I gather there must be around ten or twelve of them who seem to be Joshua's closest companions. Then Salome and Rebecca say they're tired. Ben persuades Anna finally to let Joshua go and Susannah leads her back to one of the women's tents. And all of a sudden I find I'm alone with Joshua.

'Well, Mother? Were you upset as well? I didn't mean to hurt you, I wanted to drive home to those listening how important to God they are. Most of them are poor farmers. They don't understand their worth. They need to value themselves. I tell them all to love God and love their fellow human beings as much as themselves, but that's not very helpful if they count themselves to be of little value. And the women and children are just as important. You ought to know that. You know how much God valued you. You were no older than Anna here when he chose you for something momentous. But you've always known that you were special to God. I need to make these people feel special too.'

I don't argue with him. I sense he is saying something that's very important to him. I wait for him to go on, but he has fallen silent. Perhaps he is expecting me to say something.

'Joshua, are you going to come back to Nazareth at all? Are you going to give us all a second chance?'

Joshua considers what I've said for a long time.

'Will it be any different, Mother? I can't operate in an atmosphere of unbelief. And if I say things that offend our good villagers, it can't make your life very easy.'

'I don't know, son. I can't promise anything. I'd really love you to come home – well, at least spend some time with us. I don't see why people can't accept you just as these villages here obviously do.'

'Well, as you saw before, you know how hard it is for them. As they said, they've known me all their lives. Well, perhaps they think they know me. It's asking a lot from them especially after the last experience.'

'You're not afraid of what they might do to you, are you?'

'No, Mother, I'm not afraid. It's not that at all.'

'Well, then, will you consider it?'

'Leave me to think it over. I'll pray about it. I've been thinking for sometime that I need to send my friends out on their own. They need to learn that they don't need me to do everything. They should be capable of telling others about God's kingdom and healing the sick just as I do.'

'Surely they can't do that? You've learned much with the Essenes. They haven't your experience and knowledge.'

'They could do it if they had the belief and confidence. I've got to give them the opportunity to try sometime. If I came to stay with you, perhaps that's an opportunity for me to really test them. I'll think about it. I'm not promising though. I need to learn God's will, not my will or even yours.'

'I think we'd better get some sleep. It's late. You've had a long day and the crowds must tire you. Your voice must be strained after having to shout all day.'

'In a while, Mother. I need to pray first. That's where I get my rest and power from. I'll think about what you say and entrust it to my Father's will. I'm sure there'll be a sign that will convince me of what is right.'

I give up. He must be shattered and I can't understand why he can't get some rest straight away. But he must know best. I'm tired and I'm going to lie down now, whatever he does. I can keep my eyes open no longer.

*   *   *

When I awake in the morning I realise he's not here. The men are already up and about, someone's feeding the asses and Anna has gone with Rebecca to fetch water. There's only a little bread for breakfast. I'll go into the nearest village and replenish our supplies. Hopefully we can get some grapes and figs to augment our bread, then we can get more fish and wine when we're back in Bethsaida. Then I see Joshua walking down the track towards us. And Anna and Rebecca are coming too – their paths will cross in a minute.

Joshua has brought bread, olives and grapes. I don't know where he got them from – I didn't ask. Anna skips up to me.

'He's going to come back with us, he says he will.' She's really excited.

'Yes,' he says, when he reaches me. 'This young lady has convinced me. I was still uncertain, waiting for a sign from God and the first words I hear on returning to you this morning are Anna's, saying "When are you coming home to us?" So there's my answer. I'll come. We may all be disappointed, but I'll take the risk. Anna believes in me and I'll not let her down.'

When the others realise that he's returning with us, there is some surprise. James, having criticised Joshua for not coming home, is now worried that his presence will put us all in danger. Some of the other men are dubious. 'Why is he listening to Anna?' is on their lips.

'I'll follow you. I need to talk to my followers. When you get as far as Capernaum, camp there for a while. Simon Peter's wife Rachel and John's mother will make sure you're provided with everything you need, I'm sure of that. I'll go back by boat. We need to get it back to Capernaum and I need to talk to my disciples and discuss the mission I have in mind for them. They need to talk it over with their families too. Then, when I'm sure they've grasped what I intend them all to do, I'll join you and we can go back to Nazareth together. We'll spend a day or two in Magdala. There's a good friend I'd like you to meet there, you'll like her, I'm sure.'

So we're on our way home. We're giving him another chance. Or rather, I think he's giving us another chance. Let's see if this time we can recognise who he is and what he can do if we let him.

Chapter 17
Mari

This is the first time I've ever been on a boat. Forty five years and the only time I've been in water was when I lay in the stream at the stranger's request when I was thirteen years old. I'm rather nervous about this, it seems such a little boat and the lake is so large. We're out in the middle of the water now, the shore seems so far away. At least the water is calm, reflecting the blue of the cloudless sky. Joshua had told me not to worry when he saw how fearful I was as he helped me into the boat. He said that he and his friends used the fishing boats of Simon Peter and John frequently as it was the best way of moving swiftly round the villages on the lake shoreline.

'You'll be fine today,' he says. 'Sometimes when the wind gets up it can seem a little choppy and it might make you feel queasy. One night we got caught by a sudden storm that we didn't see coming and even these hardy fishermen were scared that we were going to sink, but the storm suddenly abated and we made the shore safely. But it's bright and very calm today – look, there's hardly a breath of wind. That means our journey will be a bit slow but you can lie back and rest. Keep your shawl over your head and shoulders though. The sun's strong and can burn you quickly out here. The fishermen are used to it, you can see how tanned they are, but your skin will burn.'

Anna's really excited. She's kneeling at the front bending over the side of the boat trailing her hands in the water. I'm worried that she might fall in but Joshua tells me that she was quite safe – she is chattering to the burly Simon Peter, whose boat this is, and Joshua says he'll make sure she comes to no harm. Joshua spends a lot of the journey talking to him and his brother Andrew, for they are apparently going to spend some time in Magdala and other villages in the area while Joshua is back home with us. His followers have been told to split up and go to all the towns and villages around the lake telling everyone about the coming 'Kingdom of God', the same message that Joshua had told us in the synagogue in Nazareth and that he'd instructed them about, so they could answer questions from the crowds as well as speak with confidence. I can tell that Simon Peter is keen to get on with it and is finding the slow progress of our boat frustrating. I'm not so sure about his brother. He seems a little overawed by what he's been told to do and I think is only too happy to let Simon take the lead.

Around noon it is so still that the sails go completely slack and we are almost stationary. Simon shouts that we'll need to get out the oars and row. My Simon and Judas and Salome's husband Andrew immediately get up and offer to help, and Simon again shouts and James, and my two cousins James and Jude break off the whispered conversation they are having at the back of the boat. And, reluctantly, I think, take an oar each.

'Anyone of you townies ever rowed before?' calls Simon and all of them shake their heads. 'In that case I think just a couple of you need to help – Andrew and I are used to it. You lot will just hinder us. If too many of you have not rowed before we'll get in a damned muddle and finish up going round in bloody circles. If Judas here and Andrew' – he looks at Salome's husband who is taller than the others – 'take a turn now, others can take over when they need a rest.'

Joshua picks up an oar. 'Simon, brother, I'll take your place. I'm more used to it than you. I've taken my turn from time to time, although the fishermen usually protest when I do.'

'Quite bloody right too, Master,' shouts Simon Peter. 'There's never been any need for you to row when all the fishermen are much more used to it. You stick to what you're good at and we'll do what we do best.'

'You see, Mother,' he says, 'they don't think I'm any good at it. But I'm strong enough – all of us who've worked in the carpentry shop have muscles enough though these brutes here don't think so. Anyway,' he says turning to his younger brother, 'I'm more used to it than you. I'll join Salome's husband and between us I'm sure we can give some support to the captain and his brother there and keep the boat heading in the right direction.'

They row for a good hour before a slight breeze begins to stir us coming across the lake from the Perean shore. I see the sails begin to fill out and the men let their oars hover for a moment to check the boat continues to move forwards. Satisfied they stow the oars and lounge against the side of the boat while Simon Peter adjusts the sails to take full advantage of what wind there is. My two sisters have actually fallen asleep. Anna is still alert taking it all in, pointing to distant villages and asking her father to identify them which he is trying to do, though occasionally he asks one of the fishermen. Then Joshua joins them and takes over as he knows the geography of the lake in as much detail as the fishing folk do. He points out a shoal of fish he can see for the water is so clear and Anna watches them fascinated as they move in one direction parallel to the boat then suddenly veer off in unison as if someone had issued a military command.

Magdala is a large town and I can see distinct houses and other buildings now as we get closer. It's a bit hazy, the town shimmers in the heat and the whiteness of a larger building stands out – Joshua says it's the largest synagogue in the town. He comes over and sits beside me.

'Mother, when we make harbour, I'll lead you all to the little house of my friend Mariam who was born in this town though she lived for a while in Jerusalem where I met her a couple of years ago. I was able to do something for her then and she came back to live in her home town. She's been so grateful, that she always opens up her home to me and my followers when we are in this neighbourhood. Her house is too small to take all of us, but I'm sure she'll house you and the other women. The men have tents and I'll join them.'

'How did you get to know her? What did you do that makes her so grateful to you?'

'It doesn't matter, Mother. She had certain problems. Some things are best kept confidential. She's changed her life completely and I'm sure you'll like her and will find her a good friend.'

We are now entering the harbour. Joshua is helping Simon Peter and Andrew thread their way through the myriad other vessels, some with nets down, others anchored and a few already moored at the dockside. All other conversation ceases and all the men are now alert, watching the activity with interest. We are apparently going to tie up here, leaving the boat for Simon Peter and his brother when they've finished their mission in the area. Joshua has told them to sail back to Capernaum afterwards and he's promised to join them there to get their report on how they'd fared.

James has said absolutely nothing to me since Joshua joined us on the journey home. I don't know what he is thinking. He seems deliberately to have had as little to do with his elder brother as possible and has confined his conversation to James and Jude and occasionally to Andrew. He's said nothing to any of us women. I know Ben has found the lake crossing much easier on his bad leg than the tramp around the lake edge though he did ride one of the donkeys when his leg pained him too much. We left both beasts in Capernaum on our return there and Joshua gave them to the charge of a couple of his other followers who were going to bring them to Magdala and leave them for the continuation of our journey before they branched off inland towards Kana and villages further north.

Simon Peter and Andrew secure the boat and make sure their fishing equipment is stowed away, sheeted and roped. We walk past the hubbub of movement on the dockside – men unloading fish, even at this hour, others selling them by the quayside, merchants bartering, officials checking the catches, apparently to assess the taxes for the Romans. The smell of the fish is overpowering and I'm glad when we move into the town away from the lake, though this town has an unpleasant odour in the heat. I can see the problem. There are open ditches where sewage is dribbling. In our village such refuse and mess is removed outside the village. People here, at least in the poorer areas, do not seem so fussy. Then, as we get further from the lakeside, the air seems purer and the streets are wider and clean and we pass the large synagogue we could see from the boat. There is an open square and a number of impressive colonnaded buildings around it, and we branch off it down a narrower street and walk for a further twenty minutes or so until I think we must be reaching the edge of the town.

'Nearly there,' I hear Joshua tell Anna who has been walking with him all the way. I've been with Salome and Rebecca and for the first time since we saw Joshua in the flesh working with the crowds, we are able, without interruption, to share our views of all we've seen.

They're believers, both of them. Of course, they've been privy to all my secrets since we were children. They shared in the excitement of my pregnancy, though they didn't realise all the ramifications it raised at the time. They tell me they don't talk about Joshua too openly for their husbands are sceptics and neither has wanted to stir up controversy within the family. But with me, they are open and quiz me about everything that Joshua is doing. I wish I could tell them more because most of the spectacular things he says and does only reach me by hearsay. We are interrupted though, because we've arrived at Mariam's house. She's seen us coming and is waiting at her threshold. As soon as we are near she rushes forward and greets Joshua, then stops and looks at all of us.

She is a striking woman. I suppose she must be in her late twenties. She is quite tall, taller than me anyway, and my eyes are drawn to her unusual auburn hair which is flowing untrammelled by her loosely fastened and beautifully embroidered shawl. She doesn't look like a Jewish woman – perhaps she has some Roman or Gentile blood in her. At first I think her eyes look sad, but when she smiles they lighten and twinkle as if in mischief. I give her a smile and she responds immediately.

'You must be the Master's mother. It's a privilege and pleasure to know you. Come in, you must be weary from your journey. Come in, all of you and at least share a drink and bite of food. I was expecting some of you for the Master sent word on ahead through a couple of his followers who passed through here yesterday.'

Then she apologises for the inadequacy of her house to provide full hospitality. She needn't of course, for she is not wealthy and her home is spotlessly clean. After she has served us with bread and some grapes she moves to sit next to Joshua and immediately asks him how his latest stay in Capernaum and Bethsaida has gone. They are in animated conversation for some time, although I can't pick up everything they are saying for my sisters are talking too, then Anna joins us full of questions about the town for she's not been anywhere so big before. I sense some unspoken tension in the crowded room. Joshua's two followers are talking with James and Benjamin and I catch an occasional word which suggests to me that they resent this Mariam monopolising Joshua so much and are saying that he's too soft with her and lets her talk when she should be active in more womanly pursuits. I'm quick at picking such implicit criticism up, for I've had more than my share of muted comment in the past suggesting I was entering into areas that were the preserves of the men. I begin to feel that she must be a woman after my own heart. Perhaps, I suddenly think, seeing how intimate the conversation between

195

her and Joshua is, perhaps he will get married after all this time. Perhaps this woman is the companion and wife he needs. But, of course, I keep my views to myself. After all, I've only just met the woman and first impressions can be misleading.

After our meal the men move out and set up the tents on grazing land opposite causing the goats nibbling at the dusty grass to budge a little and find new fodder, meagre though it is. Joshua had been still in conversation, but Simon Peter interrupts him, a bit rudely in my opinion, and indicates it's time to leave the confines of the house. But they go and I ask Mariam if she wants any help.

'Goodness me, no, Mariam – may I call you that? I can sort out the house when you've moved on. There's no need for you to do anything, that's not a priority. Let's sit and chat. I'd like to get to know you all. The Master has said so much about you all to me.'

'Of course you can call me that, but most just call me Mari for short. And why do you all call my son 'Master'? He doesn't employ you in any way, does he?'

'No, he doesn't although I'd do anything he asked me to for nothing. Being near him is its own reward.'

'Why, what has he done that makes you such an admirer?'

'Let's just say that he met me when I was at my lowest ebb and helped me see my problems for what they were and gave me the confidence that I could overcome them. I truly owe my life to him, that is what I believe and I don't care who knows it.'

'Are you a follower of his?'

It's Anna who suddenly asks this question, one perhaps that had been hovering on our lips and Anna with the brashness of youth has come out with it.

'Yes, Anna, I believe I am, although I'm not sure his male followers agree with me on this. They call themselves his 'disciples' and they don't count me among their number,

196

because rabbis' disciples are always male. But the Master doesn't treat me any differently from them. And it's not just me. He is happy to talk to Simon Peter's wife and the wives and children of his other disciples on the same level. When he talks to the crowds he lets everyone come and ask questions or just thank him. Sometimes the disciples get quite irritated. They say they're trying to protect him but I really think they want him to themselves and he doesn't like being confined to a small group but opens himself to everyone.'

'We have the same problem in our family. Some of my sons resent him treating us no better than everyone else. They think because we're family he should give us priority.'

'What's more he takes the questions and comments of women and children seriously. That's more than the priests ever do in the synagogue. Last time I was in Capernaum he was talking to children and telling them stories and a couple of the disciples tried to shoo them away, but Yeshua took no notice. Then more children arrived, encouraged by their mothers and the disciples went to remonstrate, and Yeshua stopped them. He was very indignant, I've never heard him so cross before. Then he told them that unless they trusted God like these children trusted him, they'd never understand what he was on about. The disciples were quite upset at being told off so publicly. Yeshua made them wait a long time before he stopped talking to the children.'

'Yes, I can well believe that. He's always been popular with the children in our village.'

'He told me that he wished children never lost their trust and their idealism. We all have to be like children, he says. Be childlike. Sometimes the disciples think he's talking nonsense or in riddles and he has to explain what he means as if they were children. 'I think the children understand me better,' he said to me on one occasion!'

'Do the disciples let you join in with them or do they try to exclude you?'

I sense that Mariam is not as accepted as she'd like to be.

'They don't tell me to go away, but I can tell that they don't take me seriously. They tolerate me, I suppose, but if I try to express an opinion, they quickly make it plain that my views are worthless. But they wait until Yeshua is out of earshot because they know he would listen to me. They're not all the same, of course. I quite like John, he's one of the fishermen, but he's younger and easier to talk to. I think the Master finds him more open than some of the others to his new ideas.'

'What do you make of Simon Peter and his brother? My family wonders why my son chose such people as his closest companions when he was educated in rabbinical schools.'

'Simon's alright. He's a bit of a loudmouth but his heart is in the right place. At least you know what he thinks. If he doesn't like something, he comes out with it. We have arguments, but he doesn't bear any grudges. I know he comes from a village and community which just sees a woman's place is looking after the home and children and he's had difficulty in changing his views, but he tries to understand the Master's point of view and if Yeshua tells him to do something, he obeys. He's very loyal.'

'What about the others?'

'I trust Simon more than one or two of his other friends who say little to your face but I know resent my presence and that of the other women and complain behind our backs. There's a man called Matthew who used to be a notorious corrupt tax collector for the Romans. I know he's changed, but he reckons he knows all about politics and the business world and makes it plain that he doesn't expect me to understand. And then there's a guy called Judas, he's the group's treasurer, I find him a bit devious. I never know quite what he's thinking. Sometimes I think he just worries about the costs incurred of feeding all us women followers and it's no more than that. He's happy enough when one of us entertains the group at our expense. Then at other times he fancies himself as

198

the thinker in the group – he reckons he's more educated than any of them except the Master himself. He thinks it strange and undignified that I can read and write as well as he can. You can too, can't you? The Master told me that sometime. He's very proud of you.'

'Yes, I was lucky. One of the rabbis in the Nazareth synagogue said he saw my potential and educated me with his own daughter. I used to pass on what I'd learned to my sisters. And I know my brother Benjamin has taught Anna here to read and write and take an interest in more than an ordinary housewife needs to know. She's getting married soon. I hope her new husband will not stifle her interests.'

Later that evening I'm chatting with Rebecca while Salome and Anna have gone with Mariam to check that the men have everything they need.

'What do you make of this Mariam?' I ask my sister.

'I like her. She's an intelligent woman. But she could be quite dangerous. You can see she's in love with Joshua and I don't know what she might do if he rejects her.'

'What makes you think that? She's clearly very grateful to him for something, but in love?'

'Haven't you noticed how she looks at him? She's nearly thirty I guess. She needs a husband and I think she's set her heart on Joshua. I don't know if he's realised it. I think he's a bit naïve sometimes, he likes to think the best of everyone. I hope she doesn't betray his trust.'

'I'm sure Joshua's more astute than you give him credit for. I think he likes her and finds her opinions balance those of his male companions. And would it be a disaster if he married her? I've often thought he needs someone to look after him since he's left home. He doesn't care enough for himself.'

'Well, Mari, what do we know about her? She's hinted at some big problem in her past. Perhaps there was a scandal she's trying to forget. Perhaps she had a husband – or even still has.'

'But if she's as close to him as it seems, then Joshua would know her secrets if she has any. If she is unworthy, or dangerous as you put it, Joshua would have sensed it and kept her at arm's length.'

'I'm not sure. He has the reputation of not condemning anyone. I've heard James saying that he's tolerant of people who've committed serious crimes or been completely immoral. I don't go as far as my nephew, but I do wonder if people take advantage of him sometimes.'

Mariam, Salome and Anna come back then and we cease our conversation. I'm uneasy that Mariam seems unwilling to talk openly about her past but just hints at something. It's aroused my curiosity, I know it shouldn't but I can't help it. Yet I must trust my instinct for I like the woman. I feel I can talk to her about important things. I must l learn to trust my son's judgment.

*   *   *   *   *

We've come back to Nazareth and Mariam has come with us. She shut up her house in the morning and just said 'I'm coming too.' 'I told you,' said Rebecca, 'she's after Joshua.' Yet she spent all the journey chatting to me and Anna. Joshua has tried to spend time with his brothers and with Benjamin and Mariam has made no attempt to join them. As soon as she said she wanted to join us, I invited her to stay in my house and she accepted at once with great joy. She knows Joshua won't stay long, so will she go with him when he returns to Capernaum? If so, why didn't she stay in Magdala, so she could travel back on Simon's boat?

James is in the workshop seeing what Joseph and the other young men have been up to while we've been away. He doesn't trust them, despite the competence of Nathan, Isaac, Matthew and Reuben. I've told him not to get so worried time and again. Simon and Judas have gone back to their families.

Benjamin has stayed with me because we found our mother's health had deteriorated markedly during our short absence. Deborah met us as soon as we returned to say how worried she was. It was not just the arthritis. She was not eating and was just lying half asleep most of the day. She'd been unable to interest her in anything. Even Esther had been unable to attract her attention which was a bad sign. Anna has been in with her and has just returned and pulled a face.

When James came back he hurried in to his grandmother. I follow him in to where she is lying. She doesn't stir. Her eyes are open but she doesn't respond to us.

'Why doesn't Joshua come and see to her. He makes out he cures everyone else. Why not her?'

'You know why, James. You don't believe he could and he needs everyone's faith.'

'Well, even if I don't believe, apparently you do. Isn't that enough?'

Joshua has been to visit Joel at the synagogue. I guess he's offering to interpret the scriptures again. I'm sure Joel will let him if the other rabbis agree but Jonas will be against and I don't know who Jethro will be swayed by as he seems to have no opinion for himself these days.

James grabs Joshua as soon as he steps into our house.

'Joshua, you have a duty to cure your own grandmother if you can. You owe it to her. He says he can do such things, doesn't he, Mariam?' James looks at Mariam seeking confirmation.

'Yes, of course he can, can't you Master?'

'Does Grandmother want to be cured? Have you asked her?'

'Well, we can't, she doesn't say anything, but obviously she wants to be cured.'

'How do you know that, James?'

'Well, it's obvious. That's what everyone wants, isn't it?'

'Is it? And is our grandmother everyone? Perhaps she's had enough and is weary and wants rest. She's had a hard life. She married early, had a husband who spent more time away from her than he was ever near. She brought up four children in difficult circumstances. She's seen her children married with their children and now their children's children. If she wants healing and has the faith that I can help her, then it is possible, but can you tell me in all honesty that she both understands, and believes? And if not her, do you need her better and do you believe?'

'That's just an excuse, brother. You can't do it, can you? Forget my lack of belief. Our mother believes in your powers and I'm sure she wants her mother restored, so why don't you use her faith. Don't rely on me.'

Meanwhile young Anna has gone in with a cup of water to try to coax old Anna to drink something. She comes rushing out, spilling the water, her hand shaking.

'Come and look! I can't get her to move. She's just staring at the roof. She's not moving. I can't hear her breathing, I think she's dead.' And Anna bursts out crying. Deborah clutches the girl to her breast and I hurry in to where my mother is lying pursued by James with Benjamin hobbling afterwards.

I bend and feel my mother's pulse. Nothing. I look in pity at my own mother's pale drawn face and think back over her life, the times when only she and my sisters defended me against the outside world. She is gone. Do I wish her back? Does she not deserve her rest? Joshua joins us.

'You're too late!' accuses James.

'Am I? Do you know what she wanted? Let her rest. Let her be reunited with the ones she loved.'

'But she loved us. We're all still here.'

'Mother, you know best. Tell me, if you are convinced she still wishes to live and you believe, tell me to heal her.'

'But she's already dead, Joshua. It's too late. I don't know what she wanted, but it's too late now.'

202

'I could restore her even now, but you do not believe I could.'

'Joshua, she's dead. Surely you can't bring people back from death, can you?'

'Not if you don't believe, Mother. Let her rest. She's fulfilled God's plan for her life. Let her move on.'

Is he saying he can actually restore the dead to life? Surely not. I must have misunderstood him. He must have been referring to the possibility of a cure if we had acted quicker. But... ? A thought comes to me. If God could enable me to give birth without the intervention of a man, could not that child conceived in such a miraculous way also perform the unbelievable? Is it too late to ask him? Is my thought, my weak faith on this enough? If my mother were restored would she be returned in full vigour and health, or would she just be alive but still suffering the pain of her limbs, the confusion of her age? It's too big a risk.

So we accept her death as inevitable. We observe the ritual mourning. We bury her body. We remember her as she was, a loving mother of four young children. I remember her support, her heartrending love when she thought I was all but lost. Joshua is with me. He feels my sorrow. We all accompany her bier to her resting place. James has said no more. He tries not to sour the occasion with recriminations against his brother. Anna has stayed with us and cries. We suggested she went back to her mother while Benjamin stays with us but she will not hear of it. I notice that Benjamin's leg is really paining him as he follows our mother's body and that Anna has noticed and is walking with him, letting him rest his arm on her shoulder.

We go through all the motions. I suppose I do things automatically without thinking. Well, I am thinking, but my thoughts are far away. They are of my mother sewing to keep us, of washing the neighbours' clothes, of standing up to Eli, of pleading for me disdainful of any consequence for herself.

203

Mariam has been quietly at my side. She has said little but she seems to understand. I'm sure she's experienced a great tragedy, but she will say nothing. She concentrates on my concerns, bless her.

*   *   *   *   *

It must have been a week later when I notice. Joshua had kept a low profile. Joel had deemed it imprudent to risk asking him to speak in the synagogue, seeing what happened the last time. I think he'd have let him, but I'm sure Rabbi Jonas would have objected strongly. Joshua visited some neighbours. Someone said he'd healed old Ishmael, the former potter, who'd crippled his hands and now he could move them again. Others said it was a coincidence. There were others suffering from various diseases and Joshua'd not healed them.

Then, one day, Benjamin walks into the room and I suddenly see it. He walked! Normally. He wasn't limping. He observes my surprise.

'I wondered when you'd notice, sister!'

'You're not hobbling. Your leg is better!' I'm stating the obvious. It must be ten years since his injury that he sustained in the attack as he returned from Sepphoris.'

'Yes, my leg is healed. And I can see through both eyes again.'

'How?'

'Guess!'

The truth dawns on me.

'Joshua healed you?'

'Yes, he really did.'

'And it's not got better of its own accord?'

'Did you ever see any sign of it improving, Mari?'

'Well, no. When did he do it? Why didn't you say anything?'

'Because Joshua asked me not to.'

'Haven't you even told James how it happened?'

'No, especially not James. I wanted to, to prove that he's been wrong about his brother all along, but Joshua said, especially not to tell James.'

'Why on earth not?'

'I think he wants James to discover the truth for himself and not be convinced just because he's seen a miracle. James would probably find a rational explanation for it anyway.'

'Hasn't he noticed yet?'

'No. Well you hadn't noticed till now either!'

'Did you ask Joshua to heal you? Did he find you had sufficient faith after all?'

'No, Mari, I'm ashamed to say I didn't. It was all because of my daughter. Joshua came to me and said that Anna had pleaded with him to heal my leg. And she told him about my headaches and my bad eye. He asked me if I believed he could do it. I said that I wanted to believe but found it hard. And he said that I was honest but anyway my daughter believed and he could use her trust. He placed his hand on my leg and prayed and then covered my bad eye with his other hand and thanked God for Anna's faith and told me to cherish her. But he knows I do that anyway. At first I felt no different. Then my leg felt warm and I found it was easier, I could almost feel the pain seeping away. And I didn't have a headache at the end of the day for once though my sight was not immediately restored. But when I woke up next morning I could scarce believe it. I could see clearly with both eyes, everything seemed so sharp and focussed. I got up and tested my leg and it too seemed fully restored.'

I stare at him and look intently at his eye that had always seemed bloodshot and realise it is indeed clear and is looking at me with meaning.

'Of course I told Anna and she was overjoyed and wanted to rush in and tell everybody. But I told her that Joshua had demanded silence. She found that hard, she wanted to tell everyone what Joshua had done. I know she went to thank him, and he told her that it was her trust in him that had made the healing possible. Joshua asked her to keep it a secret between us. I know she's been dying to tell everyone, but equally she's been watching you all to see who noticed first!'

Of course. It had to be Anna's doing. My own eyes are misting over. I scarcely hear him as he continues.

'And he asked to meet her husband to be. They met yesterday. Joshua spent a long time with him. I don't know what he said, but he came back to me and reassured me. I was worried that he might think I'd done the wrong thing for her. But he said she'd be alright, but I was not to rush the wedding. Let her betrothal stand, but give her another year or two before she bears the responsibility of a family. And encourage her to speak her mind, be inquisitive for she has a maturing understanding of what is really important. The last thing he said to me was that he thought Anna was so like you, Mari, when you were her age. I've no idea how he knows that. I suppose you've told him many a time of your experiences.'

I'm so relieved at what my brother has just said. Of course I'm pleased for him, his injuries have been a great burden to him. And I'm pleased that my son has been able to carry out a proper healing here. But I'm especially glad at what he's said about Anna and her wedding. I've worried about her, that she would be tied down too soon. It's silly really, I was even younger than her when I was married and I survived.

I share that thought with Ben and he says 'You were an exceptional girl, Mari. We all knew that. You were strong and had an unshakable faith in God that he was looking after you.'

'Then Anna is like me', I say, 'for she's strong in her faith too.'

*　　*　　*　　*　　*

Two days later I'm sitting chatting with Mariam when Joshua joins us.

'It's time for me to leave. I have much more work to do. I need to return to Capernaum to see how my followers have fared and to help them cope with any problems they might have encountered. Then I need to go to Jerusalem. I must share my message with the people of that city. They are not hearing the true message from God through their priests and rabbis. They need more practical help, they need to act to bring in the kingdom of God, not dispute endlessly about religious trivialities and ignore the poor and the vulnerable whose needs are paramount.'

That night I lie awake thinking about what he's said. I'm worried for him. If he delivers such a strong message, won't he upset the authorities there? Look at what happened here in our sleepy village, I say to myself. If he could stir up such opposition here, what might happen in Jerusalem itself? Then I realise that I've no real ties here any more. My mother doesn't need me any longer. I can accompany my son. I tell Mariam of my resolve the very next morning.

'That's funny,' she says, 'I was going to say exactly the same thing. We'll go together.'

'What will Joshua say? Will he let us?'

'We'll not give him a choice, Mari. His disciples will follow him. We'll be disciples too. There are other women who'll join us.'

We tell Joshua that afternoon. To my surprise he voices no objection.

'Of course, Mother dear. You and Mariam. I'm sure you know the risks. But you're not needed here now. Your brother is well and will support your sisters and his own family. Your other sons are established. One day they may see other priorities but they're content now. I'll come back in a few weeks' time with the disciples and their wives who want to come with them and we'll all travel to our capital city together.

And with that we make such a momentous decision. It is only after he's left us that we realise just what we've committed ourselves to.

Chapter 18
Mari, AD 25

I wanted to go with him back to Capernaum straight away. We'd been unable to persuade him to stay any longer with us in Nazareth.

'I'm wasting my time here,' he'd said – not angrily, but sadly. 'The people here find it difficult to believe in me. They think they know me too well. Roman soldiers and tax-collector collaborators have shown more faith in me.' James overheard this last remark and I thought he was going to explode on the spot. Instead he curbed his tongue at the time, but castigated me in no uncertain terms later.

'I trust you know just what you're letting yourself in for. You can see the morality of the man now – he's not even trying to hide his contempt for us. First he snubbed the family. Now he seems to be rejecting his own nation in favour of the hated occupying army. Old Eli would be turning in his grave if he knew. You'll be sorry. It will all come to a bad end. Don't come crawling to me for comfort later. I'll just say I told you and you wouldn't listen.'

Joshua persuaded me to remain at home and Mariam, the Magdelene, to stay with me.

'Be patient,' he said. 'It'll be a long and stressful journey back to Jerusalem. Save your energy for that. I won't be long. Just a few weeks. I need to ensure my followers are trustworthy enough and ready to support me, whatever problems may arise. I need a bit more time with them privately away from the crowds. I'll take them further north towards Mount Hermon and Caesarea Philippi. There's no need for you to join us there. I know you, Mother, and I have confidence in Mariam too.'

I feared it would be more than weeks before Joshua rejoined us.

'The crowds won't let him go,' Mariam told me. 'And he's too soft with them. It doesn't matter how long he's been out in the hills or in the synagogue talking and healing, there's always more waiting to grab a word or to ask for a healing for some relative or friend who's too sick to come to him. So off he'll traipse, no matter how tired he is. He never turns anyone down if they really need him. And on top of that he'll spend time with children who come flocking to him. The mothers should really stop them, but Yeshua won't hear of it.'

'Do you think that wears him out further? My guess is that the children rejuvenate him. He's always loved the company of children and is brilliant with them. I doubt if that really tires him.'

'Perhaps he misses having children of his own.'

'Perhaps he does, Mariam.' I thought hard before asking the next question but decided to come to the point that had been exercising my mind. 'And what about you? Do you seek a husband and children? Do you see Joshua as a prospective husband for you?'

Mariam looked confused at this and blushed. Her answer was obvious without saying a word.

'Would you object?'

'I would be pleased for him. I've felt guilty that we could not find him a suitable wife. Family responsibilities would settle him down. I've not known you for long, but Joshua obviously cares for you. Has he ever spoken to you about the possibility?'

'No, never. I don't think it's even occurred to him. He's too tied up with his ministry to everyone.'

'Why don't you speak to him?'

'I couldn't, Mari. But you could! Although, frankly, I think he wants to avoid family responsibilities. He sees that everyone has claims on him. I don't think he will allow himself to restrict his care to one person. I know some of his disciples are already jealous of me and think he listens to me too much.'

'Do you want me to say something to him, Mariam?'

She thought for a long time. Eventually she shook her head.

'I think he'd refuse me. And that would be more painful than not asking. And he might feel bad about it and it could spoil our present relationship.'

'Is that enough for you? Don't you feel frustrated that you are in one sense so close to him, and in another, removed from intimate contact?'

'I know what you're thinking, Mari. Believe me, I've had enough experience of a superficial kind. I'll settle for a meeting of minds.'

I thought she might say more. She was so near to telling me about her past. She was clearly hinting at some sexual relationship but she volunteered nothing further and I felt it inopportune to press her further. Perhaps one day she'd trust me enough to tell me her secrets but she clearly was not ready yet.

So we jogged along together without baring our deepest secrets to each other. My sisters joined us often and my daughters too, but it was Anna who spent most time with us and took every opportunity to squeeze each detail of Joshua's sayings and activities from Mariam's memory.   Brother Ben was full of vigour, his leg injury totally healed, and free from the headaches that had plagued him. Despite all the evidence, James obstinately refuses to acknowledge the miraculous healing of his brother. 'Time heals' is his explanation every time. 'Just a coincidence' he argues when I point out that nearly ten years had gone by since the attack in which he'd suffered the injuries and there had been no sign of any improvement at all until Joshua tended to his leg and eye at Anna's insistence.

My neighbours seem to treat me with some reserve now. They know all about Joshua's reputation and the claims about him that reverberate around Galilee and they know I believe. I suspect they don't want to show obvious support or credence to the claims, as most of the menfolk of the village still feel slighted by his words in the synagogue last year, egged on by Rabbi Jonas who makes no bones about his contempt for Joshua and his mission. He is a true son of Eli whose malign influence still holds fast so many in this village. Thank heavens his brother-in-law Clopas has been so generous to us. Then I hear scandalous rumours circulating about my friend Mariam. I think someone is deliberately spreading dirt to upset me and get back at our support for Joshua. Someone apparently has whispered that Mariam was a prostitute in Magdala and only met Joshua when he went with her. It's absurd the lengths people will go to spread slander. I know my son and he'd never put his mission and calling at risk by being compromised in such a manner. I know he is accused of spending time with drunkards, collaborators and fallen women, but that's because he wants to help them change. The Pharisees and others who accuse him say they have no need of repentance because they haven't sinned, so who do they expect Joshua to turn to if his urgent message is the need for change and forgiveness?

Then, suddenly, Joshua comes home one evening. We were not expecting him then, he'd sent no word in advance. He looks very upset. Other men are with him, Simon Peter and some of his followers that I recognise, and they all look sombre and concerned. Something has obviously gone very wrong.

I throw my arms about my son.

'What's the matter, Joshua? What's happened?'

He kisses me on the cheek and puts his arm around me.

'Bad news, I'm afraid, Mother. There's no easy way to say this. I've received news that our cousin, John, has been killed. Executed by that tyrant, Herod Antipas.'

My heart lurches into my mouth. Instinctively my first thought is for my own son and the danger he might be in.

'I don't know the details but I'm sure it's true. The messenger is a very reliable fellow. I'm glad that his mother is not alive to hear it.'

'But he was so famous, wasn't he? Doesn't the Tetrarch respect the people's opinions about him?'

'John's been outspoken for many years. He always was a brave man. He was quick enough to criticise the corrupt religious authorities in the capital, which would have lost him any support of influence. Then he condemned Herod's marriage, so his arrest and imprisonment was not unexpected. But I must admit, I'd not thought Herod would have risked the wrath of the people by actually ordering his execution.'

'So why have you come back here so quickly? There's nothing you or anyone else can do now if John's already dead.'

'I need to get to Jerusalem as soon as possible. John's disciples need support. Someone else needs to speak up about the wrongs perpetrated by our leaders.'

'But, Joshua, won't that be putting yourself at risk? Surely now is the time to lie low. Herod will be expecting trouble. Why tempt him to act against you?'

'Mother, you've always known that our calling was dangerous. We achieve nothing without risk. You learned that as a young girl and it never stopped you from doing what you felt you had to. What is different now? We have God's will to obey. You as well as me. You know that in your heart of hearts, don't you? You'll come with me and Mariam. My disciples know what is at risk and they're coming too. They tried, just like you, to dissuade me initially, but they know what has to be faced. We can't shirk it.'

'When shall we go?'

'Tomorrow, as soon as possible.'

'But, Joshua, I've got to get ready. Can't you give me longer to let everyone know?'

'What have you got to do? You've no responsibilities now. Your family has grown up. Your sisters have their own families. My brothers and sisters too. Uncle Benjamin is fit now. He will take care of everything necessary here.'

'But what about telling everyone and saying farewell? I can't go without telling Salome and Rebecca and my daughters and their families. And what about Anna?'

'Anna already knows I'm here, so Benjamin will know and you can be sure that Salome and Andrew will soon hear. Benjamin will tell your sisters. And you're not leaving here for ever, are you?'

He's taken me completely by surprise. I haven't got my head around things yet. I know I agreed several weeks ago to join him in Jerusalem, but I'd expected a few days' notice. I haven't given it the thought needed. Joshua expects me to just drop everything and go with him, just like that. I suppose I'll get used to the idea in a minute. He's right, I don't really need to think of much. I just need a change of clothes. Joshua says we can stay with his friends, Lazarus and his wife and sister, in Bethany. But what about a bedroll and surely we need to take gifts?

Then I have another surprise. James comes in from the workshop. He's obviously been listening to my exchange with Joshua.'

'Don't worry, Mother. I'm coming with you. I won't let you go with that madman on your own.'

'But I won't be alone, James. Mariam will be with me and Joshua of course, not to mention all of his disciples. I'm sure they'll look after me.'

'I'm coming. Whatever I've said in the past, forget it. You're still my mother. I'll not let you loose with that lot without someone to take care of you properly.'

'But you're against everything that Joshua stands for. Have you changed your mind?'

'No, of course not. All the more reason for someone to look after you. I don't trust them. They'll get caught up in controversy and it won't be safe. I'm not having our neighbours saying that I failed to do my duty.'

'James, your duty is to Deborah and Reuben and Esther. How will they manage without you?'

'Joe is here and Simon and Judas. And Uncle Benjamin will see nothing goes wrong.'

'Have you told Deborah?'

'Not yet, I haven't had a chance.'

'Won't she object?'

'She'll do as she's told. She won't object.'

'That's hardly fair on Deborah and the children, is it?'

'I doubt if Deborah will mind anyway. She'll probably be only too pleased to be rid of me for a while. So stop arguing. I'm coming.'

'But Joshua might stop you.'

'No, James can come if he wants to.' Joshua has been present throughout this conversation. 'He might learn something and even change his mind.'

James makes a noise, which I interpret as a dismissal of that idea. So I need to get my mind around this new development. Joshua has gone out to talk to his disciples who are camping just outside the village. I'd forgotten Mariam. She's been standing there ever since Joshua came in. I think she might be feeling a little put out that Joshua has not spoken directly to her.

'Do you want to go out with Joshua and the others now?'

'No, I'll stay with you. The disciples won't want me around. Why don't you spend the evening with your brother and his family or with your daughter? I'll see to myself here. In fact, I might go out to see which women from Capernaum have come with their husbands. Several go around with them, and the mother of John and James, the fishermen, often comes with us.'

So I do as I'm told. Salome is worried for me and Andrew expresses his reservations. Benjamin is reassuring though. His wife says little but Anna wants to come too. I tell her that her duty lies with her new husband. She can't disappear just before her marriage. I do hope she really settles – she just seems to want to be with Joshua all the time. I will raise it with Joshua in the morning. I think he encourages her too much. He ought to make clear to her where her priorities lie.

I wish James wasn't coming. He'll be constantly reminding me that he doesn't believe a word of what Joshua says. It's so sapping of my energy, to have to face such opposition from so close to home all the time. But he's made it quite clear that he won't be dissuaded. The annoying part is that he makes it out that it's for my own good. I wish Joshua wasn't so philosophical about it all. Why won't he do something to make James believe? I'm sure he could, even though he says he can't unless he believes, which just makes James even more adamant, despite all the evidence, that it's all complete dangerous nonsense. There is an element of danger, I grant him that, but nonsense? Surely he's not so blind that he can't see the evidence all around him?

So we go. Joshua has a dozen of his male followers with him and five of their womenfolk, plus James, Mariam and myself. I thought we'd go along the Jordan route as our destination is Bethany at first, but Joshua wants to use the journey to continue his message of the 'Kingdom of God' and there are many more towns and villages along the road through Samaria than along the Jordan valley. This has already got James's back up.

'There he goes again,' he sniffed this morning when he discovered Joshua's plans. 'The foreigners come first as usual. What good does he think talking to that Samaritan scum will do? When we've travelled to Jerusalem by that route, we've had as little to do with the natives as we could. We've just had to buy bread and fruit from the villagers and I'm sure they've inflated the prices and cheated us. We could have loaded up asses with all the supplies we could get from here, but Joshua said we'd rely on trade with the Samaritans of goodwill as we journey. Fool!'

I say nothing. I think one or two of Joshua's followers are of the same opinion, but Simon Peter, overhearing James and seeing my unease, comes over to me.

'Don't you worry about it, Mari. We've got used to following the Master's wishes. We've learned a damned hard way that he always has a purpose and it usually works out so that we see afterwards that he was right. Yeshua's brother is only saying what some of us said at first, but we all accept his guidance and advice without any quibble now. Well, most of the bloody time, anyway. And most of us. You can usually rely on Judas over there to think he knows best. He worries all the time that we won't have enough sodding money to do things Yeshua's way but it always works out. Yeshua just smiles at him. He doesn't argue. But we do it his way and Judas gives way with bad grace and then we make him admit afterwards that Yeshua was right!'

When we get under way, I seek to escape James's attention and walk for a while with this Simon Peter whom the others seem to accept as the leader of the disciples. James assumes I'd spend all my time with the women. Well, there'll be plenty of time for that, but I want to ask this man what he really thinks. After all, he's given up a lot to be with Joshua all the time. He had a good fishing business with his brother who's with us also. And he's left a wife and brood of children at home. It must be hard for them. Only the younger fishermen, James and John, are unmarried and I gather James was already betrothed when he decided to leave and throw his lot in with Joshua.

So I don't beat about the bush.

217

'Can I ask you frankly, Simon, why you follow my son?'

'Because he asked me to!'

'That's no proper answer, Simon, and you know it. You don't follow everyone who asks you.'

'Fair enough, Mari. I'd seen a lot of him before he asked me. He'd preached in our synagogue often, I'd watched him healing people brought to him. I'd been impressed at the way he dealt with opposition, especially the bloody awkward questions asked by the local rabbis. I'd gone to hear him preach out of curiosity. He must have noticed me and I'd asked him a couple of questions from which he knew I was really after an answer and not just wanting to trip him up.'

'Simon, answer me this. Who do you really think he is? Do you think he's our promised Messiah?'

'Odd that you should ask me that. Yeshua asked us that very question a few days ago when we were alone with him. Some of the others said they thought he was a prophet, but I stuck my neck out and said straight out that I was sure he was the Messiah. The others were shocked. However, I noticed John nodding his head and Yeshua congratulated me and said that he'd always trusted that I would be the leader. I was surprised at this because several others are cleverer and speak better than me – Matthew for example and ruddy Judas in particular. John and James too have had more education than me. Their father Zebedee had the opportunity to hire men for his vessels so they could attend the synagogue school, while my father died while I was still a boy, so Andrew and I had to go and work from an early age.'

'So you believe he really is the Messiah?'

'Yes, Mari. I wouldn't have said it unless I believed, though I must admit I was a bit hesitant. I wondered if he would laugh at me and the others would call me a bloody fool, but he seemed really pleased. This is it, I thought, now we're going to spread the news and really go to town. Then he shocked me by making us all swear that we'd tell no-one what I'd just said. It seemed a nonsense. Why doesn't he want it known?'

'Perhaps he was being cautious, Simon. It might be dangerous for him if it became known that he was the Messiah. What would the Romans do? And Herod too? If he's anything like his father, he'd have us murdered rather than risk his throne.'

'Well, in my view, it would be better to reveal that he's the Messiah here where he has a lot of support and the crowds would protect him. I worry that he's going to declare his role when we get to Jerusalem, even in the Temple itself. That'll set the cat among the damned pigeons. If he wanted an army, we could have raised thousands here in Galilee that would really scare the pompous asses in Jerusalem, but he says that's not his way. He says he can rule his kingdom without violence. Well, I want to bloody well see that. I'd love to believe him, but I don't believe the bosses are ready to give up their power easily. I think sometime we're going to have to fight.'

This frightens me. Joshua has never talked about fighting or throwing the occupying army out. Do these men think that's what Joshua intends? If so, they've misunderstood him. Unless I have. Surely I haven't been so wrong about my own son all these years? And if these men think Joshua is going to lead a rebellion against the Romans, James is right. The Romans will crush us without mercy.

I don't argue with this Simon. All the others call him Peter, a name that Joshua apparently gave him when he became a follower. I'm getting confused about names. When I hear the others talk about Yeshua, I often don't immediately remember that they're talking about my son. And they call him Master, or Teacher or Rabbi. I find that strange too. And several of the followers have similar names. I think there are two called Judas. Some of them call the clever one Iscariot because of where he comes from, but often they refer to him as the Zealot because he used to belong to one of the nationalist rebel groups like my father. That makes me worry about the possible use of violence even more. He obviously thinks that he'll achieve his dream of a nation ruled by Jews alone by nailing his colours to Joshua's mission. I hope Joshua knows what he is doing.

I feel better when I talk to the women. They're full of commonsense and clearly adore my son. They talk about his healing powers and his sensitivity and the way he values them and the compassion he obviously has for all who suffer or are oppressed in any way.

We set off the following morning and for some reason unknown to us or his disciples Joshua has decided that we will stop for a time in the village of Nain. Joshua can't seem to explain to us the reason for this. We all thought he was keen to get to Jerusalem as quickly as possible, but he says now that he only needs to be there for the time of Passover and that is months away. It's only late autumn now and at least we will not suffer the worst heat of the day at this time of the year, although we may get rain storms. After we've been on the road for a couple of hours, Joshua confides in me that the two disciples who covered Nain in their testing expedition had somewhat sheepishly admitted that they had failed to heal some of those who came to them seeking a cure for their afflictions. They had been particularly distressed at their inability to cope with the convulsions of a young boy whose desperate father had brought him to them. Joshua had therefore decided to stop for a while in Nain, partly to restore the confidence of the two followers, but also because he felt for the disappointment and despair of the boy's father who'd had the faith to approach the disciples with the plea for his cure.

I was pleased as the proposed stay in Nain meant that I would see my sister, Salome as well as her husband Jacob and also my cousin Susannah. In fact, when we arrive, Mariam and I become the objects of rivalry between my sister and cousin as to which home will give us hospitality and in the end we are allowed to stay with Salome only when Joshua agrees to be Susannah's guest instead of remaining in tents with his followers. After being royally entertained by Salome and her husband, and hearing all the latest news about my nieces Mariam and Lydia and their children, we are asked after Isaac who is with us in Nazareth and probed for further news about Joshua and the reputed sensation he is causing throughout Galilee. He came to Nain in the early days and apparently great things were expected when two of his disciples, Thomas and Matthew, arrived last month proclaiming that they were undertaking the work of their Master and Teacher, Yeshua. Then they tell us how great an anti-climax it had been.

'They started off with eloquent words so a crowd had soon formed and they then announced that Yeshua had given them the power to heal any with afflictions. A queue soon formed and that's when they ran into trouble. The first couple who sought help went away reasonably satisfied as the two men said they would find themselves healed although there was nothing visible at the time.'

Salome interrupts her husband. 'Then Matthaeus, one of the scribes at the synagogue, brought his son, Philip, to be healed. We all knew that he'd been having serious convulsions since birth and had frequently put himself in great danger, throwing himself into fires and nearly down the well once. Naomi, his mother, says the boy has the devil in him, but Matthaeus knows it's really just his illness. But they couldn't do it.'

'I really felt for Matthaeus. In front of the whole crowd the boy started attacking his father and threw himself on the ground frothing at the mouth. I know his mother and father had tried to hide his condition from everyone but the close family and they'd taken the risk of exposing what they thought of as their shame in front of everyone, only for the worst excesses of his condition to be made public.'

Salome nodded as her husband continued.

'Thomas made a great show of appealing to God for the boy's healing and it was obvious nothing happened. Then Matthew attempted to heal the boy and that was when he had a fit and fell writhing to the ground. It was awful. After that Yeshua's two disciples lost their confidence completely and had to send away everyone waiting to be healed. They left the village that night amidst much grumbling and mockery from those who had witnessed their failure. Matthaeus and the boy's mother left in tears and the lad was worse than ever.'

Salome asks me, 'Do you think your son has come back here to make amends?'

'I'm sure he has,' I reply.

Next day Salome is bursting with the news when she comes back from fetching the day's water.

'I saw Susannah at the well. She said that Joshua took Thomas and Matthew with him to visit Matthaeus privately last night and drove the madness from the boy. Susannah went with them and saw everything. She said that at first they thought the boy had been killed because he reacted so violently when Joshua commanded his healing. He lay so still on the ground that his mother began wailing. Then Joshua had helped the boy up and restored him to his father and the boy had smiled and was so calm.'

The news of the healing has spread like wildfire throughout the village and by the time that Susannah had got back to her house there was a crowd forming outside clamouring for Joshua to come out and heal others. Mariam and I go to Susannah's house and find we can't get near the place because of the numbers gathered there. I can't see any of the disciples and I can only just see Joshua's head as he stands on the steps of the house. A lot of the women present have brought children to be blessed and it's well into the afternoon before the crowd eventually disperses. Then I see the disciples assembling. James is among them. I wonder now just what he's made of everything he's seen. How can he continue to deny the evidence of his own eyes?

Then suddenly I hear the sound of wailing in the distance. My ears prick up and I look at Salome with some concern. What is happening?

Salome notices my alarm and says, 'Oh, that will be the funeral procession of the widow Sarah's son. It's a tragic case. He was such a virile young man, his mother's sole support, then last week he was suddenly struck down with a severe fever and to everyone's shock, deteriorated fast and died yesterday. The poor woman is distraught and has no idea how she'll survive. It was a shame that no-one thought to tell her of Joshua's presence yesterday, although I think the young man was already gone before daybreak.'

The sound of mourning is getting closer and the procession comes into view with the widow, in black, staggering beside the bier, supported by a couple of villagers to prevent her falling. I notice Joshua is watching them approach and as the procession draws near, he suddenly steps out onto the track in their path and holds up his hand and the procession, barred by his presence, halts. We all hold our breath. What on earth is he going to do? Some of us heard a rumour a year ago that he'd brought back a young girl from death, but when I'd asked him about it, he'd just said that she was sleeping. Well, I'd assumed she was ill and unconscious rather than actually dead despite the rumour.

I watch Joshua as he bends and speaks to the woman and the men supporting her. Then he stands tall and says in a very loud voice, 'Young man, stand up!' There is a sudden hush and then a huge gasp from the crowd as the body on the bier stirs, then staggers to its feet, the white burial cloth beginning to fall away from the body. A couple of the men grab the robe before it exposes the naked body of the youth. The hideous chants of grief are stilled and suddenly there breaks out a shout of joy and cheering and applause, then everyone is singing and a spontaneous dance starts. The youth is being clasped by Sarah, and I notice tears streaming from her eyes. She is quite overcome. The young man just looks dazed. Everyone has surged forward to see the miracle and hear what is being said.

'He's telling her to give the young man something to eat', I overhear several people say. We go back to Salome's home, shaken to the core. We say nothing to each other, we are just too full of what we've seen. When we arrive back at the house, Salome says, 'I want to come with you.' Susannah nods. 'Yes, I will join you too.'

I tackle James later.

'Well, James? Are you still in denial?'

'I have to admit he's a gifted healer.'

'Is that all you think?'

'Well, he's an exceptional healer. I have to admit that. But he's a dangerous man. Heaven knows where the emotions he's stirring up will lead him and us. If he does this in Jerusalem he'll cause a riot. Then see what the authorities will do. I don't like it, Mother, I don't.'

Chapter 19
Mari

We stayed in Nain for a few weeks to cope with the crowds who'd come because they'd heard of the miracle of the young man's restoration to life. One night, when I've slipped out of my sister's house to gaze at the stars and think quietly, I nearly bump into Joshua. I'm able to get a few minutes alone with him at last. It's already dark and he's told his followers that he wants to be alone to pray, a routine that they accept as normal.

'Mother, are you alright? There's quite a tough walk ahead for you. We ought to be on our way soon as I need to get to Jerusalem before the Passover and you've seen how difficult it is to leave a village once the people know I'm here. It'll be the same all the way, even in Samaria.'

'Yes, son. I'm just enjoying the peace of the night. After the crowds and constant activity of the day, I find it a blessing to be alone. I say alone, but I find now is the time I can sense God is around me, protecting me, leading me. So I'm not really alone. I'm sure you know what I mean.'

'Exactly. We share a similar need and experience.'

'I don't know how you keep going. You're in constant demand from morning until darkness falls and even then your presence at various evening meals is expected and I'm sure you can't relax then. People will want to ask you questions and even bring more sick people for you to heal. Doesn't it tire you out?'

'Yes, it can be exhausting, especially when so many need healing – that takes power from me. But how can I refuse? When I see so much suffering, I cannot turn my back on it. I can only keep going through this time I set aside for prayer. Sometimes I use this late hour, other times I enjoy the freshness of dawn, when only a few people are about and I can lose myself in my father's presence.'

'Joshua, I know you spend much of your time healing so many of their afflictions, but why is it necessary? Why are so many ill or possessed by madness and delusions? Why does God allow so much suffering? You can't heal everyone, how do you choose who to heal and who not to?'

'That's a hard question, Mother. I often ask my father the same question. I know some men say that such afflictions are punishments for sins committed. There can be an element of truth in that – I have healed men and women crippled by guilt which has not just corrupted their minds but has caused physical symptoms also, sometimes quite severely. At other times the innocent become victims of the sins or neglect of others. Many illnesses are caused by the conditions endured by the poorest and most vulnerable, which the more fortunate members of our communities ignore. In such cases I feel that I'm being asked to right the wrongs perpetrated by our nation. But there are cases that baffle me. Last year I was moved to restore a young girl who'd died from a fever. Her home was clean, her parents caring. I looked at her and my heart nearly broke. Then I realised that I even had the power to overcome death itself. Perhaps that was why she died – to teach me more of my own capability if I trusted my God to the uttermost.'

'That seems a bit hard on the parents and those who loved her.'

'I'm not saying that God caused her to die so that I could learn. But he certainly used the opportunity to open my eyes to what was possible. I expect there was a reason that could be explained. Although her home was clean, the town's streets were not. Insects carry disease and poor and dirty places provide the right conditions for such to breed and multiply. And man has had the opportunity to apply his thinking and his resources to tackle such problems and find solutions to reduce such innocent suffering. But what does he do? Where are his priorities? He bends his mind to greed and acquisitiveness. He devises ways of out-smarting his fellow human beings. He wages war. If man's ingenuity had been applied to the health and welfare of all, rich and poor, for the last centuries, then perhaps this sea of suffering we experience now would not exist, or at least be so much less.'

'So you think you can now put it all right?'

'Of course not, Mother. I can only show the way. I will not be around for ever – indeed, the next few months could see me imprisoned or even killed like Cousin John. No…, don't protest, Mother, you know that's true. I want to show that such healing is possible for all who believe. My disciples, they are learning. Most of them succeeded in healing diseases when I sent them out in pairs recently. I know Matthew and Thomas failed, but they will succeed. And they will pass on their faith and gifts to others who in turn will offer the world such gifts – gifts that God is offering us now to save many from the sins and neglect of their ancestors and the failures of leaders and governments to prioritise their resources.'

'Why did you restore that young man to the widow Sarah? And yet you've ignored others who've died in all the places you've been. You can't keep everyone alive surely? Why him, why the young girl you talked about?'

'Because I was there, Mother. Because I saw the distress and I could see their needs. Because the people accompanying the widow were concerned for her and had seen me and believed I could heal. Because I was asked.'

'Who asked you?'

'The girl's parents asked for help. The eyes of the crowd following the young man's bier pleaded for him. I will not act unless people ask me and believe I can help them. The same will be true for my followers. The same applied to what I did for your brother Benjamin. None of you really asked me to heal him with confidence on your hearts that I could do it. But Anna did. She pleaded with me. I ignored her at first to test her, but she persevered and implored me. 'You can do it', she kept repeating. 'You can if you want to.' And of course I wanted to. So I did. Why didn't you ask me to, or Benjamin himself or Rachel, his wife – or even Matthew or Thomas? They all saw me enough times. But it was left to little Anna. I find this time and time again. You have to trust God just as when you were a young child and trusted your father and mother.'

'Does it always work? Does it mean if you don't heal someone that their faith was insufficient?'

'Not necessarily. Sometimes I tell someone that I will not heal them. Perhaps there is a lack of faith. But sometimes I don't feel it's right. There is another reason why they cannot be healed. Perhaps their life plan is complete. Perhaps they are healed in their mind by coming to terms with their affliction. Some people can overcome big handicaps and live a worthwhile life demonstrating that possibility to others so afflicted. We cannot live on this earth for ever, we have to move on. This is not the end. Sometimes I feel that my main mission – to invite people to live in the kingdom of God on earth and in heaven – is becoming swamped by the people who seek only to see the miracles. I have limited time. I cannot spend all my time healing, for that is but temporary. My message is for eternity. But most people do not realise this and would deflect me from my main purpose.'

We are silent for several minutes. I'm trying to absorb all he's just said to me. I've watched him being surrounded here by the crowds and I know what he's just said is true. They want miracles. Yes, they find what he says interesting and arresting for the moment, but they've really come to see something spectacular.

At length I decide to open up on the subject that is bothering me.

'Is that why you won't do something to convince James? It's embarrassing sometimes how much he disputes with you and demonstrates to others how our family is divided.'

'There's nothing unusual in that, Mother. The things I say and do divide many families. It's inevitable unless I take away their power of choice. James has seen me restore Sarah's lad to life. He can't deny the evidence of his eyes any longer. If he believes in me just because of that, then he will not see the need to change his own life, his relationship with you, with Deborah, his brothers, his neighbours, and above all, with God. He sees his relationship with God through religious practices, through saying the right words and observing the right rituals.'

'Is there no hope for him then?'

'Of course there is. He'll change, Mother, you'll see it one day. But let any change come from the heart, not from the superficial persuasion of a healing miracle. You'll find it hard one day. You'll need your deep-rooted faith, not one that can be blown away by the first setback received.'

'James says that what you're saying and doing is dangerous for all of us. Are you telling me that you think the future dangerous too? Are you saying that to save this country we're going to have to fight?'

'Not physically. But mentally and spiritually, yes. I'll be misunderstood. Many who understand me will not like what they understand. The authorities in Jerusalem will seek to silence me.'

'Then why are you going there? Could you not do more good by staying away from there?'

'To do what, Mother? To spend more time here and in other places healing the sick? I'm not called by my father just to be a doctor. I have a message to proclaim and it will not make me popular with the rich and influential. The only way to stay out of danger is not to proclaim the message. I can delay until the time is right, but I cannot put off the inevitable conflict which will come. Do you want to turn back? It's going to be a hard journey ahead in more ways than one.'

'I'm frightened for you, Joshua, but I'll be with you. Do these followers of yours all understand what you're saying?'

'I don't think it's dawned on them all yet. One or two still think I'm going to lead a revolution against the Romans, but I think the majority have let that idea go. Our revolution is harder than that, it's to fight against evil, selfishness, obstinacy, prejudice and pride and to conquer all with love and compassion. That's a stronger and weaker weapon at the same time. In the short term we may seem to lose the battle. But God will ensure that love wins out in the end. You, of all people, should know that. When you were a young girl, you learned that lesson well. You've not allowed age to dampen your faith, dim your idealism, have you? Of all my family, you are my rock, the person I can trust. Anna too, but she is still young and untested.'

'Can you trust all your followers though? You call Simon Peter your 'rock' too. Will he cope with what you say is going to happen? Is he really the best?'

'He'll fail once or twice, but I trust him to come through in the end. There are others who are firmer, but are less demonstrative, not so articulate in their faith. I trust young John. He's thoughtful and caring, but he doesn't find it so easy to express himself before large crowds – Simon Peter is fearless like that – and, I have to say, blunt. John is better at thinking things through, talking to me quietly to ensure he's understood. He'll write things down and what he says and thinks will last longer. You should talk to John more. You two can strengthen each other, I'm sure of that.'

I make a mental note to spend time with John.

'What about the others? One of James's constant complaints to me is that he doesn't think you've chosen your friends well. He says that with all your education, he'd have expected you to seek out the scholars and those who've had more education.'

'You've probably heard me say that it's difficult for rich men to enter the kingdom of God because they're too constrained by their wealth and possessions. It's unfortunately somewhat similar for the intellectuals. Their constant questioning and disputing makes it difficult for them to trust and act on truth when they hear it. They test it to death and never get round to acting, even if their intellect finally accepts the truth.'

'Are you saying that clever people can never accept you?'

'No, Mother, but sometimes it's harder for them. I have met several who have helped me though they seem strangely reticent to be open in their support. They tend to see all sides to any question. But if and when they do fully accept what I tell them, they can be very valuable for they appreciate what is important and can act with sensitivity.'

'Who are these people? Do I know them?'

'There's a couple I've met in Jerusalem, one is a man called Nicodemus who's a member of the Sanhedrin and will speak up for me if necessary. Our friend, Lazarus, in Bethany. He's had a good education and he and his family are great supporters. And you knew and were helped by Zechariah who was a very learned priest well respected by all at the Temple many years ago. It's not impossible, Mother, just more difficult. But the kingdom needs all sorts.'

'Are any of your followers educated?'

'John and his brother James are reasonably educated – for fishermen I hear some say - but I have more problems with the two of my followers who are probably the brightest, Judas and Matthew, than all the rest put together.'

'Why, how are they a problem?'

'They think they know best. They subject everything I say to their tests of reason, and whilst that is sometimes appropriate, it is not always so. Sometimes you have to see beyond reason and take a risk for what you value most.'

'Why did you choose them then?'

'Because they are representative of many people. I cannot restrict my appeal to only one class of person. All have to be invited even if not all will accept. And I saw that Matthew wanted desperately to change. He was in an occupation that made him hated and I saw how motivated he was, so I took the risk. And he is succeeding. I said he could be difficult, but he can be won over. He is a useful foil for me, he makes me express my reasons for actions that some of the others would just accept without thinking. That's good.'

'And Judas?'

'Ah, Judas Iscariot. Now he's an interesting man. He probably has more potential than all the rest. But I'm not sure if I'm winning him over yet. He's the only one who asked me if he could become my disciple. All the rest were invited by me and then responded. He has his own agenda and it doesn't always correspond with mine. He thinks that I am a means to his end and tries to manipulate me sometimes. I usually win him over, but I'm not sure of his reaction when we get to Jerusalem. I'll need to rein him in, as he is the most politically motivated and he could set events in motion that run counter to my intentions.'

'What is his intention then? What does he think you can do for him?'

'He believes I'm the Messiah, I'm sure of that. But his interpretation of the Messiah's role clashes with mine. He was active as a Zealot in his youth. He foreswore violence and joined me, but I believe that was his realism at work rather than a change in his views. He is desperate to rid our country of the Romans and now believes he can support me to achieve this politically rather than with force of arms.'

'And how does he expect you to do that?'

'He wants me to harness this great support I have in Galilee and the far side of the Jordan and negotiate with the Romans from strength. He thinks if I can convince the priests and rabbis in the Temple that I'm the Messiah, then they'll side with me and issue the Romans an ultimatum that will lead to a much lighter Roman presence that can be whittled away until the Jewish nation stands proud and independent once more.'

'Is there any chance of that?'

'Frankly, no, and I've told him so. The priests and rabbis and the Sanhedrin have their influence and power from the Romans and whatever they say privately to Jews for political reasons, they'll always act to preserve their own interests. Despite his intellect, Judas is naïve. I'm going to have to challenge the religious authorities in Jerusalem for the kingdom I'm talking about is not one that interests the Romans. I foreswore that sort of earthly power a long time ago. I'm going to have to battle the religious authorities to rescue men's souls – that's far more important.'

'You accept the Roman presence then? You don't see driving the foreign power out as the mission of the Messiah?'

'No, Mother. I can live with the Roman occupation. I sympathise with those who feel exploited or harassed by the Romans but there have been worse. I've had contact with a number of Roman officials and soldiers and found some of them remarkably generous men and just. There are cruel and bad men among them, of course, but all nations have their would-be tyrants, given the opportunity.'

'How do you interpret the scriptures then that talks of the Messiah's saving of the nation?'

'Don't you remember my words when I was invited to interpret the prophet Isaiah's words in the synagogue in Nazareth? I told the congregation there that the kingdom of God was already installed whenever justice, love, care and compassion were present – as a gift and right of all, not just to the wealthy and influential. The saving of the soul of the nation is a far more vital task than the saving of its own sovereignty – and incidentally, much harder to achieve.'

There is a long silence while I savour his words. On the one hand I feel a sense of relief that he does not foresee any physical fight or violence. But I 'm uneasy all the same. I can see his determination and although I've no knowledge of the Jerusalem priests and their views, I'm prepared to accept what he says, even though it conflicts with my experience there – for the only Jerusalem priests I've met were my lovely Uncle Zechariah and the two rabbis who brought Joshua back to us when we'd lost him and had expressed such admiration for his intelligence. However, I know different attitudes from my own experience in Nazareth. Despite Rabbi Joel's support, I remember Eli's obstinacy and Jonas's present opposition.

I'm wondering if this is the end of our conversation, whether I should let him go to pray as he said was his intention. I don't want to tire him further. But there is one other issue I want to raise with him and this is a good opportunity.

'Joshua, what do you want me to do? How can I and the other women help you best?'

'You're all my disciples too, aren't you?'

'I thought only men were allowed to be the disciples of rabbis?'

'That may be our culture and custom. But it's not a very good custom. There is no formal ceremony for making anyone a disciple. A disciple is a person who is with me, spends time with me, listens and follows me, tries to learn and put into practice what I say. Are you any different from Simon Peter or John in this? You probably understand me a lot better than most of the men. And certainly Mariam of Madgala does.'

Ah, Mariam. Should I broach that subject with him now?

'Why is Mariam such a close follower of you? Is she a disciple or something more?'

'What do you mean, Mother?'

'Is she your wife? No, I didn't mean that, obviously she's not. But she seems at times so close to you and you often talk to her on your own, that she seems as intimate as a wife would be. It wouldn't be a bad idea, you know.'

'Is that what you want?'

'No, I'm really asking if that's what you want.'

'Is that what Mariam wants? Has she asked you to speak to me on this?'

'No, actually she asked me not to.'

'I'm glad of that but I do value her, Mother. Her support and devotion to my cause is so strong. She is as good as any of the male disciples and I treat her as such, even though I can see that it sometimes irritates the men, whose minds are slower to move on from our traditional culture. But marriage? That would create problems, diversions from my purpose. It would create tensions within the group and deflect me from the things I need to say and do in Jerusalem. It would tie me to one person when my mission is for all. You know the family problems that I've already caused. James and others of my brothers think already that I should put my own family first rather than treat you all as equals to the rest of mankind.'

'I think Mariam suspects that too, which is why she won't say anything to you.'

'Then leave it, Mother, as it is. Let us not hurt anyone unnecessarily. She knows I care about her. She's already hugely grateful for how I've helped her. Let that suffice.'

'How did you help her?'

'That's hers to tell you if she wants to. I'll not betray any confidences, even to you.'

'But has her past the potential to hurt or damage you? I don't want your mission undermined by what people can say about your relationship with her.'

'Ah, people have been talking, have they? They don't know what she's said to me, so they're probably wrong. Ignore them, Mother. I know her as she is now and so do you. And I need her presence and yours and that of the other women. When things get difficult, as they will, I'll need your presence and support. I suspect you may be more use than some of the men.'

Chapter 20
Mari, AD 26

It's seemed a long winter. Not because of adverse weather or family problems, but so much has been packed into the last few months. After our stop in Nain, my sister Salome and my cousin, Susannah, both now free of family responsibilities, decided to come with us. Our travelling party therefore consists of nine women – the five relatives of the male disciples, Mariam, Salome, Susannah and me – and the dozen male disciples, my James and Joshua himself. Our progress through Samaria has been so slow as every village on our route has sought to detain us to listen to Joshua and bring their sick for him to heal. We've had to divert to other villages off our track too, as Joshua received pleas for him to go to them. At every stop, more people have joined us, mainly men, but some women too. We now resemble an army on the march – well, a very ragged and undisciplined army, it's true, for this army ambles and stops and meanders.

We really started this growth after an incident in a little village on the highway to Jerusalem after we'd rejoined it from our sojourn in Nain. I suppose we were only just into Samaritan territory and we'd camped and some of the disciples had gone to buy food while the rest were putting up the tents. Joshua had been exhausted by his labours in Nain and had asked us to stay in this camp for a few days as he wished to rest and restore his powers by reflection and quiet prayer. We hadn't noticed that he'd gone at first, then someone said that he'd left just before noon to find a deserted place to pray. The others of us were resting from the heat of the midday sun, and looking forward to the opportunity to stay a while to find water and wash the dust from our clothes and bodies.

We found out later that Joshua had found a lone Samaritan woman drawing water from the village well. He'd apparently asked for a drink and got into conversation with her – typical of him. She'd been mesmerised by what he'd said to her and had rushed back into the village to tell her family and friends. Before he'd finished his prayers he found half the village gathered wanting to see this man that had so astounded the woman. When he'd talked to them and had healed a couple of cripples who'd limped out to see him, the village went crazy and virtually imprisoned all of us until Joshua had spent days telling them about the kingdom of God and healing all those in the village who had any kind of ailment. When the villagers found the rest of us camping nearby, they invited us into their homes and would not hear of us coping on our own or buying food, but were lavish in their hospitality. Poor old James – the welcome and generosity of these folk challenged every prejudice he had and he was speechless. I've never known my son to be so quiet!

After that, the fame of Joshua preceded our every step. We were greeted in nearly every village with the same rapturous welcome and when eventually we were allowed to move on, we found nearly half the population of the village would trail after us. Most of course only followed us for a day or two, but others have followed us all the way until we must be a throng of several hundred. I'm beginning to get a bit nervous, although not half as much as James, who sees this crowd as a threat to order in the capital city – even if we're allowed to get that far. I know we're no threat in fact, but James says that the Romans will see us as such and disperse us brutally before we can do anything that might really upset them. I think Joshua is a bit concerned too, for he spends a lot of his addresses to the crowds stressing his peaceful mission, praising peacemakers and abhorring violence as I think he suspects that many in the crowd have been inspired by the Messianic rumour and, whatever, he says, think they are about to throw the Romans out.

I stay to hear most of his talks to the crowd although occasionally I join the other women buying food for our journey – although, as I said earlier, we are usually given hospitality by the villages we pass through. I'd expected Joshua to be giving the same talk everywhere we went, but as so many people followed us Joshua kept unearthing new things to talk about and thus they stayed interested and continued to follow us. I thought that such a crowd advancing on each village would have provoked fear, but word of Joshua's presence seemed to run ahead of us and we were welcomed by the local population of every town and village. Today he talked about the hypocrisy of the authorities and contrasted the attitude of the priests and Pharisees he'd met with the sincere confessions and desire to change of some of the sinners and criminals he'd come across. This won't go down well with the authorities although the crowd today lapped it up and we have a couple of hundred people or more camped in a field on the edge of the village ready to follow us tomorrow. Goodness knows how they're feeding themselves – the village shops have been stripped bare of everything edible.

And so we progressed slowly. We spent several days in the Samaritan cities of Shechem and Sychar and seemed to lose some of our followers there, although Joshua continued to be a sensation everywhere he went. When we finally crossed the border from Samaria into Judea, we diverted from the main route to Jerusalem by taking the Jericho road through Ephraim. By now many of our Samaritan followers had returned home but a core remained despite the fact that we were – to them – in hostile Jewish territory and we now found villagers from Judea joining us in considerable numbers. At one village we crammed into the local synagogue and saw Joshua heal a man who had a crippled arm that prevented him from working. That provoked immediate uproar from the local synagogue authorities and they accused him of defiling the Sabbath by carrying out unlawful activity on that day of enforced rest. I thought our Nazareth synagogue experience was to be re-enacted all over again, but most of the congregation cheered when Joshua challenged them about the priority of immediate compassion over strict observance of the law.

We arrived in Ephraim itself and we stayed for several days. The town is a lot bigger than our Galilean villages; it must be about the size of Magdala. It has several synagogues and Joshua was invited to talk in each, with large crowds crushed in each one to its limited capacity. Today we are invited to the main one in the centre of the town, and I notice with some trepidation that there are a large number of priests and rabbis present, obviously from all the local synagogues and not just this one. They've obviously ganged up together and I sense there might be trouble. They've sought safety in numbers to stand up against the pressure of the crowd and I wait with bated breath to see what will happen. Yesterday he humiliated some of them when a woman was hauled before him who'd been caught in an adulterous situation and he'd been challenged as to whether the legal penalty of death by stoning should be carried out. They knew of his compassion and soft spot for sinners and were clearly trying to show him up as being too lenient and undermining their traditional laws. He then hit them where it hurts by telling any of them who were confident that they'd never sinned in their life could throw the first stone. That stymied them and one by one, embarrassed at his response, the threatening crowd had melted away. They were now gathering to get their own back.

I am not surprised therefore, when Joshua is interrupted before he's got into his stride. They start asking questions about marriage and divorce, clearly trying to get him to say some things which are at odds with the law so they can accuse him of encouraging law-breaking. This Joshua counters by emphasising the sacred nature of marriage, then saying that people cannot live up to that standard so that the Mosiac law allowed divorce. However, he only cites unfaithfulness in marriage as a valid reason and many other excuses that some men use for reasons for divorce merely make them adulterers in practice. The challenge peters out and Joshua turns once more to his theme of hypocrisy, contrasting the outward words and actions of many with the evil thoughts simmering in and polluting their minds. He is making the religious elite squirm once more, for it is clear he is getting at them. He knows why they're asking these questions, trying to trap him and not because they really want his advice. The crowd knows this too, and many are grinning at the authorities' discomfort.

Afterwards, when the crowd has eventually dispersed, we manage to snatch an hour in the house of a man and wife who have provided Joshua and a couple of his disciples with lodging. We are all there – the disciples and our women plus our host and his wife. The subject of marriage is quite a tricky one for several here. Some of the disciples, I know, have been criticised for leaving their families and following Joshua. Some women have had to choose between staying with their husbands and leaving their children with relatives or staying with their children and not seeing their husbands for months at a time. One of them, Thomas I think, shouts above the general murmur of conversation.

'Yeshua, you've set a high standard for marriage in what you said today. Many people find it difficult to live by that standard. In that case, isn't it better that we shouldn't marry at all? If it's that hard, perhaps we shouldn't risk it.'

The room falls silent. With the wives of five of the disciples present, this could be a little sensitive. Joshua is clearly thinking carefully before replying.

'This teaching can't apply to everyone – not if they don't accept God's laws and don't even try to live by doing God's will. There is a higher standard for those that wish to follow me and be part of the kingdom of God. And marriage is not for everyone. There are those who deliberately decide not to marry because they are called to put their work on behalf of the kingdom first and marriage would then create conflicts of priority. My cousin John did not marry for he spent years in the Judean desert preaching and baptising. John here,' – he points to his disciple sitting next to him – 'John has not married. I don't know if he will, but his priority at the moment is to follow me and those of you who are already married know how hard are the choices you have to make between coming with me and being with your families. And as you know, I have not married.' He glances at Mariam at this moment and all of us turn to look at her. 'For the same reason. It's not that I don't want to, but it's a sacrifice I have to make if I'm to spend my life carrying out the plan that my Father God has for me, taking risks that would be too selfish for a married man to make. There will be many others who will not marry for that very legitimate reason. But there are others too who will prefer not to marry, because they're just made that way or they are influenced that way by others.'

'What do you mean?' It's my son, James, who asks this question, bristling.

'Well, some men are physically not capable, they may be infertile or impotent. They may be emasculated by their families for some specific reason or traditional role. Others may have no inclination for women because of their make-up or because of earlier experiences that may have damaged or changed them. For such men to marry would cause not only distress to themselves but disappointment and frustration to their wives.'

'What are you saying? Are you condoning departure from the sacred union of men and women?'

Joshua just smiled at James. Then he said, 'I told you what is the ideal state for those who wish to follow me. But I'm realistic. Compassion is the greatest priority. There are many virtues and sometimes they conflict. When that happens the greatest rule I'd ask you to follow is to love your fellow human being. Love others as much as you value yourself. Treat others as you would want to be treated. Look at my words and interpret them if you will in the light of that.'

We are all silent then. No-one wants to get drawn into the implications of this, least of all my son, James. But I can see my son Joshua is going to cause all sorts of problems with the traditional religious authorities if he continues to be as controversial as this in public. But Joshua tends to leave people to draw their own conclusions from his words. He rarely spells out exactly what he is thinking. He doesn't like dogma like some of the Pharisees. Dogma too often clashes with compassion.

We ran into more opposition as we got further along the road from Ephraim to Jericho. News of our arrival went before us to both those who would welcome us and those who came to scoff or argue. There were one or two incidents where our motley group of followers were ready to commit violence against those who laughed or derided Joshua, but my son was quick to calm the crowd indicating that all had a perfect right to express their views without being threatened with fists or staves. Such rebukes would be followed by the departure of a few of the hotheads, much to my relief really, because I could see some of them were eager for the opportunity to stir up rebellion which I, unprompted by James, could well see the danger of.

Joshua was very patient with some of the Pharisees and teachers from the synagogues who tried to trap him into saying things that might antagonise the crowd at every opportunity. He would always give an answer and usually it was one which disarmed his critics and sometimes caused the crowd some merriment if the pompous official or rabbi got an answer which deflated him. This only upset the authorities who would retreat for a time and then turn up at the next village redoubling their efforts to trip him up. They never learned and would only retreat once more humiliated and angrier than ever.

We eventually reach the city of Jericho with its Roman army garrison and many imposing buildings rebuilt in the Roman style since the damage to the city caused by the invading army many years ago. Joshua did the rounds of the synagogues, as was his habit, though he found himself initially refused entry to a couple and banned from speaking there until our crowd of followers threatened to turn ugly and the priests and rabbis relented for fear of starting a riot that the Roman soldiers would seize as an opportunity for cracking a few skulls open.

At one of these synagogues we were greeted by a couple of rabbis who seemed more sympathetic than usual and were invited to dine back in the house of one of them, a man named Simon, who had also brought some of the other synagogue officials, both scribes and teachers, to the meal. I think this Simon was a little put out when we all turned up, the women as well as the men, and he hastily set aside a room for the women only, where some food was assembled, though not, I noticed, as handsomely displayed or of such fine quality as that prepared for the men.

We are now therefore reclining in the next room and can hear the conversation between the men. We have soon finished the food put before us by the servants – this man must be very wealthy, I keep seeing another servant I've not noticed before. Goodness knows how many servants or slaves he owns! The men are still eating next door – I fear my Joshua can't be eating much because the other guests all keep plying him with questions, which he politely answers. They must be talking about one's duty to give alms to the poor, because I hear one of Simon's guests, possibly one of his sons, asking if any rich man could get into the kingdom that Joshua had been describing. There is a sudden guffaw of laughter when Joshua cracks a joke about it being easier to get a camel through the eye of a needle than a rich man to get into the kingdom. I don't get it at first, but Mariam explains to me that one of the narrow gates into the city is nicknamed the 'Needle's Eye' because it's so narrow and only pedestrians can walk through it. They obviously don't take Joshua seriously, because I hear him emphasise afterwards that he means it.

'I'm sorry to labour it, but I mean it. You're all wealthy. I know you give alms to the poor, but you make sure you keep more than enough to keep yourselves in this style of comfortable life. If you really wanted to experience the joys and satisfaction of the kingdom, you'd give it all away and come and be my disciple like these men here.'

'It's easy for them,' I hear someone shout above the hubbub that has greeted this statement. 'They didn't have much to start with, so they didn't have much to give up. And they're used to your nomadic lifestyle. We couldn't cope with that.'

'Exactly, that's what I'm saying. That's why it's so hard for someone who's wealthy. There are too many things to protect and maintain so that the priorities in life get swamped. That's why the poor and oppressed find it easier to accept my teaching. They've little to lose. Little of material wealth anyway. Don't think it's that easy though. These men have given up much to be with me. Their families, their homes, their jobs and they are ready to risk the dangers we face when I speak of things that are unpalatable to the rich and the influential.'

At that moment Mariam mutters something to me that I cannot catch and then I see her draw a jar from her bag and she gets up and without a further word pushes past the servants into the room where the men are reclining. A sudden hush falls and I hear a chink and gasps of horror. What has happened? What has Mary done? Has she assaulted someone? Has she hit someone with the jar? What has suddenly made her so angry? Are we all going to get involved in a brawl and

245

be thrown out? Then I hear Simon, in the deathly silence, exclaim.

'What is she doing? What a waste!'

There is a sudden pungent smell of exotic ointment, a fragrance that fills both rooms, is almost overpowering, blotting out the smell of food and sweat.

'The stupid woman, if she didn't want that ointment, she could have sold it and given the money to the poor. That's what you've just been talking about. Why can't you get your own followers to live up to the things you're saying? Don't expect us to do as you say if your own disciples and their women don't.'

'Don't criticise the woman. Mariam is my friend and she is showing her love and gratitude to me for the way I've been able to help her these past few years. Don't you give gifts to those you love? You can do that and give to the poor as well – they won't go away. And she's just done what you, Simon, or your servants, failed to do. We've had a long and tiring day. We are hot and sweaty, our feet are dusty and no-one gave us the courtesy of the usual cooling water at the door to refresh us and cleanse our feet. Mariam has just made up for your lack of attentiveness and what's more, she's done it in a way that – whilst it might seem excessive to you – is a symbol of her complete acceptance of my message and the existence of the kingdom in her very heart. Don't moan about her. She's an example to you and all your guests here.'

'But how well do you know this woman? Is she purified? Has she been a sinner? Why are you letting her do this to you? Are you not in danger of being unclean yourself? If you continue to live with such people you can't expect us to let you into our synagogues and talk as a rabbi yourself unless you can prove to us your repudiation of sin and loose living just as John the Baptiser did near here a couple of years ago.'

'Now you praise John. Did you go out and hear his word? Were you baptised?' There is a silence. 'No, I thought not. So he was an ascetic. He kept himself pure and challenged others to turn from their wrong-doing. I do it a different way, but to the same end. So I mix with sinners, the so-called riff-raff you and colleagues like you often accuse me of mixing with. But if I don't go to those who need to hear my message, how will they hear? So I do mix with them, I'm not ashamed of that and many do respond to my words. Which is more than you and some of your fellow priests and rabbis do. You think you are sinless, you have no need of my message. So be it. It was interesting though that when some of your colleagues brought a condemned woman to me in another town and I permitted anyone without sin to throw the first stone, no-one felt able to look me in the eye and take up the challenge.'

These words have silenced most of the conversation and there is obvious embarrassment.

'Are you admitting then that this woman is a sinner?'

'No, her past is no concern of yours or of my followers or of mine now. She is a faithful and loyal follower, the giver of hospitality. She is kind and considerate. The love she has for me and my cause has eradicated any fault she may have had in the past. And if your attitude was like hers, your past sins would be forgiven too.'

'What right have you to forgive sins? Surely that's the prerogative of the Lord God, Jehovah, only. Your speech is treading dangerously close to blasphemy.'

'If you are part of the kingdom of God, you are children of God. God is your father. You are part of the family. The family can forgive, indeed must forgive if the family is to live in harmony.'

I expect James is bridling now. Joshua will soon have upset them all. I'm not sure accepting this invitation was a good idea. At least Joshua has his own disciples around him. Most of them are burly men, I don't think Simon and his well-to-do guests will try anything silly, but it's not going to improve relationships with the religious authorities if potentially sympathetic rabbis like this feel upset. Then one of the younger of Simon's guests tries to break the embarrassment by asking another question.

'So how will we be judged? Are you saying that God will automatically condemn any of us who've not given all our worldly goods away? Isn't that a bit extreme?'

'I didn't say it is impossible – just hard. I have friends who are comfortable and learned. One is even a member of the Sanhedrin though he doesn't shout about it, as he feels he can be of greater help if he's not counted as an obvious follower of mine. Your colleagues force that on him by prejudging what I say and do, so that if he declares himself as a supporter and believer in my message, his views would immediately be discounted. And not all rich men are obsessed with the maintenance and expansion of their wealth. Some are satisfied, are thankful for what they have and use their resources to help others. If you feed and cloth the poor, tend to the sick, seek justice for the oppressed and the wrongfully accused, show mercy to those who admit their faults, God will accept you. If you see the divine in each person that you meet, however wretched their circumstances, then you are blessed indeed and a member of God's kingdom, whether you recognise it in your words or not. On the other hand, there are many who say the right words, obey their religious rituals and scruples, who think themselves saved, but if they are not compassionate, if they ignore or neglect the pain and needs of their fellow human beings, what is their religion worth? It becomes words only, an empty shell – and an empty shell is what such a person is.'

We leave in the end. They are civil to us, but there is palpable tension. I relax as we go out of the house. Some of the disciples are shaking the dust from their feet as they put their sandals on. Despite the hints, still no-one has offered them any water to wash in. At least we know we all have hosts who are generous and gracious and are solicitous of our welfare.

It's already dark and Joshua, who's been leading the way, nearly stumbles across a young child beggar lurking in the doorway of a wretched hovel that's been thrown together against the wall of a villa. He turns to Judas.

'Give this child some money from our purse. She's been here all day and no-one has given her anything. He stoops and picks up the child and looks into her eyes. At first she looks frightened.

'When did you last eat, child?'

The little girl, filthy dirty, just shakes her head.

'John, fetch the Rabbi Simon and tell him to bring some of the food we left to feed this child and to take back to her family.' Simon Peter immediately offers to go.

'Master, I'll go. He won't bloody refuse me.'

'No, Peter, let John go. He'll be more diplomatic than you and Simon will come out with him. You'll just bully him into giving you food. I want him to notice this girl and realise that she's here near his gate every day. It may stir his humanity.'

So we wait. And Joshua's right. John comes back with Simon and one of the servants carrying two baskets filled with meat and bread and grapes and figs. They hand them both to the girl. She looks unbelieving at both baskets laden with such food as she's never seen before. She can scarce lift them from the ground for they're so heavy and she's so undernourished.

'Accept a child like this, Simon, and it's as if you receive me. You laid a feast on for me. Feeding this child, even if you think she's of no value, is just as important. She's as valuable to God as I am. She's here every day. I'm not.'

'I'll see she and her family are fed each day. I'll have one of the servants send a basket of food here daily. And I'll check if there are others nearby. You're quite right. I'm fortunate and I have a responsibility to the poor in this neighbourhood.'

'You see,' says Joshua turning to all of us, 'our meal in Simon's house has been worthwhile. Simon, in helping this young girl, you've done me the honour. God created her, she is of his family. So you must see God in her. Every day you help her, just think that you are feeding me.'

I think Simon is a little embarrassed at what's just happened. Joshua has put him on the spot and he's reacted the only way he could without refusing co-operation outright. I wonder if Simon will be as good as his word when we are no longer here.

'He will,' says my son when I tackle him later and air my doubts. 'He's learned a lesson. He'll change. One of his sons will keep him up to it. That was not a servant who came with him. Didn't you recognise he was one of his sons?'

I shake my head. There were so many men in Simon's dining area I wasn't sure which were family and which guests.

'That's a rich man who might just squeeze through the eye of the needle,' he says grinning, 'though he'd better not try to bring too many camels with him!'

*   *   *   *   *

After a number of days spent in Jericho, where the news of Simon's lesson spread and a number of other rich Jews started looking to the welfare of some of the beggars found daily on their streets, we moved on taking the road back towards Jerusalem, planning to stop off with our friends Lazarus, Martha and Mary in Bethany on the way. Magdalene Mariam told me all about their last visit to this home – it was apparently shortly after Joshua had met and helped her and had taken her under his wing out of the city and had stayed for a while with our friends. I'd heard rumours that Lazarus had been unwell and that Joshua had cured him, but apparently that was nothing as dramatic as the real story – not how Mariam told it anyhow!

'He was dead,' she stressed with great emphasis. 'He'd been in the tomb for several days. They'd sent for us because they knew we were in the city, but we thought we were too late. Well, at least I and the disciples did. Yeshua seemed very upset when he found out and Mary and Martha were distraught, then Yeshua actually summoned him from the grave and out he came, just like a ghost. We were petrified. Martha was the only practical one and rushed off to get him some food. Yeshua actually told us to tell no-one about it, but the story sped like wildfire because nearly everyone in Bethany had attended his funeral so his appearance caused a sensation.'

I studied Lazarus closely, I couldn't help feeling curious. He looked quite normal to me and he acted as he'd always done. I found it difficult to believe that he'd had such a dramatic experience. It was his sister, Mary, who confirmed it. My mind is just reeling. The widow's son in Nain, the story about the young girl who was a daughter of the synagogue official, and now Lazarus. If he can do that, can he do anything? How does he decide who to help? He could spend all his time bringing the dead back to life. I asked him later that evening.

'I do bring people back to life all the time, but not literally in the way you're thinking.'

'But why these? These three? Have you brought others back to life?'

'Because I was there and there was a particular distress at their deaths. And, I have to confess, I was moved to tears by the outpouring of grief that I encountered. I just could not stand by and do nothing when it was within my power to help. And perhaps too, although it was not my prime motivation, there was the opportunity to demonstrate by that vivid symbol that my words, or the obeying of my words, could bring the souls of men to life – even those considered to be totally lost to decent society.'

We attended the local synagogue on the Sabbath and Joshua was given the opportunity to speak – he'd been speaking every day in the market place, but he was well known in Bethany and the local rabbis and scribes could not deny his powers as they had been so vividly demonstrated in their midst. Joshua had taken the opportunity once again to stress the need for justice and compassion to all people, obligations far greater than the religious rituals that so dominated the daily lives of many of the people, particularly the older more traditional Jews. He'd been a little upset that many of the Samaritans that had joined us had been excluded from the synagogue. One or two of the Samaritan women had sneaked in with us and we'd made no effort to prevent them and I think a few men had pretended to be Joshua's disciples and had got in too.

Anyway, he's completed his talk and handed the scripture scroll back to the priest and sits awaiting the usual questions. He's obviously made his point about the priority of some religious observances over others, because the first question comes very quickly from a rabbi in the congregation – presumably not a local man, but possibly one of the argumentative ones who harassed him in Jericho.

'Well, teacher, you've told us that it's most important to have compassion rather than obey the religious duties laid down by Moses and other prophets in our holy scriptures. So, get to the point. What, in your opinion, exactly is the most important law of all?'

Joshua doesn't hesitate.

'There are two that are equal and above all others – in fact, these two sum up all the intentions behind the other laws and commandments. The first is to love God with all your faculties – your mind, your heart, your very soul and spirit. And the second, which is equally important, is to love your neighbour as much as yourself. If you obey these two commandments everything else will follow.'

'Of course the rabbi decides to quibble. He can't let Joshua appear to get away with that and better him. So he comes back with another question.

'So who is my neighbour? What do you mean? The person who lives next door to me? Someone from my village? Do you include my neighbour's wife and children?'

'Everyone who needs you, everyone. Let me put it this way. There was once a traveller on the road up to Jerusalem who got attacked by thieves – a not uncommon experience on this road as I guess you know. The bandits wounded him and robbed him of everything he had and left him lying on the roadside unconscious. Then a priest came by and looked and crossed the road to the other side because he was hurrying to take part in a sacrifice in the Temple and he didn't want to be contaminated by the man's blood that he could see on his body. Then, a little later, a Levite came upon him, and he scurried off also without helping him, because he feared that he too might be attacked by the bandits if he stopped and he was conscious of the religious artifacts he was carrying which had been entrusted to him. Finally, a Samaritan, yes one of the nation despised by so many Jews, came by and he went over and looked and saw immediately the state the man was in and took pity on him despite the danger and cleaned his wounds and lifted him onto his own donkey and stopped at the next lodging place where he asked the innkeeper to look after him and paid for the man's stay. Who, then, do you think was neighbour to the wounded man?'

'Well, obviously the man who took pity on him. But your story is a little far-fetched. What Samaritan would dare to come to the assistance of a Jew? You're not really including them in your commandment, are you? Presumably you're saying that any Jew is our neighbour and not just those of our own street or village?'

'Look! Many Samaritans have welcomed me and accepted my message. And Romans! God is the Father of mankind, all men, women and children, Jew and Gentile. Love and respect all people. Only then will you be truly children of the Lord God, Jehovah Almighty. My message to you is that you can all

253

become the children of God, your Father God. Therefore everyone will be your brothers and sisters, all we be related to you because of your relationship with God, the Father.'

The rabbi who asked the questions looks crestfallen. He is silent, doesn't, can't answer Joshua. He looks sullen, frustrated and just shakes his head. Others in the congregation who might have asked further questions are then silent. No-one wants to say any more. Perhaps they don't want to be seen to be as foolish as the rabbi. Even James seems amused. Perhaps they feel Joshua has just said it all and there is nothing more to say. As Joshua says so often, 'Stop arguing about religious and ritual niceties, just go and do as I say!'

Chapter 21
Mari

Only five more days to the Passover meal, which we will celebrate in Jerusalem with Joshua. I'd thought we would have it here with Lazarus, Martha and Mary but Joshua has apparently made arrangements with a supporter of his he's known since his last visit to have the meal in our capital city. He seems to think it important though I'm not sure why. We're going up to Jerusalem today as Joshua wants to address the crowds who are swarming into Jerusalem from all over the country. I hope he knows what he's doing. I sense some of his disciples are a bit nervous about it and fear he might stir up controversy and opposition that could bring down the wrath of the authorities on us. We still have a large contingent of supporters with us and most are determined to follow us into Jerusalem. I think some of them think Joshua will, despite all his protests, declare open rebellion against the Romans and expect the city to rise up in support of him.

I know Joshua is concerned about that. I overheard him last night talking to Simon Peter and Andrew and I gathered he was making plans to try to calm a potentially volatile situation. I didn't catch the precise plan but I know they were discussing what they might do as they reached the main city gate. At least we have no worries of the type in the story Joshua told yesterday. No bandit in his right mind will tackle a crowd of the size that looks as though it will accompany us all the way. Joshua and the disciples lead the way and a group of men from Ephraim, Jericho and Bethany have pushed in front of us women, then the disciples' wives, Susannah, Salome and now two Maryiams – Lazarus's sister as well as our Magdalene has come. Then there is a motley crowd, women and children as well as men, which includes a sprinkling who've come all the way from Samaria as well as a good number from the Judean towns and villages, Jericho and Bethany.

We set out early this morning and it's hard work as the road climbs steeply between the stark barren rocks, which reflect heat from the scorching sun, now blaring from a cloudless sky. Luckily, because of the size of the crowd, we are progressing relatively slowly. Joshua is mindful of the women and children in our midst and is resisting some of the younger men who are impatient to reach the city. I'm getting a little breathless, as are Susannah and Salome, but the two Mariams make us hand over the baskets of food we've brought. We pass the Mount of Olives high to our right and get our first view of the city walls as the road turns north and runs parallel to the city boundary. Around midday we reach the green and shady garden called Gethsemane and Joshua indicates that we should sit under the shade of the olive trees in the garden and eat some of the produce we've brought with us and drink before we become faint from the heat. We're now quite close to the city wall and the Golden Gate is clearly visible, as are the Temple walls high above, shimmering in the haze. I notice that as soon as we sit down Joshua has a word with a huddle of his disciples and Simon Peter and Andrew set off towards the gate.

While we're eating, my son James comes over – he's been with the other disciples all morning. He's had little to say recently for which I'm thankful. He seems satisfied that I'm being looked after by the other women and he's left me in peace.

'They've gone to fetch a donkey, a colt for Joshua to ride into the city. He thinks it will send the right message to the authorities, rather than getting a horse which some of the men from Jericho had been advocating. He seems to think that the authorities will recognise that he's come in peace rather than declaring rebellion and war. I don't think it will make any difference. I think that message is too subtle for the crowd, they'll go mad and so will the Romans and the Jewish leaders. They'll see it as a challenge, the priests will read it that he's claiming to fulfil the prophecy of Isaiah. Since I couldn't persuade you to stay at home, I implore you to remain at the back of this mob and if there's any sign of trouble I'll come and fetch you, Susannah, Salome and Mariam and we'll get back to Bethany as fast as we can and before real trouble brews up.'

'Surely we'll be safe in this crowd?'

'Mother, nothing can be guaranteed. I don't trust this crowd. It'll only take one of them to utter some stupid challenge or shove a priest or Roman soldier and then they'll retaliate. Before you can decide what to do, you'll find they've arrested Joshua and will come storming into the crowd to disperse us, staves and spears flung indiscriminately. The fact that you're an older woman will make no difference. If you're in the crowd, they'll just lash out and if any innocent gets caught they'll just say you were in the wrong place at the wrong time and have no sympathy.'

'James, I've come all this way with Joshua. I've always known he would be seen and recognised as the Messiah one day. I'm not going to run away from him at this stage. I've trusted God so far. I'm going to trust him now.'

'I've warned you enough times of the danger Joshua's in. If you insist on staying with him, you'll be tarred with the same brush. If trouble starts, I'm getting out. You can come with me if you like. If you stay, I'll take no more responsibility for you. You're not my mother any more.'

I wince at his vehemence. Surely he doesn't mean what he is saying? Why has he come all this way against his better judgment if he intends to give up and leave me to my own devices now? He's trying to bluff me and get me to weaken. I won't.

'James, if you must, so be it. I'm staying, no matter what!'

He stamps his feet in annoyance and turns away. I watch him go back to Joshua and the group of disciples around him. I'm sure he is only trying to call my bluff. He doesn't really mean it, does he?

We've finished our meal for the moment and the crowd is getting restive. Someone starts singing and then the whole crowd bursts into song, it's one of King David's songs of triumph. If they keep singing as we go into the city, the claim they are making for Joshua will be only too obvious. Some of the younger folk have started tearing leaves from the trees, then others go and find palm trees and rip great swathes of fronds down and start swinging them in time with the song. The crowd is at fever pitch and shouting that Joshua is King David's son. Then we see Simon Peter and Andrew coming towards us leading a young colt and the crowd goes mad. Grown men are tearing their cloaks off – someone has flung one over the donkey's back and the surge in the crowd bundles Joshua on to its back, then others fling their cloaks on to the ground in front of the animal and they are actually worshipping him, some shouting out that he is God. This is insane. We shall have a riot on our hands as soon as we enter the Gate – that is if we are not met by Roman soldiers or the Temple Guard before we even reach the city wall.

I'm really frightened now. We've set off and there is nothing I can do but follow and pray. Joshua is riding ahead and the men and children are racing ahead making an arch over him with the palm leaves and picking up the cloaks strewn on the ground and slinging them again in front of the beast. It's a wonder the animal hasn't bolted with all the screaming and hullabaloo. Joshua hasn't done anything to stop them. Well, I suppose there's little he could do now – the crowd wouldn't take any notice of him. They're too excited, totally carried away. Then I notice people are streaming out of the city and coming to join us. They're singing and laughing too. The people around me are euphoric. I can hear the shouts.

'The Messiah's come!' 'Praise God, the Messiah's here at last!' 'King David's back to rescue us!' I'm thrilled and scared at the same time. The adulation, the recognition is all I've sought for him, but the very violence of the welcome is out of control and I fear the consequences.

Where are the authorities? We go in through the Gate unopposed and the citizens of the city are flocking to us and join in the procession. Where are we going? I watch the bystanders carefully and notice that not everyone is sharing in the general celebration. There are a few men in rich robes I see muttering to themselves, but they seem unwilling to tackle the mob. They'll wait for the crowd to disperse and then they'll act. I find myself being even more concerned for my son. Doesn't he realise that not all the crowd is so enthusiastic?

We reach the Temple and Joshua mounts the steps to address the crowd. There must be nigh on a thousand people now before us in the square, all cheering and shouting. I notice a few soldiers appearing and taking up positions on the edge of the crowd, but they stand there, weapons at the ready, and just watch.

Joshua holds up an arm and the crowd falls silent. His voice rings out.

'Citizens of Judea and Samaria, citizens of Jerusalem, God's kingdom is here. If you love God and obey his commands, if you care for each other and act justly in all your dealings, you are already citizens of that glorious kingdom, a nation of peace where the lion shall lie down with the lamb and war shall be no more. You call me the Messiah. Even the stones shouted out as we passed by...' – the crowd erupts at this point and the cheering and screams of 'Hosannah' drown out his attempt to finish the sentence. For several minutes the uproar continues and his attempt to silence them so he can continue is thwarted. Eventually he manages to say, 'I come in peace to rescue your souls, not to overthrow the government,' but clearly many in the square do not believe him for the shouting and singing

259

breaks out once again. Eventually he resigns himself to allowing the crowd to continue their singing and cheering and comes down to mingle with them. At this the crowd surges round him and attempts to lift him to their shoulders. This carries on for a whole hour. The priests I saw earlier have disappeared. The soldiers are making no attempt to intervene, but they are watching closely. I'm sure they're noting who the mob's leaders are and are biding their time. They'll be reporting back to the Roman Governor and to the Tetrarch, Herod Antipas, tonight, I'm sure of it.

Then word goes round that Joshua intends to return to Bethany before darkness falls and the crowd begins to calm down. There is still singing, but it is more tuneful, less lusty and the crowd begins to become more good-humoured, linking arms, perhaps relieved in their heart of hearts that they've not provoked retribution from the soldiers. The crowd begins to disperse and some of the families who've come with us are beginning to make their way back to the Gate and the Jericho road. Then I see Joshua escaping from the adoring group straining to listen to him and he comes right over to me.

'Mother, it's time we went back to Bethany. Are you not tired? We'll come in again tomorrow. You'll see, the numbers will drop off and it will be more manageable. There are serious messages I want to get across to the citizens here and I need a little more privacy and a chance to speak without all this noise.'

James comes too. 'Well at least we're still here and unscathed. But they're watching. We won't get away with it for long. Let's get back to Lazarus and Martha and get a good night's rest. If you're intent on coming in again tomorrow, you need to get some rest.'

He's right, at least on this occasion. I do need to rest, but we've a good couple of hours' walk first. At least it's downhill nearly all the way.

When we get back to Bethany, Joshua tells me he's been talking to many of the families that accompanied us today.

'I've suggested to them that they stay at home tomorrow – or at least the women and children. I need to start confronting the authorities there and it could put some of our followers in danger. I need space to get down to the serious part of my message too – I can't do that if I'm surrounded by hundreds of people wherever I go. I need to get my message to new people in the city. We'll go in tomorrow morning – we'll set off early to give a longer time in the city. Do you want to stay here with Martha and Lazarus?'

'No,' I say. 'I'm coming too.'

*   *   *   *   *

We set off at sunrise. Our party is much smaller today. All the disciples and their women, Susannah, Salome, the two Mariams and me, of course, and around thirty or forty men, mainly those who've come with us all the way from Samaria, Ephraim and Jericho. The walk is easier at this hour of the day and the hills look strangely beautiful in the low rays of the sun, the beams picking out the different contours and valleys, the deep clefts looking black and sinister. We are in the city by the middle of the morning and Jerusalem is already full of pilgrims from all over Judea and further parts, all come to celebrate the Passover festival. We make our way immediately to the Temple for Joshua will take his place once more on the Temple steps as it is one of the best places to catch the attention of the passers-by. As soon as Joshua begins to speak, a crowd begins to form and word spreads quickly for his fame is acknowledged here as well. He addresses the crowd for many minutes on his favourite theme, the coming of the kingdom and its nature, that it will be a society of the caring and the just where wrong-doing will be renounced and forgiven and the oppressed and the poor will have a rightful place, honoured and respected citizens equal to all in the

261

kingdom, sharing together the privileges of the children of God.

Then one or two in the crowd begin to shout out questions and comments to him.

'What about justice here? Are you talking about now in Jerusalem or some time in the far off future?'

Other voices are raised.

'I want justice now!'

'You won't get much reaction from this lot here!'

'You'd better start with those in the Temple!'

Then someone shouts out a specific demand.

'I've been cheated. The rogues in the Temple forecourt charged me double for the sacrificial doves!'

'And me,' calls another. 'The money changers are charging extortionate rates. It's criminal!'

Before long Joshua is besieged by a gaggle of angry men all complaining of the way they've been treated by the traders inside the Temple walls. Joshua is listening carefully to them, asking them questions. Then I hear him calling to us.

'We're going inside. These people feel cheated. I'm going to sort things out.'

Joshua strides off ahead surrounded by his disciples and some of the men who've been complaining to him. James comes back to us women.

'I think you'd better stay here. There may be trouble if he intends to challenge the traders. They're protected by the Temple Guards who'll expel Joshua and his followers from the Temple precincts if they don't like what he's doing.'

'No, I'd rather stay close to him and see exactly what's happening. They won't hurt a group of old women.'

'I wouldn't trust them, but if you must, stay close to me.'

We enter the Temple's outer court. It's pandemonium in there. The noise is horrific with the cries of the traders hawking their wares mingling with the bleating of sheep and goats, the calls of doves and the screeches of animals being slaughtered ready for sacrifice. The floor of the courtyard is dirty with animal droppings and rivulets of blood and the stink is horrible. There are angry shouts coming from men as pilgrims barter and argue over the prices they are being charged. Joshua watches all this with a look of sheer contempt on his face. Encircled by many of the men who have complained to him, he goes up to one of the traders who is selling doves and listens to the customer who is trying to buy a bird for sacrifice. The man is saying that the price is more than double of that in his own village.

'Well, you should have bought one there and brought it with you. I've got middle-men to pay and the Temple tax on top.'

'But it's outrageous. You're taking advantage of all the pilgrims. I'll find another stall.'

'You won't do any better. We all charge the same. The priests make certain there's no undercutting. They have no intention of being squeezed.'

Joshua is seething, but he moves on to the next stall where a money-changer is having a similar row.

'Why do I have to change my money for Temple currency, just to give it away as my donation. What's wrong with good Jewish coins?'

'It's the rules. Don't complain to me, mate. I don't make them.'

Another trader pipes up.

'It's purified money. You don't know where your common currency has been. It might be contaminated by buying unclean food or paying for a whore.'

'I'd like to know what's pure about money sold in such a scandalous manner, cheating these poor people who can ill afford it.' Joshua has spoken up after listening carefully to the customers' complaints. 'How much is your mark-up? What percentage do you add on for your own profit?'

The first trader will not answer, but another stall-holder shouts out.

'It's not us. Don't think it's our fault. The priests take three quarters of the profit and we only get a quarter for our time spent here in the heat and noise all day.'

The dove-seller has overheard and comes to join in.

'It's the same with us. We have to pay rent for every day we're here. The priests make a packet from us. If you don't like it, go and complain to them and don't stop us making our legitimate pittance here.'

'Pittance? Don't make me laugh! You're all scoundrels, you're in league with the priests. I know how much you make.'

Joshua is getting really angry. I've never seen him so furious as he is now. He storms off round the courtyard watching the other traders, listening to similar arguments raging everywhere. He spots one poor woman weeping.

'What's the matter?' he asks her.

'I can't afford a dove,' she mumbles, 'and I didn't realise I'd need to change my Temple gift into a different currency. I'd saved up to make a generous gift for so long and people tell me that half of it will go to the pockets of the money-changer and the value to the Temple will be so much less.'

'Don't worry,' Joshua says gently to her. 'It was your intention that counted. You have made the sacrifice, your love was sufficient. God desires your loyalty and service, not bits of dead birds and valueless Temple currency. Go and worship God in the Temple and leave this travesty of religion behind. If they demand a sacrifice from you, tell them that Yeshua, the prophet from Nazareth, has received your sacrifice and blessed you.'

The woman smiles weakly and looks at me. Joshua notices.

'Mother, take this lady inside to the Women's Court and see she is treated fairly.'

So the group of us women accompany her and we are scarce at the gateway to the Court when we hear shouts and screams and the noise of coins clattering to the ground and rolling on the stone tiles. I look round and see Joshua striding to every stall in turn and sweeping his hand across the tables scattering the coins in all directions. His disciples are joining him and our other followers take up the action with great enthusiasm, opening the bird cages and releasing the flurry of doves now taking off into the air, untying the sheep and goats so soon there is utter confusion of people and animals, a total madhouse. The traders' tables get knocked over. The Temple Guards coming running, but there are only half a dozen of them and the crowd with Joshua, there must be fifty, is growing by the second as the pilgrims see what is happening and join in, some releasing the animals, some grabbing at the rolling coins or snatching a bird or animal for themselves.

The crowd is now out of control. And the first guard that attempts to stop them is overpowered by the mob and the others cower back in fear.

Joshua suddenly stands still and shouts at the top of his voice for silence. The hubbub subsides and everyone stands still as if frozen by his command.

'This is meant to be a house of prayer. Look at all of you! You have turned it into a den of thieves. You are all guilty. The priests and Temple authorities who permit and organise such flagrant exploitation of the devout and humble. You traders who profit from it and hide behind the excuse that you are only doing the business of the priests. And those of you who've now taken advantage of the chaos to steal the money and the birds and animals for sacrifice. I tell you, these beasts and birds are tainted. If you try to present them at the altar, I tell you, God will not accept these gifts, for they did not come from your heart.'

I can still hear a coin rolling on the stone flags. The doves have flown and circled in the air and some have returned to settle on the Temple ramparts or strut haphazardly round the courtyard. The other animals are wandering aimlessly around while their would-be sellers are frantically trying to round them up again. The Temple Guards have grouped but they look askance at Joshua who now has a crowd of maybe a hundred men around him and they decide they can do nothing. Joshua, surrounded by his supporters, now moves back to the Temple steps where a large crowd of curious onlookers has assembled, hearing the noise from the precincts of the Temple. The guards have not followed, but are watching as the traders attempt to restore their stalls for business. All the pilgrims seem to have followed Joshua out, intent to see and hear what happens next.

'Fellow Jews and friends here for the Passover from other nations or parts of Israel, those of you who value true religion and not the commerce and betrayal of our faith that you see here, I beg you to offer prayers for the cleansing of our nation and of our great Temple here which should be the spiritual centre of our faith and not the cesspit of all that's misguided and wrong in it. When I was a boy, I found scholars and men of faith who listened to and obeyed God's will. I had a relative, much revered as a caring priest here, Zechariah of Ein-Karem. What has gone wrong? Many of you will have heard my cousin, John, known as the Baptiser, and heard him call for the nation's repentance. Even then, I heard him complain about the hypocrisy and avarice of the priests and Temple officials, but now I see it with my own eyes and am appalled. How can supposed men of God defraud and cheat the poor? Those in charge of us should be our servants, not our exploiters. Have you not read of Isaiah's prophecy that declares God's messenger, the Messiah, to be the servant of all, suffering with his people? Do these priests and Pharisees who are meant to be our teachers and our guides not know these things?'

Joshua spots a white-robed Pharisee on the edge of the crowd holding his arms aloft as if in prayer.

'Why is that Pharisee thanking God that he's one of elite and not sinners like he thinks all of us are, because he believes we desecrated the Temple? God will not hear his pompous self-justifications. Better the men and women who retire privately into their own abode and fling themselves on God's mercy imploring him to forgive their sins that seem to them so great but pale into insignificance compared with that man's self-righteous pride.'

The crowd turn as one and jeer at the man, who gathers his robes around him and flees. Men are shouting out their support to Joshua's words. I'm surprised that Joshua has made his contempt for the man so obvious. He's usually so sensitive but he's made an enemy of this man who could be influential. No-one will tackle Joshua now, the crowd around him is too great. I see rabbis and officials scurry past, a few huddled together in deep conversation, pretending not to notice us or hear what Joshua is saying. As Joshua continues in similar vein, speaking out against the corruption of our rulers and the way in which the religious authorities not only condone but are often the chief perpetrators of what's wrong, James finds me and grabs me by the arm.

'He's done it now. He's signed his own death warrant. He's made an enemy of every man of influence in the city. If the Romans take action against him, none of the Jewish rulers will lift a finger to help him. How could he be so stupid? You're coming back with me to Bethany now before the priests and Pharisees return with a contingent of Roman soldiers to arrest him for stirring up the mob. Every trader in the Temple courtyard will be a witness against him. You can bet that the Pharisee he so publicly humiliated just now will be complaining to his peers at this very moment, plotting how to avenge himself.'

The disciples are gathered in a huddle. The excitement of the violent action in the Temple courtyard is draining away, as they realise the offence that's now been caused and the threat to the very source of so much income that the priests and Levites have relied on for several years. They want to get Joshua back to the comparative safety of Bethany before the Temple Guards are strengthened by the Roman forces. After a long debate, Joshua is persuaded to go along with their wishes. We walk slowly back towards the Jericho road, still accompanied by many of the visitors to the city who see Joshua as a spokesman for their discontent. I don't get a chance to speak to my son until at length we're back in Bethany and Martha is ministering to his physical needs, bringing him a cup of wine and fruit while her only servant carefully washes his feet. Before I can speak, Joshua looks at me and smiles ruefully.

'You think I was unwise, Mother. They all do. It's not just James. Even Simon Peter has had a go at me. Do you think I should have ignored such corruption in the Temple of all places? Do you think I should have condoned such practices by saying nothing?'

'I'm sure the traders who were cheating the pilgrims deserved what they got. And their masters too. The racket they are running is a disgrace. Wise or not, I'm sure you had to say it. I do not criticise you for that. But why did you single out that praying Pharisee and publicly humiliate him? He won't forgive you for that. It's not like you to condemn anyone so publicly.'

'You think I was too harsh.'

'Well, certainly unwise. Did you really have to do that? Couldn't you have had a quiet word with the man?'

'You obviously didn't hear what he was saying, Mother. He was taking delight in condemning those around him. He knew they could hear and he was so obviously praising his own standing before God whilst judging everyone else. I had to take him to task in the hearing of those whom he was condemning. He's like many of the religious leaders that have made compromises with the Romans, not for the benefit and protection of the people, but for their own greedy ends. The Romans don't respect them. They use them to control the people but privately they hold them in contempt.'

'I understand. But is it wise?'

'No, of course it's not wise. But I have to trust my father. I have to stand up for the oppressed, those for whom justice is an unknown concept. This will bring me into conflict with the rulers of this world, the abusers, not the abused. It will cause trouble. I always knew it would. I've told you all often enough. I've told my followers to be ready to sacrifice themselves for what is right and good. I don't think they've ever really realised just what I meant. It's coming home to them now.'

'I understand you, Joshua my son, but it's hard. I fear for you, you're my own flesh and blood, why should I not be afraid on your behalf?'

'My brother James is not a great help, is he? He feeds your fears and worries. You should spend more time with my disciple, John. He is one of the few that really understands me and he would help you. And Mariam of Magdala and Lazarus and Mary in Bethany. I'll have a word with John. It is going to get tough, I know that, Mother, even in the next few days. I've not come to Jerusalem and addressed the crowds openly like this before because I knew where it would lead and I wasn't ready. Or, more truthfully, my disciples weren't ready. Even now, I worry about some of them. But I can't postpone the challenge for ever. When we go into Jerusalem tomorrow, walk with John. There will be no danger to us during the day. The crowds are too strongly in our favour – the authorities won't risk anything that could cause a riot for fear of upsetting their Roman masters.

That night I have a good look at John. I've never singled him out before. He's the only unmarried one – his brother got married last year as his betrothed family put pressure on him. I'll do as Joshua says and try to get to know him.

269

Chapter 22
Mari

We didn't have much to eat for breakfast this morning as we left Bethany so early and John told me that Joshua had been out alone praying well before dawn. He must be hungry now. There's not much vegetation beside this road but I can see a fig tree in the distance and with a bit of luck there may be ripe figs we can pick. Joshua and most of the disciples have gathered round the tree, but Andrew and Nathaniel who've gone to pick the fruit, shout back that they can see nothing – either it's barren or someone has beaten us to it. Then something extraordinary happens. Joshua curses the fig tree and declares it will always be barren. Why? What has the poor tree done to him? Has tiredness got the better of Joshua and put him in a bad mood? Has he really lost his temper just because he was hungry and it was bare of fruit? It's not like him at all. Losing his temper with the traders in the Temple yesterday, and now this. Yesterday I could understand, his anger was justified, but this? It seems so petty.

I didn't hear much after that. John walked back to me and we continue uphill towards the city.

'John, did Joshua really curse that fig tree and make it barren?'

'Yes.'

'Why? It's not like him. What was the point?'

'I think he was trying to teach us something. I think he was trying to demonstrate to us - not just his disciples, but some of the other followers as well - that he had power over nature, but that if we followed and obeyed him, we could utilise such power ourselves and do similar things. And what's more, I'm not sure if he really made that tree barren. I have a shrewd idea he'd seen signs of blight on the tree and knew it would be barren and die in the next season or two. He's pretty sharp in his observation and knowledge of nature.'

I suppose that's an explanation. It seemed a very odd thing for him to do, out of character, but John doesn't seem too bothered.

Eventually we get to the Temple. We buy some bread and figs from a trader on the way – Joshua will certainly not let anyone buy things inside the Temple courtyard after yesterday's near riot. He's so angry at the hypocrisy of the outwardly religious that he won't let any of his followers open themselves to similar criticism that could be used against him. When we arrive, we find a large crowd already gathered. He's been expected. I notice in the crowd several blind men and a couple of severely crippled women. Joshua spots them and calls them forward. They are helped through the surging crowd by those accompanying them. Clearly they'd come in the hope that Joshua would heal them and they're not disappointed. He spends time with each one, talking quietly to them – I can't hear what he says for the crowd is noisy. But there are exclamations, and cheering and singing breaks out as one after another shout that they can see, and the elderly women seem to be transformed from stooped huddled beings into upright mature women, in fact one now seems to be no more than a slip of a girl. A rumour spreads round the crowd – she had been born deformed and no physician had ever been able to help her. I could guess the accuracy of this because she is now radiant, beaming at all of us and bubbling with laughter. She is quite transformed.

Some in the crowd start dancing and lots of children suddenly seem to be there running around all over the Temple steps, nearly bumping into a knot of white-robed bearded men looking on in disdain at this frantic activity. Then the children make it worse by yelling out 'Praise to King David's son', a clear reference to the Messiah. The men, I suppose they're rabbis from the Temple, remonstrate with the children's

271

parents or anyone near at hand, that what the children are shouting is sacrilege, blasphemy and they must be stopped. Joshua hears this and steps across and defends the children. Typically he takes the children seriously. He speaks directly to the complaining men.

'Let the children be. They're just doing what comes naturally. No-one's put them up to it, which I know is what you're thinking. Children are intuitive. They say what they think without dissembling. You should listen to them sometimes. You might learn something!'

One of the men turns furiously to him.

'Are you claiming they're right? Are you really accepting what they say in their ignorance and using babies' words to strengthen your dubious claim to be our Messiah? Just look at you, nothing but a peasant from Galilee with a smattering of knowledge of quackery!'

This makes those who overhear this exchange angry and the rabbis decide to beat a hasty retreat before they get jostled further. They depart muttering to the jeers of the crowd.

Joshua then starts again to teach the crowd and tells some stories, then contrasts the behaviour of the humble pilgrims with the pig-headedness and obstinate pride of the elite Pharisees, priests and rabbis. It's a popular message but it won't make him any friends in high places. I can just guess what James will be thinking now.

Later, in the afternoon, a group of rabbis from the Temple turn up at the edge of the crowd. Joshua has been answering questions from men in the assembled throng, which is growing every hour, and, confident now among several of their peers, one of the rabbis decides to challenge Joshua.

'Yesterday you were condemning the payment of donations to the Temple. What do you think we should do with our money then? Pay it all in taxes to the Romans to let them occupy our land in luxury and send our wealth back to layabouts and slave-owners in Rome?'

They're trying to trap Joshua. They want to goad him into saying something that will give them reason to denounce him to the Roman authorities. I'm sure Joshua realises this, he's not that naïve. Joshua is thinking hard and the crowd falls silent waiting to see what he'll say. He turns to Judas.

'Give me a coin from our purse!'

Judas scrabbles in his bag and produces a silver coin. Joshua peers at it, holds it up, glinting in the sun. He turns to the rabbi who questioned him.

'Well, learned teacher, whose head is inscribed on this coin?'

'The Emperor's, Caesar Tiberius, I think it is.'

'Perfectly correct. So then, give to Caesar what belongs to him, and give to God what's his.'

The rabbi doesn't know what to say. Joshua has wriggled out of his trap. Those nearby who heard everything give a laugh. The rabbi tries to recover and redeem himself.

'Well at least I do give to God, I'm a generous man and pay a handsome donation regularly to the Temple.'

'Yes, I guess you do, from your more than ample resources. I saw an elderly widow here yesterday. When she thought no-one was looking she put a tiny coin in the Temple donation box. I tell you, that woman was more generous than you.'

'Don't be ridiculous, man. I give more in a day than that woman would have acquired in a year.'

'Exactly, you've just proved my point. She gave all she'd got. You just give a small proportion of your wealth. So she's fully committed. You're not!'

Joshua turns back to the crowd of those eager to hear him, while the thwarted rabbi tries to slip unnoticed back into his own.

'Do you want some stories?'

'Yes!' roar the crowd in unison.

'Right. There were two sons. Their father was a farmer. He asked them to help him one day harvesting in the fields. It was going to be hot work and both were reluctant, and the younger one was honest and told his father he wouldn't go. The other chipped in at once and said he would certainly go and smirked as his father patted him on the back and said 'Good lad'. But it didn't quite work out that way. The younger boy, when he really thought about it, felt ashamed that he'd left his father to do all the hard work, and despite what he'd said, he turned up and worked hard. However, the elder son, having said all the right things, got distracted, forgot his promise and then, later, when he remembered, thought it was too late and couldn't be bothered. He'd make his excuse later, his father knew he'd intended to, unlike that ungrateful brat of his younger brother. Which one then pleased his father?'

The bright ones in the crowd soon grasp that he's comparing the priests and rabbis with the elder son who is outwardly obedient but inwardly a sinner. They're still debating who the other boy represents when Joshua starts another story.

'You've all been to wedding feasts,' he exclaims, grinning. 'I'm sure you are delighted to receive an invitation and go and celebrate with the bridegroom and his new wife. But not the guests in this story. They all made excuses. The groom's father thought they were his friends and he was so disappointed in them. So he told his servants to go out and bring anyone they found in the streets to the feast, he didn't want the hall empty.' He pauses to let the story sink in. Some are getting his meaning. I suspect the priests and rabbis think he's getting at them. 'God invites everyone, but not everyone accepts.'

Just to make sure everyone gets his meaning, he tells yet another story.

'A wealthy man had a vineyard and let portions of it out to tenants who tended it and were entitled to some of the harvest, a set proportion of that owned by the man. So at harvest-time he sent his slaves to collect his due. The tenants ganged up against them and sent them away empty-handed.

274

So the landowner sent paid servants and they were similarly rejected, some were beaten up and a couple died from their injuries. The landlord was furious and sent his own son, thinking that they would at least respect him and hand over the proportion of the harvest due to him. But these scoundrels saw their opportunity and murdered the son, thinking they could now claim the land as the owner had no other sons who could inherit. So the owner, in great distress and anguish, had the villains arrested and jailed and gave instructions that the vineyard was to be divided and given to the local poor villagers.'

Some people are looking a bit puzzled.

'God has sent many prophets to the nation of Israel. Many have been rejected, some mistreated, some actually killed. Even now some are plotting to kill me.'

Shouts of 'No!' and 'Never!' rend the air. Joshua looks at the group of rabbis at the edge of the crowd.

'Yes, they are. And they know who I'm talking about.'

The crowd is growing restive and I notice that most of the rabbis and priests have slipped away. But one who is more courageous – or perhaps angrier than the others - decides to challenge Joshua further.

'You say all these things. You get the crowd on your side. But on what authority do you speak? Who trained you? What qualifications do you have? You sound as though you believe you're speaking the words of God. What makes you think you're a prophet?'

'You all went out to hear John the Baptiser at the Jordan River. He was no better educated than me. Do you believe he was a prophet of God?'

The man finds it difficult to quarrel with this as many from Jerusalem had gone to hear him, and it is widely acknowledged that he was a prophet.

'So on whose authority did John preach? Did his authority come from God?'

The rabbi says nothing for he doesn't want to upset the crowd.

'Since you say nothing, I assume you accept that his authority came from God. So if I say the same, why do you challenge me?'

The rabbi remains silent.

'So you can't answer that. If you stay silent and won't answer me, I'll do the same. I won't tell you where my authority comes from. You can work it out for yourself.'

The embarrassed man finally leaves, the crowd now laughing at his discomfiture. But no sooner has he gone, than a group of Sadducees from the Sanhedrin turn up. People say they don't believe in people rising from death to an afterlife and they begin to question Joshua about this. But they're easy for Joshua to counter. They pick a rather silly argument.

'Rabbi, if you say human beings can rise after death, what happens if a man has had seven wives in his life, all of them dying one after another before their husband? Which is his wife in the afterlife?'

'You take things too literally. The afterlife is spiritual, not physical. Gender doesn't matter, it's not a spiritual state.'

These Sadducees are soon bested. They don't ask him any more questions for fear of looking fools. We go home in safety, the cheerful laughing crowd following us, people still bringing sick children and adults for him to bless and heal. Has Joshua really got the better of them? Will he now be left in peace?

Chapter 23
James

They think we're out of the woods now. Joshua's disciples and followers were laughing all the way back to Bethany. Poor fools, they're deceiving themselves. They actually think the Jewish religious leaders will allow themselves to be beaten by a Galilean peasant, for that's what they think he is. I was beginning to have second thoughts about my brother as we came through Judea and into Jericho and Bethany. He has a gift for healing, I can't deny that. The story about him bringing Lazarus back from the dead is too much though. I know Lazarus thinks that happened as do his sisters, but I'm sure he was just in a coma, as the young man he healed in Nain must have been. And I had a certain sympathy for some of the things he was saying about the obligations of the rich to the poor, though I think he played too much with the crowd's emotions and managed to attract men who are too foolhardy and dangerous for my liking. But he's insane now. What does he think he's doing? He couldn't have tried harder to upset the authorities these last couple of days. They won't have it, I know they won't and we'll all suffer the consequences. My brother is either terribly naïve or quite mad. And my stupid mother still trusts him.

They all think we're going back to Jerusalem tomorrow and there'll be no trouble. We'll see. I don't want to be right, but I fear the worst. And Mother's going to be in the thick of it. I'm damned if I stay to help her and damned if I abandon her for they'll never forgive me back home. The disciples are as bad as Mother. I'd have thought practical fishermen like Simon Peter and his brother would have seen sense but they're as besotted with the man as my mother is. And as for John, who seems to be hovering around Mother all the time, and is encouraging her foolish opinions, he's as daft as they come, a right dreamer. How he ever got to be a successful fisherman, I'll never know. Probably relied on his brother James, a tad more worldly, and the hired hands they say they had.

Anyway, I've got little choice. Lazarus's sister, Mariam, tried to persuade Mother to stay there today on the grounds that she must be weary with all the walking, but she wouldn't hear of it. Even Lazarus is coming today. When we get to the Temple steps, we find a crowd already gathered. I look round. I can't see any priests or rabbis at the moment. There are one or two Temple Guards about, but they look bored. I'm sure it's just a façade to put us off. They'll gather their forces and hit us when we least expect it, because we're complacent.

Joshua starts off by healing the sick they've brought first. That always excites the crowd – I'm sure some of them only come to see him do that. Then he starts preaching. Is he conciliatory? Has he learned any lessons? Of course not. He's worse than ever. Even I did not expect the vitriol he's spouting about the very people who could squash him like a fly if they wanted to. Perhaps they're not here today because they deem him beneath their contempt. I doubt it though. They'll be in some back room in the Temple hatching their plots.

Anyway, what's my saintly brother think he's doing? 'Teaching' time? 'Making more enemies' time, more likely! He's starting by calling the priests, rabbis, scribes, Pharisees and Sadducees – the lot – all hypocrites. He hasn't left anyone out. Well, yes he has. He's left the Romans out. Not enough to flail our own Jewish leaders, he has to side with the occupying army and their collaborators. Well, perhaps he doesn't explicitly, but they're about the only ones he doesn't crucify with words. He's having a go at our law now – the Law of Moses. He's breaking every taboo he can think of. All our laws and customs, an unnecessary burden on the common people, he calls them. The priests and others who obey our traditions, he ridicules them. He complains they have the best seats at feasts and in the synagogues and Temple. Well, of course they do. They're the most important people there and we should pay them that due respect. He's meant to be a rabbi himself. He left me doing the work at home while he went off to the rabbinical school – you'd think he'd at least take advantage of the status he's earned. But no, the greatest must be your servant. How absurd can you get? Just listen to him now.

'These men, in their flowing robes and tassles, think they are the most important people round here. They conveniently forget the Romans, but in any case I tell you that their servants and slaves are just as important. Those who claim the first place will have to wait till last, and the humble who wait at the back will be called forward and come first. Don't spend all your time worrying about your earthly status – it'll count for nothing in the kingdom of God. Until you learn to serve, you will be as nothing.'

And he goes on in this vein for a long time. We've got the message, brother. Popular with half the crowd who cheer his remarks. Not very practical though. Don't know how he's going to apply it. I expect he means in the next life. I think most of this lot think he's talking about now and are waiting for him to start the revolution. Silly fools!

As if this wasn't bad enough, he's now back on the theme of the hypocritical priests and Pharisees. He's telling us all their religious rituals and practices are useless – and he calls himself a prophet, man of God. How can he be when he's so contemptuous of our religious leaders?

'All you that trust solely in your religious observances, keep yourself ritually pure, don't lift a finger to help your neighbour in trouble or have apoplexy if your child picks up a ball to play on the Sabbath, you're blind, I tell you, you've missed the whole point of existence. You strain a tiny fly from your drink and swallow a camel!'

There's a roar of laughter. This brother of mine's quite a comedian. Don't know when he developed that, I used to

279

think he was so serious when we were boys. On he goes. Listen to the rubbish.

'These hypocrites, they're like white-washed tombs, pompous and grand to look at and full of decaying bodies, riddled with maggots!'

Ugh, where does he drag these crudities from?

'Your leaders will bring down the wrath of God on the nation. They'll incite retribution. They'll cause such anger that the people's patience will end, their fury will boil over and in destroying the guilty they'll destroy us all, innocents and guilty alike, for the Romans will wreak a terrible carnage if we become ungovernable, and I tell you, these leaders are arousing such emotions that that is what will happen. I can see it coming. All these grand buildings you're so proud of will one day be destroyed, even the Temple itself. And this destruction is not in some distant time – it'll happen in the lifetime of many of you standing here.'

Where's he off to now? He's upsetting his followers and supporters. As long as he harangued the priests and Pharisees at least he had the crowd on his side. But the cheering and laughter has noticeably stopped. There's a stunned silence at his latest words.

Someone calls out 'Defeatist!'

Another shouts 'Where's your courage, man? Give us a lead and we'll follow you and throw the bastards out!'

More talk from Joshua about the destruction of so many buildings and landmarks we hold dear is treated with gasps of horror, then he starts telling everyone to go home and look after their family for the time is coming when family ties will be destroyed and even our children will be at risk. It's depressing and shocking and turns the crowd right off. That's not what they came to hear. Where did he get these views from? I haven't heard him so gloomy before. One minute he was joking, the next he's almost despairing. What's he heard?

Has he got wind of a new Roman army initiative? Has he heard the priests' secrets in the Temple, heard their fears?

'When's it all going to happen?' someone shouts. 'You said some of us would live to see it. Tell us so we can escape with our families.'

'I don't know when, but it will happen. Ten virgins are waiting with their lamps at a wedding. The bridegroom's procession is running late and their oil is running low. Five have prepared for this and brought a spare supply with them. Five girls are foolish and have no spare oil. 'Give us some of yours,' they beg, but the wise girls have only just enough for themselves for they still don't know when the bridegroom will come. So the thoughtless virgins rush off to buy some more and, of course, the groom turns up while they're away and they get shut out of the wedding feast. Destruction will come like that. Be prepared, live for the kingdom of God and you and your family will be saved.'

'How do we know who will be saved? You obviously don't think our priests and teachers will be among that number. Will we all be judged unworthy and suffer the destruction you speak of?'

It's very apparent that many of the crowd have lost interest in Joshua's latest pronouncements and have drifted away. The remaining ones move forward to fill the empty spaces and wait to hear how he will answer this.

'The king will divide the people just as a shepherd sorts out the sheep from the goats. To those whom he invites to enter his kingdom, he will say that they fed him when he was hungry, clothed him when he was naked, visited him when he was sick and in prison, gave hospitality to him when he was a stranger. They will be astonished and say that we never saw you in such a state and he will say 'just as you cared for one of the least of my children, you did it for me!' And to the others he will say that you never helped me when I was hungry or naked or sick or in prison or homeless. And they will protest that they never saw him and failed to act. And he will say that he was there in those who needed help and didn't get it. And some will try to argue and say 'we've always read your word and been assiduous in attending synagogue on the Sabbath and have kept all the commandments' and the king will reject them and say 'I never knew you. Just because you called out 'Lord, Lord' and said the right words does not reserve a place for you in my kingdom.'

'So you are saying only those who serve their fellows will be saved?'

'I've said it many times before. Love God and love your fellow human beings as much as you value your own life. Do that and you won't go wrong. God will welcome you into his kingdom.'

It's a chastened crowd that disperses now. The excitement of the morning has evaporated. We can go home before the Temple Guards are sent out to arrest us. I'm sure there were spies in the crowd who'll go back and tell the priests exactly what Joshua has said. There'll be no mercy now, it'll be outright war. He's given them the ammunition they need. They'll accuse him of being a traitor ready to hand over Israel to the foreigner and find some pretext to get the Romans to execute him as a common criminal.

I walk back with the disciples. They're arguing of all things about who is the greatest among them and will be most important in this kingdom of God. Really, haven't they listened to a word he's said today? Joshua looks pretty fed up, someone says the argument was started by James and John, someone else said it wasn't their fault, it was their mother seeking their preferment. The disciples are pretty annoyed. There's a family going in the opposite direction with a couple of small children. Joshua beckons them over.

He picks up one of the children, smiles at her and says, 'This child is more important than any of you. Be trusting like her, trust God, find and follow his plan for you, put your own will and desires last, then you will be important. If you think you are, you won't be. If you think little of yourself, God will call you to an important place in his kingdom.'

He hands back the child to her mother. She doesn't flinch from him, he seems to have a sure touch with children. The mother makes no protest and it becomes obvious that she knows who he is. As they go on their way, I hear her telling the little girl, 'That was the famous prophet from Nazareth. He called you important. You'll remember that all your days.' And she smiles at Joshua, who thanks her.

John's very embarrassed about the whole incident. James, his brother, dashes off to find his mother and tackle her for apparently causing the ructions between the disciples with her request, although some of the disciples are saying that it was James himself who sought to push himself and his brother to a primary position among the disciples. It has been clear to me that Joshua is inclined to confide more in these two and in Simon Peter, although I think he seeks out the company of Magdalene Mariam most of all, which certainly has caused some eyebrows raised among the men.

As we continue down the road, the barren hills either side looking threatening as the sun sinks behind us, Joshua tries to pacify his disciples, then reminds them that life is not going to be easy. It's just as I thought. He knows full well the effect his words and actions will have had on the authorities. He's not naïve, but he is crazy. He can put his own life in danger as much as he likes as far as I'm concerned, but he's not justified in putting us all at risk, especially not my mother and the other womenfolk. At first he talks about his own fate.

'You think today has gone well because none of the authorities challenged me and the Temple Guards took no action against us. They were watching though and they'll act. Before this week is out I'll be arrested and killed.'

'What? Stuff and nonsense, Master! Not while we're around!'

It's Simon Peter, as usual, boasting. What hope does he think he has against armed soldiers? If they try to resist, the army of followers we have will fade away.

'It's inevitable, Peter. I've challenged them. I've hit them where it hurts. They won't forgive me, because the truth hurts more than vague accusations. They know in their heart of hearts that what I've said is true and they have no answer, so they'll resort to violence, the refuge of the weak.'

That's a fine phrase but it's meaningless. Violence is for the strong, that's what's effective. You only have to look at the Roman army to understand that.

Joshua looks at me. It's as if he read my thoughts.

'You're wrong, James. Men whose moral authority is weak will bluster and use their physical power because their words, their powers of argument, are weak. The priests and rabbis and Pharisees have no answer to the things I say, so they'll retreat to the only area where they have an advantage – in physical force. And we must be prepared and not hide our heads in the sand.'

'So are we going to leave Jerusalem? Go back to Galilee now while we can and before disaster overtakes us?'

'No, James, that's not an option.'

'Of course it is. If we go tonight we could be the other side of Jericho before they know we've gone. Back in Galilee you stand a chance. You're popular with the people. Stay with the crowds and don't get caught on your own. Surely your friends here see the sense of that?'

'I've told them that I had to confront the religious leaders. They're leading people, ordinary humble and worthwhile people, astray. These people need to be told and shown God's way. If I have to die in the process, it will but have a more lasting effect. My words will live on even if I die.'

Some of the disciples have been listening to this exchange. Several of them chip in and try to support my words but Joshua rebukes them quietly. He just seems resigned, sad, but

284

not angry or indignant. I can feel my own anger rising, for he is only thinking of himself. What about Mother? What about Mariam whom I thought he respected and cared for? Doesn't he care if they get caught up in the backlash against him? What about me? What about his disciples? Are we all to be condemned? I've seen the Roman crosses with so-called terrorists dying in agony and if the Jewish leaders think we are undermining their authority, they'll not hesitate to denounce us to the Romans and we'll all find ourselves victims. Simon Peter can bluster as much as he likes – I bet he'll be a coward if the soldiers come for him. And I make no bones about it, I'm certainly a coward if that's what's in store for us.

One or two of the disciples attempt to continue the argument in favour of flight, but quickly get squashed by Simon Peter and Andrew and James who now say that if Joshua is in danger, they'll share it. Listen to them! I bet I hear a different story when the soldiers come to arrest them. Except I won't be around to listen – I'm off and I'm taking my mother and any others who are still sane with me.

Chapter 24
Mari

Lazarus's sisters spent yesterday gathering together the ingredients for two Passover meals. They are going to celebrate the feast at their home with cousins and neighbours, while we go into Jerusalem with Joshua and the disciples. Mariam, Salome and Susannah and I are going to get the meal cooked and laid out while the men spend another day at the Temple. Joshua has arranged a place where we can eat the meal undisturbed. He's told us how to find it, but it all seems very secret as he doesn't want to risk being found and stopped before he's had this meal with us.

I had the most almighty row with James last night. He told me I had to go back with him to Nazareth and leave Joshua to his fate and of course I refused. He said he'd physically force me to go with him, and I said 'How? Are you going to tie your old mother up and kidnap her?' And he told me not to be a silly old… I won't tell you what he called me – it was most unseemly for any son to address his mother that way and I was ashamed of him, especially as Mariam and Salome both heard him. Then John heard him and came to my rescue only to get lambasted by James in his turn. Finally Joshua overheard the row and told James to shut up in a very decisive way. I've never heard him so commanding with his brother before, it finished the argument there and then and left James astounded and floundering. In the end James just said weakly that he was going home and that I could go with him if I changed my mind. He stalked off to bed in a great sulk and Joshua stayed with me. He saw how upset and shaken I was.

'Thank you, Mother, for being determined to stay with me. I value your support and love, especially now. But you know at one level he's right, don't you? The next few hours will be very hard for us all. They will arrest me. They will execute me. I've said too much to damage them and they will not accept such criticism. They're jealous of their authority, their power and they're afraid of the reaction of the Romans if they let me get away with it. They're petrified that I'll stir up the population and cause riots, a rebellion and bring the Romans down on their heads and sweep away all their privileges. They've not understood my message at all. They've not listened. Their hearts are like stone, they're deaf to God's message to them and the nation.'

'Do you have to say these things? If you know the consequences, can't you find any other way?'

'I've been thinking about this moment for over three years, Mother. I knew it would come to this sooner or later. I can't escape the consequences of my purpose on earth. I've got to show that God's way is a way of love, not power or force. I have power, yes, but it's a very different type of power from that understood by my opponents, James and even my disciples on occasions. I have to stand up to evil. I have to stand for the downtrodden and the oppressed. I have to show that the power of love is stronger than the power of force or greed or ambition. If I were to retreat now I would be bowing before these earthly powers and accepting defeat. My power is a spiritual one and I want others to recognise and share that power. It will ultimately overcome even though things may appear dark and broken. You'll need all your strength, Mother, but don't despair, however black things look. Trust me, hang on to that. God loves us and he will not let us down.'

'But aren't you afraid, Joshua? If what you say is right, won't you suffer dreadful things? I can't imagine the pain and distress. There must be another way for you.'

'Yes, I am afraid. I wouldn't be human if I wasn't. You must realise that I've spent the last few months figuring out if there was an alternative. There isn't, not without destroying the very purpose for which I've come.'

287

'Who are you?' I asked. 'Just who are you?'

He looked at me.

'Mother, you've known since you were thirteen years old who I am. Do I need to spell it out to you?'

I thought back to the visits of the stranger in Nazareth, the mysterious conversations with him, the encounter in the stream, my outburst before the rabbis in the synagogue, the strange visitors at Joshua's birth, that time in the Temple when I asked him if he knew the answers and he replied, 'I think I do.'

Before I could answer, he asked me, 'Do you know who I am?'

'I think I do,' I answered.

*   *   *   *   *

So, as I said, we set off early this morning. Despite insisting he'd leave on his own, James has come too. I really didn't think he'd carry out his threat. We all walked together as far as the Golden Gate, then Joshua directed Mary to the room where we were to have the Passover supper. I watched Joshua and the others go with some trepidation. Will I see him again or will his enemies pounce before he's even had the special meal with us? We soon find the room, an upstairs room in a large house near the edge of the city nearest to the Jericho road. To my surprise there's no sign of life in the rest of the house, which is locked. Mariam has the key to the room where we are to eat the supper and we find cooking implements laid out near the stove as though we are expected.

When the herbs and bread are placed on dishes and put on the low table in the centre of the room and the lamb offering is gently stewing in the large cooking pot on the stove, we rest. A group of disciples' wives are bored and decide to go into the city crowds and watch the pilgrims coming from all parts of the Roman Empire, Jews talking a host of unknown languages.

I'm invited to join them, but I say that I want to stay and rest and Mariam, Salome and Susannah decide to remain with me. There is little to do, but await the meat to be done, just giving the stew an occasional stir. Someone has put two large water jars in the corner of the room. There are jars of wine. Someone has been here and got everything ready for us. I wonder who it is; perhaps the owner of the property, obviously a wealthy man, is secretly an admirer of my son. We all look at each other. Then I notice that Mariam has been crying.

'What's the matter, Mariam?' I ask.

She looks at me, then all of us. Her eyes are very red, she must have been crying for sometime and none of us have noticed. I feel bad about that.

'I have a nasty premonition, Mari. Joshua has been so sad these last couple of days, despite the adulation of the crowds. I think he knows what is going to happen and I'm frightened for him. I even wonder if we'll see him again. What if the Temple Guards are waiting to arrest him this morning as soon as he arrives?'

'Surely not,' says Susannah. 'There'll be crowds again just like there have been all this week. They wouldn't dare. If they tried, the crowd would go mad and they'd have Roman soldiers to contend with. They won't try on anything today.'

'I wish I had your confidence.' It's my sister, Salome, who intervenes now. 'I don't like it. I expected to see rabbis and priests throwing questions at Joshua yesterday, but they were absent. They're up to something. What do you think, Mari?'

Shall I tell them what Joshua has said to me? It'll only upset Mariam more, but they'll soon guess that I'm hiding the truth.

'I think the situation is bad. Joshua told me himself last night. He expects to be arrested. I hardly slept a wink worrying about it.'

'What will they do to him? Will he be put in prison like John was?'

Again, I wonder whether to tell them everything Joshua said to me.

'They could kill him. They'll accuse him of blasphemy and the penalty is death.'

Mariam bursts into tears again. I shouldn't have said that.

Between her tears she mumbles, 'They can't do that here, not in Jerusalem. Only the Romans can authorise an execution and they don't recognise blasphemy as a crime.'

I don't like to tell her that if the Jewish leaders are determined to kill him, they'll trump up some other charge that does carry a penalty of crucifixion. But I do pass on the conversation that Joshua had with me last night.

'He is expecting the worst. He is determined to face up to them and not flinch. It's admirable in many ways but I do wish he was not so single-minded about his mission if it has these consequences.'

'But doesn't that put all of us in danger? Won't they arrest his disciples too?'

'I don't care. If they kill him, they can kill me too! If he dies I might as well be dead.' This outburst comes from Mariam's lips. Her eyes look wild, her eyes bloodshot, she's torn off her shawl and I see her hair is tangled. I guess she didn't have much sleep last night either.

We try to change the subject and find another topic of conversation but we cannot concentrate. There are long silences then suddenly two of us will speak at once. Time is dragging, we are waiting for our menfolk to return, but it's barely noontide yet. We eat a little of the bread and take a few mouthfuls of water, we want nothing more. Then we lie down and try to get some sleep but no sleep will come to me. I think Susannah and Salome have dozed off, but Mariam, like me, just tosses and turns. My imagination is running riot. I see again the mangled corpses on the crosses in Nain when I went there as a girl to the festival and remember looking with pity at a young man contorted in agony and feeling such pain myself until my mother called me away. And, in my imagination, the face of that young man I saw so many years ago changes to the face of my beloved son, then I awake for I realise I must have dozed off. Then I know it was the sound of the disciples' wives returning, Susannah heard them and got up and unlocked the door and they are around us now, all talking at once. I wait for their excited chatter to moderate a little, then I ask the question we all really want to put.

'Did you see Yeshua, Joshua, my son?'

'Yes, we went to the Temple. He's talking to the crowds on the Temple steps. There are more people there than ever.'

'Were the priests and Pharisees there? Did they ask him any trick questions?'

'No. We saw no sign of any of them.' It's John's mother, Dorcas, who replies. 'It was good-humoured, the crowd was excited at what Yeshua was saying. And we saw him heal a couple of beggars that had been brought to him – I think they were both blind.'

'Are you sure there weren't any priests or rabbis?' Mariam is not satisfied and shows her anxiety. 'They could be deliberately keeping their heads down.'

'Well, if that's the case we wouldn't see them, would we?' It's Thomas's wife, Lydia, who speaks up now. 'All I can say is that it all seems calm so far. I know Yeshua has been warning the men of the dangers they're running, but my husband says that he's just testing them and he doesn't really believe the authorities will dare arrest him while there are so many in the city up for the Passover. It could inflame the crowds and cause a riot. In any case, Yeshua goes out of the city every night. He knows what he's doing. He's been saying similar things for three years now and despite upsetting the Pharisees and rabbis in many places, no-one has dared do anything about it other than engage him in argument. And then they always lose,' she adds.

Mariam is shaking her head. She doesn't believe this. She knows what Joshua has said and how accurate he's always been in his forecasts. And she's sensed how determined he is now and the depth of his anguish. I feel it too, although I try to find a glimmer of light. But in my heart of hearts I have to admit to myself that it doesn't look good. I've been praying, but for what should I pray? Just for my son to be saved from this situation? It's not what he's praying for. I heard him yesterday – he's asking for the courage to go through with it. I want him to be able to stand up for what is right, to tell out God's message loud and clear and I want the outcome to be a miraculous acceptance of this message by everyone, especially the authorities, but I know this is just wishful thinking.

So I don't say any more and put my mind, as much as I can, to the practical job of finishing the preparation of the meal. The stew is ready now and can be served any time Joshua and the disciples return. We are just sitting here waiting, wondering. I'm so nervous, I feel sick. The smell of the food is upsetting me. I get up and want to wander out into the street and get some fresh air. I go to the door several times and look. There are many people sauntering by, a few hurry as if they are aiming to meet someone, but I can't see any sign of Joshua or the disciples. Mariam comes to the door with me too, she's probably as churned up as I feel. Neither of us says anything, but we both know.

I've actually just come back in getting more panicky by the minute. The light is fading fast, he should have been here by now. I'm so tense, I can't stay still and I'm muttering a prayer under my breath, trying to control my breathing and trying not to betray my fears to the others. Then I hear the steps and I get up and rush to the door and see Joshua just mounting the final step. He steps forward and embraces me.

'Mother, don't fret. I'm here. It's all in God's hands now. Leave it to him.'

He holds me for some time, then as he steps back Mariam flings herself at his feet.

'Mariam, can you help me, I've something I want to do. Can you bring me over one of the water jars and a towel?'

'Oh, Master, let me wash your feet, you'll be filthy treading through the muck of the city in this heat.'

'Not now, Mariam. It's my job this time. I want to give an example to my followers.'

The disciples troop into the room and discard their outer garments and make themselves comfortable. Andrew goes to find water to wash himself, but before he can, Joshua addresses them all.

'There was an argument yesterday about who took precedence in God's kingdom, which of you was most important.'

James and John look particularly uncomfortable.

'You know it's the job of the lowliest servant to wash the feet of guests when they arrive for a meal. You also know that the ritual of washing is particularly important before eating the Passover meal. There is no servant in this household, so I am going to carry out this role for you, for although you call me your master, in fact I am your servant too.'

They all look shocked, every single one of them. Mariam hurries over with the towel.

'No, Master, please, no. Let me do it, I have the towel.'

'Mariam's right, Master, you should never do this. It's absurd. It's just not right. I'll not have it. Let her do it as she asks, or I'll do it myself. Not you, I won't let you.'

'Peter, what I'm doing is a demonstration of my love for all of you. If you love another, you serve them. It's the greatest expression of love there is. I want to show you, in the most memorable way I can, an example of how you should treat each other and all with whom you come in contact. Don't you want me to express my deep love for you? Are you going to reject me and all I stand for?'

'No, of course not, Master! It is just such a shock to see you doing this deed. I thought it was humiliating for you. But if it really is an outward sign of your love for me, then I accept it – wash all of me if you like for I love you too – as everyone here does.'

'That's unnecessary, Peter. This little act is symbolic enough. You all know what it means and you'll remember it long after I'm gone.'

And he takes the water bowl and towel from Mariam's hands and begins to wash our feet, one by one, slowly and with great tenderness. He even washes the women's feet much to their embarrassment. When he gets to me, he looks straight into my eyes and he knows I cannot hold back my tears. It's as if this is a farewell, it's charged with great significance and it's too much for me. He rises and kisses me softly on both cheeks.

'Mother, don't cry. I'll be with you always. Whatever happens, don't let go of that. Your spirit is strong. My spirit will be with you.' And he squeezes my wrist. I can hardly see him now, my vision is blurred. It's as if he's saying goodbye to me and I can't bear it. But I pull myself together. I can't break down in front of the others.

'God bless you, my son,' I whisper to him, and he passes on to wash the feet of my sister, his Aunt Salome. I think she senses what I feel, for, after he has moved on again, she leans across and gives me a gentle hug as well.

After Joshua has completed the round of everyone, he takes the bowl of dirty water to the window and empties it slowly to the courtyard below, handing the damp towel back to Mariam. The men begin to take their places at the table, while James comes over to me, unsure of whether he should be in their number. The women are going to serve the meal and find a space in the corner of the room where we can eat also.

'No, friends, I want everyone round me at this table. Peter, John, Thomas, make room for the women to join us. And you too, brother, I know you don't agree with much of what I'm doing, but you are part of this Passover meal.'

A couple of disciples move aside and James helps me to the table and take a position beside him. One or two of the disciples are muttering about the women being given an equal place, but they dare not say much for they know my son has strong views about the right of women to be as involved as men in the worship and service of our God. If any challenge him, he'll put them in their place at once, for he makes it obvious that he values the opinions of Mariam and of me and talks often with Susannah and Salome and his disciples' wives. If there had been any children here, he'd have had them at the table, just like any family would at Passover. Of course, we lack a child to take the symbolic role of asking about the meaning of the feast. Who will take that part?

'Where's the roast lamb?' James whispers to me urgently as we stoop to recline.

'It's in the pot. It's a stew.'

'That's not right. It should be roasted.'

'James, be practical! We've a large number to feed, only one lamb and limited cooking facilities.'

'He should have organised it better. He knew how many we were going to be. It's poor if our so-called Messiah can't even get the Passover meal right.'

'Shush, James, don't embarrass yourself. You know Joshua doesn't put much store in the literalness of outward symbols. It's a meal with his family and friends and it's special. The food is not that important.'

'We always manage to do it properly at home.'

'James, we're not at home. We're in a crowded city, guest of an unknown supporter, trying to take an important meal with someone who could be discovered and arrested at any moment.'

James stops complaining but he isn't happy. He mutters to himself and it's probably just as well that neither I nor anyone else can make out his words. Luckily I don't think anyone else has been watching him or listening to us, all eyes are on Joshua as he settles at the table. He waits until everyone appears to be comfortable, then stands and recites the traditional blessing and calls for our cups to be filled to drink the first draught of wine. The wineskin is passed round until we're ready and we drink the sweet sticky dark liquid together. A bowl of water is then passed round and we all wash our hands before each taking a piece of celery and dipping it into a small bowl of salt water that I prepared earlier. Joshua then takes the unleavened bread and breaks it in the familiar way I've seen him do so often, opening his hands displaying the broken pieces so all can see. He sets the largest portion aside and breaks the remnant into small bits, which are passed round till all have a share.

'John, I think you're the youngest here. Will you enact the part of the child?'

He is taken by surprise. He thinks for a moment, but soon recovers for he knows the ritual by heart.

'Why is this night different from all the other nights?'

All turn to Joshua, expecting him to answer but he looks at all of us and indicates that we should all join in. So suggestions are thrown out, 'it's the first night of the Passover'; 'it's the night we remember our flight from Egypt'; 'it's the night we remember how the Lord God rescued our nation'.

Joshua listens.

'It's significant for me too. I recall my family's flight to Egypt, in order to survive Herod's jealousy. But this is the beginning of a second rescue of our nation, a spiritual one, rescue from the sin and evil that men do.'

He doesn't explain any further and John asks a second question.

'Why do we eat unleavened bread?'

The answers come tumbling. 'The Israelites had no time to wait for the bread to rise.' 'Such bread lasted longer in the desert.' 'It's our law.' 'It's our tradition.'

'Tonight we have to hurry too. We shall need to eat quickly and gird ourselves to leave before we are interrupted. I have to go on a journey. This will be my last Passover meal with you.'

Several voices are raised in protest and I hear a choking sound, which I realise has come from Mariam on my left. But before more can be said, he urges John to continue.

'Why do we eat only bitter herbs tonight?'

Joshua does not wait this time.

'Bitter tears were shed that night many years ago when the Egyptian families awoke to find their firstborn cold in death. And there will be bitter tears again tonight for my time has come and the same fate awaits me, to be sacrificed by the nation's leaders just as the Israelites were told to sacrifice a lamb that fatal night to save themselves.'

They don't know what he is talking about. I can see disbelief and puzzlement spread over all their faces. They want to ask what he means, but no-one dares ask the question.

'Continue, John.'

'Why do we dip our food twice on this night?'

Silence. All await Joshua's words.

'We are celebrating a re-enactment of that bitter night. The second dipping is an immersion into our present travail. And the one who will set it all in motion, who will start the night's sacrifice shares the dipping with me.'

'What do you mean?' many call in alarm. 'Are you blaming one of us? Surely not?'

We have already dipped the parsley herb into the bitter juice and no-one noticed who acted at the same time as Joshua. Is that what he meant? That one of us would betray him? I went cold suddenly all over. Surely my own son, Joshua's brother, would not stoop to such a deed? I look at James. He looks as mystified as the rest. If he is the culprit – if that is

297

what Joshua means – then he's a good actor for he shows no sign of guilt or embarrassment.

In the flurry of questions and anger as the disciples realise that he is suggesting one of them will be the instrument of his betrayal – intended or not – the last question gets lost until John is prompted.

He remembers.

'Why are we all reclining tonight instead of standing?'

'Because we remember death. The death of the firstborn laid in their graves. My death. But it is temporary, for I shall rise and defeat death. It is not the end. You have seen me raise the dead. So shall it be for me too and you in turn. Let us drink the second cup!' We lift the cups to our lips mechanically, we are not thinking about what we are doing for our minds are elsewhere.

We are stunned into silence. No-one is protesting or arguing. There is a sombre mood. Mariam is weeping softly. I hear Judas mutter quietly to his neighbour, 'Why does he just accept it? Why is he so passive? Why won't he get up and fight? That's why we joined him, wasn't it?'

We wash our hands and Joshua now takes the larger loaf of unleavened bread and begins to break it also, handing a piece to each of us.

'Remember what I'm doing now. I shall be broken just like this bread but even so, just as this bread is life-sustaining for you, so am I for your soul. Whenever you eat such bread, remember that. I am offering you the bread of life – if you do all that I have taught you, you shall enter my kingdom, the kingdom of God that I have promised. God my father will receive you. So whenever you sit down together to eat this bread, do it in remembrance of me and all I've done for you. By eating this with me, you are sharing my life, you are continuing my work.'

And we eat, slowly, thoughtfully. We really can't grasp what it all means. Perhaps we will one day, but not now. I'm just overwhelmed at the thought that Joshua seems resigned to his own death. It seems so unjust. There must be a different way. I resolve I will fight, though I am weak. I don't know how, I'll think of something. I'll not accept it.

Now it's time for another blessing and the third cup of wine. He's going to say something else. There is absolute silence.

Joshua takes the cup of wine and tips it slowly so that the wine dribbles out and stains his garment and forms a pool of red on the floor, just like a puddle of congealed blood. We stare at the crimson stain, which is spreading slowly as the liquid eats into the rough wooden floor.

'This is my blood which will be shed this night, sacrificed like the blood of the Passover lamb. You will all leave me because it is too hard, it is asking too much of you. But I forgive you, I know the pressure you'll be under. No matter what you do or say, I'll always forgive just as God forgives the sins of those that truly repent. So when you drink the Passover wine in future, remember me. Remember that I love you so much that I'll forgive. I'll be your sacrifice – don't worry about doves and lambs. God accepts my love and sacrifice for you and for other misguided and weak people who will regret what they have done and try to start again. With my help you will, they will. Drink then, drink this cup and remember what it symbolises.'

Nearly everyone has been stunned into silence. But not Peter, oh no!

'Master, this will never happen to you! We won't let it. Well, I won't anyway.'

'Peter, I know what you want, but that's not God's way. What is going to happen, has to happen. It's inevitable. I have to face down evil and if that means that by so doing, I'm sacrificed, then so be it. I would rather it not happen, but I cannot turn away and postpone this moment, not let evil think it's triumphed.'

'Then if that's the only way, I'll join you. I will not let you be taken alone!'

'Brave words, Peter, but easier to make in the stillness and safety of this room. When the crunch comes, you'll forget those words. You'll flee like the rest of them.'

'Never, Master, never!'

'Peter, you'll deny you even know me before this night's out. Before the cock crows at dawn, before then you'll have refused to acknowledge that you're my disciple!'

Simon Peter is shaking his head vigorously. He's very upset. The others are looking at him in dismay. Joshua's words are beginning to sink in and all are perhaps now realising that he's serious. He means it. For the first time the reality of Joshua's impending fate is occurring to everyone. The mood changes and all look extremely sombre, even melancholy.

We should now sing the psalms that are traditionally sung at this juncture in the Passover meal, but no-one wants to sing. We begin to chant the well-known words but the phrases of victory over Israel's enemies ring false from our lips and only the voice of Joshua himself holds firm above the mumbles. When we get to the words 'The Lord is not praised by the dead, by any who go down to the land of silence', the low chant is broken by the sound of Mariam sobbing and later 'How painful it is to the Lord when one of his people dies!' brings tears to my eyes. Suddenly the voice of Joshua rings out above all of us as he declaims, 'I will not die; instead I will live and proclaim what the Lord has done. He has punished me severely, but he has not let me die.' 'Please God,' I pray silently, 'please let this be true.' I'm still praying this, not listening to the next words, when I hear Joshua again chanting, almost as if he is defiant, 'The stone which the builders rejected as worthless turned out to be the most important of all.' How often recently have I heard him use those words. Only the other day when his disciples were arguing about who was the most important of them, he quoted that verse from the scriptures. Then further words break into my consciousness. 'This is the day of the Lord's victory; let us be happy, let us celebrate!' and I look around at everyone. No-one is celebrating.

The chanting dies out. No-one is looking Joshua in the eye. I look round the room. Judas is missing, where has he gone? I think no more about it because Joshua raises the cup of wine once more to his lips.

'Drink this all of you. This is the final cup of the Passover, a covenant that I share with all of you who believe my words and act on them. Every time you drink this wine, remember me and the sacrifice I make to confront the evil of this world. Overcome evil with love, all of you, and this remembrance, my Spirit, will live in you and strengthen you. You will be in communion with my Spirit and I will be in you. Do not be afraid, my brothers, my sisters, my mother. We will meet again.'

'We break up slowly. Joshua comes over to me and gives me a big hug.

'Thank you, Mother, for giving me life, for your courage and belief often in the face of adversity. Be strong now. Stay here tonight and go back to the care of Lazarus and Mary tomorrow. James will take you and look after you and see you're safe, won't you James?'

'Of course, Joshua. I have no idea what you think you're doing but rest assured, I'll see our mother comes to no harm.'

'And you, Salome and Mariam and my other sisters, stay here together and pray for me tonight. Pray that I have the courage to fulfil God's plan without ever faltering.'

Then he turns to his disciples.

'We'll go quietly into the garden just outside the walls. You can keep me company. I want to spend the night in prayer.'

And I watch him go, dread in my heart.

Chapter 25
Mari

The night is long. None of us sleep but sit talking about all that has happened this week and our fears based on the predictions Joshua made. Only one or two voices dismiss these as nonsense. James listens for a while.

'The fool has brought it on himself. I always said he would. If this is the best way of bringing in his beloved 'kingdom of God', then I'm as mad as he is. And he's put all of us in danger too.'

The other women look alarmed.

'Yes, we're in danger if they arrest him. Do you think they'll leave the other men with him alone? Of course they won't. They'll arrest the lot and torture them until they reveal our hiding place, then they'll be here and we shall be delivered into their snares as well. I'm sorry, but that's what'll happen. And if it doesn't, as soon as it's light, I'm taking my mother back to Bethany and I strongly suggest the rest of you join us. You women have got families to go back to and look after. Don't stay here and throw yourselves away as well – that is if we're given any choice.'

'I'm staying. I'm going nowhere until I know what happens. If Yeshua needs me, I'll be here.' Mariam has spoken and she means it. She looks quite fierce as she says it.

'Me too!' I say this scarcely without thinking. I do not care about the consequences. It's all in God's hands now. He's looked after me so far and I can do no else but continue to place my life in his hands.

'Don't be stupid, Mother. You're not thinking straight. You're tired and overwrought. Get some sleep while it's still dark. I'll wake you at first light and we'll start back to Bethany at least. Then we'll get back to Nazareth where the rest of our family can make up for this sorry episode here.'

There's no point in arguing. I won't go and he can't make me, but words are futile now. And there's no way that I'm going to get any sleep. Even as James is about to say more, there's a sudden sound of footsteps on the stairs outside and a loud pounding on the door. We shrink in fright until we hear familiar voices, albeit with an element of panic in their shouts.

One of the women unlocks the door and three dishevelled disciples are standing there, Philip, Thaddaeus and Thomas. They burst in and one of them shouts, 'Lock the door quickly. I don't think we're being followed but you never know!'

The chorus goes up, 'What's happened? Where are the others?'

When they've got their breath back, Thomas tells us.

'A huge band of soldiers have arrested Yeshua. I think they were Temple Guards but I'm not sure, it was so dark and we didn't hang around to find out. We went to the garden called Gethsemane just the other side of the city wall and the Master said he wanted to pray alone. Then he asked three of us to keep him company and Peter, James and John went with him deeper into the garden. Nothing happened for a long time and we grew bored and tired so some of us lay down and went to sleep. Then a sudden noise woke us up and there was a mass of soldiers all around us. In the confusion we managed to get away but I'm not sure about the others.'

'What about Simon?' It's Peter's mother-in-law, who looks shocked.

'I don't know, I last saw him still with the Master and I think he was struggling to free him, but it was hopeless, there were just too many soldiers.'

'And my sons?' Dorcas is worried about James and John.

'I don't know. They were with Peter and Yeshua when the soldiers came.'

'I'm sure I saw Judas with the soldiers. He wasn't with us in the garden before. I don't know what he thought he was doing.' It's Philip who's interjected now.

'What should we do? Do you think we're safe here?' Susannah voices our fears.

'There's not much else we can do while it's still dark. We'll be too obvious if we venture out now. The streets are deserted. At least stay put until dawn. I think you women should go back to Bethany. You should be alright if you go with Yeshua's brother, you'll just be like other Passover pilgrims on the road. No-one will recognise you as followers and relatives of Yeshua.' The three disciples are agreed, Thaddaeus and Philip nodding at Thomas's words.

It's not good enough. I want to know what's happened.

'Where have the taken my son?'

'I have no idea, Mariam. If they were Temple Guards, I presume they took him to the Temple or even the High Priest's house. If they were Romans, he'll be in the city gaol.'

'I want to go out to find him. Who'll help me?'

Everyone looks aghast at me. No-one says anything.

'Please, we can't abandon Joshua. We must make our voices heard. What has he done that warrants his arrest? All he's done is criticise some priests and rabbis who've abused the trust of pilgrims. Surely there's nothing wrong in that? He's not hit anyone or threatened violence. He's restrained his followers who would have done more. We need to go and find out where he is, then we must find someone in authority to protest.'

'Mother, stop being so idiotic. You can't go out now. It's pitch dark. Even if you found where he is, no-one will let you near anyone of authority. And in the unlikely event that you did get to someone, they'd just arrest you, so what's the point?'

A few minutes later there's another banging at the door and two more wild-eyed disciples come barging in – Andrew,

Simon Peter's brother and Matthew. We beg for more news. There's not much more they can tell. They confirm it was the Temple Guards.

'I last saw my brother and John trailing off after the soldiers. Yeshua had been bound and was being dragged away. All the rest of us fled into the trees of the olive grove and watched, but the soldiers only seemed bothered about Yeshua himself. Judas was with the guards, the filthy swine. It must have been him that the Master was indicating at supper when he said someone would betray him. I can't think what possessed the bloody man.'

Really, no-one's bothered about that now.

'Will nobody come with me? I'm going to the High Priest's house to see if I can find out anything.'

'I'll come with you, Mari. I can't sit around here doing nothing till daybreak.' Mariam is impatient like me.

'No-one's going anywhere. Stay where you are. Do you want to get arrested too?'

'Do you know where the High Priest's house is?' Andrew asks me. I don't. I'd need to rely on one of the disciples and they have no intention of going out again. And James doesn't know and wouldn't tell me even if he did. Mariam comes over and clings to me.

'Please, Mari, let's go. I'm sure someone will know.'

'Mariam, the only people on the streets are soldiers. You'll have to wait.' Andrew is harsh. He's clearly angry and upset and is barely controlling his temper.

So we wait. I can't sit down, I can't stand still, and Mariam is worse than I am.

'Mariam, just bloody well shut up and sit down. You're sending me crazy charging up and down the room.' Andrew daren't speak to me like that. I still hold their respect as their Master's mother. It's clear that the disciples are irritated by Mariam's presence though, and see her as an interloper who has no right to spend as much time with my son as she does,

305

nor be so intimate with him, often going for long walks together.

I want to scream but force myself to be still. I shut my eyes and pray, but no words will come, except 'help us God' over and over, no pretty words now. The time drags. Eventually I sit down and try to sleep. Salome and Susannah seem to be dozing. So are some of the other women, although Dorcas is still wide awake. I try to shut my eyes, but my ears are listening to every sound, especially anything from the road outside. At one point I hear the trudging of feet and guess that a group of soldiers are marching past. Then I hear a cock crow. The city is stirring. I hear a flock of sheep being driven down the road. Dogs are barking in the distance. The wind is getting up, a storm is brewing. Some of the women have woken up and look to see if there is any food left over from last night. We're meant to have eaten everything from the Passover meal, but many of us were not hungry and there's a little cold stew at the bottom of the pot and some crusts of unleavened bread. James is wide awake.

'Get something to eat, Mother, and then we're leaving for Bethany.'

I ignore him.

'Mother, do as you're told. I'm master of our household now and you'll do what I say.'

'Mariam and I are going to look for Joshua. We'll enquire for the High Priest's house. People here will know.'

We've reached an impasse, which means that neither do we set off for Bethany, nor do we escape the house to seek out Joshua. Then I hear more footsteps on the stone stairs outside and there is a tapping at the door. It doesn't sound like the tread or summons of the military. Someone unlocks the door and we see it's John, alone. Dorcas cries out in relief and rushes over to her son and embraces him. Eventually he frees himself from her clutches.

'Where's James? Have the soldiers got him?'

'Calm down, Mother, don't worry so. No, as far as I know the soldiers haven't got him. I last saw him rushing off into the olive grove in Gethsemane, but that was hours ago. I thought he'd be back here, but don't worry, he'll be alright. He knows how to look after himself.'

'Where have you been? Have you seen Simon?'

'Peter and I followed the soldiers in the distance, we wanted to see where they were taking the Master. They went to the house of Caiaphas, the High Priest and into the courtyard there. We slipped inside before they closed the gate. There were plenty of people about and we mingled with the crowds, and tried to pick up what was happening by overhearing the conversations round a big fire in the centre of the courtyard. We found out that someone had gone to wake the High Priest up and that Yeshua had been taken through to the man's private quarters and I managed to slip through with a couple of servants. Peter stayed in the courtyard and I haven't seen him since. I looked for him when I came back out, but he was nowhere to be seen.'

'What did you find out? What's happened to the Master?'

'He'd apparently been questioned but I couldn't find out what he's been accused of. After a couple of hours he suddenly came out chained to Temple Guards and I heard someone say that he was being taken to Herod Antipas. Presumably that's because Yeshua comes from Galilee.'

'Weren't you under threat there?'

'No-one seemed to notice me. It was dark and there were lots of people milling around. I don't know who they all were, but nobody tackled me. When Yeshua was led through the gates with the military escort I followed with a number of others and nobody took any notice of me. I didn't know whether to follow them or come back here. I thought it probably best to come and put you in the picture because if I went to where Herod is staying, I wouldn't learn anything. I'll go back to Caiaphas's courtyard later and see what I can find out.'

'Be careful, John. They will notice you in daylight and you'll not find it so easy.' John's mother is clearly worried.

'John, when you go back, I'm coming with you.'

'And me!' Mariam joins in my plea to John. James comes over and grabs John by the shoulder.

'No, John. They come back to Bethany with me. You can stay and find out what happens if you will. Join us at Bethany tonight.'

'John, I want to come with you. I'll never rest until I know I've done everything I could to help my son.'

'What can you do, Mother? You'll just get yourself beaten up by the Roman thugs if nothing worse.'

'No-one said he was a prisoner of the Romans.'

'He soon will be. If the priests want him executed they'll have to get the Governor's permission.'

'Then I'll demand to see the Governor.'

'Are you out of your mind? Don't even think about it. You won't get near him. Try to approach the Governor's palace and you'll get a spear through you just for looking.'

'You're just going back to the High Priest's house, aren't you, John? What's the harm in that?'

'Mother, you don't understand these people. Joshua's threatened their livelihood, their accommodation with the Romans. They think he's a danger to them, therefore anyone connected with him is a danger too. I know it sounds silly to us, but that is what they think. If you go with John, you'll be putting yourself at risk.'

'I don't care. He's my son and he's done nothing wrong. And I'm going with John and Mariam. Salome, Susannah, are you coming too?'

'I'm sure they'll be more sensible than you and come back to Bethany with me.'

'What are the disciples' wives going to do? I think we're safer with them.'

Apparently they've all agreed to stay in Jerusalem until their husbands return. Susannah and Salome agree quickly to remain with them.

'Can we stay here? Whose room is this? Will we not have to vacate it anyway?'

'I've no idea whose it is.'

Andrew overhears. 'It belongs to a friend of the Master, a posh man in the Sanhedrin. He keeps his friendship secret in case he's embarrassed to be seen to be a supporter of a mad prophet from a backwater in Galilee. I think the Master agreed with him that we could have this room for the whole Passover festival.'

'If he's influential, can't we go and see him and plead for Joshua?'

'Mariam, I wish we could but even I don't know who he is. The Master apparently promised him secrecy and he's never even told us.'

'Andrew, what do you and the others intend to do? Are you going to stay with the women here or come looking for Yeshua with me?'

'I think we should all stay put. When the Master's friend hears what's happened he'll come and find us and see what he can do. At least some of us should stay. If you want to risk going to the High Priest's house to find out what you can, I'll not stop you, but I think it's madness to take any of the women with you.'

'Andrew, I can't stay cooped up in this room. I'm going with John and so is Mariam here, aren't you?'

Mariam and I pull on our cloaks and go to John, who looks us in the eye and sees our determination.

'James, let them do as they wish. You've done what you feel is your duty, but I can understand their feelings. I'll see they come to no harm.'

'You can't promise that, John. You've no idea what the authorities can and will do.'

John shrugs his shoulders and I go to his side.

'He'll do his best and that is good enough for me. I can't stay here and do nothing.'

James gives up and goes to Salome and Susannah.

'At least your sister and cousin have some sense. Be careful. Don't tell anyone where we are and make sure you're not followed when you come back.'

And so Mariam and John and I step outside into the cool morning dawn. Gusts of wind are stirring up flurries of dust. There are already several groups of people hurrying to buy provisions for the day or making their way to the Temple to offer their morning sacrifices before the crowds turn it into a madhouse. We have to pass the Temple steps and courtyard on our way to the High Priest's house and we hang around there for a few minutes to see if we can glean any rumours about Joshua, for each day the crowds have gathered there to hear him speak. Indeed there are already several sick people lying patiently at the foot of the steps, brought by friends and relatives who've heard what Joshua's been doing this last week. They obviously haven't heard of his arrest. Even as we watch, one of the Temple Guards walks over to them and presumably tells them, for they slowly pack up their belongings and struggle off, clearly disappointed. We walk over to the soldier and John, feigning to be a visitor to the city, asks if the soldier knows at what time the Galilean prophet will appear to speak to the crowd.

The soldier laughs at us.

'Don't waste your time here. He won't be coming back. He's a fraud and the authorities arrested him last night.'

'Where have they taken him?'

'What's that got to do with you? Good riddance is what I say. He's made my job impossible here, stirring up the crowd. If I lose control, I'll be on a charge. Just get on your way and don't loiter here unless you intend to go inside the Temple courtyard to get your sacrifice.'

'Please tell us where he is?' John is looking at me, I know he thinks I should be quiet, but I have to find out.

'Who are you? Why do you want to know? Are you a follower of his?'

'I'm his mother!'

'Then you'd better get out of my sight before I call more guards to arrest all three of you.'

We move on before he can carry out his threat. I don't know if he meant it. John doesn't say anything. James would have sworn at me by now if he'd been here, but John understands, I think. I apologise to John but he doesn't scold me or complain. When we finally reach the gates of the High Priest's house, we find them firmly shut and the courtyard inside seems deserted. We're just wondering what to do, when we hear shouting and see a column of soldiers marching towards us with a prisoner in their midst. It must be Joshua. John looks at both of us.

'Don't do anything silly now! There's a couple of dozen hefty soldiers. If you try anything they'll overpower you in moments and rough you up. I promised James I'd take care of you. Don't make me break my word.'

They're dragging Joshua in chains. I'm horrified, he looks as if he's been beaten. One eye is virtually closed, there's blood on his garment, then I realise it's the stain from when he poured the wine from the cup last night and let it trickle down his white robe. I don't think he's seen us, as there are many people coming to see what all the fuss is about. Suddenly a cry of 'Master' rends the air and all heads turn to stare at Mariam who's stepped forward and ripped the shawl from her head. Joshua, who's almost past us, turns and notices us, I think, only to receive a savage blow from one of the soldiers across the head and in the same movement receives a violent shove which nearly makes him fall. One of the guards at the end of

311

the column leans out and aims a swipe at Mariam catching her across her face and she falls forward. The soldier mutters 'whore' under his breath and does a double-step to catch up his comrades and all disappear into the courtyard, the gate shutting firmly behind them. We can't follow and the crowd that's formed is staring at Mariam who's trying to retrieve her shawl from the dusty road. One or two men avert their faces and one spits at her. I go forward and help her up and someone gives me a shove and I nearly overbalance, but John grabs my arm in time.

What now? We stare at the departing prisoner escort, which disappears into the house itself and we are left at the gate, a few people staring at us curiously. Someone asks us if we are followers of that prophet and I say that we are. The person shrugs, then speaks.

'I should make yourself scarce if I were you. I don't know what he did but it doesn't look good for him. I heard some were saying he'd been accused of blasphemy but I don't know if that's right. I'd find myself another prophet to follow. I think you'll find you're wasting your time if you try to stick with him. He's a loser.'

Mariam looks angry at this but John tries to calm her down. When this bystander has moved on, John just says, 'Best not to say too much. Just listen and see what we can glean.'

We retreat further back down the road to a place where we can keep watch on the High Priest's gates, without making it too obvious. The sun is well up into the sky now, though it's obscured from time to time by scudding clouds as the wind is now really turning into a gale and I'm sure a storm is coming. I pull my cloak about me and try to shield my eyes from the grit being hurled into the air. The thoroughfare is blocked now by pilgrims and their pack animals, not to mention a caravan of camels plodding by, causing the crowds to scatter out of their way.

'Can't we get into the High Priest's house and make our plea for him?'

I know what I say is useless, but what else can I do? I'd go in if I could, whatever the consequences, but the gate is firmly shut and a couple of Temple Guards are stationed either side. My guts are churning, I feel faint, but I must not let John and Mariam see this for they'll want to take me back to the stranger's room. Perhaps the owner of the house is there now. If so, I'm sure Salome and Susannah and Andrew and the others will press him to do what he can. Best to stay here and see what happens. The crowds are getting denser by the minute and when the gates are flung wide and the soldiers emerge once more, we can scarce keep up with them because of the throng. I've no idea where we are going now. Many people have poured out of the High Priest's house and are following the soldiers. Most are white-robed priests and rabbis and there is a lot of scurrying around, youths being pressed into service as messengers by the look of it. One comes close to us and John reaches out and grasps him by the arm.

'What's going on, young man? What's happening? Where is everyone going?'

The youth struggles to break free, but gabbles as he makes to dash off.

'They're off to the Roman Governor's palace. They need the Governor's sanction to an execution order.'

My heart lurches when I hear this. What can we do? Is there a way of getting an audience with the Governor himself? Perhaps we can find an official with whom we can speak. I look to Mariam. She's crying again. It's getting desperate now. How much time have we got? I don't think John has any ideas. I'm praying wordlessly although the pleas are stabbing at my stomach. I mustn't panic. That will not achieve anything. We follow the crowd. The spacious forum outside the palace is full of people. They seem to know something is going on. There's a lot of talk, people seem to be passing purposefully through the throng and whispering to others. The crowd is restive, it is not good humoured.

John steers us to a space near the edge of the crowd in the shade of one of the taller buildings opposite the entrance to the Governor's palace.

'Wait here – don't move. I'll mingle with the crowd and see what I can find out.'

He's gone a long time. The crowd is thickening all the time and I don't like the look of many of the men who look hostile. There are hardly any women and many of the men are looking at us with disdain as though we have no right to be here. Well, we have, it's Joshua who has no right to be inside that wretched building where the Roman Governor lives. It's big and bullying, towering over our Jewish homes, next to the more decorative palace that Herod, the tyrant father of the present Tetrarch, built for himself along with the Temple itself. John has said that Herod Antipas is there at the moment, visiting the capital for the duration of the Passover, even though he's not a Jew. Why is the crowd so large? Why have they come here? I would expect a large number of pilgrims outside the Temple at this time, but why here? It's as if they are expecting something to happen. Surely they haven't come to see what is happening to Joshua like us?

Then I notice some young men near the front of the crowd are shouting slogans. I can't hear everything they're saying, but I notice Mariam is looking alarmed.

'What are they saying, Mary? What's happening?'

'I think they're young Zealots, they must be foolhardy to come and shout anti-Roman insults in front of the Governor's palace. The Roman guards outside will surely stop them.'

Then I hear muttered expressions of like-minded thoughts from some of the men near us, grouses about the Roman presence and I begin to think that we're in the middle of a Jewish nationalist protest against the Roman occupation. Surely they wouldn't dare, not at this festival time? I'm getting very nervous. I don't feel our presence is welcome here, although I can't put my finger on the reason. Then I see John wending his way back to us, pushing through the throng.

'What's happening, John? What is everyone waiting for?'

'There may be a chance of rescue. Apparently the Romans, in order to improve their popularity with the crowds who've come up for the Passover, grant an amnesty to a well-known prisoner every year. Many of the men here are supporters of the Zealot movement, some of them have risked coming to the capital and mingling with the pilgrims, because there's a rumour that the prisoner to be released this year is their leader. He's a man called Barabbas. The Romans captured him last month up in the hills north of Galilee and brought down here for public execution during the Passover holiday as an example to other rebels. Many of the crowd are here to greet their leader and celebrate his release. But I'm told that there may be the possibility of a change of mind and that the Romans might decide to release Yeshua instead. The Governor will not want to let such a prize prisoner go and Yeshua's presence here might give him a way out.'

My heart leaps at this news, but before I can get too optimistic, a man standing nearby, who has overheard John, turns to us.

'You're right. They led us to believe that Barabbas would be freed and tempted his supporters to the city. It's a ruse, they just want to flush the Zealots out so they can arrest and execute the other ring-leaders. Now they say they're going to free another prisoner instead, some wretched peasant preacher who's upset the local priests. That won't worry the Romans at all, he's harmless as far as they're concerned. They'll be in trouble back in Rome if they've let a key catch like Barabbas loose again when they've spent the last year trying to catch him. Governor Pilatus will fear for his job. Well, we've all come now to protest if this rumour's true. We'll turn nasty if the decision goes against us. The Romans won't want a riot at

Passover time, that won't go down well in Rome either. And the Jewish authorities will like a riot even less, so they'll be on our side. They'll happily push Pilatus to let Barabbas go in order to get their own man.'

My optimism is dwindling. When John said they'd be releasing a prisoner, my hope was raised. Perhaps the Romans would release him just as this man said they might in order not to have to free this Zealot leader. But if the whole crowd is hostile? What will they do if the Romans give back Joshua to us? This mob looks as though it might get violent.

'Come, both of you, let's try to get nearer to the palace entrance so we can hear what's going on. We won't hear anything back here.'

So we try to push through the crowd. We are jostled and shoved and men look angrily at us as we try to advance. But we persevere until we are near the front and have a good view of the portico and veranda above it. John says that apparently the Romans produce the prisoner they are to release there in full view of the crowd in order to milk the maximum goodwill from the Jews. They normally have some sort of rebel whose release will be popular. Not usually a man of violence, as this Barabbas apparently is, more often an outspoken advocate for Jewish independence or other nuisance, a political prisoner. Joshua apparently would fill this role ideally as far as the Romans are concerned and I have to cling to this faint hope. But I get the feeling that if the Romans don't produce Barabbas, this crowd is going to turn very ugly. John tells me that we should hide our relief if Joshua is released as the crowd could take out their frustration on us if they think we're not supporters of their leader.

The sun is beginning to climb into the sky and appears at length above the Temple walls to the east of the city, casting its rays directly onto the palace veranda. There is an expectancy now and the hubbub of the crowd has fallen to a low hum. The announcement is clearly expected any time. Then we notice the door to the veranda is moving. The crowd falls silent. Then the door shuts again and there is a muttering of frustration all around. Then, eventually, the door opens and to everyone's surprise the guards push out two men in chains into full view of the crowd. My heart lifts when I see one of them is Joshua. He still looks pale and beaten, he has a black eye and his white robe is creased and dirty as well as still having the visible crimson stain where he spilled the wine. The other man, who must be Barabbas, is rough and bearded, he must be about ten years older than Joshua at a guess. He looks defiant and salutes the crowd who let up a great roar and start chanting 'Barabbas, Barabbas' and go on and on, until a Roman official holds up his hand, signalling he wants to speak. The chanting carries on for a few more minutes, until eventually it is silenced when Barabbas himself holds up one of his chained arms. The crowd cheers again, then falls silent.

'I, Marcus Aurelius, Chief Administrator of Governor Pontius Pilatus, bring to you two prisoners as it is the custom of our sovereign Roman munificence to the Jewish people to release a prisoner in honour of your great annual festival.'

He pauses while cheers let rip once more. Are they going to release both prisoners this year? Is that why Joshua and Barabbas have been paraded before us? Then my hopes are dashed.

'This year the Governor has instructed me to bring two prisoners before you so that you, the Jewish people, can make a choice. To my left is the Zealot brigand Joshua bar Abbas, a native of the town of Bethlehem in Judea, found guilty of murder, robbery with violence against many Jews as well as against the forces of your Tetrarch Herod Antipas and the Roman Emperor, and sentenced to be executed by crucifixion. To my right is your so-called King of the Jews, the prophet Yeshua ben Yosef, native of the village of Nazareth in Galilee, who has been accused by the Jewish religious authorities of blasphemy, for which they seek the sentence of death. The

Governor offers one of these men to your mercy with a strong recommendation to release Yeshua ben Yosef as he has not been found guilty of any crime against Roman law.'

As soon as he's said this there is uproar. Shouts of 'Barabbas' rise in a crescendo and wave after wave of noise swamps the forum. I realise that nearly all these men are Jewish nationalists, hundreds of them, supporters of the Zealot leader, and they will call for Barabbas no matter what the Romans recommend. In fact, by pushing the case for our Joshua's release, they have further inflamed the crowd. This band of extremists will not be quelled. The Chief Administrator is trying to stop the shouting, but it goes on for minutes until the Roman soldiers guarding the palace entrance seize a couple of the crowd and threaten to kill them unless the noise subsides. When this Marcus can make himself heard, he steps forward once again.

'Which of these two men do you wish Governor Pilatus to release? Joshua bar Abbas or Yeshua ben Yosef?'

It's hopeless. Mariam, John and I shout 'Yeshua' as loudly as we can but our voices are drowned by the tumult around us as 'Barabbas!' is screamed by everyone. I don't even think those immediately around us heard our call. Just three small voices against the throng. Did no-one else call for Joshua? Where are the other disciples? Where are the crowds who came to cheer him in the Temple courtyard and on its steps? Where are those whom Joshua healed? Where are those who'd been cheated by the Temple traders whose need for justice Joshua had championed? Perhaps they just don't know. They don't know he's been arrested. They don't know he's been brought here to the Governor because the priests and rabbis he's offended want the Romans to sentence him to death. They don't know that the Romans release a prisoner every year. Or they don't know it's happening now. They don't know that they could shout for my son, their Messiah. They don't know...

The cries of 'Barabbas' go on and on and on. The Chief Administrator looks concerned. He gives an order and the guards seize the two prisoners and drag them back inside the palace. The crowd roars its disapproval and boos loudly. The crowd then starts chanting rhythmically, 'Barabbas, Barabbas, we want Barabbas'. Minutes pass. The crowd is still chanting, louder than ever. I notice now that there are priests and rabbis in the crowd and they are shouting as loudly as the rest. Eventually the door reopens, and the Chief Administrator appears accompanied by an imposing individual dressed in a white toga. It must be the Governor himself.

A hush suddenly descends on the expectant crowd. The official steps forward again. The prisoners are not in sight.

'By order of the Governor, I ask you. Who should be released? What is you will...?'

Before he can finish, the shout begins, 'Barabbas, we want Barabbas!' The Chief Administrator battles on trying to make himself heard above the din.

'Do you wish the Governor to release your king, your Messiah, who is guilty of no act of violence or the murderer and bandit, Barabbas?'

The noise from the crowd increases until it is deafening. They are all screaming for the Zealot leader. There is a hurried consultation between Marcus Aurelius and Governor Pilatus and then the Governor makes a rapid exit back inside his palace. There is a hiatus at the palace balustrade, but the crowd continues to call for Barabbas. The Chief Administrator calls for silence and eventually the noise subsides sufficiently for those near the front of the crowd to hear him declaim.

'The Governor has decided in accordance with your wishes to release Joshua bar Abbas.' The announcement is greeted with a huge cheer from those who've heard it, and as the news ripples round the audience the volume of cheering and applause swells swamping all other noise. Marcus Aurelius has continued to speak but almost unnoticed by the crowd. I hear him say, 'And what is your wish for the fate of your Messiah?' Those nearby who catch what he says start to yell back, 'Kill him, crucify him!' Others shout, 'He's a fake, a blasphemer, he's no Messiah of ours.' I notice that a bevy of white-robed priests and rabbis are in the front, leading this call and others nearby repeat the refrain. Mariam is screaming 'No' by now but no-one can hear her. I'm confused, I'm suddenly exhausted, everything is very blurred, then I feel John holding me firmly by the arm.

'Mari, can you hear me? Hold tight, I'll get you out of here. Take deep breaths.' I can hear Mariam vaguely in the background. She's wailing, shouting 'No, no, he's innocent. You're condemning an innocent man,' but nobody is taking any notice of her. There is a sudden roar and I manage to ask John for its meaning.

'Barabbas has been brought out and they're removing his chains. It's a travesty of justice. I thought the Romans were in charge. I never thought they'd be swayed by a crowd like this one. Come, Mari, there's no point in waiting here. We must go and tell the others.'

'No, John. We must do something!'

Mariam joins me. 'Please, John, we must protest to the Governor.'

'How?'

'I don't know. We must do something.'

John hesitates a moment, then, with us in tow, approaches one of the soldiers guarding the entrance to the palace.

'We need to see the Governor. A grave injustice has been done. You've just condemned an innocent man.' At first the soldier does not answer, so John repeats his request.

'Go away before you get arrested. The Governor has decreed. He won't change his mind. You heard the crowd. They're convinced of the man's guilt, so the Governor's hardly likely to change his mind.'

'But he's innocent!'

'Get lost. If Pilatus says he's guilty, then he's guilty.'

'But he didn't. It's the jealous Jewish priests who want him condemned. They must have bribed witnesses to provide evidence against him.'

'If you don't go away this minute I'll arrest you for rebellion against the Roman Governor. Then you can be crucified alongside your innocent Messiah if you insist on calling him that. You're becoming a nuisance. Go away.'

'No, I want to see the Governor!' I surprise myself with the boldness of my words.

'And the same applies to you, old woman. We may not crucify silly old women yet but we've a few decomposing in damp and dirty cells and you can join them if you insist on your stupid protest. And you!' he says looking at Mariam, 'although some of the guards will enjoy your favours first before you're slung into the pit.'

'Mary, Mariam, you must come away. You will not save Joshua this way. Perhaps he'll save himself. You know the powers he has. If he really wanted to use his powers to save himself, he could, you know....'

Chapter 26
Mari

We've somehow got back to the room where we celebrated the Passover just yesterday evening. It seems already an age away. The women try to make me eat but I cannot. John has told them what we've experienced and was heard out in doleful silence. All the disciples seem to be there now, well, with the exception of Judas. No-one knows where he is or seems to care. Simon Peter is there, but is very silent for him. He looks as though he's been crying, something I don't associate with that big man. I know he's a close friend of Joshua, but I hadn't expected tears from him.

No-one knows what to do. The owner of the house has not appeared – some say that we could try to get him to plead for Joshua's life as apparently he is a man of influence. But nobody knows who he is or how to get in touch with him. That was Joshua's secret.

Time passes. We sit around. Some are in despair. Mariam has not ceased her weeping. Some of the other women are near tears. Susannah and Salome are very concerned about me. They try to say words of comfort but it is all meaningless. It's all passed so quickly I can hardly appreciate what's happening. It's strange that no tears have come for me. It's just like a nightmare that perhaps I'll wake up from in a moment. We can't sit here like this forever. It must be the middle of the day by now, though it's difficult to tell in this dark room – there is but one small window and that is on the eastern side. The sun's rays have long since ceased to penetrate the room. Thomas and Bartholomew eventually pluck up courage and say they'll go out to try to establish what's happening. My son James says he'll accompany them. If they're accused of being Joshua's disciples, he can honestly say that he's not. I doubt if they'll discover anything. It's the Sabbath tomorrow and the

Romans will not want to do anything that will offend the Jews with all the pilgrims in the city. I look out of the window and stare at the sky over the roofs opposite. The wind has dropped suddenly and I realise that the sun is not shining. The clouds are ominously dark and it feels so sultry. A rainstorm is in the offing.

John has been telling me to seek some rest, but I refused. I wish to stay awake, to know everything that is happening. But I've had no sleep now for many hours. And despite my attempt to stay awake, I must have dropped off, even as I was staring out of the window. For, suddenly, the door crashes open and James and the two disciples are in the room.

'It's too late, we're too late. There's nothing we can do. He's finished!' Thomas shouts to everyone. The man is beside himself, tearing at his clothes as he speaks. 'He's already been executed. We nearly got caught up in the procession of condemned prisoners being led out to execution and the Master was among them.'

'He was in a dreadful state,' says Bartholomew. 'He was so weak he collapsed on the way to the execution site. He must have been flogged, his back was lacerated, a bloody mess.'

'There's no need to distress the women further,' says James trying to shut the two disciples up. 'There's nothing anyone can do, so I suggest we all go back to Nazareth and Capernaum as fast as we can before the authorities realise many of us are still here and decide to arrest us all before we can make mischief.'

'Where is he? I want to be with him.'

'Mother, forget it. It's no sight for you to contemplate.'

'It doesn't matter. I should be with him. I'm his mother.'

'No. No. You can't. It'll kill you to see him like this. You should have listened to me ages ago and had nothing more to do with him. You can't go now, I forbid you!'

'I'm going. It's a mother's duty. He must see someone he knows and loves. He'll think we've all abandoned him. I'm going. Who'll come with me?'

'You don't know where to go.'

'Thomas will tell me.'

'He won't.'

'Yes you will, won't you, Thomas?'

'I'll come with you, Mari.' It's my sister, Salome.

'Are you coming, Mariam?'

She shakes her head. Through her tears she mouths, 'I can't, I just can't!'

A couple of the disciples' wives say they'll come too. Not one of the men. What are they afraid of? Do they think they'll be arrested as one of his followers? I don't care. Without Joshua, I don't care what happens to me. Then John says he'll accompany us to see we're safe. Thomas tells John where the crucifixion site is, just outside the Damascus Gate near the area where refuse is disposed of, alongside the highway as is the custom of the Romans, apparently, in order to create a deterrent for the maximum number of people to see.

'Don't go, Mother. I implore you not to go. The sight will be too much for you. Try to remember him as he was, not as he is now. You won't recognise him. It's pitiful to see him like this, even though I've always despised all he stood for. I wouldn't wish this on anyone, not even my worst enemy.'

He stands before me, barring my way to the door.

'I'm going, James. I don't care what you say. Stand aside and let me go.'

'James, let her go. I'll be with her and the others. It's distressing, yes, but it can't be worse than they'll imagine if they're kept in ignorance here.' John is emphatic and James gives way.

Six of us – Mariam Magdalene, who has changed her mind at the last moment, Salome, Susannah, Joanna, Bartholomew's wife, another Mariam, the mother of another disciple called

James and me - escorted by John, hurry through the congested lanes towards the Damascus Gate. The sky overhead looks very threatening, it's dark in the narrow streets and sultry and I'm perspiring. We can't progress as quickly as we want because the crowds are ambling and my mind is scarcely on what we are doing. I bump into people, I mutter apologies, I blunder my way forward, I scarce know where I'm going but follow the others blindly. There's a queue at the Gate, we have to wait because of the horde of people and animals trying to get in. I want to scream at everyone, let us through, let us through. Why so fast – because I want to reach my dying son, don't you understand? And if I shouted this, they wouldn't understand, and if they did, they'd block my path. Why should they make way for the wretched mother of a condemned man?

And when we at last squeeze through against the heavy flow of people in the opposite direction, we find nearly everyone on the Damascus road coming towards us. And I can see the crucifixion site ahead, ugly black crosses against a filthy sky and black figures milling around the bases, strangers come to gawp at the death throes of the condemned men, chatting, laughing while my son dies in agony. The stench from the nearby rubbish tip, nicknamed 'Gehenna' or 'Hell', adds to the dreadful scene.

'Are you sure you want to go on?' John is anxious. Salome comes to me, puts her arm around my waist and holds me tight.

'Mari, you don't have to. I'll stay here with you, while the others go on.'

'No, I must get there. He must see me. He must. I must get there. Please, let it not be too late!'

'Mari, don't panic. There's no need to rush. Your son will not be dead yet.' I know he's trying to tell me that the agony will go on for hours, sometime for days, but he doesn't want to remind me of this. But I know. I've seen crucifixions before.

I shall never forget that first time when we visited the festival in Nain and Uncle Pharisee Eli made me look, and I thought it might have been my father. I'm helped to the edge of this motley crowd. I suppose there might be relatives here of other dying men, but the figures nearby don't care. They are curious, indifferent. If they are angry, they are resentful of the Romans who devised this torture to afflict their countrymen. They have no pity for those condemned to die, they assume they've deserved it. Some are mocking, treating it all as a repulsive joke. I push forward until the distorted faces of the dying men come into focus. I'm searching, horrified that I can't recognise him, perhaps after all they've got it wrong and he isn't here.

Please God, please let it be wrong!

And then I see him. His eyes are closed. Blood is trickling from his brow. His naked body is contorted obscenely like the others. Some are moaning, groaning. Some are shrieking in their agony. Joshua is quiet, almost asleep? He can't be. Unconscious already? Am I too late to bid him farewell? Has he already gone?

Then, at last, the tears come. I can't stop them now. Something has released them. The stark reality before me. It's as if the pain I see is mine too.

'Mari, please Mari, don't, don't!' Why, what am I doing? What does Salome mean? Then I hear my voice, disembodied, nothing to do with me, my conscious self. There's a strange noise, a groaning, a keening. Both Salome and Susannah hold me tight. I look up at him, and the tears flow so that he's only visible as a blur. Then I'm conscious that he's opening his eyes and looking straight at me. Someone nearby is shouting something. They're laughing. It's horrible. Voices are telling him to come down from the cross, heal himself like he healed others. Could he? Could he perform this last miracle, the greatest miracle of all? Could he? I look up at him. He's not reacting to the jibes. He's still looking at me. He knows I'm here. He doesn't say anything, perhaps he can't. But he must know I'm here. I feel I need to say something, but what can I say? What should I tell him? Can I offer comfort? I feel helpless. God, where are you? Why this? Why this? You said he was to be the Messiah and now you let this happen. Why?

I'm right by the foot of his cross now. There are Roman soldiers milling around, chatting, gambling, looking bored. I'm just staring at him. He is still looking at me. Sometimes he shuts his eyes as if a new wave of pain throbs through him, then he's looking at me again. Someone has just touched my arm. I think no more of it, it's John or Salome. But there's a voice, a different voice, low, with a heavy accent.

'Lady, do you know this man?'

I start. I look at the owner of this voice. He's a soldier. Is he going to mock, insult me too? Salome whispers to him, tells him that I'm his mother.

'I'm sorry, lady. Something's wrong. He's not like the others. I feel bad about it. I don't like this job. I'm in charge and I have to order my men to carry out these executions. Most of the condemned scream and curse and struggle, but this man? He is very different. He seems sad, he even apologised to me and the soldiers while they were nailing him, apologising that they had to do such a hideous thing. I don't understand it, I've never had to execute someone like him before. Who is he, who are you?'

Is he mocking me? Is he teasing? I can't take this. But I manage to look him in the face and his eyes are kind. My eyes well up again. I try to speak, but the sounds stick in my throat. John answers.

'He was a prophet, sir. We thought he was the Messiah, sent from God to save our nation. And this lady is his mother.'

'So he was condemned as a rebel? He raised soldiers to fight us Romans?'

'No. He sought to save men's souls. He was a peaceful man, renouncing violence. But the Jewish priests were jealous of him, he criticised their greed and hypocrisy and they made out to the Roman authorities that he was a threat to them, claiming to be their king.'

'But the inscription scribbled on the head of the cross says he was their king.'

'He never claimed that.'

'But the Governor insisted that the inscription was placed there. I assumed that was the reason for his conviction. Some here tried to get me to change it because they said he was a fake, but I had my orders and I have to obey them.'

'Well, I suppose he was a king, in a way. He was always speaking about God's kingdom, but he described it as a place of peace and love and care for each other, a place where we would all be one family, Jew and Gentile, men and women, boys and girls.'

'If that's right, it hardly seems a reason for condemnation. It seems to me like a miscarriage of justice.'

'There's nothing you can do about it now.'

He turns to me.

'Lady, I'm so sorry. I cannot save him, but I can try to reduce his suffering. I'll order my men to give him a drink laced with herbs that can deaden the pain and I can hasten his death, so as not to prolong his agony.'

He looks me in the face again and I see his eyes are watering too. A hardened Roman soldier, an officer! There is a sudden gust of wind disturbing the dust at our feet and it is getting even darker. There is a storm coming from the north, an occasional flash of lightning on the horizon. Some of the crowd are scurrying for shelter, but we stay still.

Suddenly I hear him call.

'Mother, mother!'

I look up and his eyes are searching for me.

'John will look after you. He will be as your son. John, look after my mother, take her as your own.'

John looks at me.

'I promise. If that is what you need and want, I'll do it gladly.' He looks up to Joshua. 'I promise. I'll care for her as you have asked.'

I even think he smiled. How could he?

It's getting so dark now that nearly all have fled the storm. Thunder is crashing all around, and the rain starts, large single drops spattering the dusty earth at first, then a deluge. In no time we are soaked through, but I ignore it. Only our little group and the soldiers are still present. We stand there amidst the storm and cling to each other, the storm cleansing us, even to our very souls. That is what it seems.

The Roman officer is still beside me.

'It seems even the heavens object to what is happening. Perhaps your son was right. Perhaps he was your nation's Messiah and look what they have done to him. His God and theirs protests. I wouldn't like to be in the shoes of those who condemned him when they need to face the consequences before the judgment of the God they worship.'

The rain eases after a while, but the darkness remains. The wind has dropped and the storm stays stationary, even circles round us, the lightning illuminating the sky and the ramparts of the city. The officer has been as good as his word. His soldiers have offered Joshua a drink.

'Lady, don't look now. We'll help him to finish his agony.'

There is a sudden cry of anguish and I shudder. He's shouting something but I can't catch what he's saying. Then, quite clearly, I hear the words.

'It's over. I've done what had to be done.'

And then he looks down at the soldiers.

'Father, forgive them. They are ignorant of what they are doing.'

Does he mean the soldiers? Is he just referring to them? Or is he thinking back to those who condemned him? Is he even forgiving them?

'Father, I'm coming back to you. Take my spirit into yours.'

329

And I look at him, and his whole body has gone limp, relaxed, the strain in his face is gone. It is over.

*   *   *   *   *

And as I stand there, staring, hardly conscious of my surroundings and my sister, cousin, friends just hold me, I hear another voice. A man, a stranger, speaks quietly to me.

'You don't know me but I'm a friend. I was a friend of your son. I tried to save him, but I couldn't. Let me do now what I can. I have a tomb where you can lay his body in the city. It is a quiet place, in a garden, peaceful where I had planned to be laid myself. But it is for him now. I'm so sorry that we never met in happier times. But I offer you now all I can. My name is Joseph. I live here in the city but I come from a Judean town called Arimathea.'

I nod. He takes over and goes to speak with the Roman officer.

'Come, mother.' There is a quiet gentle voice. It is John.

Chapter 27

Joseph of Arimathea

I failed. I tried to save him, but I failed. Offering the family the use of my tomb is the least I can do for him. It seems insensitive to interrupt them now in their grief, but I need to tell them, to save them worrying what will happen next; to let them know that his body will not be thrown with the corpses of the other criminals onto the rubbish tip and just covered with a thin layer of earth to deter the crows but which will hardly deter the foxes and wild dogs. I recognise the young man from Yeshua's description of him, it must be John, the youngest of his disciples. I don't know the women with him, but I assume one is his mother.

John is already trying to persuade the group to leave the dead man, so I call him and tell him that I have the burial of his body in hand. I give John details of the location of the grave so that Yeshua's relatives can prepare the body properly when they feel ready. I have written permission from the Governor's chief official to take possession of his body and arrange its burial before the commencement of the Sabbath. The official didn't argue. He didn't seem to care. I'd had a word with the Centurian in charge of the execution party too, asking for his help to ensure the Master didn't suffer the agony for too long dragging on overnight and then be left hanging and exposed throughout the Sabbath, to await disposal the following day.

Surprisingly the soldier seemed understanding and sympathetic. I'd expected to receive abuse or scorn and be treated as a criminal myself for making such a request, but once he'd seen my official authorisation, he became quite chatty and quizzed me about the condemned man. He expressed the opinion that Yeshua was highly unusual, a man who bore the humiliation, indignity and pain of the crucifixion in a restrained and passive way as if he'd accepted his fate. He'd even seemed thoughtful about the rough soldiers who were forced to pin him to the execution cross, although he must have been in agony for his back was raw from a flogging he had received just prior to the final act. The Centurian asked me about the inscription he'd been commanded by the Governor to nail to the upright – that the man was the 'King of the Jews'. 'He didn't strike me as a terrorist or member of a nationalist group. We've crucified a number of those recently and they either die full of bravado and yelling nationalist slogans or they curse and swear at the soldiers whom they despise as the occupation force. Several of my soldiers, uncouth as some of them are, remarked on this man and felt uneasy about what they were doing.'

So I told him about the Master. How he'd been a famous prophet, renowned in Galilee, but had fallen foul of the religious leaders here in Jerusalem who'd been jealous of his following and resented his criticism of them. How they'd had to bribe witnesses to give evidence that Yeshua had claimed kingship, so that he could be condemned under Roman law. That really they'd accused him of blasphemy, but no Roman court would convict a man and sentence him to death just on a Jewish religious law. They observe the niceties here under the noses of you Romans, although they'd apply their own barbaric practices unhindered in the remote villages. The Centurian asked in that case why they'd not dealt with him outside the capital and I said that his following was too strong outside Jerusalem, the priests and Pharisees would have to face the mob themselves who'd never let them get away with it. 'So was he a king?' he'd asked and I talked to him about his spiritual message. I'm not sure the soldier understood, but he grasped the fact that he was innocent of the crime for which he'd been condemned and assured me he'd do his best to minimise his suffering as far as he could.

So the Centurian orders his men to take down the body of the Master and help me to take it to the tomb, which is inside the city walls. The soldiers express surprise as executed criminals are not allowed to be buried within the city, but the Centurian assures them that I have the appropriate permission. Luckily I had to get this only from the Roman authorities. The Jewish leaders would never have permitted it. It doesn't take them long. We've covered his body so that bystanders do not realise that this is the corpse of a crucified man and ask awkward questions. We've only just laid his body to rest on the stone slab within the tomb, when another delegation of soldiers turns up with a couple of rabbis, whom I recognise from the Temple establishment.

'Why are you allowing this? You know the regulations concerning the burial of criminals. You must remove this body at once, it's an insult to Jehovah that he, a vile blasphemer, should find a place inside the city of David.' One of the rabbis has rounded on me and intends to use force if necessary to get his way. I show the commander of the Roman patrol who has accompanied the rabbis my official letter of authorisation, signed by the Governor himself and the soldiers who've brought the body of Yeshua from the execution site back me up and the new group of soldiers accept that and ignore the protests of the rabbis. These two say they'll complain of my actions officially in the Sanhedrin and get me censored, but since the military will take no further action, they go away muttering that they'll complain to the Roman official, saying that if there's evidence that I've bribed anyone, they'll have me barred from the chamber meetings.

We're still securing the tombstone across the entrance when the rabbis return, flustered and out of breath.

'We've obtained orders from your official to place a military guard on the tomb. We can't get him to have the body removed but here are the written orders for at least two soldiers to remain by the tomb here for the next few days until the body has decomposed sufficiently to make it impractical for removal.'

'Why on earth do you want that? It seems a nonsense. I trust you're not going to bribe the soldiers to remove the body and take it out of the city as soon as our backs are turned?'

'On the contrary. We fear his disciples will come and steal the body and say he's risen from the grave.'

'Why on earth would they do that?'

'There's a rumour that he predicted he'd be destroyed and rise again. Most think he was talking about the Temple, which was one of our complaints about him, but some say he was talking about himself. We can't take that risk. If his body disappeared and the disciples spread the rumour that he'd come back to life, then people all over the country might take it seriously and cause all sorts of problems and heresy.'

'So you just want to be sure he's still here?'

'Yes'

'In that case you'll presumably not mind if I ask the Centurian to permit one of his soldiers to remain on guard as well. I don't trust you'

'It's a poor reflection of your Jewish faith if you can't trust the word of senior rabbis attached to the most important temple in the land.'

'You've done little to justify that trust in that you lot conjured up witnesses to lie about the prophet in order to get the Romans to confirm the death penalty you were determined to impose.'

'We'll ignore that remark. And if you make it again, I'll have you accused in the Sanhedrin of slander and expelled.'

I don't know if I can get the Centurian to agree. However, one of the soldiers agrees to stay while the others return to their commander to seek his permission for my request. The rabbis wait until the soldier returns and says the Centurian has approved. The soldiers agree the coverage among themselves and I leave satisfied. I trust the Centurian, which is a poor comment on the behaviour of my own countrymen.

I had better return to my house in the city now and see if the Master's disciples and family are still there. They don't know me, but it was Yeshua himself who asked me if he could borrow a room in which they could all celebrate the Passover. We've had a series of meetings of the Sanhedrin in the days leading up to the festival and I've been with my brother and his family for the ritual meals. It's been good to be at the meal with them, for I have no family of my own since my wife died in childbirth and I treat my brother's children as my own.

I said that I'd tried to save the Master. I thought I could use my influence in the Sanhedrin to argue his case when I heard of his arrest. There had been earlier debates about the phenomenon of John who was condemning the hypocrisy of the religious leaders and baptising those who repented of wrongdoing in the Jordan river. Then there had been a couple of references to Yeshua's actions in the Temple and complaints about his disturbance of the Temple traders. I had defended him then, and they'd let the matter drop as they were unable to assure me that the traders were not charging excessive prices to the pilgrims and that they, the priests, were not themselves benefiting greatly from the trade. When I heard that they had arrested Yeshua, I was prepared to defend him once more, despite the risk to my own reputation, but I was not prepared for the speed with which he was condemned. The matter was never brought to the Sanhedrin, but was dealt with by the High Priest and his religious court and they got him to the Romans that same night because they said they wanted the matter cleared before the main festival was in full swing. I think it was their plan to move so swiftly to pre-empt any move to speak on his behalf and challenge their arguments, for their mind was already made up.

So I've come here to witness the execution and see to his proper burial as befits a man of his integrity and holiness. It has been a rebuke to me to have to witness my friend in such agony, drumming into my brain the magnitude of my failure to speak up for him and save him. I'm ashamed that I was unprepared to speak openly earlier. I've since discovered that I'm not his only supporter in the Sanhedrin. Nicodemus stopped me after my last timid intervention there and said that he too had been impressed by the Galilean prophet but had been nervous of admitting it openly for fear of criticism from the High Priest and his faction in the assembly. What might have happened had the two of us spoken out more boldly? Would we have found others of influence prepared to defend him? We might have saved him. We might even have made it difficult for the priests to have had him arrested at all. I think of my weakness now, my lack of courage, as a direct cause of his death, as great a sin as that of those who actually condemned him, or drove the nails into his hands and feet. So I'm now trying desperately to atone for my failure to act and all I can do is to offer him my own tomb as his last resting place. What an admission of failure!

And now I've had to watch the grief of his own family and followers. I daren't admit to them my lack of timely action. Indeed, it's embarrassing that in their grief they were so effusive in their thanks for this little service I could undertake. And, now I've had his body laid to rest, and secured some assurance that nothing untoward will happen to it, seen the heavy stone rolled across the entrance, I suppose I'll have to face his followers who'll probably still be in my home where I promised Yeshua he could celebrate the Passover. His followers may not be so grateful as the women, they may suspect that I could have done more and challenge me. Yeshua told me about some of them, especially the rough outspoken fishermen from Capernaum. I guess I'll get the rough edge of their tongues. But I must face up to that – part of my penance perhaps for not having faced up to my responsibilities earlier. I must make my way there now, for the Sabbath is almost upon us.

Chapter 28
Mari

What a miserable Sabbath we've just celebrated! We've all be crowded into this one room. No-one has felt like eating anything, although a couple of the disciples' wives cooked something earlier to eat on the Sabbath. Many of the men are petrified that the Temple Guards will come for them next. They're all ashamed that they fled when Joshua was arrested and did nothing to try to protect him. Simon Peter is especially upset although he won't say why. I suppose it was that Joshua seemed to look to him to be leader of the disciples and he feels he should have done more. I tried to comfort him, but he hinted that there was something far worse he'd done and was too ashamed to tell me about. Then the man we'd seen at the crucifixion, who'd taken Joshua's body to his own grave, arrived and we discovered that he owns the house we are in. And he was as miserable as the rest of us, he kept blaming himself for what had happened although I've no idea why.

Then Simon Peter said it was all his fault and others joined in – they seemed to be having a competition on who could accept most blame. It was not very helpful. Mariam spent the day in tears. I was just so weary, I felt drained as though I'd no fight left in me. Tears should have come to me too, but I felt numb, cold, depressed. I felt an overwhelming sense of disappointment, I suppose, somehow I'd assumed God would intervene even at the last moment and fulfil his promise that my son was the Messiah. What am I to believe now? That my whole life thus far has been a huge delusion, a fraud, that I've convinced myself only of my own wishes and missed God's will entirely?

The day dragged on forever and all our minds were mired in pointless recriminations. At one stage some of the disciples vented their frustration on their absent member, Judas, whom some seemed to think had betrayed Joshua to the Temple Guards. Others could think of no reason why he would and thought that perhaps he'd been arrested too. He'd disappeared anyway and a couple thought he might be imprisoned still. John and his brother ventured out at one stage and went to the Temple and brought back a few people who'd been searching for Joshua and were unaware that he'd been killed. They were upset then of course and we went through everything that had happened all over again for their benefit. At first light this morning, now we're free of the Sabbath restrictions, most of them set off back to their own villages. They didn't feel like staying in the city to celebrate the rest of the festival as their hearts were now not in it.

Last night the owner of this house, Joseph, showed us some of the herbs and spices he owned and offered them to us to take and use on the body of Joshua. Some of the women said they'd go, Mariam among them. I was in two minds at first. I'm not sure I can bear seeing my son lying there, cold, his body bearing the signs of the torture he's undergone. But Mariam has persuaded me. Salome has said she'll come too. Joseph offered to come, but I think was hesitant at being alone with a group of women he hardly knew. I thought Simon Peter and John might have come too, but after the sleepless nights we've had they were both slumbering deeply at dawn and we decided we wanted to go before many people were about.

There are four of us. Salome, Mariam and the mother of the other disciple called James, yet another Mariam. Joseph has told us exactly where to go and we progress through the nearly empty streets unhindered. After the storms of the last two days, the sky is clear and washed out, just a tinge of pink from the rising sun. As we reach the garden where Joseph said we could find the tomb, the same thought hits all of us at the same time. The tombstone will be too heavy for us to roll away to gain entrance. How stupid of us not to think of this! We should have accepted Joseph's offer to accompany us. But it's my sister who points out that Joseph said that there would be guards at the tomb and we could ask them to help. Of course, I'd forgotten that. I remember Joseph telling us now. He'd know that we could get help. We expected therefore to see the guards first, but I was surprised that they were not obvious. Perhaps they had hidden themselves away, but I can't think why.

Then we see it. Instead of the tombstone, there's a great gaping hole in the rock-face. Someone's been at the grave already. His body has been removed, the authorities have not allowed his body to remain within the city walls after all. This is awful, how will we know where to find him? Mariam bursts into tears when she sees this and we all stop in our tracks. Then I go forward. What are they fearful about? I'm going to make sure. I stoop and enter the darkened tomb. It's difficult to see in here. I can just make out a ledge against the far wall, where his body ought to be, but I can't see anything. I grope forward and find there is cloth on the cold stone. I feel it. The cloth is folded, it's like the cloth that we wrapped his body on when it was taken down for us from the scaffold. I'm puzzled. If his body has been moved, why has someone taken the trouble of stripping the body and folding the cloth? You'd have thought that either graverobbers or soldiers would have taken the cloth as well as the body, it must be of some value. I go back outside and find the others talking to two young men I'd not noticed before. They are asking them where Joshua's body has been taken. Poor Mariam Magdalene is distraught. Salome and the other Mariam are looking incredulous.

'It's empty, his body's gone!' I shout as I emerge from the tomb. The others don't seem to take any notice of me. They're still talking to these two men. Perhaps they know what's happened.

'Mari, listen! These men are saying that Joshua isn't here...'

'That's obvious,' I interrupt. 'I just told you.'

'No, they're saying he's alive. That he's come back to life.'

'You misheard,' I say, 'what do these men know? Who are they?'

'Mariam, are you the Rabbi's mother?'

How do they know that?

'You mean the mother of Joshua, the prophet from Nazareth?'

'Yes.'

'Yes, I am.'

'Then we have a message for you from your son. You won't find him here. He's not dead but more alive than ever! Go and tell his friends and followers. He'll confirm it with you all later.'

My mind is reeling. Am I hallucinating? Is it wishful thinking, is my mind playing me tricks?

'Are you telling us the truth? You're not making fun of us, are you? Who are you? How do you know?'

They are saying nothing more. I suppose it could be true. I've watched Joshua bringing others back to life – that widow's son in Nain, our friend Lazarus. If he could do that, could he actually restore himself to life? But he was dead, I know he was. How could he heal himself if he was dead? It's too much to take in. Salome is gaping open-mouthed. Mariam is itching to get back to tell the others. Mariam Magdalene has disappeared, I don't know where she's gone. The men have gone too. I was just about to ask them another question to be sure, then I saw them hurrying away. Perhaps they've gone to search for Mariam. I can hardly believe what has happened. Already the doubts are creeping in.

'Salome, tell me I didn't imagine that. That they said Joshua was still alive. Did they? Did they really say that? It was not a trick? That would be too cruel.'

'Sister, that's what they said. They said he'd prove it to us and his friends. We must go back and tell the others.'

Of course. You'd think I'd be over the moon now, but it hasn't really sunk in. I've heard the words but really? Joshua is really alive after all that was done to him? He was dead, I know he was. He can't just have been unconscious. The Centurian made sure of that. He'd be in trouble if he let any condemned man escape.

'Come on, Mari, what are you waiting for? Let's go and tell everyone.'

'Where's Mariam? We've got to find her.'

'She wandered off convinced that his body had been abducted. The men tried to tell her that it wasn't true but she was so upset, I don't think she heard them. She knows where we are staying. She'll come home when she realises we've gone.'

So the three of us hurry home. There's a spring in our step now despite our tiredness. I'm beginning to hope despite the unlikelihood of what we've just been told. I still worry that it's a trick, that some cruel men who saw us at the crucifixion have decided to jest with us and laugh at our credulity.

Salome and Mariam are up the steps to the room on the top floor two at a time – I can't manage that, but I'm not far behind. We bang on the door and I hear movement. The door opens a margin and a face peers at us. They think we're soldiers come to arrest them.

'It's the women! They're back already. What's the matter? You all look exhausted!'

'He's not in the tomb. We saw some men there who said he's alive.'

Others crowd round us now. Everyone starts talking at once. They make us repeat what the men had said.

'You misunderstood. You heard what you wanted to hear. It can't be true.' Simon Peter is voicing everyone's thoughts.

'He said he'd rise again,' says John with a sudden burst of insight. 'We didn't understand, but he did say it. Peter, let's go and see for ourselves.'

John rises and moves rapidly towards the door.

'Alright, John. Hang on, I'm coming too. A couple of other disciples get up to follow, but Peter and John are already through the door.

'Come on, Mother, sit down and calm yourself. I don't know what you and the other women are babbling about. Your imagination has taken over. It's crazy. You're all going mad. Even Salome now.' James is trying to throw cold water over our experience. His usual scepticism has full rein now.

'Mother, answer me this. Did you actually see Joshua?'

'Well, no. But we saw the empty tomb, I saw folded graveclothes and I heard the men tell us that he was risen.'

'Who do you think these men were? They were making fun of you. Of course it's untrue. It's a hideous joke. You need to get away from here as soon as possible.'

Everyone is gathering round arguing. Most don't believe us, though a couple of the disciples agree with John and confirm that he talked of rising again although they didn't take him literally at the time.

'Where's Mariam?'

'She disappeared while we were talking to the men at the tomb. We ought to go and look for her. She was in as pretty dreadful state and I don't know what she might do if she's left on her own.' Salome is concerned and I am too.

'Let's go and search for her, Salome. You're right. She needs close watching at the moment.'

'I'll come with you.' It's Thomas, who volunteers to accompany us. We hurry back to the garden where we last saw Mariam. Just as we arrive, we meet Simon Peter and John.

'You were right,' they chorus. 'We met the same men – well, I presume they were the same ones. They said Yeshua wasn't there. They even said 'Why are you searching for the living among the dead?' Then they told us to go back and he'd find us. What are you doing back here?'

'We're looking for Mariam,' says Thomas. 'Have you seen any sign of her?'

'No, she isn't here. We didn't see her on the way either.'

'You go back and tell the others what you've been told. We'll continue to look for her. We can't leave her to wander alone round the city in the state she was in.'

Simon Peter and John hurry away and we continue our search. If she's not in the garden here, goodness knows where we can look for her. The garden is quite big and covered with shrubs and olive trees so we decide to have another look in the garden before searching nearby lanes. And there she is, crouching behind a large bush, weeping copiously. I rush up to her.

'Mariam, cheer up. Stop weeping. Haven't you heard that we've been told that he's still alive? Peter and John saw the same men as told us. Don't be so sad.'

'I'm not! I'm just overwhelmed. It's true. He is alive. I've seen him!'

'You've what? You've seen him? Are you sure? Was it really him?'

'I didn't think so at first. I just saw a man, I assumed he was the gardener here, my vision was too blurred from so much crying. Then he spoke to me. I'd recognise that voice anywhere. It was him, it really was.'

'Are you sure, Mariam? After all, you said your vision was blurred. Could you have been mistaken?'

'I'm sure. He just said 'Mariam' like he always does, half affectionate, half exasperated like when I fail to understand something he's just said.'

'Where is he now?'

'I don't know. He stayed with me a moment or two and then I just looked up and he wasn't there any more!'

'Mariam, are you sure you saw him? It sounds to me as though you just imagined him. You saw what you wanted to see. The man could have been the gardener, you know.'

'It was Yeshua. I know it was.'

'What now? Will you come back with us?'

And so we make our way back to Joseph's house, hope within our hearts. It seems too good to be true, but if Mariam has really seen him…

When we get back, we find the door unlocked. We are scarce inside the door when everyone pounces on us.

'He is alive. He's been here. We've all seen him. The door was locked and suddenly he was right in the middle of us. At first we were really frightened. We thought he was a ghost. Then he asked us for something to eat and had a piece of bread right in front of us. Ghosts don't eat solid food, do they?'

At least I can really believe. Lots of them have seen him.

'You're all hysterical,' cries Thomas. 'I'll not believe until I see him myself, and make him prove that he's our Master and not some joker playing tricks upon us.'

We're all excited and talking at once. All day we prattle on, talking about everything that has happened, trying to make sense of it all. Someone goes out to buy some food, but we're still not hungry, we're too excited now. Darkness falls before we even think about cooking a meal and we're finally just about to eat when the door bursts open once more. One or two look up in alarm, but it's only a couple we saw earlier in the day who left to go to their home village. They're exhausted, but they shout out, 'We've seen him. We've seen the Master. He joined us on the road home and recounted all the scriptures and prophecies and how they'd all come true. We asked him in to stay – we hadn't recognised him, then as we ate together, it dawned on us who he was. You know how it is, we hadn't expected to see him, we thought he was dead, so we didn't dream it was him, then it was the way he broke and blessed the bread. We couldn't wait, we had to come all the way back to tell you.'

'We've seen him too! Just a few hours ago he was here with us in this room.' Simon Peter explains to the couple from the distant village, heaven knows how far they've run to get back to us so soon.

Then, as everyone is rejoicing, James comes up to me, and puts his arm round me and squeezes me.

'Mother, I've seen him too. It really was him. He spoke specially to me. After all this time! All the time I've never believed either you or him! I'm really sorry, Mother, please, please forgive me! I don't know how to say this after everything I've said about him in the past. And the things I've accused you of. Can you ever forgive me, Mother? I'll have to tell everyone how wrong I've been. I will.'

And I suddenly realise nearly everyone's seen him, except me!

Chapter 29
The Watcher

I'm very patient. I know she'll come here one day, under the fig tree in her native Nazareth. She'll remember me. She's never forgotten that forbidden moment when we met and she dared to take the risk. I warned her then that the path she was accepting was far from easy. She knows the pain now. She thought I was talking about the immediate consequences of her premature pregnancy, but the agony of the last few weeks has surpassed that, yet she has remained faithful and now needs reassurance. She knows everyone else has been blessed. Even her rebellious son, James, has seen his resurrected brother and is now as much an enthusiastic believer as he was a vehement mocker of his brother's claims. All the disciples, even that arch doubter Thomas, have seen him several times. Mariam of Magdala, Mariam, mother of the disciple James, followers in Jerusalem, and all round this Galilean sea have seen him. But not his mother, Mari. Of all people, why has he not come to his own mother? Was he so sure of her that she was the one person who did not need to see him? The one person who had not seen, but yet believed, extra blessed?

She does believe, of course, despite all opposition, despite all mockery, despite flouting her traditions and daring to challenge, question those in authority. Even when she alone believed, she somehow persevered. During the darkest days when all seemed lost, defeated, when the disciples fled, cowered in a locked room, her belief flickered on. Of course doubts assailed her. She would not be human had she not wondered sometimes whether her calling was not of her own dreaming. But in the end she always held on tightly to her faith. She knew

God. *She still knows him. I am his messenger and she will know me still.*

She has come to celebrate a marriage here in her native village. Anna, daughter of her brother Benjamin. Little Anna who wanted to follow Joshua on his journeys through Galilee, Samaria and Judea, but she was betrothed already and had to stay at home. 'Wait' Joshua had advised her kin, and she has waited. She has been avid for news of her uncle's mission, elated and despondent in turn as news filtered back to Nazareth. Now even she has seen the 'Master' as they call him and her young husband to be. They intend to join the ranks of the believers who are following the disciples all over the land. They are so different now. James, Mari's son, Joshua's brother, has stayed in Jerusalem and is a controversial and fearless figure there, both revered as the Master's brother and held in awe as he is so bold, so headstrong that he causes reactions that some worry that he will stimulate violent opposition. Simon Peter is there too, but others have moved on to other towns and cities and tell of Joshua's new life and kingdom.

Only John has not left his home. He returned to Capernaum to nurse both his parents, for Dorcas, his mother, had a stroke and was semi-paralysed in the days following Joshua's appearance to her and the disciples in Joseph's Jerusalem house, and old Zebedee was struggling to walk far and wanted John to manage his fishing business that was their sole income. And John, as he promised Joshua in those last hours, took Mari into his own home in Capernaum, where she helps him care for his ailing parents and is a revered mother figure for the wives and children of the disciples who now spend their time in far distant places. John has his own calling. He is a thinker, a writer. He has been writing down stories of the past three years and asks Mari from time to time for her memories. But he is more of a poet. He thinks about the meaning of things. He is not interested in the literal truth, no historian he. Instead he seeks out the reality underlying those remarkable events.

But Mari is here now among her own siblings, children and grandchildren. She visits often, but this is the first time since her return from Jerusalem that they are all together. She will be in the thick of things, all will come to her and want to hear her stories. The children especially will gather round her knee and she will tell them of marvellous happenings. She will not need to invent her stories now for she has such a store of memories that will enthral the children. Stories they will tell to their children and will go down many generations. But she needs some solitude. She needs her private time to talk to God, as she always did, and does. She will need to escape the bustle and the noise and she will come here, to this lone fig tree in the meadow where she used to graze her Uncle Eli's sheep.

It is early morning. There is a little mist hanging over the valley, although the sky above is clear. I can see the lone figure walking slowly, silently along the track. She walks past this meadow. I know where she is going. She is visiting the little stream, the stream where she'd take the flock to drink, but that stream has other more vital memories. That is where, as a young girl, she lay in the water and allowed it to flow throughout her being, where she obeyed God's call to her – for which I was the messenger. She is staring at the ripples in the stream, watching the clear water bubble and gurgle over the rocks and thinking of that time nearly thirty five long years ago when she said 'yes' to her God and changed her life irrevocably. Everything that has happened in those years is imprinted on her mind as she watches the living water flow. She is praying now. Is it thanks for her life? Is there any tinge of regret? Would she have accepted the commission that I entrusted to her if she'd known all it would entail? Is she even now sad that her son did not return to see her personally, that she has to rely on the witnesses all around her that he is alive?

At last she rises from the mossy turf and comes in my direction. Yes, she's coming to sit beneath the tree where she so often communed with God, where she would fling care and all inhibitions aside and come naked before her maker to bare her soul to him. Where he knew that she was the one, the one he'd been waiting for, to intervene in this world of his. She is coming in my direction. Will she notice me? Am I visible to her, or is it one-sided and I'm only the one allowed to see?

Out here, all alone, she's taken off her shawl and loosed her hair. No-one will see her here, she thinks. The rituals of village life can be cast aside. She is changed of course. No longer the twelve year old virgin with those huge brown eyes and that chortling smile that she could hardly suppress. But those eyes are still fresh despite all they've seen. A few wrinkles at the edges, but the smile hovers on her lips as she recognises the old tree. Her long dark hair is tinged with grey now but for a few minutes the lines on her face are smoothed in relaxed contemplation of the place where she learned to meet her God. Her body is older now, for it has born seven children, but it is the same soul that lies within. Any moment now she will see me. I'm sure she will. Her discernment of the spirit life is still as sharp as ever and she will see me and remember. Will she be frightened? I think not.

She has seen me. She starts a little at first, then she smiles. She has recognised me, I know she has. She does not speak but waits for me to utter the first words. She has learned patience now, the foolhardy eagerness is held in check. What shall I say? What can I say?

'Mari!'

Her eyes brim over. She is transformed into a young maiden once more.

'It is you! I should have known. Did you know I would come here?'

'I knew you would return.'

She is silent a long time. She is not embarrassed now.

'Do you have regrets? Would you change your mind?'

She thinks. She does not rush to answer. She picks a fig from the branches and offers it to me.

'You kept your promise. You told me that I would face pain and hardship. I did. But I would not go back. God has been very close to me.'

'Perhaps, Mari, you do not realise how close. I watched and wanted sometimes to be by your side and tell you that he cared, but he said you knew. Your son is with you now. He is with us here in this meadow. He knows your fig tree as well as you yourself.'

'Can I see him? Everyone else has seen him. Will he appear to me now, alongside you?'

'Do you need to see him, Mari? He came to so many others because they needed to believe. You're not like the others. That's why he chose you.'

'So I shall not see him?'

'He's with you all the time. He was with you more than four and thirty years. He knows you. You know him. What more do you need?'

'Is this the end? Have I done everything that God planned for me?'

'Who knows, Mari? You might yet be surprised. Perhaps it's the end, perhaps it's just the beginning.'

She is silent.

'Are you tired? Do you want it to be over?'

'If God wants more of me, then so be it. He will give me the strength.'

'More than that, Mari. He loves you. God loves you. He always did. He always will.'

'Then whatever the future holds, I accept it.'

'I know you will, just as that time I challenged you in this very spot, I knew you'd accept.'

I have said enough. It is time for me to go now. I do not know the future but I have carried out my God-given mission. My task is completed. I have to say 'farewell'.

Then she looks me straight in the eyes, hers mirroring my own.

'You always said you were nothing but a messenger. But who are you? Who are you really?'

It is time to go.

'Your name is Mari. All will know your name. And my name is Gabriel, it is for you alone to know.'

Postscript

Was it fair? Was I wrong to treat you so? Did I exploit you, manipulate you to do my will? Did I take advantage of an innocent? You were so young, so open, so trusting. I knew you'd not refuse the call I made of you, so did you have a choice? You had free will, of course you did, that is how I created you. I had to give you the chance to refuse, yet I knew you would not. But I loved you then and even so, knew the pain that I'd inflict upon you. But then I love all men, and by their very circumstances I know that they will suffer. You are at once the archetype, the very symbol of my dilemma, and yet are a very personal painful individual creation. All I can say to you is that I share your pain. If you had to have a choice, then others would need that same freedom. And very few will make choices that do not lead to suffering, albeit not necessarily their own. I could have withheld the apple, denied you knowledge, pre-empted the very reason for which I needed your conscious co-operation, indeed, submission.

So you have lived a full life, tasted the ecstasy and the agony of that knowledge, devoured the whole apple, the unblemished white and the bruised brown flesh and the scars inflicted by the grubs. And you did it with your eyes open, knowing this time it was not forbidden fruit but one I'd offered you. And by taking it you enabled a healing of so many. You did not do it by yourself, but made it possible. You were a necessary precursor, like John in the Wilderness. I needed to share your flesh, experience your pain to be truly one with mankind. I am your son, your father, his father, the sacrifice I made for you, through you, and thus made you that sacrifice as well. We are one now. You never saw your resurrected son? He is in you just as he is in me and I in him.

Look at you now. Most of your earthly life is long since forgotten. Who now knows of your persecution as a young girl, your flight as a pauper refugee, the arguments and disbelief you had to face from your own family? Men are humbled and saved by the suffering of your son, they forget the grieving that wracked your body at the foot of the brutal gallows. Yet many now venerate you for what you never were. Pure, spotless, sinless, a pale distorted image of the precocious, foolhardy, gutsy girl you really were and the faithful, understanding and sensitive woman that you became, culminating in life as the revered mother, the wise counsel, the inspiration of so many of the apostles and early believers.

Some adopted you as their version of the earth mother that early man perceived, maintaining you as that feminine image that so many patriarchal societies tried to expunge. Perhaps in a way you were and are. For the earth suffers too. It nearly dies under the ravages of storms and floods, earthquakes, ice and heat. Yet from that it still creates new life, fruits and nature in profusion. Perhaps you were and are that earth from which my creation, my love for the world was manifest. Your son talked so often of the mustard seed, that tiny seed from which great trees are created. You were a mustard seed, Mari. Look at what your son achieved. Your real memory is not in those great cathedrals, the 'notre dames', the Virgin Mary statues and paintings. It is of a small often frightened girl who obeyed her call. It is in the little incidents and encounters in life that trigger a reaction to my love, and from that little seed, heroic actions flow. You are not in the plaster images, even in the haloed masterpieces or the iconic sculptures. You are the seed that is germinated in each individual that starts the search that will culminate in my life, the life of the spirit, filling and empowering that person. You are the starter, that first pinprick of conscience, that first misty vision that gradually becomes realised in the full rebirth of our son in the lives of myriads around that still fill this earthly creaking sphere, this damaged home of all, with hope and love.

You are no longer the young girl or the old widow, the mother or the apostle. You are with me and with my people, with my son and your son, with my spirit. You still inspire.

I called you and you took the risk.

Thank you, Mari.